FALLING TOGETHER

Falling Together

MARISA DE LOS SANTOS

WILLIAM MORROW
An Imprint of HarperCollins*Publishers*

FALLING TOGETHER. Copyright © 2011 by Marisa de los Santos. All
rights reserved. Printed in the United States of America. No part of this
book may be used or reproduced in any manner whatsoever without
written permission except in the case of brief quotations embodied in
critical articles and reviews. For information address HarperCollins
Publishers, 10 East 53rd Street, New York, NY 10022.

HarperCollins books may be purchased for educational, business, or
sales promotional use. For information please write: Special Markets
Department, HarperCollins Publishers, 10 East 53rd Street, New York,
NY 10022.

FIRST EDITION

Library of Congress Cataloging-in-Publication Data has
been applied for.

ISBN 978-0-06-167087-9 (hardcover)
ISBN 978-0-06-210635-3 (international edition)

11 12 13 14 15   OV/RRD   10 9 8 7 6 5 4 3 2 1

For my first family,
Arturo, Mary, and Kristina de los Santos,
with all of my heart

FALLING TOGETHER

CHAPTER ONE

P EN WOULD NOT USE THE WORD *SUMMONED* WHEN SHE TOLD
Jamie about the e-mail later that night. Additionally, she would
not say that the e-mail dropped like a bowling ball into the pit of her
stomach, and at the same time fell over her like a shining wave, sending
arcs of sea spray up to flash in the sun, even though that is precisely
how it felt.

Across from Jamie at dinner, forkful of rabbit halfway to her mouth,
Pen would cock an eyebrow, cop a dry tone, and say, "Leave it to me
to get the e-mail of my life while wedged between Self-Help and True
Crime, listening to Eleanor Rex, M.D., recount her career as a paid
dominatrix."

The truth is that Pen was not giving Dr. Rex her full attention, even
though she should have been. She liked Eleanor. She liked her Louise
Brooks bob, her large, smoky laugh, and her impeccable manners. In
the nine hours she had spent driving Eleanor around to radio inter-
views, stock signings, and an appearance at an upscale but vampire-
den-looking private club called Marquis, Pen had come to view the
dominatrix gig—no sex but a lot of mean talk and costumes—as an
utterly valid and even sort of nifty way to put oneself through medical
school. Even if she hadn't, she should have been listening. As a general
rule, she listened to all of her authors. It was part of the job.

But this evening, Pen was unusually tired. She stood with her head tilted back against the bookstore wall, her ears only half hearing a description of how to single-handedly lace oneself into a leather corset ("There's an implement involved," she told Jamie later. "There always is," he said.), her eyes only half seeing the otherwise lovely store's horrible ceiling, paste-gray and pocked as the moon, while the weary rest of her began to fold itself up and give into its own weight like a bat at dawn.

Yesterday, Pen's daughter, Augusta, had come home from school with a late spring cold, and Pen had recognized, her heart sinking, that they were in for a rocky ride. Augusta's sleep, disordered in the best of circumstances, could be tipped over the edge and into chaos by any little thing. To make matters worse, it was her first illness since Pen had purged their apartment of children's cold medicine following newly issued, scarily worded warnings that it might be harmful to kids under the age of six. When Jamie got home at 2:00 A.M., he had found Augusta cocooned in a quilt on the sofa, wide awake, coughing noisily but decorously into the crook of her arm the way she had been taught to do in school, and a pale, wild-haired Pen staring into the medicine cabinet like a woman staring into the abyss.

"I hate the FDA," Pen had spat viciously. "And don't tell me I don't."

"I would never tell you that," said Jamie, backing up. "Noooo way."

In the bookstore, Eleanor's voice grew fainter and fainter, and Pen was so completely on the verge of sliding down the wall and curling up on the hardwood floor that she was planning it—how she would tuck her knees under her skirt, rest her head on a very large paperback book, possibly some sort of manual—when she felt her phone vibrate against her rib cage. Jamie, a sucker for gadgets, had given her the phone just a few days earlier—a "smartphone" he'd called it—and he had since realized what Pen had known the second he'd handed it to her: that it was far, far smarter than she required or deserved.

A hummingbird, Pen marveled through her sleep fog, *in my purse*.

A second later, she thought, *Augusta*, and then, *Oh no*, and her heart began to do a hummingbird thrum of its own. Generally, Pen's girl was as healthy as a horse, and her cold had been of the messy but aimless variety. But anything could happen. A couple of months ago,

Pen had sent Augusta to her father's house for the weekend and, apparently seconds after Augusta had stepped over his threshold, her flimsy sore throat had flared like a brush fire into a serious case of strep.

"Pustules all over her tonsils," his wife, Tanya, had hissed. "*Pustules. Everywhere!* And you never *noticed*? I've got news for you, lady: strep can turn into rheumatic fever. Just. Like. That."

Anything could happen with children. No one had to tell Pen this. Anything could happen with anything. Pen didn't even bother to check the message before she was punching in her home phone number and snaking her way through the small crowd of people who had gathered at the back of the store to hear Eleanor. In every bookstore audience, there were those who stood on the fringes instead of taking a seat, even when seats were plentiful, folks Pen called "lurkers." Usually, this label was both unkind and unjust, simple snideness on her part, but in the case of Eleanor's lurkers, perhaps not so much.

One ring and Jamie picked up.

"Jamie," Pen whispered frantically into the phone. "What? Fever? Pustules? What? Just tell me."

"You," Jamie told her calmly, "are insane."

Pen breathed, and her eyes filled with tears of relief. She swiped at them with her finger.

"Well, you *called*," she said, clearing her throat. "Naturally, I was worried."

"I called?" There was a brief pause and then Jamie said, "You didn't check the voice mail, did you? You didn't even check the *number* of the person calling, even though it was right there on the screen. Just hauled off and called me in a panic like a crazy person."

All true, but Pen was not going to say that to Jamie, so instead she said, "Not that many people have this number, Jamie. It's new, remember? You and Amelie and Patrick and Mom and Augusta's school. The school is closed; Mom's in Tibet or wherever the hell; Patrick never calls in the evenings; and I just talked to Amelie twenty minutes ago. That leaves you."

There was a small silence as Jamie considered this, then he said, a sly note sliding into his voice, "Let me ask you this."

"No," Pen said. "Whatever it is, no."

"Did your phone even ring?"

"It didn't ring," Pen corrected. "I'm in a bookstore. It whirred."

"Repeatedly? Or once? One long whir?"

"Who knows? Could've been one whir. Maybe. So *what*?" She gave her phone an accusatory look.

Jamie groaned. "E-mail." He enunciated the word as though it were composed of three distinct syllables. "Didn't we go over this? Check your e-mail, Penelope. We're fine. Augusta's fine. No fever and she ate like a champ. We had a long, and I'm talking about crazy-long, dance contest, and then she conked."

Pen swiped at her eyes again. "Oh. Well, thanks. Sorry."

Quietly, Jamie said, "The world doesn't spin out of control the second you turn your back, Pen."

Oh, yes it does. That's exactly what it does. You know that as well as I do. Pen thought this, but she didn't say it.

Jamie sighed. "Listen, if she busts out in pustules, I promise you'll be the first to know."

After she hung up, Pen almost didn't check her e-mail. She glared at her phone and stuffed it into her handbag. Contrary to what Jamie probably thought, she knew how to check it, but anyone who needed urgently to reach her would call, and the mere thought of pecking out an answer on the phone's microscopic keyboard made her fingers inflate to the size of baseball bats. Besides, she needed to get back to Eleanor.

Pen was walking toward the rows of chairs when she heard someone ask, "So I know you're, like, retired? But do you ever, you know, make an exception if the guy's, like, really special? Like really cool or whatever?" The person's voice had an unfinished, squawking quality: a boy, about twelve years old, thirteen at the outside. He was talking to Eleanor. Pen winced, stopped in her tracks, and there, in the heart of the Animals and Pet Care section, she checked her e-mail. The new one was from Glad2behere, an unfamiliar moniker but one that struck Pen as cheerful. *Good for you,* she thought.

```
Dear Pen,
I know it's been forever, but I need you.
Please come to the reunion. I'll find you
there. I'm sorry for everything.
                                    Love,
                                    Cat
```

Pen did not draw a blank or have a moment of confusion or have to read the message twice. She didn't think, *Cat who?* There was only one Cat. What she did was sit down on the floor between the shelves of books, shut her eyes, and press the cell phone to her sternum, against her galloping heart. Out of the blue sky and after more than six years of waiting—because no matter how hard she had tried not to wait, that is exactly what she'd been doing—Pen had been summoned. As soon as the merry-go-round inside her head slowed its whirling and jangling enough for her to think anything, she thought, *Oh, Cat,* followed by, *Finally.*

Chapter Two

*C*AT WOULD BEGIN IT: "WE MET CUTE."

"No," Pen would correct. "We met terrifying."

"And hostile," Will would add.

"I wouldn't say 'hostile,'" Pen would say.

"You were yelling," Will would remind her. "And swearing."

"And pushing," Cat would add. "Although not that hard."

"How would you know?" Pen would demand. "And I wasn't the only one swearing."

"I *know*," Cat would insist. "You were hostile. *I* was cute."

"You were terrifying," Will would correct.

"Through no fault of your own," Pen would concede.

"But cute," Cat would assert, "nevertheless."

And no one would disagree.

This was the way they told their story.

IT WAS THE FOURTH DAY OF THE FIRST WEEK OF THEIR FIRST YEAR OF college, immediately following a lecture on *Beowulf.*

Weeks afterward, when their friendship had become an ageless and immovable fact, Will would remark that he had noticed Pen during the lecture, specifically the way her hair had looked all of a piece, a glossy brown object hanging next to her face as she tilted her head to write.

"God," Cat would say, grimacing, "don't tell me you were checking her out. Don't tell me that Pen piqued your sexual interest. Because the thought of that is just nauseating."

"Thank you," Pen would say.

"Nope," Will would assure them. "It was just that hair. It was so brushed that it didn't even look like hair. Who has hair *that* brushed?"

"No one," Cat would reply. "No one has hair that brushed. And no one cries over *Beowulf*. No one but Pen."

Pen had not cried exactly, not out and out cried, not during the lecture anyway. She had cried the night before when she had gotten to the part about Beowulf's death. It wasn't so much the death itself, since Beowulf had never, during the hours she'd spent reading the poem, felt particularly real to her. Instead, it was the moment immediately following his death, a still and private moment near the end of an epic's worth of action and fighting, appearing suddenly and taking Pen off guard. The smoke cleared, and there was Wiglaf, the youngest of Beowulf's warriors, exhausted and blood-spattered and out of options, sprinkling water on the face of his dead king to wake him up.

During the lecture, Pen had waited for the professor to cover this moment, its bottomless sadness, but he had not even mentioned it. Still, while he spoke in cool tones about Beowulf's death marking the beginning of the end of an entire civilization, Pen had envisioned the boy's cupped hands full of water and had not burst into sobs, thank God, but had felt her eyes flood with tears. Her embarrassment at displaying emotion in front of what appeared to be hundreds of strangers was compounded by the fact that she was wearing mascara for the second time in her life. Her high school boyfriend, Mitchy Wooten, had liked her lashes "plain," but he had abruptly broken up with her fewer than twenty-four hours before they'd left for their respective colleges. Mascara was part of the new, college Pen, but as her dampened eyelashes began to gum, Pen vowed to throw the stuff away forever, a vow she would keep.

However, before its absolute exit from her life, the mascara had a role to play because when the professor ended the lecture a half hour early so that the class could break into small groups and meet with their respective teaching assistants, Pen did not go directly to her assigned classroom. Instead she wandered through the belly of the old, neoclassical, externally gracious, internally dank building in search of a bathroom in which to repair her smeary eyes. It took some time, but she found one, and as soon as she opened the door, she found Cat.

The bathroom was tiny, just two stalls, one sink, a paper towel dispenser, a trash can, and a large radiator. Lying on the scarred black and white tiles, face-up, her head jammed against the radiator, was a small girl in big trouble. Pen did not immediately identify the exact kind of trouble because the second she opened the door, the scene slammed into her senses, scattering them: a spill of black hair, limbs in terrible motion, a rigid face, a gasping, prolonged moan, a banging, banging, banging.

Pen yelped and fell back against the paper towel dispenser. For a few seconds, her hands flapped stupidly. Then she squatted down and took hold of the girl's thin ankles. She had expected them to stop moving, but they bucked inside her hands like two animals.

"Oh, God," Pen squeaked. "It's okay, it's okay, it's okay." But it wasn't.

Pen leaped up, wheeled around, and shoved open the bathroom door.

"Help," she said, not as loudly as she'd meant to. She saw a sweatshirt, grabbed it, and pulled it into the bathroom. Inside the sweatshirt was a boy.

"Shit," the boy said breathlessly and with what Pen would later discover was a relatively rare display of profanity. "She's seizing."

"Of course she is!" Pen shrieked, even though, before the boy said it, she had not hit upon a name for what the girl on the floor was doing. "We have to call 9-1-1!"

"Wait," said the boy.

"Wait?" squealed Pen.

"She's got one of those bracelets."

"A bracelet? Are you insane?"

The boy *was* insane she decided. Insane and useless. She yanked open the zipper of her backpack, fished wildly inside it, and snatched out a pen.

The boy pulled off his sweatshirt.

"Oh, great. Are you *getting warm*?" yelled Pen. "Are you a tad *uncomfortable*?" She pushed past the boy and leaned over the girl.

"What are you doing with that pen?" demanded the boy.

"You're supposed to put something in her mouth, so she doesn't swallow her tongue."

To Pen's amazement, he grabbed the pen out of her hand.

"That's a myth, the tongue thing," he snapped. "You'll hurt her."

Pen launched into a rant about the boy not being a doctor, damn it, and about how everyone knew the tongue thing was true and about how he needed to return her pen right now, this second, but the rant petered out before it really got started because what the boy did next was drop to his knees and tuck the sweatshirt under the girl's head, placing part of the shirt on the floor, part of it between her head and the radiator. It was among the most restrained and gentle gestures Pen had ever seen.

"Look," the boy said softly. "She's stopping."

Pen and the boy stayed still, waiting, and in a few seconds the noise emptied out of the room and was replaced by an opalescent quiet.

Eventually, the girl's eyes batted open. She looked from the boy to Pen, bewildered. She turned her head to the side, looked at the base of the sink, and groaned.

"Oh, bloody hell," she said hoarsely. "Give me a minute, okay?"

"Sure," said the boy, and Pen added, ridiculously, like a person on TV, "Take all the time you need."

Minutes passed. The girl might have fallen asleep, she lay so still. Her blouse was gauzy and peacock blue, scattered with yellow flowers. Pen caught sight of her own reflection in the mirror and gave a start at how haggard she looked, before she realized it was mostly because of the smudged mascara. Surreptitiously, she touched her forefingers to her tongue and rubbed under each eye. It helped a little.

When the girl opened her eyes again, she said, "So tell me who you are."

Relief and the sudden sound of the girl's clear voice sent Pen's adrenaline flowing again.

"Pen," she said. "Penelope, actually. Calloway. My grandmother's name. Penelope, I mean. Not Calloway. She was my mother's mother, so you know, different last name." The words hopped out one by one, *flip flip flip*, like goldfish out of a bowl. Pen sighed.

The girl smiled, and Pen noted that the smile managed to look exhausted and sparkling at the same time. "Got it," the girl said.

The boy wiped his hand on his gray T-shirt and held it out.

"Will Wadsworth," he said.

The girl's eyes widened.

"Get the hell out of here!" she cried.

Will froze for a second, then put his outstretched hand on the back of his head and rubbed. When Pen looked at him, she saw that under his tan, his cheeks were turning red. "Oh, right," he said. "Yeah, yeah. Sure. No problem."

He started to stand, made a slight move in the direction of the sweatshirt, still underneath the girl's head, then seemed to change his mind.

"So, uh, I'm glad you're okay and all," he said and turned sideways to squeeze past Pen and head for the door.

Pen giggled, a slightly hysterical sound, and Will Wadsworth turned toward her, startled.

"What?" he said.

"I don't think she meant for you to really get the hell out," Pen told him, still giggling. "I think it was an expression of incredulity. Disbelief."

"I know what 'incredulity' means." Will looked at the girl on the floor. "Yeah?" he asked.

The girl smiled again. "It was the name!" she sang out. "Will Wordsworth! Like the poet!"

"Uh, it's Wadsworth, actually," said Will, his face relaxing. "Like the other poet."

The girl laughed, a chiming sound, and said, "Well, you sure know how to make a first impression."

Will crouched down next to Cat, his elbows on his knees.

"When *I* first met *you*," he pointed out, "you were having a grand mal seizure."

The girl laughed again and sat up, her back against the radiator. She hooked her tangled hair behind her ears with her fingers, a snappy movement.

"Tonic-clonic," she told them, inscrutably but with great charm, her black eyes twinkling. "And I'm Cat."

WHEN CAT, PEN, AND WILL EMERGED, IN THAT ORDER, FROM THE over-conditioned air of the English-department building and stood blinking in the sudden sunlight, Pen stood and looked out at the saturated greens of the grass and trees, the white columns blazing against the red brick of the buildings, the cobalt sky stretched tight as a tarp overhead. Ever since she had arrived at the university, she had walked around, heavy (like a soaking wet pathetic tea bag, she'd e-mailed her mother) and dull, missing her parents every waking second and also in her sleep. She had watched the other new arrivals, resenting the pact of eager chipperness they all seemed to have signed. Now, standing between Cat and Will, a veil lifted; she felt engulfed by the electric beauty of everything around her. She gasped. It was a loud gasp.

"I *know*," moaned Cat. "The *heat*! Ugh."

"It's like walking through Jell-O. Hot Jell-O," observed Will, shedding the sweatshirt he had put back on only minutes before.

Pen peeled off her red cardigan sweater and said, "It really is awful, isn't it?" But she didn't feel awful. She tipped her face to the sun and smiled.

Will carried Cat's backpack. He offered to carry Cat herself.

"Not to be a jerk or anything," he said to Cat slowly, "but do you think you can make it walking? Because I can carry you, no problem."

Cat looked at Pen and rolled her eyes. "God, that was jerky, wasn't it? What an offer."

Pen peered at Will. "Do you know what 'jerk' *means*?"

Will laughed. "Okay, okay. Just answer the question. Carry or no carry?"

"No," said Cat thoughtfully. "I used to be one of those small people who liked to be carried. Up on people's shoulders usually. I'd also sit in laps. But I'm done with all that."

"Gave it up for college?" asked Pen.

"Exactly."

"I gave up not wearing mascara, but then just a little while ago, I gave up wearing it."

"Good choice. With your kind of eyelashes," said Cat, squinting at Pen, "mascara just muddies the waters."

"Good choice to you, too," said Pen, and the three of them, Will and Pen with Cat in between, set off together, amid the people, under the bright sky, and straight into the whites, greens, reds, and blues of the day.

THAT EVENING, THEY ATE A CHEESE PIZZA ON THE LAWN IN FRONT OF Pen's dormitory. Plain cheese was Pen's favorite kind of pizza; she found it pure and unencumbered. But in the argument that preceded the placing of the pizza order, Pen had not advocated for cheese. As Jamie had pointed out to her for years, it was a boring preference, reflecting underdeveloped, kindergarten-like taste. So she kept quiet about cheese and let Will and Cat battle it out to a stalemate.

"Forget it," Will finally said. "I'd rather have no toppings at all than eat anchovies."

"She did have a little bit of a rough day," Pen reminded him. "Maybe you could tough it out this once?"

"No chance."

"Hatred of little fish is a reflection of a little mind," said Cat primly. "But fine. No toppings. Cheese me, man. Let's do it."

They ate, slathered in citronella and sitting atop Pen's bed-spread on the cropped, prickly lawn. Late summer life—young and gold-edged—crackled around them: footballs and Frisbees cutting parabolas into the sky, club music undulating out of someone's window into the humid air, and it seemed to Pen that she, Will, and Cat were part of the action and also separate from it, so that when Will leaned back on his elbows and laughed, the sound rang through the quiet the three of them had made at the same time that it was just another noise.

"Tell us what's funny," Pen ordered.

"'Are you *getting warm*?'" said Will. He shook his head in amazement.

Pen put her pizza slice down and covered her face with her hands.

"Oh, no," she said from behind the hands. "I was a nightmare, wasn't I? Totally inept and screeching."

"Oh, yeah."

"What are you talking about?" demanded Cat. "No fair you two knowing something I don't know."

"That's what she said," explained Will. "In the bathroom. When I took off my sweatshirt."

"Oh, God," said Cat to Pen. "You said that?"

"I was a little freaked out, Cat."

"You were *enraged*," corrected Will.

"That's what happens when I get freaked out," said Pen, truthfully. "I get enraged."

"And hurl insults," added Will.

"I'm sorry," said Pen. She looked at his face in the fading light and realized that ever since she had met these two people, she'd been too busy at first and then too comfortable later to really notice what they looked like. Will's hair was wavy, but the rest of him was all straight lines: straight eyebrows, a straight mouth, his cheekbones two arrows pointing to the straight line of his nose. Even his eyes were somehow straight. It was a good face, but severe. When he smiled, though, with his straight, straight teeth, everything softened and lit up.

He smiled and said, "No problem. It got pretty scary there for a while."

"Wait! I don't think I thanked you guys, did I?" cried Cat. "Oh, God, I didn't!"

Pen looked at her, too, and found that she was bird-boned and broad-faced, not pretty in an ordinary way, but a joy to look at. Her delicate brown hands danced when she talked. She knee-walked over to throw her arms first around Pen's neck, then Will's, planting kisses on their foreheads.

"That doesn't usually happen," she said, "the tonic-clonic thing. Grand mal. I haven't had one in aeons. But I got thrown off last night."

"How?" asked Pen.

Cat wrinkled her nose. "Ooh, well, a little party happened in my dorm, I guess."

"You drank?" asked Will, then quickly added, "Not that you shouldn't. I meant does drinking do it?"

"I don't know if it was the drinking exactly. I think it was more of a triangulation."

"Like in trigonometry?" asked Pen.

"Of course not," said Cat. "I hate math. As in three things." She counted them on her fingers. "I drank three beers, even though I hate beer. I stayed up too late. And I forgot to take my medicine."

"So maybe you shouldn't do that anymore," ventured Will. "You think?"

"I definitely shouldn't," said Cat, nodding. "But I probably will."

Then she reached out, grabbed one of their hands in each of hers, and squeezed. "Thank the Lord in heaven you didn't call an authority figure. Or 9-1-1! Gosh, that would've been bad."

Even in the heat, Pen felt her face grow hot, as her own voice yelling about calling 9-1-1 echoed in her head. In a flash, she pictured the ambulance screaming up to the building, Cat being slid into it like a batch of cookies, the hordes of gaping undergrads, Cat known forever after as the girl who mysteriously malfunctioned in the English building. Pen shot a don't-rat-me-out-please look in Will's direction, but he was already talking.

"It was pretty stupid of us not to, given the fact that we didn't know what was wrong with you. A kid at my high school had epilepsy, so I sort of thought the seizure would be over fast. But we didn't know for sure."

Pen smiled her thanks at him. She wasn't ready to tell Cat the whole story, yet, but she knew that she would tell her before long. Maybe tomorrow. Maybe the day after that. There was plenty of time. She watched the sunset settle itself into dark pink and apricot layers behind the faraway trees.

"Your bed's going to smell like citronella for weeks," remarked Will.

"I don't mind," said Pen.

CHAPTER THREE

*Y*OU'LL GO," TAUNTED JAMIE, LEANING BACK IN HIS CHAIR. "You know you'll go. You know-know-know you'll go-go-go." He played the kitchen table like a conga drum, ending with a flourish.

Ignoring him, Pen focused on the food on her plate. It smelled winey and still held the shape of the take-out container: a tiny, brown, glistening mesa. Pen wheeled her knife and fork like birds looking for a place to land, poked wearily, took small, snapping bites. She set the knife and fork down with a bang.

"Why rabbit?" she asked irritably. "Why French? Again? I mean, I appreciate your bringing me leftovers, but enough with the rabbit and the snails and the congealed butter and the soggy crepes. Crepes don't travel well; I thought we'd established that."

Jamie shrugged. "It's Nancy. She thinks if it's not French, it's not sophisticated, and if it's not sophisticated, it's a bad date."

Pen narrowed her eyes. "If it's not *French,* it's not *sophisticated*?"

"Yeah, yeah, I know."

"Why work so hard to please Nancy, anyway? Isn't she just one of the Jims?"

"She was." Jamie snagged a bite of Pen's rabbit and grinned, chewing. "I just tonight asked her to call me 'Jimmy.'"

Pen shook her head. "You are hopeless. Hopeless and bad."

Roughly two years ago, shortly after Pen and Augusta had moved into

Jamie's apartment in what was meant to be a temporary arrangement, Jamie had devised a system that he called a work of genius and on which he congratulated himself with a glee and a frequency that Pen believed spoke volumes—and nothing good—about his moral development.

Upon first meeting a woman, he would introduce himself as James. At some point in their relationship, and this point could come within minutes or after several dates, whenever Jamie decided it was time for a phone number exchange, he would ask the woman to call him something else: Jim, Jimmy, Jay, or Jamie. For example, he might tell her, "I always introduce myself as James, but, actually, my friends call me Jim. I think maybe we should be friends," or something along those cornball lines. Occasionally, if the relationship continued for long enough and the necessity arose, Jamie would initiate what he called, obnoxiously, "an ancillary nomenclatural shift."

While the women took the changes to be a sign of growing intimacy, they were actually unknowing participants in a scheme that involved a reluctant Pen and the use of a code. In the drawer of the telephone table that had once belonged to their grandmother, tucked beneath the folder of take-out menus, Jamie had placed a laminated sheet ("Laminated?" Pen had said upon seeing it. "Are you kidding me?") delineating the code:

```
        If she asks for . . .

 Jimmy:   act like an aggrieved girlfriend; demand
          to know the identity of the caller; request
          that the caller refrain from future calls;
          in the best of all possible worlds, you will
          cry, yell, and/or hang up on the caller;
 Jim:     don't identify yourself as girlfriend,
          but be terse and businesslike when
          taking message; take message even if Jim
          is home; if asked your identity, say "I
          live here" in an ambiguous tone;
 Jay:     be friendly; if Jay is home, turn the
```

```
         phone over to him; if asked to identify
         yourself, say "Penelope";
Jamie:   identify yourself in a friendly manner
         as Jamie's sister, Pen; turn the phone
         over to Jamie if he is home; feel free
         to submit funny anecdotes from childhood
         or beyond that speak well of Jamie's char-
         acter.
```

Most of the callers asked for "Jim." There had been just three Jimmys (Pen had neither cried nor hung up on any of them) and two Jays, although Pen knew that the number of callers did not accurately reflect the number of women Jamie had met or dated because the majority of those women did not progress past the James stage. In two years, Pen had never once fielded a call from a woman asking for Jamie.

Pen was ashamed of her participation in the system, and every few weeks, she railed at Jamie for his treatment of women in general and for the system in particular, saying things like "You will burn in hell for this," or "You suck," or "You are hopeless and bad." Just once, after a particularly fragile Jim had broken down on the phone, sobbing apologies to Pen, she had said solemnly, "Jamie, what would Dad say? He treated Mom like gold. He treated everyone like gold," but when she saw Jamie's eyes change, she knew she had gone too far.

The truth is that when Jamie first proposed the system—he had a brainstorm one day as he watched her answer the phone: "Hold on," he said, squeezing his eyes shut, pointing at her with one hand, pressing his other palm to the side of his head, "I can use this. I *know* I can use this"—Pen hadn't felt repulsed, but touched, even grateful. That her older brother would invite his emotional wreck of a sister and her sleep-disordered toddler to live with him at all was kindness enough, but that he would figure out a way to view Pen's presence as an asset, something to high-five her over, rather than as the liability it clearly was, moved her nearly to tears, even now, whenever she thought about it. It was such a quintessentially Jamie thing to do.

When Pen was twelve and the despairing victim of mean-girl awfulness, sixteen-year-old Jamie had scooped her up and let her live for a whole fall in the reflected glory of his perpetual coolness, even letting her walk around the track at football games with him and his beautiful friends. Pen could still see Mary Anne Riddle's evil face in the dazzling stadium lights, the dual stripes of her blush, her jaw actually dropping in an expression of envy and shock. Jamie had not discussed beforehand with Pen his decision to do this, had not set down ground rules or made her feel like she owed him. She was pretty sure he hadn't even thought about it much. Under Jamie's lawyer suits and caddishness, Pen knew he was still that carelessly generous boy, so that even when she called him "hopeless and bad," she never really believed it.

"So we were talking about how you're going to the reunion," said Jamie. "How there's no-no-no way you're not going."

Pen pushed her plate in Jamie's direction. "Take it," she said. "I'm through."

"I thought you'd be eating dominatrix food with the dominatrix anyway," said Jamie, digging in.

"She was tired and decided to order room service."

Through a mouthful of rabbit, Jamie said, "I *thought* you'd be eating with her, but just in case you weren't, I got you your own order of profiteroles. Check out the white box on the counter."

Pen hooted with joy and began to sing a rough approximation of "La Marseillaise." She paused and said, "Chocolate sauce?"

"In its own separate container for do-it-yourself, type-A-freak drizzling."

While she was in the middle of chewing the first ungodly good profiterole, Jamie said, "It's your ten-year college reunion, which is a big deal, right? Why weren't you planning to go even before you got the e-mail?"

Pen swallowed, her throat suddenly tight, and, briefly, pressed her fingers to her eyes.

"You know why," she said.

"The kid and no husband thing? Forget about it. Patrick sucks. Augusta's awesome. You made out like a bandit with that deal."

"You think I don't know that?" demanded Pen, her eyes flashing. "And who gives a nit about what anyone thinks?"

Jamie smiled at "gives a nit," one of their mother's stock phrases, along with "shut the cluck up."

"Good. So why not go?"

"Don't pretend you don't know."

Jamie looked down at the table for a few seconds, fingering his napkin. Pen watched his brow furrow and relax. The sound of a siren swirled in the distance, first faint, then louder. Jamie's eyes met Pen's.

"It's not like it's on the same day as the thing for Dad."

As soon as Jamie said the word *Dad,* Pen saw her father's face, yellow under that streetlamp, felt the stillness of his hand inside hers. She remembered the way he lay on his side, as though he were asleep. She put her hand over her mouth.

"Come on, Pen," said Jamie, sighing.

" 'Come on, Pen'?" Of its own volition, her voice rose. Jamie glanced over her shoulder at the hallway that led to Augusta's room. Pen took a breath and said more quietly, " 'The *thing* for Dad'? The *thing* means he died two years ago. Remember that?"

Jamie ran a hand across his forehead. "Yeah, I remember."

"Do you?"

Jamie shook his head, picked up the plate with the remains of Pen's rabbit on it, and pushed back from the table. Pen watched him as he scraped, then rinsed the plate, first one side then the other, and slid it into the dishwasher. Jamie had always performed small tasks this way, ever since he was a kid, as though he were being graded for thoroughness.

"I'm sorry," said Pen. She looked down at the profiteroles, the chocolate sauce in its plastic cup, and she ached for Jamie and herself and her mother in Tibet, and her father, who deserved better than to die on the dirty ground.

Jamie leaned on the counter with both hands, his shoulders hunched.

"You think I don't miss him?" he said finally, without turning around. "You think you're the only one?"

"No."

Jamie turned around and looked evenly at Pen. "Forget moving on or getting over it or whatever because who does that? But I gotta tell you, it would be really good if we didn't have another anniversary like last year's. Good for Augusta, especially."

At this mention of Augusta, Pen turned her face away sharply, as though she'd been slapped.

Jamie's voice softened. "Good for you, too. Right? For all of us."

Pen didn't look at him, but said, "I know."

"The bike ride is supposed to be a way to celebrate Dad, right? Everyone together?"

"I *know*. All right? I know. I don't have any plans to fall apart again, so you can stop worrying." Pen's voice was bitter, but she wasn't mad at Jamie.

Their father, Ben Calloway, had been a passionate cyclist, getting up before daylight for decades to ride with a group of people who, over the years, had become like family to Pen and Jamie, a tribe of aunts and uncles with sunglass tans and articulated calves. The rides would begin and end at the Calloway house in Wilmington, Delaware, and for Pen's whole childhood, before she got old enough to ride with them, Saturday mornings meant watching for her dad and his friends through the screen door and then coming outside in her pajamas to greet them. She loved it, the clack of their shoes on the front walk, the way they'd drop onto their backs on the lawn and squirt her with their water bottles, her mother coming out to laugh and offer them breakfast.

To mark the anniversary of Ben's death, two of the riders, David and Tracy Hersh, had organized a long bike ride through the countryside. More than thirty people, including Pen and Jamie, had met that May morning in front of the house. Pen would never forget how perfect it felt just before they took off: the dewy grass, the laundered scent of her mother's lilacs, everyone poised, one foot on the ground, ready to begin.

Pen's mother, Margaret, was still home then, hadn't yet been chased off by grief or loneliness to faraway places, and the last thing Pen saw before she set out was her mother standing on the porch with Augusta half-asleep in the crook of one arm, her free hand pressed to her mouth, then waving in the air.

But a few miles into the ride, as they came around a curve and the trees opened up to a vista of fields and stone barns and streaked-silk sky, Pen was overcome by a bleakness that made it hard to breathe, a comprehension that this road, this sky, the bikes rounding the curve together, swooping like a flock of birds, even the faint twinge between her own shoulder blades and the air filling her lungs, all of it belonged to her father, was rightfully his, except that he was dead, and so it belonged to no one and meant nothing.

Pen had not finished the ride. She had slipped to the back of the pack and stopped her bike by the side of the road, willing the others not to notice, to keep going, but they turned back, all of them.

"I don't feel good," she explained, forcing a smile. "A stomach thing. You guys keep going. I'll be fine."

Even though she had tried to avoid looking in Jamie's direction, he had pulled alongside her and stopped, leveling a gray-eyed stare at her that was fierce and pleading at the same time.

"Stay. You have to," he'd said in an urgent voice that only she could hear.

But she had turned around, gone back to the house, stumbled past Augusta who sat at the kitchen table, a cup of milk in her hand, her eyes round and surprised, past her mother who stood at the counter, coiling dough into cinnamon rolls, and up the stairs into her old bedroom. She tossed her body onto the bed like bags of sand, and she stayed there for the better part of three days.

When her mother tried to coax her to get up, she cried and said that she was too tired. When Jamie raged at her for being selfish and for scaring Augusta, she turned her face to the wall. When Pen woke to find the hard knot of her child jammed against her back, she turned over, put her arms around the little girl, and said, "I'm sorry, baby. Mama's sick," in a hoarse, remote voice that even she knew was the opposite of comforting. For weeks afterward, after they were home in Philadelphia and back to their regular routine, Pen would catch Augusta watching her with a mixture of hope and worry, an expression no one should ever see on a four-year-old's face.

"I wouldn't do that to Augusta again," said Pen, more to herself than to Jamie.

"You sure?"

Pen rested her chin on her palm and looked at the vase of flowers in the middle of the table, tulips, barely open, like little folded hands in white gloves.

"I didn't get it," she said. "For that whole first year, I knew that he was gone from us and how unfair and sickening and sad that was. But I didn't get that what was worse, the very worst thing, was that he was gone from himself and all the things he loved. The day of the bike ride, it fell on me like an avalanche."

She looked up at Jamie and shrugged. "So now I know. And it can't fall on me again."

Jamie got a bag of coffee beans out of the freezer and poured them into his expensive coffeemaker with its built-in grinder and timer. Pen listened to the oily click of the beans, waiting.

"Your reunion doesn't start until, what, a week, week and a half, after this year's ride?" said Jamie finally. "So if you're not planning to be incapacitated, why don't you go?"

Pen stood up, slapping crumbs off her skirt in annoyance. "Why are you so sure I'd want to see Cat, anyway? It's not like I've been holding my breath until she and Will came back."

"Uh, actually, if you think about it, that's exactly what it's like."

"Nice," said Pen. "Very nice. They walked out on me. Why would I want to see either of them?"

"Because they're Cat and Will." Jamie flopped onto the sofa and snagged a remote control out of the bafflingly large collection on the coffee table. Before he began pushing buttons, he added, "And you're you."

WHEN PEN WAS STILL NOT ASLEEP AT 3:00 A.M., SHE GOT OUT OF BED and walked, as silently as she could, into Augusta's room, a thing she almost never did. For Augusta, the state of sleep was a frail construction, something you could send toppling with a misplaced footfall or clearing of your throat. But every now and then, Pen risked it. Now, she closed the door behind her and stood, allowing her eyes to adjust to the powdered-sugar sifting of moonlight and streetlight on the windowsill and the thin blue glow of the nightlight that Pen allowed as a concession to Augusta's fear of the dark, even though she'd read that nightlights could cause nearsightedness later in life. Glasses later, she decided, beats terror now, hands down.

Augusta lay in one of her customarily untranquil positions, as though she'd been struck by sleep mid-snow-angel, her duvet and sheets heaped in drifts on the floor around her bed. Pen resisted touching her, but leaned in close to listen to her breath and smell her smell: honey soap, apple shampoo, and a fundamental Augusta scent that reminded Pen of dandelion stems.

Without taking her eyes off her daughter, Pen lowered herself by increments into the chair next to Augusta's bed and thought what she had thought so many times before: *How can Cat and Will not know you?* For weeks after Augusta was born, Pen had expected them to come, even though, when the three of them parted ways, first Cat leaving, then Will, they had all agreed to make it final, to never get in touch, not years later, not ever.

"We're all or nothing," Cat had said, tears streaming down her face. "We can't be fake or partial or now-and-then. That would be wretched." Pen hadn't been so sure, but she had agreed to it anyway.

Even so, and even though she had no clear idea of how they would've found out about Augusta's birth even if they had wanted to, she had waited for them to come. She had waited again after her father died. At the funeral, she had sat between her mother and Patrick, Augusta on her lap, feeling broken and absent, her body numb inside her black dress, and had suddenly felt them there, behind her, the certainty of their presence running like electricity along her shoulders and up her neck. She had stood and spun around, searching through the crowds of people who had loved her father, for Will and Cat who had loved him as much as anyone. Nothing.

After that, over and over, for two years, Pen had imagined what she would say to them if she ever saw them again, all the ways she would be angry or indifferent, clever or cool. But from the beginning, from the very first day each of them walked out and for every second since, what she would have said if she were speaking truthfully was this: "Since you left there's been a you-shaped space beside me, all the time. It never goes away."

"All right, then," whispered Pen into the darkness of Augusta's room. "What the cluck. She wants me to be there, so I'll go."

CHAPTER FOUR

*W*ILL COULD STILL CONJURE THEM UP. LIKE NOW, FOR IN-
stance, as he worked at his desk, he could look through the
window and watch them emerge from between the guesthouse and the
japonica bushes and walk across his backyard, past the weird village of
staked birdhouses his mother had set up, past the crab apple snowing
white onto the grass. Pen all spare, pliant lines, with her hair pulled
back, her hard cyclist's legs. Tiny, animated Cat with her usual bird-
of-paradise plumage: lapis-blue scarf, flame-red dress, green shoes.

Sometimes, he had nothing to do with it; they showed up out of
nowhere, with the fast sting of a static electric shock. Just yesterday,
after he'd gotten the e-mail, he had seen Pen's long, oval-nailed fingers
wrapped around a stranger's coffee cup in the Bean There, Done That
Café. These visitations didn't happen often, a few times a year maybe,
but they always left Will a little out of breath, the sudden yank backward through time: Pen's surprising, childlike laugh bubbling up over
restaurant noise or her almost comically perfect posture ("Tut, tut!
Chin up, shoulders back, stiff upper lip," Cat would tease in a very
bad British accent. "For God and Empire, you know.") inhabiting the
back, neck, and shoulders of a woman across the room at a party.

Once, a couple of years ago, as he stood in line for a movie, he had
heard Cat's voice, winsome, tinny, and unmistakably off-key, singing
a song he didn't know but that was exactly the kind of sappy love song

Cat would adore. He had left his place in line to find the singer, who turned out to be teenaged and blue-haired with a nose piercing that looked fresh and painful, a detail that had annoyed Will unaccountably, almost to the point of anger. How stupid of him, he had thought, how moronic, after so many years, to look for Cat and find this silly, attention-hungry kid instead.

Now, though, he let himself fall into the act of imagining them, of hearing Cat's silver bangles add themselves to the morning music—birds and, already, a distant lawnmower—of watching them balance each other the way they always had, Pen shortening her fluid, stalking stride, Cat stepping fast and light, like a sandpiper, so that she seemed, from this distance, to just skim the ground.

Will shifted his gaze to the bulletin board on the wall next to his desk. He had read Cat's e-mail once, then printed it out and pinned it to the bulletin board. Pinning e-mails to the bulletin board wasn't something he usually did, and he didn't analyze his reasons for doing it now. "You're trying to make it more actual," his mother had said when she'd seen it. "You're filling a space," which was just the kind of thing his mother said these days, although in this case, as in others, he had to admit that she might have a point.

> Dear Will,
> I know it's been forever, but I need you.
> Please come to the reunion. I'll find you
> there. I'm sorry for everything.
>
> > > Love,
> > > Cat

It didn't sound like Cat. Will had thought this as soon as he'd read it. A flat, sparse e-mail from a girl (Will still thought "girl" when he thought of Cat) who was never either of those things. The Cat Will had known was effusive and playful, hardwired for flirting. "Buckets of love," Cat would have written. "Aeons, oceans, and mountains of love forever and ever." "I need you," though, that sounded like Cat.

The e-mail was pinned next to a poem that Kara had given him, left for him to find there on the bulletin board, when they had first started dating. "I Knew a Woman" by Theodore Roethke. Funny, Will had thought at the time, for his girlfriend to give him a love poem in the voice of a man worshipping a woman. "This is what I want," the gift suggested. "Love me like this."

Will liked the poem for its rhymes and because it didn't praise the usual body parts—eyes, lips, et cetera—but the woman's body in action, her specific way of moving or of holding still. After Kara had gone, moved out without ever having entirely moved in, Will had left the poem where it was. In his mind, it had never had all that much to do with Kara, who was pretty and smart, but not exactly graceful, a fact she freely acknowledged. Still, when the man in the poem asserts, parenthetically, more to himself than to anyone else, "(I measure time by how a body sways.)," Will had always known exactly what he meant.

" 'I'm sorry for everything,' " Cat had written in the e-mail. *Why should you be sorry?* Will thought, and looked out the window again to see, not Cat or Pen, but his mother, in the flesh and saluting the sun. Even though she had been this woman for almost five years, Will still felt amazed at the sight of her, sturdy, lean, and clear-eyed. She traced arcs in the air with her arms; her gray hair flashed. Abruptly, she broke her posture to wildly shoo a fly away, hands flapping, elbows stabbing the air. When she gave the retreating fly the finger, Will grinned.

He remembered the conversation they'd had on the first anniversary of her sobriety. They were celebrating at the summerhouse where his mother had lived year-round since the divorce. His sister, Tully, was upstairs napping with her new baby; his brother, Philip, and Tully's husband, Max, had driven into town for lobsters, corn, tomatoes, and blueberry pies. Will had been working at his computer on the porch. He liked it out there, even though it was smotheringly hot and breezeless that day, the wind chimes hanging, listless, in the sticky air. His mother had come up behind him and pressed a cold glass of iced tea against the back of his neck. When he reached around for the glass, she'd given his hand a little slap.

"Talk to me," she had ordered, "or no drink for you."

Will had laughed, closed his laptop, jumped up, and pulled out a chair for her, into which she settled like a cat, tucking her feet underneath her, leaning forward, and eyeing him determinedly.

"Oh, man, what are you up to now?" Will said warily.

"I asked Philip and now I'm asking you."

"Uh-oh."

"It's just this: I've done a lot of changing this past year, and I'm wondering how you feel about it all."

Her eyes were hazel, like Will's, coppery brown near the pupils, shading to amber and ending with rims of dark green, and they were looking at him with a combination of patience and insistence. *We will have this conversation*, the look said, *if it takes a hundred years*.

"Good," answered Will. "I feel good."

The eyes waited, unblinking.

"Proud of you," he went on. "Relieved. Uh, happy at how happy you are. I'm glad you're painting."

"Thank you," said his mother. "All very nice. What else?"

"Else?"

"Yup."

He slapped his neck. "Mosquitoes."

"William."

"What was Philip's answer?"

"William."

Will thought for a few seconds, looking out at the wide lawn, the blue-purple hydrangeas and thick, leaning stands of black-eyed Susans, the blown-glass hummingbird feeders hanging from the trees, and, yards away, the vegetable garden looking like a tiny campground, with its stakes and bean teepees. He loved this place. It had been the setting for some intense family ugliness over the years, and this very porch was the spot where his friendship with Pen had ended, smashed to smithereens, but the place itself had stayed pure, calm and unstained. Will felt oddly glad for it, glad that its days of bearing witness to meanness or betrayal or to the icy, cutting conversations that had been his father's specialty were over.

"Okay, how about this? Sometimes, I worry that you'll change so much I won't know you anymore," he had said finally. "Some of those friends of yours, they're nice, but they're a little . . ."

"Humorless?" his mother offered. "Annoyingly earnest? Overly huggy?"

"Yeah, that," said Will, laughing.

"Say more. What else worries you?"

"Apart from your maniacal insistence on openness and communication, you mean?"

"Yes." She folded her hands and smiled innocently, waiting. "Apart from that."

"All right, all right." He thought for a few seconds, listening to the bees hum like tiny engines. "I'm getting used to the yoga and the vegetarianism. I can see the point of them. But the really hard-core New Age stuff makes me—" He searched for the right words (*itch uncontrollably, vomit, run like hell*), then gave up. "I want you to be happy, and you should do whatever it takes. I'll adjust."

"But from a purely selfish perspective . . . ," prompted his mother.

"You should get a job with the KGB. Seriously."

"I believe the KGB was dissolved some time ago. As you were saying."

Will picked a leaf of mint off the surface of his iced tea and chewed it.

"From a purely selfish perspective, I'd say that I just want to keep feeling like we speak the same language. And I want you to stay funny."

His mother slapped the table and laughed. Then she leaned toward him and said, "How about this? Yoga, vegetarianism, and maybe just a bit of Buddhism. Tibetan. The joyful kind. But no crystals, personal gurus, or star charts."

Will raised his eyebrows. "Goddesses?"

"Nope."

"Vortices?"

"Don't know what they are."

"Wicca?"

"Never."

"What's your position on modern medicine?"

"All for it. Deal?"

"Deal."

Now, out in his backyard, his mother finished her sun salutation, started walking toward the house, and then leaned forward, squinting, her hands on her knees. Will wondered what she was looking at. It was so much brighter outside than it was in his office; no way could she see him. Then she smiled and blew a kiss in his direction. Will was highly skeptical about things like sixth sense and intuition, but when it came to her kids, his mother could be downright uncanny. This hadn't always been true, but it was true now. Even though he didn't believe she could possibly see him do it, he waved.

She didn't come straight to the office but went instead to the kitchen. Will heard her turn on the water, then clatter around, unscrewing the lids off the small, round metal canisters that held her loose tea leaves and herbs.

Will knew that she would come into his office in a few minutes, would lean against the doorjamb in her paint-streaked shirt, and tell him that she'd finished the last illustration for his new book. She had been close to finished last night, and he was pretty sure she had gotten up before sunrise that morning to paint. It amazed him, how little sleep she needed now, especially since one of the primary ways he remembered her from his childhood was as a long, sloped lump under sheets. He could see himself—he could transport himself into himself—at six, ten, fifteen, standing next to the guest-room bed or next to the couch in what she called her studio, even though she almost never used it for making art, staring at her and churning with worry and anger, his hands dangling, as full daylight sliced in around the drawn curtains.

Soon she would come in with her tea, say she had finished the painting for the book, and tomorrow or the next day, he would drive her to the airport and she would go back to the summerhouse. This visit had been her longest, almost four months. During the last book, she had come for three and had been staying in the guesthouse when Kara finally left him for good.

Having his mother, or anyone else, around to witness firsthand his getting dumped should have been a nightmare of humiliation and awkwardness, but it wasn't. He remembered how she had waited a few days, staying nearly invisible and quiet as a cat, before weighing in on the breakup. Then all she'd done was tilt her head to one side and say, "I liked her."

"She liked you, too," said Will. It was true. Some women might have minded—might have *detested*—having their boyfriend's mother living in the backyard, but Kara had repeatedly told him how much she loved it, even going so far as to ask her to eat dinner with them nearly every night, an invitation that, most of the time, his mother graciously refused. In fact, Kara seemed to have a crush on his mother, blushing in her presence, agreeing with her about the smallest things, asking her what kind of perfume she used ("Eau de paint" his mother had said, laughing). Once, Will had come home to find Kara wearing the cardigan his mother had left in their kitchen the night before. Will hadn't completely understood this enthusiasm, but sincerely hoped—and almost believed—that it had nothing to do with what Kara had once referred to, with a complete and disturbing lack of irony, as his mother's "pedigree."

"I liked her," his mother continued, "but, if I may be blunt, I didn't think she would stay."

"Why not?" Will had asked. Forty-eight hours earlier, he might have asked this defensively, but now he felt more exhausted than anything else. Besides, he was curious.

"The way she cleared out a separate shelf in the pantry for her own food, instead of mixing hers up with yours. I thought it was a bad sign."

"Oh."

"Also, she always seemed to be a little mad at you."

Actually, Kara had seemed more than a little mad, a fact that Will had asked her about exactly five times during the nine months they were together. The first time, she had laughed it off. The second time, she had cried and apologized and blamed her anger on her own moodiness. The third time, Kara had yelled, thrown a magazine in his direction (it didn't hit him), and slept in the guesthouse (his mother wasn't staying in it at the time), but at four that morning, he'd woken up to her hands pulling up his T-shirt, her mouth on his chest. "Forgive me," she'd murmured, and he had.

But then, just days later, when her anger came slashing toward him out of nowhere again, and he'd asked her about it, she had pressed her lips into a line, walked out of the room, walked back in, and said matter-of-factly, "You're just a closed-off person. That's your right, of course. But I'm passionate; I wear my heart on my sleeve. Sometimes, I get frustrated that you aren't the same way."

This had surprised Will because he had never considered himself closed-off. He wasn't a secret keeper, for the most part; he disclosed. He expressed his feelings when it seemed important to express them. When he tried to explain these things to Kara, she had cut him off, tenderly, saying, "Please. I didn't mean to put you in the position of having to defend yourself. You are who you are. I love you, and I value you, and I'm sorry," which pretty much put an end to that conversation.

Then, one night, on their way out to a dinner party, he had kissed her and said, "I love you in that dress," and she had pushed him backward with both hands, slapped the kitchen table, and snapped, "Well, that's just great, Will. That's just peachy," shoved her handbag over her shoulder, and slammed her way out the front door. Will had stood in the kitchen, listening to the screen door creak on its hinges in the aftershock of her slamming, suddenly feeling his own anger nearby, crouching, like something misshapen and ugly in his peripheral vision.

He had looked down at the kitchen chair in front of him, a fragile thing, and gripped it to steady himself, even as the urge to lift it up over his head and hurl it against the wall rushed up from his hands, into his arms and shoulders.

He'd done the breathing, the visualizing, employed all the strategies he hadn't had to use in years to calm himself down. Then he'd gone out to the car, where Kara sat in the passenger seat, opened the door, and said quietly, "Why are you so mad at me all the time? The real reason."

Kara had stared straight ahead for a long time before looking up at him with sad, sad eyes and saying, "I lied."

"What?"

"That time I said you were closed off, not passionate enough."

Will knew all at once what she was going to say, the general gist of it, and he braced himself.

"You do wear your heart on your sleeve," she told him in a hollow voice. "It's right there. You just don't love me as much as I love you."

"Kara," Will began, then stopped.

"You love me," she clarified. "But only a little bit. Not enough."

WILL'S MOTHER STOOD IN THE DOORWAY TO HIS OFFICE.

"How's the tea?" he asked.

" 'It tastes like licorice,' " his mother said, smiling. " 'That's the way with everything.' " It was a Hemingway quotation, one Will had been hearing for as long as he could remember. Even though it made no sense for his mother to love Hemingway (Woolf maybe, Austen definitely, Hemingway no), she always had. She knew that particular story, every word, by heart, and could quote whole chapters from *The Sun Also Rises*. When Will had finally read those stories on his own— he'd been in tenth grade—it had made his stomach hurt to think about his mother feeling so at home with all those unhappy, disappointed, disconnected characters.

"I finished the last painting," she said. Jokingly, she threw her arms out to the side and said, "It's brilliant!"

"Same as always. Thanks, Mom."

She leaned over and kissed the top of his head.

"Have I told you lately how I adore you?"

"Yep."

"Adore," she said. "Not just like a lot."

"Adore. Got it."

"Good."

"You still need to do the book cover," Will reminded her, "for the novel."

"I'll come back," she said.

She turned to face the bulletin board, and Will knew she was read-ing the e-mail again.

"It still says what it said the first five times, Mom."

"You know, it's really too bad Cat ever left in the first place," she said.

"She wanted to get married," said Will. "It seemed like a fair enough reason to go."

His mother turned around and said suddenly, "You know, I thought that after she left, you and Pen might fall in love."

Will leaned back in his chair, startled.

"Oh, yeah? I never knew you thought that."

"I guess it wasn't in the cards, though?"

Will straightened some papers on his desk. He could feel her watch-ing him.

"Nope. We were friends." He gave a half-baked smile. "Until we weren't."

His mother's cheeks reddened, and she made a gesture with one hand, as though she were brushing away the past.

"Anyway, I think you should go." She tapped a finger against the e-mail on the bulletin board. "Cat needs you. That's not a small thing, is it? Even after so long?"

"No," admitted Will.

"You never could say no to Cat. You and Pen. Could you?" She was smiling.

"I don't know. No," said Will, with a shrug, "I guess we never could."

Chapter Five

As Pen parked her car at the curb in front of Augusta's father Patrick's house, or in front of the uniformly rainforest-green ocean of lawn on which Patrick's house floated like a distant ship, Pen thought what she had thought the very first time she had seen the house and every time since: Patrick was living the wrong life.

Although it's true that this thought initially came to her during a time in her own life when thinking such a thing was suspiciously convenient, she persisted in thinking it long after she'd stopped wanting Patrick to live a different life in a different house with a radically different wife, a thing Pen had wanted ardently for a while there, or at least had thought she wanted. It was clear to her now: she had been confused and only *thought* that she wanted to be married to Patrick—although she had to admit that, at the time, thinking and actually wanting felt like one and the same.

But Pen couldn't imagine anyone who knew Patrick reconciling him—perpetually messy, boyish, slouchy Patrick—with all this newness and gleam: the dazzlingly white driveway lined with still-scrawny trees, the landscaping carefully choreographed for staggered, three-season blooming (crocuses, then forsythia, then tulips, then azaleas, then a bewildering sequence of flowers and flowering bushes, then, finally, dahlias and mums, and somewhere in there, for years, twined delicately around the mailbox, clematis—starry, purple, and hope-ful—until Tanya had declared it "folksy" and had it yanked).

The first time Patrick had shown her the house, Pen thought he was joking. She had given his shoulder a playful shove and said, "Yeah, right. Now take me to the real house."

"What do you mean?" he'd asked, with what Pen had assumed was faux surprise. "That's it. That's our house."

This remark would only sting later, after they'd driven back into the city and she was lying next to him on his simultaneously rock-hard and rickety Ikea futon in his small, unbeautiful, rented South Philly row house, watching him sleep. He had only been living in the house for a few weeks before Pen met him, but already it looked more lived-in than the apartment a few blocks away where she'd lived for years: houseplants on the kitchen windowsill, *New Yorker* cartoons stuck to the refrigerator door, a grove of candle stumps above the imitation fireplace, the mantel studded with coins of wax.

"That *was* our house," he should have said, or "That's *her* house," or even better, "That's the house I barely remember living in for two years, if you can call what I was doing before I met you living."

Pen had watched his eyes move under the heartbreakingly thin skin of his eyelids and tried to remember what she knew about REM sleep. He was dreaming, right? Watching things invisible to her. It seemed possible that in such a state, his brain might be especially susceptible to suggestion. "You live here," she had whispered fervidly. "Got that? *Here.*"

But because at the time, sitting next to Patrick in the car, Pen thought the whole thing was a joke, she had laughed and said, "Trust me, that is not your house."

"It is," he'd insisted. "I lived in it for two years."

"Please," she'd said, rolling her eyes. "You did not live there."

"Why do you say that?"

"Because people don't really live in houses like that. It's not pos-sible."

"Houses like what?"

"You know like what. Like oversized and soulless and planted in the middle of what used to be someone's cornfield."

They both looked at the house. Because Patrick had slunk down in the passenger seat to hide from the neighbors (although why he bothered was a mystery to Pen, since the neighboring houses were set so far away that, unless the people living in them had high-powered binoculars, they couldn't have seen a 747 landing in Patrick's yard, or what Patrick was pretending was his yard, which was almost large enough to accommodate such a landing, should one ever occur), he had to scoot himself up so that his eyes were just above the base of the window.

It had been July, just after twelve noon, and the high white sun pounding down wasn't doing the house any favors. Pen remembered imagining how, in mellow afternoon light, the stucco might have looked buttery instead of bad-teeth yellow and the tall windows might have seemed welcoming rather than flashing and blind. Despite her old-house snobbery, Pen might have found it sort of pretty or at least impressive. As it was, the house appeared creepily phony, like an enormous photograph thumbtacked to a vast blue wall. Even the flowers looked plastic.

"I think it's fake," Pen had said in a stage whisper. "I think if you went up to it and pushed it with one finger, it would fall down flat."

"I guess I can see how it wouldn't be everyone's cup of tea." Something in his voice caught Pen's attention because it sounded like sadness. But before she could ask him about it, the yard was suddenly alive, blossoming with tiny, silvery, geranium-flower-shaped fountains and crisscrossed with rainbows.

"Whoa," breathed Pen.

"Hey!" said Patrick, sitting up in his seat. "That's not supposed to happen." He didn't sound sad anymore; he sounded concerned.

"I guess it's the sprinkler system. For the grass?" said Pen, figuring it out. She felt a bit deflated. For a few seconds there, the lawn's abrupt transformation had seemed like a minor miracle.

"Yeah, but it's set for morning and evening. If you water in the heat of the day, the sun soaks it all up. Tanya must have set it wrong before they left for the beach."

Pen stared at the back of Patrick's neck.

Crap, she thought, *crappity crap crap shit.*

"Um," she said in a small voice. "So, gosh. You really did live here, in this place I just completely demolished?"

"Until I was thrown out on my ass, yes." He turned and smiled at her. "Demolished? You doused that sucker with gasoline and set it on fire."

"I'm sorry. I really and truly didn't think it was yours."

Patrick took off his ancient Phillies cap, put it in his lap, and looked at it.

Pen said, "Guess I was pretty harsh."

Patrick looked back at the house, "You really think it's soulless?"

Absolutely and entirely soulless, thought Pen, *barren and treeless and pretentious and soulless.* "I shouldn't have said 'soulless.'"

"Because that's the house Lila's growing up in, you know?"

At the time, Pen hadn't yet met Lila, who was three years old, and whenever Patrick mentioned her, Pen experienced an odd and intense mix of reverence, curiosity, jealousy, and irritation. It was just the way she had felt back in elementary school, when her devoutly Catholic friend Shelby talked about the Blessed Virgin. ("We have the Virgin Mary, too," Pen could remember protesting. "You don't pray to her, do you?" Shelby had shot back. "And if you don't pray to her, you don't have her. You have God and Jesus, that's *it.*")

Pen looked at Patrick's longish curly hair, the stubble on his face. His T-shirt was transparent in spots and so decayed that the figure on the front looked more like a Cat in the Hat zombie than the Cat himself, and his Phillies cap was a dull pink, the ratty white buckram poking through all along the brim.

"I don't know. I guess I just can't imagine you in that particular house," ventured Pen finally.

"Why not?"

"Patrick, you shave once a week, tops. And look at you. Every single edge on you is frayed."

Patrick looked down at himself, fingering the hem of his khaki shorts.

"I'm clean, though. I make a point of being clean." He smiled at her, but his eyes weren't happy.

"You are. You do."

"I let Tanya pick the house. She cared, and I really didn't. Besides, it was mostly her money."

Pen wasn't sure that this was true. Despite his threadbare appearance, Patrick was a partner in a marketing and design firm that even Jamie (who had loathed the Patrick situation from the beginning) had grudgingly acknowledged "did well." But Patrick liked to think of himself as a "regular Joe," a trait Pen had found endearingly down to earth, initially, and annoyingly affected later. ("I should have known he wasn't trustworthy," Pen told her friend Amelie, after Patrick had broken off their engagement and gone back to Tanya. "The first time I saw him in a mechanic's shirt with another man's name on it, I should have known.")

The house seemed to suit Patrick no better now, almost six years after he'd left her and gone back to it the first time, two since he'd gone back to it for good, than it ever had, but now Pen had her own reasons to regret calling it soulless, since, for one weekend out of every month, Augusta was growing up here, too.

Before she got out of the car, Pen smoothed her already smooth hair and put on lip gloss, stabbing at her mouth with the sponge-tipped wand and cursing herself between clenched teeth for caring, even a little, about Patrick's and Tanya's opinions of her. She started to check for food in her teeth, then stopped. *Enough,* she thought, *enough, enough, for God's sake,* and she set off briskly down the long driveway, *pat pat pat,* her dark red ballet flats flashing against the white. It was strange, Pen thought, how coming to this house never got any less awkward, especially strange when you considered that she hadn't hated Tanya for a long time, not for years, and was ashamed that she ever had.

The trouble was that Tanya still hated Pen. She hid it, most of the time, or, rather, camouflaged it as cold dislike or stony indifference or mocking disdain (the woman had Joan Crawford eyebrows and knew how to use them), but then, as sudden as a slap, it would hit Pen: a blazing, palpable, ever-fresh hatred that whipped around and raged inside Tanya's eyes like twin electrical storms. *If you ever get diagnosed with terminal cancer, if you get hit by a freight train or just drop dead for no reason at all*, the look told Pen, *I would rejoice in my soul.*

Certainly, this was disturbing, but Pen had to admit that she found it kind of admirable. She could imagine sustaining certain emotions at that pitch for that long—love absolutely, grief probably, guilt maybe—but hatred was exhausting and gave so little back. Once, after her father died, Pen had tried to keep hatred alive, but it kept losing its firm shape, kept smudging and blurring until it became an immense, black, impossibly heavy sadness that lived inside her body and made it hard to move, so she had given it up. Sometimes she missed it, though.

When Tanya opened the door, the eyebrows were telegraphing a patronizing impatience, but nothing more.

"Finally, she arrives," said Tanya.

Pen didn't apologize or glance at her watch. Her habitual lateness was a fiction Tanya had maintained for years, despite the fact that Pen was chronically, even annoyingly punctual. ("It has to end," Amelie had ranted once. "This arriving *on the dot*. Good Lord. It's an *affront!*") But Pen couldn't help it. It was family law. Her parents had caught her young and brainwashed her. Even Jamie was never late.

"We said five," Pen reminded her. Then she made the snap decision to smile and did it, slowly, beginning with her eyes, ending with the corners of her mouth, throwing a tiny nose crinkle in for good measure. What the hell; she had a favor to ask Tanya and Patrick and could use a boost, even a cheap one. She held the smile for a few seconds, letting it ripen on her face like a peach. She waited. Whenever Pen was friendly to Tanya (and sometimes she was even friendly by accident, rather than by design), she got the same response: Tanya was thrown off her game entirely, sometimes freezing up, sometimes spluttering incoherently, sometimes stomping out of the room. Whatever her response, for a few moments anyway, Pen had the upper hand.

Her face still beaming post-smile warmth, Pen watched Tanya

take a step back and clear her throat. "*We* have a *dinner* reservation with Lou and Bev *Byatt* at a *tapas* place. We ordered the special rice dish, *not* risotto"—she paused, searching for the word, then shaking her head, impatiently—"in *advance* because it takes an extremely long time"—her voice rose as she finished—"*to prepare!*"

Tanya didn't say, "So there," but with her raised eyebrows and fist on her hip, she might as well have. Pen had to stop herself from smiling again.

"You mean paella?" asked Pen. "Lucky you. You'll love it."

"Oh, I've had it," Tanya told her. "Many, many times!" Then she twisted her neck to bellow over her shoulder, "Lila! Time for Augusta to go!" And she turned on her heel and was gone.

Pen leaned against the foyer wall, feeling more guilty than satisfied. The truth was that Tanya was not a ridiculous person, not most of the time, anyway. She was smart, generous, and community-minded, a former ob-gyn who now worked for a women's health advocacy group. Pen had met a few of her former patients over the years, and they all worshipped her. She was pretty, too. Five years older than Patrick, which meant that she was ten years older than Pen, but no one would ever have guessed it. She had an aquiline nose and the kind of coloring that Pen's mother called "autumn redhead," auburn hair, tawny skin, and eyes the color of whiskey.

Pretty, hardworking, and good, Pen thought, *and you had to push the one button that turns her into a blithering idiot.*

She hates you, Pen reminded herself in her own defense.

Understandably, she argued back.

Understandably, maybe, but not justifiably. Look at the facts.

It was an old argument. In its first incarnation, Pen had been arguing with her mother instead of herself.

"She's a mother. And you're threatening her family. Of course, she hates you," her mother had said.

"Look at the facts," Pen had retorted. "He didn't leave her for me. She called him a self-centered bastard and threw him out. I met him afterward, when he was living by himself because she *threw him out!*"

"Even so."

"She changed the locks!"

"Oh, Pen."

The kindness in her mother's voice had been too much for Pen, who was alone, jobless, and, although she didn't know it yet, pregnant. She had begun to cry, then to sob, clenched and bent over like an old woman. Her mother had pulled her into her lap and stroked her hair.

"I wanted to keep him," Pen sobbed. "And I gave him back. I loved teaching, and she got me fired, even though I gave him back."

Her back against the wall in Tanya's cold foyer, Pen closed her eyes, remembering.

"Hey there, uh, Pen." It was Patrick, slipping into the foyer in his slinking, barefoot manner, saying her name the way he always did, as though he didn't quite have the right to say it.

"Hello."

Reluctantly, Pen opened her eyes, saw Patrick in the vintage Replacements T-shirt she had bought him when they'd first started dating, thought, *Oh, God,* and shut them again. The Replacements had been Jamie's favorite band all through college (even though they had been broken up for years even then) and, therefore, Pen's favorite, too, although Pen really only liked their major-label albums. She opened her eyes and took another look. Paul Westerberg, the first of her scrawny, shaggy-haired crushes, gazing moodily out at her from the chest of her last. *Wonderful.*

"You want to come in? Sit down or something?" asked Patrick.

Pen didn't. She preferred the peripheries—the yard, the foyer, the driveway—and rarely ventured into the rest of the house ("the family quarters," she joked to Jamie, "the inner sanctum," "the bowels"). In the five years since Augusta was born, she had never gone upstairs once. Today, she needed to talk to Patrick, though, so she nodded and followed him into what she knew was called "the great room," cavernous, a tsunami of sun cresting through the gigantic windows, drowning the room and everything in it. Pen recoiled like a vampire, arms in front of her face.

"I know," said Patrick. He made his voice flat and instructional, "Don sunglasses before entering."

Pen smiled. *Don.*

"It's actually a pretty room," she said, blinking and looking around. "Sweeping. Gracious. All those words. I've always thought so." She meant it. She couldn't imagine living in such a room, but she liked the *idea* of wall-lessness: everything happening in one place, everyone together. And despite its vastness and stark light, Tanya's decorating, or her decorator's decorating, had given it warmth. Cream, sand, and sage, punctuated with garnet and Delft blue, large vases of real flowers, walls the color of coffee ice cream.

"Nah," said Patrick, with a sidelong grin, "I've seen the nest. I know your hermit thrush ways."

Pen stiffened.

Suddenly, it was winter, her parents' house, back when it was still her house, too, the first time Cat and Will came home with her for a weekend. Will and Cat seeing her old room for the first time: the bunk beds, the white swivel egg chair with the red cushions. Will pointed to the bunk beds and asked, "You and Jamie shared a room?"

"God, no," said Pen, making a face and ducking backward into the chair. She looked up at them, her legs swinging. "I just like bunk beds. Upper bunk. I used to pretend I was sleeping in one of those train compartments from a Hitchcock movie." She thought for a second. "Actually, I still do pretend that."

Will eyed the bed. He rapped his knuckles lightly on the fiberglass shell of the chair and nodded.

"You're a nester," he'd said. "You like to fold yourself into little spaces. Armchairs. Library carrels. I've noticed this."

"Restaurant booths!" added Cat, catching on. "I like an open table myself, but you!" She leaned over and poked Pen's forehead with her finger. "You always want the booth! I bet you get in the bathtub and close the shower curtain."

"Tea parties *under* the table," said her mother's voice from behind them. Pen couldn't see her, but could hear her mother smile, and swiveled around to look.

"I think they're on to me," said Pen to her mother.

Her mother pointed to the wardrobe against the far wall of the room. "That's got a deep, low shelf, for shoes, maybe, or blankets. But when Pen was little, she used to climb out of her bed and sleep on it. The first time it happened, Ben and I were scared to death, looked for her everywhere."

"Like I said," said Will, "a nester. A hermit thrush."

After graduation, a week after the three of them had moved to Philadelphia together, Pen had come home to the apartment she shared with Cat to find that they had made her a nest. A window seat rigged with a wooden curtain rod, a green curtain, and a matching cushion, so that she could curl up inside, draw the curtain shut, and look out at her little piece of city. Pen had still lived in the apartment when she'd met Patrick, even though, by then, Cat was long gone.

So unfair, Patrick's fingerprints on her funny stories, her pet phrases, on people he never knew.

This is what you get, she berated herself, *for handing everything over.*

She had felt the same way when Cat and Will left. "I gave you two my life," she had raged at Will the last time she saw him. "My childhood, my parents, the things that scare me, the books I love, the *sentences* I love from the books I love. You went on bike rides with *my dad.* And you're *leaving*? Are you *kidding* me?"

Keep the T-shirt, she wanted to tell Patrick, *but everything else, everything pre-you, forget it; erase it from your clucking hard drive.*

"Have a seat," Patrick offered.

Pen looked at the sofas, the deep armchairs, and the love seats and could not imagine doing that kind of sinking down and leaning back in Tanya and Patrick's house.

"How about over here?" She was already walking toward the kitchen, which lay at the distant end of the great room, rising up out of the earth tones like a city, all steel, edges, and glass, its appliances mammoth, its countertops shining like lakes. She sat on one of the high stools that flanked one of the counters, feeling out of place and rigid, her back straight, her hands in her lap, becoming prim the way she often did when she felt out of place. She shook her head when Patrick offered her something to drink.

"So," she began, but Patrick grabbed her "so" and ran with it, in the last direction Pen wanted to go.

"So, *yeah*," he said, widening his blue eyes, "tell me about the weekend at your mom's. The bike ride and all. It go okay?"

Just like that: *Tell me about.* Pen stared at him. Tell *you*? *Tell* you? *He cares,* she tried to remind herself. *He has no tact and is presumptuous, but he does care.* And he had taken Augusta for an unscheduled weekend so that Pen and Jamie could go alone to the anniversary ride. *You're about to ask him for another unscheduled weekend,* Pen thought. *Suck it up.*

"I guess it went okay," she said. "It was crazy-sad, but we got through it. And it felt like the right thing to do."

"Was it different from last year?"

It had been. Jamie had been too loyal to tell Patrick about Pen's little breakdown last year, and Pen had been too ashamed, but Patrick had picked up on the fact that it had been an ordeal for everyone. This year had been different, maybe not easier, but hard in a different way. Last year, Pen hadn't been able to finish the ride; this year, she hadn't wanted it to end. With the road unspooling under her bike wheels and the trees leaning in on either side, Pen remembered doing the same ride with her father, a memory of such detail and vividness that, for several sweet miles, she almost believed he was there with her, riding just outside of her peripheral vision, his voice tugged out of earshot by the wind. But when the ride ended, he was as gone as ever, and Pen was left raw, windburned by loss.

Then, afterward, eating catered food in her parents' house with their friends, Pen kept expecting her mother to appear, to come down the stairs in a linen dress and lipstick. Pen had known she wouldn't be there (she had called the night before from Greece), but Pen kept watching for her anyway. "It's awful," she'd told Jamie. "Like phantom limb syndrome."

But to Patrick, who had lost his right to know about such things, she said simply, "Yes."

Patrick nodded his trademark nod, a movement not just of his head, but of his shoulders and chest as well. Full-upper-body empathy. *Please know that I, and my entire torso, are right there with you.*

"Cathartic, right?" he prompted. "Healing? I bet you have that wrung-out but good-wrung-out feeling, right?"

Pen stared at him. He had not always been like this; she swore he hadn't. Back when they were together, he'd had a far more distracted approach to conversation, losing track of threads, doodling while they talked, playing his own knee like a techno-pop keyboardist. Back then, he had a trick of nodding with apparent interest even as he zoned out, then zoned back in, saying, maddeningly, "So, *yeah*. Wow. *Any*way."

Somehow, since their final split two years ago, he had become a talk-show host, a conversational lobster eater, cracking open shells, twisting off legs, trying to get at every soft and hidden thing. His bright blue eyes were lit with over-interest, and Pen had to stop looking at them, focusing instead on the pepper grinder in front of her. It was a foot and a half high and appeared heavy as lead.

"Man felled by pepper grinder in own kitchen," she said.

"What?" Patrick's full-body nod stopped midbend, and his neck turned scarlet. "Oh, okay. Boundaries, right?" They'd had boundaries conversations before.

"Right."

"Sorry." He gave a little laugh, but his face shifted into the kind of puzzled hurt that you usually only see on the faces of small children. Once Pen had crumbled before that expression. Even now, her first impulse was to take back what she'd said, but she resisted. Instead, she smiled a lopsided smile at him, and said, "Man apologizes in nick of time."

Then, sailing toward her from across the room: "Mama!"

High-pitched, even squeaky, it was the most soul-catching sound Pen knew. She was turning in its direction before she had even slid off the stool, and, when she saw the girl bounding rabbit-fashion through the great room, she felt what she always felt, her body opening toward her daughter in a great whoosh of breathless blooming.

"Sweetpea," she whispered, smiling, and then Augusta flew against her with a whack, and Pen knelt down to gather all of the child into her, pressing her cheek into the cloud of dark hair, her palms against the narrow back. At five, Augusta was already losing her baby softness, was becoming pared down, almost sinewy, her back a delicate landscape of spine and shoulder blades that Pen could feel through her shirt.

"I am so happy to see you," said Pen.

"My heart leaps up, Mama." It was what they always said.

"My heart leaps up, too."

She drew back and looked at Augusta's face, which was smeared with colors, brilliant, glittery, and iridescent as a hummingbird's neck. For the first time, Pen noticed the child's outfit: black go-go boots so big they were merely drifting around her calves, a scratchy pink tutu, a silvery tank top slipping off one scrawny shoulder.

"Hey there, Pop Star."

Augusta shimmied her shoulders and sang a few lines from a song about going out with her girlfriends and leaving the boys behind.

"Sounds good to me," said Patrick.

Pen could imagine her before-kids self being utterly disapproving of this, the little girl in makeup and grown-up clothes thing, the pre-pre-pre-tween fascination with fabulousness. But seeing it in action, she found it didn't bother her. Little girls were magpies and butterflies, gaga for everything shiny, in sheer, giggly, joyful love with transformation. Pen looked at Augusta, so at home in her body, so convinced of her own gorgeousness. *Keep it up, honey,* she thought. *Hang on to it with both hands.*

"Hi, Pen." Lila stood behind Augusta, smiling and tugging at her T-shirt in a way that made Pen's heart ache. At nine, Lila barely qualified as chubby, but, despite her parents' efforts to celebrate her good points, which were many (smarts, big blue eyes, and an uncommon sweetness), self-consciousness was setting in.

"Hey, lovely," said Pen, standing. Lila's eyes widened with happiness. Pen did not spend enough time with Lila for the two of them to really be close, but Pen knew Lila regarded her with the kind of shy, eager interest that verged on adulation. She remembered feeling that way herself, about her fifth-grade teacher, her friend Sydney's teenaged sister who began loading her neck with rosaries (to her family's deep and everlasting horror) and her arms with rubber bracelets before most people in Wilmington even knew who Madonna was. Pen could not imagine Tanya's enjoying Lila's crush on Pen, but to her credit, she had never tried to squelch it.

"You guys have fun this weekend?" Pen asked.

"We totally did," said Lila, reaching out and giving her sister's hair a gentle tug. "Can Augusta come back soon?"

"You know what? I was just about to talk to your dad about another visit. You think you could help Augusta change and get her stuff together, while we discuss it? That would be a huge help."

"Definitely!"

Pen and Patrick watched the girls zigzag through the furniture and out of the room, hair flying.

"Lila's a doll," said Pen. "Aren't they supposed to get mean by the time they're nine?"

"Yeah, she seems to be sidestepping that stuff so far. Hope it lasts." He folded his arms across his chest. "So what's up? You need another weekend?"

"My college reunion, ten year. It's in two weeks."

Patrick smiled at her. "Ten year, huh? I forget what a baby you are."

"Oh, come on. You're five years older than I am, which is nothing." Five years wasn't nothing really, not necessarily, but Pen had never felt the age difference between them. Most of the time, she felt as though she were the one who was older.

"Hey, you think you'll run into Cat? It's been ages, right?"

Pen hesitated, then told him about the e-mail. He'd known what Cat had meant to her. It might give him some extra incentive to persuade Tanya to take Augusta for another weekend. Tanya liked Augusta, never failed to make her feel welcome, but she was fiercely protective of "family time" on weekends. On weekdays, too. She and Patrick both made a point of being home by 5:30 and ruthlessly screened incoming phone calls in the evenings. A couple of years ago, Tanya had asked Pen not to call, unless Augusta had a "life-threatening emergency." Wincing at the phrase "life-threatening" appearing in the same sentence with her daughter's name, Pen had quickly agreed.

"I think it'll be fine," said Patrick. "I'll talk to Tanya. But I hope that Will guy won't show up."

"Oh, Patrick."

"Seriously. I've heard enough about his temper to think you're not safe around a guy like that."

It was ridiculous, this protective posturing, this misplaced, leftover, and far too easy chivalry. When Pen had met Patrick, Cat and Will were newly gone, and Pen was still reeling, her sadness still fresh and shot through with anger. She'd told Patrick too much, probably, and he had fixated on Will in a way that she'd briefly found touching, but that made no sense. Not safe with Will. *Will?* With whom had she ever been safer?

"He never directed any of that stuff at me. He wouldn't in a million years. You know I've told you that."

"I'm not so sure. Sorry, but I just don't think he's trustworthy."

What about you? You walked out on me and our newborn baby. You gave up custody of her because your wife made you. How trustworthy are you? Pen felt like saying these things, but mostly only because they were true, only to defend Will. She wasn't really bitter anymore, not bitter-bitter, a fact that still surprised her.

"He probably won't be there, anyway," said Pen, although she knew that if Cat had written to him, too, he probably would be. Not probably. She didn't know who Will had become in the past six years, but if he was now a person who could turn down a cry for help from an old friend, Pen would eat her hat.

"It's been a long time. Do you still think about them? I mean, more than once in a while? Do you miss them?" said Patrick.

Lobster eater, thought Pen, shaking her head, *lobster eater, lobster eater, lobster eater.*

"Not really," she said.

CHAPTER SIX

$\mathscr{T}$HE LITTLE BOY IN *COUNTING BACK TO LIAM* TURNS INTO A monster when he's angry. The monster is huge and gloriously ugly, toothy as a shark, carpeted with spiky slime-green hair, sporting bat wings, stegosaurus plates down his back, and a head that is an amalgamation of buffalo, werewolf, and Gila monster. When a man walking in front of Liam and his mother down a city street unwraps his sandwich and throws the wrapper on the ground, the monster erupts into thundering life, charging down the sidewalk—clunking into innocent bystanders along the way—and confronting the man with a roar that shakes the buildings around them, shattering the window of a bakery storefront, toppling the cakes. Then the monster stomps on the man's foot. The man is hopping and stunned. The people on the sidewalk are appalled and rubbing their elbows and heads and other places the monster has bumped. The mother's head is drooping, her hand over her eyes, and in this gesture and in the wilt of her shoulders, there is a profound discouragement, a near hopelessness that tells the reader that this is not the first time something like this has happened.

When the boy turns away from the man, he is Liam again, small in his T-shirt and jeans, shaky, drained of triumph, frightened by his own loss of control. In bed that night, he tells his mother, "I thought the man was bad, but maybe I'm the one who's bad." And his mother tells him, "You? No, you are my funny sonny, my curious, story-loving, cookie-sharing boy. That monster, *he's* the one who's bad." And the boy says, "The monster makes me lonely. I mean he makes me feel alone." "The monster makes me lonely, too," his mother says.

Liam and his mother visit a wise woman. In the wordless illustrations that follow, Liam talks, sometimes laughing, sometimes sad, sometimes pressing his face into his mother's arm, and the woman listens. Then she says, "I'm not a fairy godmother, you know. I don't have a magic wand, and what a silly thing, to think that magic lives inside a wand!" "It doesn't?" asks the boy. "Magic lives in here," the woman says, placing one hand on Liam's head. "And here," she tells him, pointing to his heart. "And you are full of it and courage, too." "Courage?" asks Liam. "I don't think so. Me?" "Of course," says the woman. "Now, listen: I think I know a way to get that monster *gone*."

Pen read this book for the first time four months after her father died. She was sitting in Pollywogs, her favorite children's bookstore in Philadelphia, a place to which she had escorted so many writers that she'd become friends with the owner, a Mrs. Piggle Wiggle look-alike named Selena Bass. Selena had invited her to come just after closing to help create some displays of new books.

It was one of Pen's first ventures out of the apartment for anything other than work since her father had died, and she had walked the whole way there, a long walk. At first, she had almost turned back, shaky and tired, street noise loud in her ears, but after a few blocks, it had felt good to be out, walking among strangers, anonymous. She crossed streets, stopped at corners, shrugged her handbag more securely onto her shoulder, an oddly reassuring movement. On the busy sidewalk, she could have been anyone, someone who was grieving or not, had a father or didn't. If Selena hadn't been watching through the door of her shop, Pen might have walked right past it. She might have walked all night.

Inside, the shop was cozy and purple-walled. A former elementary-school teacher, Selena had whipped off freehand, typeface-quality signs with colored Sharpies, each sign featuring a quotation from a famous children's book (one notable example from *Winnie-the-Pooh*: "If the person you are talking to doesn't appear to be listening, be patient. It may simply be that he has a small piece of fluff in his ear"), while Pen had unpacked picture books, feeling moved and reverential, running a hand over each glossy cover before placing the books on the display shelf of the little backroom reading space called the Cuddle-upreadalotorium.

She was remembering a conversation with her father.

"Here's what happened: you got fired, then you got discouraged. Who wouldn't?" he had told her a few days before he died. "Then you started driving the writers around, you and that cute Amelie, and you liked it pretty well, and then you had Augusta, and you went with the flow. Makes sense. But my bet? You'll be back in front of a classroom one of these days."

"How do you know?" she'd asked him.

"I know because I know," he'd answered.

Holding the new books in her hands, she missed teaching kids how to read. She missed having someone know her the way her father had.

Pen didn't see Will's name on the front of the book at first. She had been too arrested by the cover: jewel and earth tones soaked in light, looking more like a Vermeer than like any children's book cover Pen had ever seen, the monster standing with one vast, clawed hand over its eyes, the other hand in the air, three fingers raised, counting.

"Ooh, that's a good one. Brand-new and bound for greatness. It'll win every kids' book award under the sun," said Selena, glancing over. "Why don't you sit down with it for a minute?"

Pen had sat. From the beginning, the language was wonderful, clean, vivid, leaping upward into poetry at just the right moments, especially in the second half of the book. Liam and his mother wait in line at the post office, their arms full of packages. Outside the window, low afternoon light rests on the snow-covered street; pearly caps of snow top fire hydrants and parked cars and the wool hat of a woman who bustles into the post office with her own tower of packages. Snow caps the tower of packages. "Excuse me," the woman says huffily. "I'm late for a very important appointment! I'm sure you won't mind!" And she steps in line in front of Liam's mother.

Slowly, Pen had turned the page and winced to find what she'd been afraid she would find. The little boy Liam is gone, replaced by the monster, who begins to take a step toward the woman, his awful, thick green leg hooked in the air, his arms raised menacingly. And then, quite suddenly, he freezes, and he puts his foot back down, the effort that it takes to do this written on his face. Then he closes his wild eyes—red lizard eyes with the dash-shaped pupils of a goat—and in a few moments, the walls of the post office fall away, the people and their packages and the snowy city turn translucent and disappear, and there is the monster, standing in somebody's backyard. It is early summer and the yard is flush with blooming; a sprinkler glitters in the background, a giant oak tree cradles a wooden tree house in its branches, purple pansies with their tiny, winking faces bloom in a pot beside the backdoor of the house, and framed by an open window—it seems to be a kitchen window—is the face of a woman, Liam's mother's face.

Liam's mother smiles at the monster, who puts one hand over his eyes. He begins to count, and something amazing begins to happen. "Five . . ."—the monster shrinks to boy-size. "Four . . ."—his bristly fur silvers, turns to dandelion fluff, and blows across the sky. "Three . . ."—each stegosaurus plate along his back detaches, folds itself into an origami bird and flies away. "Two . . ."—the bat wings of the monster who is almost not a monster anymore close themselves like black umbrellas. "One . . ."—and then they *are* umbrellas and Liam holds one in each hand.

On the next page, Liam is back inside the post office in his winter coat, packages at his feet, and he takes the two umbrellas and slips them into the umbrella stand beside the post office door. Then he walks up to the woman who cut in line and taps her lightly on the arm. She turns disdainful eyes on him and asks him what he wants. Liam says, "Excuse me, but my mother and I have been waiting a long time. Our packages are heavy, just like yours. I think you should go to the end of the line. I think it's only fair." And, for a moment, the woman's face twists in anger. She seems about to speak, then stops, closes her eyes, and takes a few deep breaths.

"You're right," she tells the little boy. "I'm having a hard day, but that is not your fault. Not your mother's, either. And, yes, it's only fair." And she steps to the back of the line. Then Liam's mother smiles as loving a smile as Pen had ever seen on any person, living or painted, and carefully bends her knees to set her bundles on the floor. She opens her arms to Liam, who fits himself inside them. "Liam 1," she whispers to him, "Monster 0."

Pen had not consciously known that Will had written *Counting Back to Liam* until she shut the book and saw his name on the cover, but what she would swear to be true forever after was that before she knew that she knew, she knew. About three-quarters of the way through the book, she had gotten the strange and specific sensation of a small light turning on inside her chest, lifting itself out of darkness like a miniature dawn, and starting to brighten and grow, so that by the time she'd found his name on the cover, she wasn't stunned the way she might have expected she'd be. Her heart didn't take off like a racehorse. Instead, she sat in the child-sized blue plastic chair and felt like one of the paintings in the book, imbued with a warm, lemon-colored radiance. It took her a few seconds to realize that what she felt was happy.

Good for you, Will, she had thought, hard. She meant for writing the book, which was wonderful, for writing it in spite of his father, who would never have given his blessing to such a thing, but more than that, she meant good for him for getting better, for learning how to get the best of his temper, which had been so nightmarish and had made him feel so bad. Because that's what the book meant, Pen understood. She lifted the book and leaned her forehead on it, briefly, eyes closed, in honor of the promise it gave that her friend was okay.

"It's gorgeous, isn't it?" said Selena.

"Yes. It's gorgeous and moving and funny. I love it," said Pen. "I know him."

"Will Wadsworth?" asked Selena. "Is he a friend of yours?"

"He was," said Pen, but the words sounded wrong, so she added, "We went to college together." Still wrong, too limited and small. It had seemed very important to find the right words to describe Will's position in her life, but the story was too long to tell. "I adore Will, actually. Just haven't seen him in a while."

"Oh," said Selena. She had smiled, head tipped to one side, and blinked her twinkly eyes. *You need a hat,* thought Pen, thinking of Mrs. Piggle Wiggle, *a boater hat and an apron.* Because she was picturing this, it took her a moment to process what Selena said next, "Then you must know his mother?"

Will's mother. Mrs. Wadsworth. Pen had flashed back to her, then, seeing her as she'd been the few times Pen had met her: flushed, faintly smiling, extremely quiet except for, now and then, a surprisingly witty remark, the fact of her drunkenness revealed only in her occasional shaky and incongruous bursts of laughter and in her clumsy hands. Pen had eaten three meals with the woman in her life, and at all three, she had knocked over a glass. But mostly, she was so lacking in presence, so overshadowed by Will's father that it had been hard to tell that she was drunk at all.

"If I didn't know your mom was an alcoholic," Cat had said once, "I wouldn't know she was an alcoholic. I don't think I've ever seen her drunk."

"You've never seen her not drunk," Will had said dryly. "Trust me on that."

The last time Pen had seen Will's mother, she had been different. It was at the summerhouse, not long after Cat had left, the only time Pen had ever been there with Will's mother and without Cat, a weekend that had started out calm and lovely and that had ended in disaster. She had been newly separated from Will's father (Mr. Wadsworth, Pen always called him, even though he had asked her more than once to call him Randall), and there was something wild in her. Pen remembered her as loud and frenetic, in constant motion, laughing, whirling across the living room, sitting on the lap of a man just a few years older than Will, a painter she had met in an art class. Damon Callas.

Pen's face had felt hot as she answered Selena, "I didn't know her. Not well. She and Will weren't really close." Again, her words felt wrong. Will and his mother hadn't been close the way Pen and her parents had been. There was no confiding, no easy camaraderie, and none of the starry-eyed hero-worship that marked Cat's regard for her father, but what was written all over Will's face whenever he spent time with or talked about his mother, while it might have been broken and sad, was clearly love.

"No?"

"You sound surprised," said Pen. "Do you know her?"

"Oh, no," said Selena. "But the illustrations and the words, they're so wonderfully matched, so one with each other. It's surprising to hear that they're not close."

Pen felt confused, trying to make sense of Selena's pronouns. Then she looked down at the cover of the book again and saw what she had missed the first time. There, below Will's name: "Illustrations by Charlotte Tully Wadsworth." Pen read the name again, tracing it with her finger. What a wondrous thing.

Pen had gone back and paged through the book, then, through each glowing, intricate, color-drenched illustration, and had stopped at the picture of the monster, mid-transformation, the dandelion fluff touched by the sun into a kind of filigree, each feathery filament of each tiny blowing seed parachute precisely shining, the whole picture full of an almost palpable lightness. Pen looked, next, at the mother's watching face in the kitchen window. The illustration had blurred, as Pen's eyes filled. She smiled. If Charlotte Tully Wadsworth had walked into the bookstore right then, Pen would have hugged her, something she had never done in real life.

"You're right," she'd said to Selena, nodding, her fingertips resting on the beautiful thing that Will and his mother had made together. "Something must have changed a lot for her to be able to do this."

Selena capped her Sharpie with a flourish. "Good. Better than good. The world could use more of that, couldn't it? Kids and parents getting closer, instead of breaking apart and losing each other." Then Selena pressed the back of her hand to her mouth for a few seconds and shook her head. "Oh, God. I'm sorry, dear heart," she said. "I wasn't talking about you and your dad, who were as close as any people could be. I didn't mean—"

Pen reached out and squeezed Selena's hand. "I know what you meant. And it *is* better than good. That's just exactly what it is."

◆　◆　◆

AFTER PEN HAD SPENT TEN MINUTES INTERCEPTING DIRTY LOOKS from her fellow diners, including one from a child in an Elmo T-shirt who feigned gagging himself with his finger, and watching Kiki Melloy, nonstop talker and bestselling mystery author, try to simultaneously talk nonstop and cut her enormous rib eye without losing her grip on the unlit cigarette chopsticked between two fingers of her left hand, she said, "Kiki, maybe you should just put that thing down."

Kiki's gaze became patient and long-suffering. "Penny, honey, no one ever said personal protests were easy. Ask Dr. King about that."

Kiki's mysteries featured amateur detective Hildy Breen, an occasionally clairvoyant exotic small animal vet (fire-bellied toads, sugar gliders, bearded dragons, and the like), living in an adorable, if corpse-riddled, southern town. People categorized her books as "cozy mysteries" but there was nothing cozy about Kiki, not Kiki's exterior anyway. Her interior was quite a different matter. She had been one of Pen's first clients and had teased out of Pen the whole story of Patrick and Tanya and of how, after a long talk with Tanya, and after talks with other parents who had talked with Tanya, the headmaster at Pen's school had suggested that she take leave from teaching to deal with her "disheveled personal life." Kiki's rapid-fire, profanity-laced excoriation of Tanya, Patrick, the headmaster, and all of "Purifuckingtanical, hypofuckingcritical, soy-slurping, 100 percent testicle-free upper-middle-class America" had caused Pen to laugh out loud for the first time in months.

Pen ignored the Dr. King remark, along with Kiki's calling her "Penny." Calmly, she said, "All I'm saying is that more of your outrageously expensive steak is flying off the table than is going into your mouth, for which your circulatory system is probably thanking you. From the bottom of its heart."

"My father said that if a steak didn't weigh more than the family Bible, it wasn't worth his time, and the man's going gangbusters at eighty-six."

"Good for him, but you've still got twenty bucks' worth of red meat sitting in your lap."

Kiki closed her eyes and issued an extravagant groan. "Have you *read* the Bill of Rights?"

"Life, Liberty, and the Pursuit of Lung Cancer? That part?"

Kiki turned to the pregnant woman at the next table, who had been shooting her murderous looks since she'd sat down. "How about you? Have *you* read the Bill of Rights?"

"You're a lunatic," said the pregnant woman.

"Only if being crazy about freedom counts," whooped Kiki. "That baby of yours will have a better future because of lunatics like me, lady."

Pen sighed. "I do not, do not, do *not* want to talk about this, but the data regarding the harmful effects of secondhand smoke are looking pretty solid."

A thoughtful expression stole over Kiki's face; her chewing slowed. " 'Data *are*,' " she echoed. "Sounds wrong. Is it?"

"I don't think so. Possibly, you can use 'is,' too. Probably."

"Interesting," said Kiki, nodding, then she jabbed the air with her fork to signal the end of their grammar facts sidebar. "Anyhoo. Data potata. Folks who don't want to expose their candy-ass asses to hazards should stay the hell home. The world is dangerous. Deal with it, people."

"I said I didn't want to talk about it. Remember?"

The pregnant woman and her friend began ostentatiously slapping their napkins from their laps to their table and signaling their waiter.

"Oh, fine. Fine, fine, fine," growled Kiki, and jammed the cigarette into the pocket of her immaculate pink Oxford shirt. Kiki swore like a dockworker, but she dressed like a Junior League president. Amelie called her a "Lilly Pulitzer fever dream."

Kiki sawed off a chunk of meat and wedged it into her mouth, squinting at Pen as though sizing her up.

"What?" asked Pen.

Through meat, Kiki said, "Tell me about this Cat character, the one who dropped you like a hot potato and is whining for your help. Whine, whine, whine."

Pen had told Kiki about the reunion by way of explaining why Amelie, not Pen, would be escorting Kiki to her speaking engagement at a big hospital benefit the following day ("the Lyme disease lunch," as Pen and Kiki liked to call it).

"You're gearing up to give me the 'You're Too Nice for Your Own Good' speech, aren't you?" Pen asked.

"No, I am not. Honest Injun."

"I don't think people say that anymore."

"Good Lord, whatever. Cross my heart, then," said Kiki, crossing her heart with her steak knife and alarming vigor. "Look, I strongly suspect that you are being too nice for you own good, but I *get* friendship, undying loyalty, all that crap. It's one of the few varieties of crap that I do get."

Because she knew this to be true, Pen thought for a moment, and then said, "Cat is the single most charming person I have ever met. She is beguiling. Bewitching. She pulls you in."

Kiki frowned. "One person's charming is another person's full-of-shit, if you know what I mean."

"I do know what you mean, and Cat likes attention, for sure. She likes to be fussed over and cuddled and adored and taken care of. She's a kitten. But she's a *real* kitten. She's genuinely sweet, but in good way."

Kiki chuckled. "Sounds like something I'd say. Okay, so what about Will? What was he like?"

Pen laughed, remembering. "Once, Cat asked Will if he was the WASPiest man on the planet."

This had been in the spring of their freshman year. Without missing a beat, Will had said, "I used to be, until my brother, Philip, showed up."

"Isn't your brother, Philip, a high school sophomore?" Pen had demanded. "Are you saying that you were the WASPiest man on the planet until you were just three years old?"

Will had nodded and said, "It was a good run, though. A really good run."

Kiki laughed when Pen told her this, then said, "I've known WASPy men. Stone face, good manners, cold hands. Getting all distant and

Episcopalian on you the second the going gets tough. Bad genes, too. Those Mayflower types are as inbred as the stinkin' Amish.'"

Before Kiki finished her list, Pen was shaking her head. "No. Good manners, yes. He was maybe a little old school, but not in a phony way. And maybe a little quiet. Not with us, mostly in big groups. But funny, dry-funny, and creative—he's an amazing writer now—and the main thing about Will is that he always had—what do I mean?" Pen rooted around for the right words for what Will had always had.

"An extremely large penis?" suggested Kiki.

"Quiet." Pen held up her hand. The right phrase came to her and she blushed at the thought of what Kiki would say about it.

"Spit it out," said Kiki.

"You'll make fun of it."

"Very possible."

"A generous heart."

Kiki absorbed this and then said, "You're saying he was nice, but in a good way?"

"And I don't know about inbreeding, but he did not get his niceness from his father, that's for sure."

"Mean?"

"Hideous."

"Hitting-mean?"

"No. But I'm pretty sure the guy was a sociopath. Or a narcissist. Not sure what the difference is, but he thought he owned other people. Or more like he didn't have any idea that other people *were* other people, especially his family. He thought they should all behave according to his will, and when they didn't, he got mean. I think Will hated him."

"Bummer. So tell me this." Kiki leaned in, her necklace of fat, unmistakably real pearls falling forward to rest on her steak. "Were you doing it?"

"Kiki."

"The three of you. You were doing it, right? Not all the time, not *nightly,* but it happened."

Pen rolled her eyes. "You aren't the only person who's wondered that."

"I'll bet."

"We weren't doing it. We were *friends*."

Kiki deflated a little and she said wistfully, "Yeah, I didn't really think you were doing it. I mean, I *hoped*. But I was almost 100 percent sure that you weren't."

"Hold on. Almost 100 percent? And why would that be?"

"Oh, come on. Why else? It's you. You're wholesome. A good girl. No getting around it. More's the pity."

"Thanks."

It was something Cat used to say, one of a few things she'd said to Pen that truly stung. "Our resident girl next door," she would sing. "Our pink-cheeked, long-lashed, straight-A, stand-up gal!" "The original brown-eyed girl!" "America's Sweetheart!" "Little Miss Perfect!" "The kind you bring home to mother!" Once as a joke, she had copied out the Girl Scout Law in semi-calligraphy on a piece of poster board and taped it to Pen's wall.

"Euphemisms for boring," Pen had observed, once, unhappy but tentative, not wanting to hurt Cat's feelings.

Cat had thrown her arms around Pen, pecked kisses onto her cheeks, and shrieked, "Never!" But she hadn't explained or taken it back. Pen hadn't stayed mad, though. She was never very good at staying mad at Cat, and she had to admit that Cat wasn't the only one calling Pen a good girl, squeaky clean; it was the sort of thing people had said, in varying tones of voice, for Pen's entire life.

"I don't feel like that inside," Pen had told Will, once.

"Of course, you don't. Why would you?" he'd said.

Now, she told Kiki, "I had an affair with a married man. Twice. Same man both times, but still. I was fired from my job for my rule-breaking ways. I have a *child* out of *wedlock*. I am an unwed mother, for crying out loud."

"Well done, too, all of that. Even so, doesn't change who you are. I guarantee that you'll go to that reunion, and Cat and everyone else'll tell you you haven't changed a bit." Kiki dabbed primly with her napkin at one corner of her mouth and shrugged. "Sorry, sister."

Pen lifted a forkful of salade Nicoise to her mouth, then put it back down on her plate. What if she and Cat and Will had changed too much? How was it that in all the years the three of them had been apart, Pen had never once, not for a moment, considered this possibility? Abruptly, she put her elbow on the tabletop and dropped her forehead into her open hand.

"Kiki."

"What?" asked Kiki, alarmed. "Oh, God. Bad tuna?"

"What if we don't know each other anymore?"

"Oh, sugar. You'll catch up. Gab, gab, gab. It's a reunion! Don't you worry."

Stricken, Pen lifted her head and looked wide-eyed at Kiki.

"No, what I mean is, what if we aren't knowable to each other anymore?"

"People don't change that much. Usually."

"What if we have? I don't know what I'll do." She had no idea.

Kiki reached across the table, pressed her tobacco-scented hand briefly against Pen's cheek, and looked at Pen in way that reminded her, with a pang, of her mother.

"Here's what you'll do," said Kiki sternly. "You'll have a quick, no fuss, no muss, three-way roll in the hay and come on back home. Understand?"

This was in no way like something her mother would have said and was at the same time exactly like something her mother would have said. Pen felt a smile start in the middle of her chest and spread to her face.

"I do," she said, and she gave Kiki a double thumbs-up to show that she did.

CHAPTER SEVEN

*D*RIVING DOWN TO THE REUNION, PEN REMEMBERED THIS: Halloween, junior year. Cold; the smell of wood smoke, rotting leaves, and beer; a fat and jaundiced moon.

The fraternity party was bad, but not as bad as most. The music was moody and decent and playing at a less-than-bone-jarring level; someone had actually made an effort, however feeble, with the decorations (jack-o'-lanterns, dry ice in a plastic cauldron, wobbly rubber bats hanging from the ceiling, fake cobwebs making their woolly way across walls and windows and the cracked bathroom mirror); and there was even—and this was the crowning glory—promotional beer from a new local microbrewery.

"Just wait," Will warned. "What begins as Beck, Luna, and amber ale will be grain punch, vomit on the dance floor, and 'Louie, Louie' by the end of the night. It's the way of all things."

They were there because of Cat, who adored fraternity parties as she adored any activity involving dim lights, music, noise, and boys. "Don't you feel it?" she would ask Pen, with a shiver. "The singing in your veins? The electric zing of possibility in the air?" And, often, Pen did feel it, not so much at the party or the club or the bonfire or the concert, but beforehand, getting ready with Cat, trying on clothes, splashing the rejected scarves, tops, and dresses onto Cat's bed, shimmying around the living room with a glass of wine. They'd walk out their apartment door, with their lipstick fresh and their hair and eyes lit by the streetlights, and anything, *anything* would seem possible to Pen.

Thirty minutes into the party, Cat left with a mummy. He had a blanket tucked under one arm and the other arm around Cat, who blew Pen a kiss and smiled a devilish smile. Cat had a rule to never, ever go upstairs with a boy at a fraternity house. This made sense to Pen (technically, she had this rule, too, although the opportunity to enforce it had yet to arise), but going outside in a flapper dress to lie on the cold ground with a guy wrapped in toilet paper struck her as a fairly bad idea, as well.

An hour or so later, after two brief, desultory, and shouted conversations, the first with a vampire Pen recognized as the guy from her British lit class who'd made a compelling argument linking the metaphysical poets with early Motown songwriters, but who turned out to be both a personal-space invader and a person who spit when he talked, and the second with a Jolly Green Giant who was losing leaves at an alarming rate and really just wanted to score some Ecstasy—("Do I look like a drug dealer?" Pen had asked, slightly flattered. "No," the Giant had said. "You look like the kind of person who'd be too polite to refuse drugs from others and would put them in her pocket to dispose of at a future time.")—Pen was ready to leave.

Her wig itched. Her false eyelashes itched. She had succumbed to Cat's demand that she be Holly Golightly, mainly because she owned a black dress and had no imagination for things like Halloween costumes. "Halloween costumes should be *scary*," she'd protested to Cat. "I hate it when women use Halloween as an excuse to glam up. All those Catwomen and go-go dancers, and flappers in tiny dresses with fringe."

"Ooh, *flapper!*" Cat had squealed. "I'm being that!"

Pen spied Will at the other end of the room flipping through CDs with his friend Gray, a guy he knew from boarding school. Gray was the guitarist for Elephants Gerald, a band that specialized in punk covers of Gershwin and Cole Porter songs and that was perpetually purportedly on the verge of being signed by a major label. Pen liked the band's name and found that there was something appealing about watching a kid with facial tattoos scream out the lyrics to "It's De-lovely," but she worried about the band members' complete lack of musical training. "When we first got together, we put our names in a hat to decide who would play what. It was totally random," Gray had once told her. He had seemed to consider this fact an asset, but Pen had her doubts.

Pen caught Will's eye and made an inquiring doorward motion with her head. She watched Will nod, give Gray a good-bye clap on the shoulder, and begin to make his way toward her. She smiled. Will's costume consisted entirely of a black eye patch and a fake yellow bird pinned to the shoulder of his shirt.

"I don't get it," Cat had said, when they'd picked him up.

"I'm a pirate," said Will.

"You're wearing a rugby shirt," said Cat.

Pen had touched the bird on his shoulder. "I think this is a canary."

When Will got to Pen, he flipped the eye patch up and rubbed his eye. "This patch is making me unexpectedly nauseated. Is that weird?"

Pen considered, then said, "It would've been weirder if you had expected nausea and worn the costume anyway. Because, really, it's not that great a costume."

"I expected limited vision. Disorientation, *maybe*. Nausea, no. I don't know how the pirates did it."

"Maybe they got used to it. Maybe being on ships all the time made them immune to nausea. Maybe not having the two-eye option made a difference. I'm just guessing here."

"What else can we do but guess?" Will's gaze shifted to something behind Pen. "Uh-oh," he said.

"What?" She turned around to see the mummy swaying in the open doorway, his toilet paper raveled and torn, his expression similarly frazzled, even stunned. But in the few seconds she looked at him, she witnessed the party soaking into his consciousness: a dopey grin wormed across his face, and he began to bob his head and pop his chest in and out to the music, first absentmindedly, then with increasing vigor.

"Yo, Jason!" shouted one of his compatriots from across the room.

"Squid Man!" bellowed Jason the mummy. "I have been overtaken by a great and powerful thirst!"

Pen glanced at Squid Man, who was sitting atop a beleaguered upright piano in one corner of the room. He was dressed as a skeleton, not a squid. Pen was struck by the fleeting thought that, as far as she knew, squids did not even have skeletons.

"Shut the damn door!" roared Squid Man.

And Jason turned around and flung the door shut, without Cat's having walked through it.

"Oh, no," groaned Pen. "Where is she?"

She and Will didn't need to consult each other; they made a beeline together through the grinding, gyrating, drink-spilling crowd. At some point the music had become earsplitting and horrible; Pen could feel the bass thumping inside her sternum. They caught Jason mid-bellow, "I repeat: I find I have been overtaken by a great and powerful—" Will thumped him on the shoulder and said, "Where's Cat?"

Jason blinked. "Who?"

"Cat," said Pen. "The girl you left with?"

Jason screwed up his face in a look of concentration that struck Pen as remarkably authentic, as though he had actually forgotten Cat. Suddenly, Pen began to feel scared. *Let him just be drunk,* she thought. *Let him not be some psychopath out of a Flannery O'Connor story.*

"Oh," said Jason finally, snapping his eyelids open, "the Hispanic chick."

"Filipino," corrected Pen automatically. Her heart was beating fast. "Half Filipino. Her dad's side. Filip*ina*, actually, is what you'd say. But she's, you know, from Houston."

Will shot her a look that said, *For the love of God, stop.*

"Where is she?" Will asked Jason, but Jason didn't answer him. Instead, he said to Pen, "Houston? Ha. She's from Crazyville is where she's from."

"What?" said Pen.

"That is one spooky chick," said Jason. He scratched his ear and shook his head for emphasis, then said, "Seriously."

Pen saw Will's hand around Jason's upper arm. "What are you talk-ing about?" asked Will. His voice was icy.

Jason tried to shrug Will's hand off and said, "We're just down in the Crater, hanging out or what have you, and she goes totally freaky on me. Sits up, says, 'Hold on a sec,' and then lies back down and gets all stiff, like a freaky-ass"—he searched for the word that would de-scribe the freaky-ass thing Cat had become—"board."

"Oh, man," said Pen, turning to Will. "She had a seizure."

"No," said Jason, "she wasn't throwing herself around or anything. She just got stiff and kind of shook, tremored or whatever, and, like, disappeared, so to speak. Scared the shit out of me, if you want to know the truth. Ow! Dude!" He slapped at Will's hand, which had evidently tightened its grip. "Get off me."

"You left her?" Will's voice was quiet and deliberate, but scary. Pen looked up at his face, which was scary, too, taut, the muscles working beneath his skin.

"You would've done the same thing, man," avowed Jason. "Believe me. Anyway, I'm sure she's fine."

"Oh, you're sure she's fine," said Will. "That's good."

"Ow! What the hell?"

Pen yanked on Will's wrist, trying to pull his hand away from Ja-son's arm. "That's not helping," she said, trying to catch his eye and failing.

She turned back to Jason. "Just tell us where she is."

"The Crater. Like I said."

The Crater was a large, shallow, scooped-out field in the middle of fraternity row, part beach, part playing field, a place where droves of students hung out on sunny days. In snow, it was a fairly lame but very popular sledding and peppermint-schnapps-swilling destination; in wet weather, to Pen's eternal disgust, it morphed into a mud-wrestling pit. "The very last—and I mean *very* last—people on the planet you would want to see shirtless, covered in mud, and slapping their bel-lies together are shirtless, covered in mud, and slapping their bellies together," she'd told Cat, shuddering, after once having walked past it after two days of spring rain. "Goody!" Cat had cried, grabbing her jacket.

Pen tugged at Will's shirtsleeve and said, "The Crater. Let's go."

"Show us," said Will, his eyes never leaving Jason's face, "exactly where she is."

"Naw, man. You'll find her."

In a single, violent motion, Will turned the doorknob and sent the door flying open with one kick. He caught it before it rebounded shut again, took Jason by the shoulder, and shoved him out of it.

"Whoa!" Jason lost his balance and fell sideways, grabbing at the first thing he found, which, unfortunately, turned out to be the arm of a rocking chair. He went down hard on the porch and the chair somersaulted onto him with a whack. For a moment, everything seemed to go still. Pen heard some people standing in the yard start to laugh, and then Will was yanking the chair off Jason and telling him to get the hell up.

"What is your problem?" Pen hissed at Will. "Enough with the Bruce Willis crap. Let's just go!"

When Will didn't even look at her, she turned her back on him, yanked off her black pumps, and, with one in each hand, took off across the lawn in the direction of the Crater, gaining speed until, before she realized it, she was running full tilt, flying by startled face after startled face, the cold burning her eyes and filling her chest. She knew she must look insane, but it didn't matter. Her legs pistoned; her breath clattered; her heart banged.

"Audrey!" someone yelled after her. "Late for breakfast?"

Let her be there, she thought. *Let her be there. Let her be safe.* A sob rose in her throat, and she thought, *This is what it feels like to be a mother,* which only struck her as a peculiar thing to think later, when everything was over.

Her wig slid backward, and she pulled it off, faintly aware of the scrape of hairpins. In the same way that she could leave off being herself and become the act of bicycling, she became the running. Even when she thought she heard someone running behind her, she didn't turn around, didn't do anything but fling her body forward through the night, until she found herself on the rim of the Crater. She stopped short and wiped her eyes with the backs of her hands.

It was hard to see anything inside the Crater. The moon was high and its light didn't clarify, but stretched tightly over everything, like the skin on hot milk, making what lay under it appear liquid and uncertain. Pen realized that she was light-headed. She dropped her shoes, and leaned over, her hands on her knees. When she straightened back up, Will was beside her, Jason a few stumbling steps behind.

Jason, who was having a manifestly bad night, knocked his fist against the seismic heaving of his chest. His breathing had an alarming seal-bark quality to it, and when she glanced his way, even in the dark, Pen could tell that he was looking bad, slack-faced, pale, and sweating. If he had been a sixty-year-old man or even a forty-year-old man, Pen would have dialed 9-1-1 without a second thought.

"Where?" demanded Will.

Jason flapped his hand weakly in the direction of the Crater's center. Pen squinted into the dark and couldn't tell for sure, but thought she saw a small spot where the darkness condensed.

"Okay, we'll take it from here," she said to Jason, although her words were really meant for Will, whose face was marble-hard and cut with shadows, more full of barely contained rage than ever, but when Will started off down the hill, he took hold of Jason's shirtfront and towed him along behind.

As Jason went by, the expression on his face startled Pen. She thought he would look pissed off, even dangerous, but what she saw was much worse: a bleak and weary resignation. *He looks kidnapped*, she thought, and, for a moment, Pen wondered if that's what he was. Then she ran down the hill, leaving Jason and the Will who wasn't Will behind.

Cat was curled up and wrapped in a gray blanket, her black hair fanned on the grass and catching light.

"Oh, thank God," whispered Pen. Cat was not confused and wandering in the dark alone. She wasn't being hurt by drunken strangers. No one had taken her, although Pen thought that anyone could have, could have so easily lifted her up like a rag doll and carried her away. In the big field, she looked tiny and abandoned, like a toy forgotten on a beach.

Pen dropped to her knees next to Cat and lifted a flap of blanket away from her face. Cat's eyes were open and she looked confused, as though she'd been sleeping, which she probably had. Pen saw that she was crying without making a sound, tears falling sideways down her face and into the grass.

"Please don't cry, Catsy. You knew we'd come to get you, didn't you?"

Cat smiled. "I like it when you call me 'Catsy.' "

She sat up and put her arms around Pen's neck. "It happens sometimes," she said, "after a seizure. Tears for no reason."

Pen thought to herself that being left alone mid-make-out-session, mid-seizure in an empty field in the dead of Halloween night would be reason enough for anyone to cry, but she didn't say this out loud. Over Cat's shoulder, she saw Will coming toward them, Jason behind him, slumped and shadowy, and she put up her hand and said, "Don't."

Will stopped.

She pulled back and scanned Cat's face. "You're okay?"

"Tip-top."

"Promise?"

"Yes."

"See, man. Told you she was okay." It was Jason.

Pen held her breath, thinking, *You are dumber than krill.*

"What happened next was like the moment in the movie when the grenade flies through the window and lands on the floor and everything stops. I swear to God, even the crickets stopped chirping. And then the grenade exploded, except that it was Will instead of a grenade, and the whole night blasted open, and everything got surreal and slow motion, and it was the wildest thing I ever, ever saw."

Cat would say this over coffee the next afternoon to a group of students from her and Pen's Twentieth-Century Women Writers class. It was how she would tell the story to other people in other places for years, and, even though Pen would be repulsed every time by the excitement gleaming in Cat's eyes, she wouldn't say a word because what had happened that night belonged as much to Cat as it did to Pen.

But what Pen knew was that it wasn't like a grenade or a movie. It wasn't surreal or exciting. It wasn't like anything but what it was: one wholly human body slamming into another one, packed dirt and spit flying and animal grunts and sobbing and the sickening sound of a fist hitting skin and bone.

It was the first time Pen had ever seen Will lose his temper, although "lose his temper" never seemed like quite the right way of describing it. What got lost was everything else, all the things that made Will himself: empathy and patience and decency, his sense of humor, his sense of justice, everything fine and good deserting him in one ugly rush.

Before that night, she had only seen the fallout. After a visit from his parents (his father handing him a box of condoms, saying, in front of his mother, who was drunk, "Learn from my mistakes, Will. One slip-up and I'm stuck with this pathetic cow for life."): broken hand, cracked windshield. After a phone call from his father ("Drop the creative writing bullshit. I'm not paying for any faggot courses."): scabbed knuckles from punching a tree. Smashed dishes. Broken chair. A ragged hole in the plaster where he'd yanked out a light fixture with his hands.

He had told Pen and Cat about how he had been suspended twice in eighth grade and had been kicked out of one boarding school after six months for fighting. But Pen had never been able to reconcile that information with the Will she knew, and assumed he had been that person in the same way that Jamie had spent his seventh-grade year as a skate punk (bad haircut, an anarchy "A" inked onto the bottom of his sneakers).

For at least a whole minute, all Pen could do was watch. Jason was a big guy, broad-chested, with the meaty muscles of someone who spent a lot of time in the weight room. Will was over six feet tall and just this side of slight, no more than 175 pounds, but he was strong and had the advantage of being both sober and unhinged by rage.

As she watched, though, Pen saw that he was not wildly out of control. After they had rolled over a few times, they ended up not ten feet away from Pen, with Will on top, his left hand against Jason's chest, the right angle of his right elbow jutting out again and again. *Not wildly out of control,* Pen thought, *controlled out of control,* which was somehow much worse.

Pen watched that methodical punching, heard Jason yell, almost scream, "Stop!" and was herself walloped so hard by a sense of wrongness that she felt dizzy. It didn't matter how much Pen loved Will, how much they both loved Cat, didn't matter that Jason had put Cat in danger and had forgotten about her like she was nothing. The why of what was happening was weightless compared to the what: a person on top, hitting, a person on the bottom, not fighting back, defeated.

Pen stood up and threw her full weight against the side of Will's rib cage, knocking him off Jason. For a second or two, she lay sprawled on top of Will, before she scrambled up and pinned him to the ground by sitting on his chest. There was no way he was getting back to Jason. She expected him to struggle, to try to get up, but he lay still, except for the sharp, fast rise and fall of his ribs.

She could feel the bones and muscles of Will's chest, could feel his heart beating under her hands, but she didn't look at him. Instead, she watched Jason painfully clamber to his feet, openly sobbing, spitting what Pen knew must be blood and hoped did not include teeth. "Thank God," she said hoarsely, so relieved that he could stand, that he wasn't unconscious or worse.

Jason walked unsteadily backward, wiping his face with one hand and pointing at Will with the other, yelling, "You're a fucking maniac. I didn't do shit to her. I put the goddamned blanket over her, you fucking maniac. I will kill you. I will bring my buddies back and kill your ass. I didn't hurt her. I put the blanket over her. I will sue your ass from here to fucking eternity, I swear to God."

He turned around and ran up the hill, out of the Crater, and away.

"Are you okay, Will?" asked Cat in a tremulous voice. She was still sitting where Pen had left her, the blanket bunched around her shoulders and coming up over the back of her head like a hood.

Will didn't answer. Suddenly, Pen didn't want to be touching him. She slid off his chest onto the sparse grass and realized how cold she was. In the name of costume authenticity and foolhardy vanity, and because they'd assumed they'd only be walking to and from the party, not sitting around for what seemed like hours inside the Crater while Will pounded a fellow human being into the ground, she and Cat had eschewed outerwear. Pen's bones felt brittle. She tucked in her knees and pulled the skirt of her dress as far over her bare legs as it would go.

"Will?" asked Cat, again. "Are you okay? Did he hurt you?"

"Did he hurt him?" Pen said bitterly. "Is *Will hurt*?"

"Stop it," said Cat.

"I don't think Will's hurt, Cat, but I'll tell you what; he is definitely not okay."

"*Stop* it!"

"I'm sorry," said Will. Even though she could hear the misery in his voice, Pen didn't look at him.

"Don't be sorry!" cried Cat. "The guy was an asshole. You were right to do it!"

Pen pressed her palms to her eyes and shook her head.

"I didn't mean to," said Will.

Pen looked down at his face, which was white against the grass. Pen saw that his lip was bleeding and that his face was familiar again. Will's face was his face, his voice was his voice, and it would have been so easy for Pen to warm to him, to tell him not to worry, that she understood. But she couldn't, and she didn't really think he would want her to anyway, not that what he wanted mattered to Pen just then.

"What does that mean: you didn't mean to?" she said, struggling to keep her voice low and even. "You did it. I tried to get you to leave him alone, back there at the party, and you wouldn't stop. How could you not *mean* to?"

"Pen, let it go," pleaded Cat, getting up and coming to kneel down beside Will. Tenderly, she placed a hand against the lean slope of his cheek, but he flinched, and she took it away.

"You're right," he said, looking straight at Pen. She didn't want to be right.

"Oh, Will," she said, and silence sprawled out between the three of them after she said it. Except for shivering, nobody moved. Pen could hear laughter and shouting spilling toward them over the edge of the Crater from what felt like a very long distance away.

"I don't know what to do." Will's voice was hollow. "I don't know how to fix it."

Because Pen didn't know, either, she unfolded herself and stretched out next to him on the grass. Cat did the same, flaring and settling the gray blanket out and across the three of them. They lay like that, not touching or speaking, in the center of Crater, with the moon like a white balloon and the ground like a cupped hand, holding them, and after a little while, they got up and walked home.

PEN TURNED UP THE MUSIC. IN A CHARACTERISTIC COMBINATION OF thoughtfulness and mockery (and because he was just a guy who liked to make playlists), for the trip, Jamie had made her a playlist of the music she had listened to in college. "The sound track of your youth. Total-body nostalgia immersion," he'd intoned, dangling the iPod in front of her nose. "You know you want it."

Because her car didn't have an iPod hookup, she had taken his Land Cruiser, mammoth, black, and gas-gulping, a ridiculous vehicle for any non-outback dweller, but particularly for a man who walked to work and almost never had cause to take his SUV out of the shockingly expensive garage in which it languished. (In moments, Pen imagined it there, waiting, like a lonely, shiny hippopotamus.) It was Pen's habit to make relentless fun of Jamie for owning it. "Who do you think you are, Puff Daddy?" she'd asked the first time he'd shown up with it, which had made Jamie shut his eyes and say, "Nobody calls him that. Nobody. For well over a decade, not one person has even considered calling him that." Even so, Pen loved driving it. She felt like a badass driving it (and she was not someone who got a lot of opportunities to feel like a badass), and the playlist was marvelous, just what the doctor ordered.

Just as Pen came to the place in the highway where the mountains appeared like magic—up and over a hill, around a curve, and there they were in lines and layers, ghostly and blue-gray, more like clouds or billows of smoke along the horizon than like mountains—she remembered how Jason had never followed through on his threats. He hadn't shown up on Will's doorstep with a gang of fraternity brothers out for blood or with a lawyer out for damages. He hadn't confronted Will at all, even though they had expected him to, Cat and Pen, fearfully, Will with a fatalism that, in Pen's opinion, bordered, disturbingly, on hopefulness.

Instead, a week or so later, Jason did something entirely other: he walked up to Cat as she sat drinking coffee with Pen in a campus café and, with a great, serious sheepishness and a ducking motion that was almost a bow, handed her a letter. They hadn't known who he was at first, having only seen him at night and dressed as a mummy. He could have been anyone: a big kid in a dark blue sweatshirt and brown cords, clean shaven, his blond hair newly cut, patches of pale skin beneath the sharp line of his short sideburns.

It was only when Pen noticed the partially healed cuts on his upper lip and the faded green half-moon bruises under his eyes and saw a wary expression replace Cat's initial smile that she understood who he was. Pen and Cat looked at each other, then down at the white envelope in Cat's hand.

"What's this?" asked Cat.

"Just something I needed to say to you," Jason said, shoulders high, hands shoved into the pockets of his pants.

Pen bristled and was preparing to say, "*You* needed? Do you think anyone here gives a shit about what you need?" when Jason surprised her by adding, in the small, taut voice of someone possibly about to cry, "I mean, something I hope you'll read, even though I wouldn't blame you if you didn't feel like it."

Cat's eyes widened, and, absently, as though it had a mind of its own, her hand lifted and started to reach out in the direction of Jason. *Oh no, you don't*, thought Pen. *Do not do it*. As though it had heard her thoughts, the hand drew back and landed in Cat's lap. Cat shrugged.

"All right," she said. "If I feel like it later, I'll read it."

Jason's mouth gave a twist, and he seemed about to say something else, but then he just tugged a hand out of his pocket, lifted it in a good-bye wave, and walked out of the café. Through the window, Pen saw him take off running the instant he was out the door, the white bottoms of his sneakers flashing.

Cat set the envelope on the table gingerly, as though it were fragile or dangerous.

"My name's not on it," she said a little forlornly. "Maybe he forgot it."

"Maybe he doesn't know how to spell it."

Cat smiled.

"What do you want to do, sweetheart?" asked Pen.

"Split a cinnamon bun."

"Okay. What else?"

"Tell Jason to shove his stupid letter up his stupid ass."

"Good."

"Then throw it away without reading it."

"Yeah, right. That sounds like you." Pen smiled.

Cat laughed. "How about this: call Will, get him to meet us at our place, and read it together?"

"Well." Pen paused. "Why don't we call and tell him we're coming to his place?" she said, raising her eyebrows. "Just in case."

She waited. The subject of Will's temper had come up a few times since Halloween, and they had always handled it with circumspection and gravity. In fact, there wasn't one thing funny about it, and, although she didn't tell Cat or Will this, Pen found the whole of Halloween night physically, chest-tighteningly, stomach-knottingly painful to discuss. ("Do you think he could have killed that guy, if you hadn't been there to stop him?" Cat had asked once. "Of course not," Pen had said, almost as sure as she sounded, but not quite.) But since the inherent seriousness of a subject had never stopped them from joking about it in the past, Pen thought it might be time to try.

Without missing a beat, Cat nodded. "Just in case he decides to throw a refrigerator through the wall."

"I like our refrigerator," said Pen. "It's shiny."

"And it has an in-door ice dispenser," Cat reminded her. "Which is extremely handy."

THEY SPLIT THE CINNAMON ROLL THREE WAYS. CAT WAS TOO NER-vous to read the letter aloud, and no one brought up the idea of Will's reading it (he seemed averse to even looking in the direction of the white envelope), so the duty fell to Pen. The letter was unexpectedly long and, more unexpectedly, lucid. Although everyone hated to admit it (and didn't admit it out loud for some time), it was quite a good letter, particularly the end:

> Like a lot of people, even though I knew I could be a jerk at times, I always thought of myself as a good guy, but after what I did to you, I can't think that anymore. A good guy does not leave a girl by herself outside on the ground at night (even if she does have a blanket over her), period, let alone having a seizure. I've done a lot of thinking since Halloween and I realize that I am turning into someone I don't want to be. I think a big part of the problem is drinking, so as of one week ago, I quit for good. I know you probably don't care about that in terms of my health or well-being because you probably wish I would drop dead (justifiably), but I wanted you to know that I will never do to anyone else what I did to you. I am sorrier than I can explain.
>
> Sincerely,
> Jason Rogers

P.S. I have a younger sister and if any
shit-for-brains did to her what I did to
you I would summarily kick his ass.

LIKE THE MUSIC POURING OUT OF JAMIE'S RIDICULOUSLY SOPHIS-
ticated sound system, the past seemed to come at Pen from all sides,
sharp and clear and real, and, momentarily, she felt the urge to turn
the SUV around and head home. *Nerves,* is what her mother would
have said, *just a minor nerve-quake.* Pen decided to buy herself some
time. She steered off the main road and drove through an ancient
town of woods, upright, stoic houses, and what might possibly qualify as the most charming post office on the planet.

She was surprised at how well she remembered the letter. Partly this
was due to, after that first, breathless, trisected cinnamon-bun reading, many subsequent readings (mostly in Cat and Pen's apartment,
mostly by Cat, who would, for months, interrupt Pen's eating, or television watching, or studying—once even her sleep—with an "Okay,
listen to this," followed by an excerpt from the letter), and partly due
to the fact that bits of the letter became, irresistibly, stock phrases for
all three of them, and eventually for their friends and family members,
for a ridiculously long time. (Just last month, Pen had scolded Jamie
by saying, "You shouldn't stuff your sweat-drenched running clothes
into the hamper, period, let alone having a seizure.")

But more than any of that, Pen knew that the reason Jason's letter
had stayed with her so resolutely was that reading it out loud that day
had triggered in Pen what could only be called an epiphany, although
she had never called it that to anyone but herself, suspecting, as she did,
that what had hit her, at age twenty, like a ton of bricks, was an understanding that most people acquired much earlier in their development.
It was simply this: for the first time, she understood that it was possible
to form an opinion about a person, an opinion based on solid evidence
and a vast quantity of justified self-righteous anger, to even have this
opinion reinforced by trusted colleagues, and to be, at least partially,
wrong.

Actually, this was something Pen had already known to be true about other people. Other people could and often did form wrong, negative, vehemently held opinions about their fellow human beings. But as Pen read Jason's letter, she was shocked to discover that she, Cat, and Will—*she, Cat, and Will*—were fallible in exactly the same way everyone else was. If a boy they had branded, once and for all, as a complete and irredeemable cad could reveal himself to be an incomplete and potentially redeemable one, what else might be possible?

With more than ten years gone and oceans of water under the bridge, Pen couldn't help but regard the long-gone college-boy Jason in yet a different way: as somebody's son. For someone out there, Jason had been the sun and moon, the basket into which someone had placed innumerable eggs, a walking, talking universe of promise and heartbreak. *You screwed up in a way that you should not have screwed up, but good for you writing that letter,* the mother in Pen said. *Well done.*

With the Replacements jangling, growling, and banging around her, Pen thought again about Halloween night, the moment after Will had told her that she was right, that he had done, on purpose, the ugliest thing that Pen had ever seen up close. She remembered the hard ground and the burning moon and the stillness and the cold seeping into them all. For Pen it had been a moment of truth, a fulcrum moment. She had stood on the fine point of all that had just happened and she had teetered. *I could walk away,* she had considered. *Get up, brush the dirt off my dress, and go.* The thought was appealing. It caught her by the wrist and pulled, but at the last second, she had stopped teetering. She had yanked herself loose from the idea of leaving and had stayed. *I'm in. For better or for worse.* She had sat on the ground thinking those words, making a vow. *For better or for worse.*

Pen realized now that she had never regretted it, not even after Cat left, after Will left. It mattered, being a person who stayed, who counted herself in, for good. Paul Westerberg rasped out a song Pen had always loved, "Hold My Life." With a sigh, but without bitterness, Pen thought, *When did I ever do anything else?*

CHAPTER EIGHT

*W*ILL WAS WISHING LIKE HELL THAT HE HADN'T COME. NOT
that he hadn't come to the reunion weekend itself because it
made no sense to regret doing something that, if left undone, would
have caused him to wallow in regret for the balance of his natural life.
He wished he hadn't come here, to Alumni Hall, his REUNION CEL-
EBRATION REGISTRATION LOCATION! as the massive banner over its
massive white doors declared it to be, but which he realized, too late,
was not only a mouthful, but also a misnomer, since his actual registration had taken place at home, online, so that his schedule and map,
even his name tag (which he had no plans to wear; he and Cat would
know each other if they met in their nineties in a snowstorm, and Cat
was the only reason he was there), were all already neatly printed out
and tucked inside a folder back in his hotel room.

Will didn't love crowds, but he didn't mind them that much, either.
Still, the prospect of seeing Cat after so long had set him so on edge
that, for a long minute or two, standing just inside the doors, next to
the inevitable bust of Thomas Jefferson, he felt like bolting, his pulse
revving up, his palms right on the verge of sweating.

Chaos, he thought, looking out at the crowd. *A seethe, a hatch.* He
remembered a spider's egg sac he had kept in a jar when he was a kid,
how right in front of his eyes, the white ball, tidy as a planet, had

erupted into a boiling mass of bodies. This was like that, he thought, but with squealing and goody bags.

Even after the initial urge to leave had subsided, he recognized that this was no place to be, the last place he would want to reunite with anyone, let alone Cat.

Still, as he turned to go and someone's hand tugged at his shirt from behind, he felt hopefulness flash through him and spun around, ready for Cat's face, almost already seeing it, her black eyes, the distinct shape of her smile. Instead, because he was looking downward, Cat-ward, he found himself looking directly at a tall woman's breasts. They weren't bare breasts, and Will wasn't exactly looking down the woman's shirt (although if he had, it would not, technically, have been his fault), but because they were definitely breasts and definitely there, inside a thin, blue, sleeveless sweater, and because they definitely did not belong to Cat, they were an unexpected and arresting sight all the same. For a few seconds, Will stared, immobilized.

"Will Wadsworth." The voice wasn't squeaky like the rest of the voices piercing the air, but languid, stretching the vowels of his name out like caramel.

Will snapped his gaze upward, to the woman's face. She was pretty, honey-skinned, blue-eyed, blades of blond bob cutting toward the corners of her glossed mouth. Pretty and vaguely familiar. Will ransacked his memory and came up with, "Kirsty?"

Her smile swung open slowly, like a bank vault. White teeth gleamed.

"You remember me."

In the nick of time, a few details floated to the surface. Sophomore year. Two months of dating. Maybe less. Winter. It had been winter. Will flashed back on a moment of holiday awkwardness: Cat and Pen studying at Will's apartment; Kirsty showing up with a gift wrapped in silky, heavy gold paper. Will had noticed that it was embossed with pears and was the kind of paper his mother and her friends used for one another, hostess gift paper, not college kid paper. Because Kirsty had insisted, he had unwrapped it right away, in front of all three girls:

a scarf the color of pumpkin soup, obviously handmade. "To match your eyes," Kirsty had explained, throwing her arms around his neck.

Mid-hug, over Kirsty's cashmere-covered shoulder, he had watched Pen and Cat wrinkle their noses, their faces bunching with stifled snickering. Will shot them a "grow up" look, but they had known he wasn't really mad. Will could stand in his living room locked in Kirsty's arms all day, but everyone knew, with the possible exception of Kirsty who at the very least suspected, where he really stood. When Pen looked at him and mouthed, "*Orange eyes?*" Will knew before she said it exactly what she was going to say.

Will smiled. "Sure, I remember you."

"You weren't leaving without your goody bag, were you?" scolded Kirsty. She lifted the blue drawstring bag next to her face and set it swinging like a pendulum, and Will remembered that about her, the way she could turn the smallest act into a flirtation. "Because I think that would be a really bad idea."

"Oh, yeah? Why?"

She leaned in, lifting her eyebrows, half-whispering, "Lanyard," then leaned closer, "Car magnet."

Will laughed. Had she been funny back in college? Will didn't think so, although it was possible that he just hadn't noticed. When he remembered college, only Cat and Pen were sharp, four-color, foregrounded. (He remembered the exact smell of Pen's shampoo, the sweater Cat's father sent her for her twentieth birthday.) And it wasn't just the way he remembered things; it was the way things had been. Cat and Pen were the people with him on the train; everyone else was the blur outside the windows.

But here, in this moment, stood Kirsty, being funny and looking extremely good. *Stay in this moment, dipshit,* Will commanded himself.

"Do you have a plan for your lanyard?" asked Will.

"A lanyard plan?"

"What do people do with lanyards? What do people who aren't high school football coaches hang on a lanyard?"

Kirsty wrinkled her forehead, thinking. "An ID card?"

"So is that your plan? Hang your driver's license around your neck so you don't lose it? Because I'm having trouble picturing it."

Kirsty laughed. "You want to know what I think?"

"Yes."

"I think we should go out for a drink and discuss it."

Will hesitated, thinking of Cat.

"Unless you're with someone," said Kirsty quickly. "Like a wife or someone."

"I'm wifeless."

"You mean, you're wifeless here?"

"Wifeless everywhere. You?"

"Equally wifeless." Kirsty smiled. She waggled her ringless left hand in front of his face.

"But I'm supposed to meet someone later," said Will, then added, "A friend." Even though this was perfectly true because Cat was certainly a friend, Will felt a twinge of guilt at saying it that he could not explain.

"At the reception?" Kirsty looked at her watch. "Because we have three hours before the reception. Three hours and eleven minutes."

Kirsty raised her arm to show him the time. Her watch was bracelet-thin and as expensive looking as the rest of Kirsty, gold against the darker gold of her skin. He looked at her fine-boned wrist, but, without wanting to, what he saw was Pen's wrist, her long hand. He had to keep himself from circling the wrist with his fingers, turning it over to see the paler underside, and it startled him, this sudden emergence of Pen. *Get a grip,* he told himself. Here was a flesh-and-blood woman, asking him to have a drink.

"Sure," he said, meeting Kirsty's arch blue gaze. "Let's do it."

"Kirsty!"

Kirsty turned around to see another blond, tan woman across the room. The woman smiled a gargantuan smile and waved with her skinny brown arm shot straight up in the air, in the manner of a first-grader frantic to be called on.

Kirsty waved back and, sideways, through the closed teeth of her bright smile, said to Will, "Oh, God, it's Sissy."

"Sissy is very, very happy to see you."

"I fooled around with her boyfriend, senior year. She never knew. I can't not say hi to her."

Will didn't question the logic of this. Feeling equal parts disappointment and relief, he said, "Hey, we'll do the drink another time. No problem."

Kirsty swiveled on her heel. "Oh, no you don't." She poked his chest with a pink-nailed finger. It wasn't a light poke. "You wait right here."

As Will watched Kirsty walk across the room like a woman who knows a man is watching her walk across the room, thoughts tumbled toward him, one after the next. He thought about Cat, small, bright, and in trouble, waiting for him somewhere out there in their old college world, thought about how little he needed the complication of a Kirsty this weekend, then followed up that thought by thinking that thinking of her as "a Kirsty" was a reprehensibly asshole thing to think, and the fact that he'd thought it reflexively (without thinking) did not make it less reprehensible. Then he cursed himself for overthinking, reminding himself that, whatever had brought him to the reunion (not only Cat, but the possibility of Pen, a possibility that leaned, slender as a birch tree, in a far corner of his mind, casting a shadow he tried to ignore), he was still a wifeless guy at a reunion and was therefore practically obligated to have drinks with a blond blast from the past. Across the room, Kirsty and Sissy shrieked and fell into each other's arms.

Will averted his gaze from the two women and found himself looking straight into the marble eyes of Thomas Jefferson. The eyes seemed disapproving, accusatory, and cold, and not just because they were carved out of stone.

This is not a big deal, Will told Jefferson silently. But Will had the uneasy sense that going for drinks with Kirsty was some kind of betrayal, although he wasn't sure what he might be betraying, or who.

You owned slaves, he told the statue. *Remember that?*

Then Kirsty was back, slipping her hand into the crook of his arm, saying, "Ready?" And even though he wasn't, even though he thought he should just go back to his hotel room until the reception or maybe jump on the bike he'd stuck on top of his car at the last minute—actually pulling out of his driveway, then pulling back in and stomping impatiently into the garage to get the bike—and ride for a couple of hours, maybe do the hilly ride past the old church that he used to do with Pen, Will didn't know how to say any of this to Kirsty, so he just said, "Why not?"

THEY CALLED IT A "RUMP SLAP." ACTUALLY, THEY CALLED IT NOTHing for a long time, didn't even acknowledge that such a thing existed between them, even though they all knew that it did. Then one day, Cat said something about a soccer player Pen had a date with that night, and Pen jumped up out of the hideous armchair Cat had bought at a fire sale ("lung-pink" Pen had declared when she'd seen it), pointed at Cat, and shouted, "Rump slap!"

Later, Pen would say that it hadn't been the soccer player but the Tri Delt who had asked Will to her spring formal that had provoked the comment that provoked the birth of "rump slap," but Will knew it was the soccer player. He remembered the soccer player's name and exactly what Cat had said about him, which was, "Trent Bly's legs are so exquisitely dreamy that I don't even notice the front teeth thing anymore."

"What front teeth thing?" Pen had asked.

"I'm sure it's not his fault," demurred Cat.

"What's not his fault?"

"It probably has to do with the way they're shaped or the way they're set or something."

"Elucidate."

"I'm sure he brushes. Of course, he does."

"Cat."

"I shouldn't have brought it up."

"Cat!"

And Cat had sighed and done the thing she did to indicate resignation that was half-shrug, half-Charleston shimmy, pointed to her front teeth, and said, "Food."

"Food? In his teeth?" said Pen.

"Always."

"I never noticed that."

"He sat next to me in psych last semester." Again, she pointed to the place where her two front teeth met. "Spinach. Bread. Lunch meat. Just the teensiest bit. But every day. Without fail."

Will laughed, and that's when Pen jumped up and said it: "Rump slap!"

She was referring, it turned out, to the Old West practice of hanging a man by setting him on a horse under a tree, dangling a noose (possibly a lasso knotted noose-fashion, possibly an ordinary rope, if there was a difference; Pen didn't know; none of them knew for sure) from a tree branch, looping it around the man's neck, and then slapping the horse's rump to make the horse run out from under the man, causing his neck to snap like kindling.

"Although I'm not sure why I think this happened in the Old West. Maybe it only happened in westerns," mused Pen.

"Do you watch westerns?" asked Will. "Because I've never watched you watch a western."

"You've never mentioned watching them," added Cat. "In all the time I've known you, not one mention."

"So maybe it only happens in novels about the Old West. I don't know which ones. I don't even know if I've ever read that kind of novel, but I must have," said Pen.

"Doubtful," said Cat. "You really aren't the type."

Pen groaned with impatience. The source of the rump-slap scenario wasn't the point. Historical accuracy wasn't the point. The *point* was the no-going-back comment, the irretrievable, irreversible, eternally damning remark, the one that broke the relationship's neck, sometimes even before the relationship *had* a neck.

"Trent Bly could cure cancer, negotiate peace in the Middle East, and reunite the Beatles, and he'd still be the guy with food between his teeth," Pen said.

"Per*pet*ually," Cat added. "Food between his teeth per*pet*ually."

"See?"

"I do see," said Cat thoughtfully. "I wonder if I rump slapped Trent on purpose. I guess I might have. I'd rather have you stay home and play with me than go on dates with Mr. Food Teeth."

"Like that thing Pen said about the Tri Delt who asked me to her formal," said Will. "Eliza."

Pen winced, blushing.

"Ha!" shouted Cat, clapping her hands. "Eliza of the constantly erect nipples!"

"Rump slap," said Will.

"I just worried that maybe she had, you know, circulation issues. Or trouble maintaining a normal body temperature, like a condition or something," explained Pen. "And I thought she could benefit from a different kind of bra."

"Pen was only thinking of Eliza's needs, Will," said Cat.

"Too bad she never told Eliza about her concerns directly," said Will. "Since, last time I checked, and I do check, she was still walking around with her high beams on."

"I should have told her," said Pen, a smile teasing around the corners of her mouth. "I was actually going to, but then I thought that having constantly erect nipples wasn't something a person could do and not notice. I mean, you'd notice at some point, right? Even if no one ever pointed them out to you, you'd at least see them in photographs and know."

"Oh, she knew," said Cat, nodding. "She definitely knew."

"You really didn't want to go to that formal, anyway," Pen reminded Will. "Remember?"

"I guess I remember that."

Pen turned down the corners of her mouth and sighed. "I shouldn't have said it."

None of them should have said, ever, what they said about each other's dates, boyfriends, girlfriends, or potential dates, boyfriends, and girlfriends, but that never stopped them.

Now, sitting at the hotel bar with Kirsty, Will remembered her rump-slap moment. It wasn't the scarf; the scarf was not insurmountable. You could still date a girl who believed you had orange eyes. It was the kind of thing that you could spin as a charming idiosyncrasy, that best men joked about in wedding toasts, not that Will ever considered marrying Kirsty or even, really, going away with her for the weekend, something he remembered her pushing for more than once.

What snapped the neck of the Will/Kirsty alliance was the voice-lowering habit, *habit* being the noun Will, Pen, and Cat had finally agreed upon, even though Cat swore that it was so euphemistic as to be nearly worthless. Will disagreed, although he did admit that, while the Will/Kirsty neck had been unusually flimsy, the voice-lowering habit would have spelled doom for even the strongest, most promising neck on the planet.

Apparently, the habit had staying power, too, because less than an hour into Will and Kirsty's conversation over drinks, there it was.

Until that moment, things had been going well. The funniness Kirsty had exhibited back at Alumni Hall turned out to be part of a bigger-picture change, which was that somewhere along the line (she had moved from the wealthy suburb of Atlanta in which she'd grown up to Atlanta itself, had been married briefly to a guy who owned "of all things!" a vegetarian restaurant, and had ditched law school after a year to become a buyer for a shoe boutique), Kirsty had acquired an edge. She swore; she had only recently quit smoking; she liked art house films "in moderation." In addition, her debutante flirtatiousness of old had grown feline and sinuous: she laughed with her head thrown back; she trailed her hand up and down her own bare leg as she spoke; she narrowed her eyes like Lauren Bacall.

At the bar, she insisted on buying Will's beer.

"I'm just so glad you decided to start drinking," she said, giving his hand a congratulatory pat. "In college, you were Mr. Club Soda with Lime, which was, to be honest, a little boring."

"You're getting me mixed up with someone else. I was Mr. Ginger Ale," corrected Will. "Way more exciting."

Most people who had known him well enough to know about his mom had figured that she was the reason for his teetotaling ways. But somehow Will had never worried about becoming an alcoholic, had intuitively understood that he was not one, and luckily for him, seemed, in fact, to have dodged that particular genetic bullet. What he had worried about—and only Pen and Cat had recognized this—was messing with what little control he had over his temper. If he could beat the living shit out of an oak tree (or a frat boy) sober, what havoc might he wreak drunk? By now, he had figured out enough about managing his anger so that he wasn't Mr. Ginger Ale anymore, but he still didn't trust himself to have more than a couple of drinks.

In the light of the hotel bar, Kirsty was soft-edged and golden. Will was bad at noticing this kind of thing, but he could swear that her hair was blonder than it used to be. *Less goldenrod, more canary,* he thought, and smiled to himself. Pen and Cat spent years making gloating, gleeful fun of him for almost only ever dating blondes.

"It's inspiring," Pen had told him dryly, "the way you're dating your way through the whole yellow section of the Crayola box."

"Better than the whole purple section," he'd answered.

"I don't know about that," snapped Pen. "I can definitely picture a future between you and a woman with purple mountains' majesty hair."

Only once, after a few drinks, had Cat said, "You're dating blond girls because they are markedly un-us. If you dated girls who were more obviously Cat-and-Pen-like, the possibility would exist that you could at some point be interested in dating one or both of us, which, of course, would mean . . ."—she'd paused dramatically—"Total. Friendship. Apocalypse."

Even though that had been everyone's cue to laughingly agree or disagree, for several beats too long, nobody had. Nobody had met each other's eyes or said a word, and Will was torn between urgently wanting and urgently not wanting to know what the other two were thinking.

Will didn't know if it was the beer or the mellow light or the new

and edgier Kirsty, but he found himself relaxing, the tangle of anticipation that had been knotting inside him for weeks loosening enough
so that when Kirsty asked, "So who are you meeting later?" Will said,
"Cat."

When Kirsty found out that Will hadn't seen or spoken to Cat and
Pen for years, her eyes (cerulean? cornflower?) widened, and she said,
"I'm stunned," and then, "Actually, I'm not that stunned."

"Why?"

"It's hard to imagine you guys maintaining that level of . . ."—she
paused—"intimacy forever," she said. "But it's also hard to imagine
you being normal adult friends."

Will didn't say anything.

"Oh, come on," said Kirsty. "Dinner parties? Exchanging the occasional e-mail? Cookouts with your significant others? Significant
others, period?"

She was right, of course, but he didn't feel like telling her that.

"Why did you break up? What was the inciting incident?" There
was a challenge in her voice.

Will thought about not telling her or about making something up,
but what would be the point? He shrugged and said, "Cat wanted to
get married."

"Ha! Go on."

"We were a pretty self-contained entity, I guess. And I guess we
could be a little hard on people who weren't part of that entity."

"On outsiders, you mean."

"I guess."

"No kidding!" Kirsty laughed. "I don't think clubs that exclusive
are even legal! I think they're in violation of the Bill of Rights!"

"You could sue," suggested Will, smiling.

"I haven't ruled it out."

"Cat wanted to give her relationship a real shot, she said. So she
broke off our friendship and moved away with her fiancé."

"What about you and Pen?"

"Without Cat around, we couldn't figure out how to stay friends."

"Oh, I'll bet you couldn't," said Kirsty, laying on the sarcasm.

Will didn't know what she meant and didn't want to know, so he ignored this and, thoughtfully, popped a couple of peanuts. "I don't think we meant to be exclusive. The three of us just knew each other in a way that made it hard to know other people very well."

Kirsty narrowed her eyes. "Biblically? Did you know each other in the biblical sense?"

Will laughed. "I just talked to my friend Gray the other day. He asked the same thing in those exact words."

"Gray who was in that band?"

"Yes."

"The one who dated the"—and then Kirsty did it, did what she had done not only once but twice in a single conversation with him, Cat, and Pen over ten years ago: lowered her voice to a whisper and said—"*black* girl?"

Rump. Slap. Snap.

I'LL FIND YOU THERE IS WHAT CAT HAD WRITTEN IN HER E-MAIL, BUT after assessing the reunion demographic as it was represented inside the giant white party tent stretched over a good quarter of the university's central green lawn, Will figured that discerning one tall, lean, brown-haired thirty-two-year-old man wearing a navy jacket and khaki pants in that crowd would be a lot like finding the real Will in a house of mirrors.

So Will spent the first thirty minutes of the cocktail party looking for Cat. Actually, he spent the first thirty minutes trying to look for Cat while also trying to remain invisible to any person there who might know him, especially Kirsty. It was hard. For one thing, although Cat, small, dark, dressed like a flock of butterflies (assuming she still looked the way she used to look, which Will did assume), would stand out in that crowd, the fact remained that she didn't literally stand out in any crowd because Cat standing was not a lot taller than most people sitting. Avoiding Kirsty was equally tough since every third woman there could have been her.

After spending a half-hour skirting the edges of the party, dodging blondes, and attempting unobtrusive, chest-level crowd scanning, Will felt too stupid to continue—and too hungry. He threw caution to the wind and cut a straight and reckless path through the crowd to the food table.

Plate loaded, a ham biscuit halfway to his mouth, he turned around and saw her, no more than twenty feet away in a dark blue dress: bare arms, straight back, smooth hair, clavicles like open wings, and Will didn't need to see her face to know her: Pen.

He had tried not to think about what it would be like to actually see her, but on the few occasions that he had slipped up and imagined it, he had gotten it all wrong. He wasn't numb or frozen or panicked; he didn't feel like he had been punched in the stomach or was having a minor heart attack. Right then, Will wasn't searching for a word for his reaction, or doing anything except looking at Pen, but later, he would recognize what he felt as wonder, the kind of baffled awe you would feel if a statue in your house came alive or if the music playing on your iPod in the next room turned out to be an orchestra.

He wasn't ready for her to see him see her, yet, and knew he would have to look away, at least briefly, but for one attenuated moment, he took her in. She was looking to the side, searching through the crowd the way he'd been doing a couple of minutes before, and he saw an earring dangling, the long tendons in her neck, her jaw's clean swoop, and when she moved, shifting the white Chinet plate from one hand to the other, looping her hair behind her ear, Will saw that she still moved the way she always had, with a fluid, all-of-a-piece grace that was unexpected in a person so lacking in softness, so sinewy and sharp-jointed.

As Will stood watching Pen, just before he turned away, his initial astonishment shifted into something quieter. *Soon, she will see me; we'll sit someplace and talk,* he thought. He felt like a kid who falls asleep on a long car trip, wakes up, and looks out the window to find that he's in a new place, or home, and that it's morning.

CHAPTER NINE

$\mathcal{I}$N THE MOMENTS BEFORE SHE TURNED AND SAW WILL (AND IT was more a shifting of the gaze than an actual turn, a movement the slightness of which would strike her as remarkable, even breathtaking, later), Pen had begun to get angry. Actually, before she had begun to get angry, she had begun to get sad because this party, like all parties, reminded her of her father.

Pen realized that not everyone would understand this because her father had not, in any obvious way, been a life-of-the-party kind of man. He didn't dance outside of his own living room, would hold the same scotch on the rocks until it went the color of weak lemonade, and was much more likely to be the (often underdressed) guy talking to one other person in a corner of the room for hours than the one in the center, telling stories, making everyone laugh. "A glower, not a sparkler" is how Pen's mother described him. But once Pen had asked Jamie if parties reminded him of their dad, and he had said instantly, "Yeah. Because Dad *believed* in parties," and Pen had hugged Jamie right then and there because that was it exactly. For their father, any place full of people talking to one another over food and drink qualified as hallowed ground.

Pen had stood under the peaked, snow-white sky of the tent, in the middle of the brightness and noise, with the wide-open, breathing spring night just outside, thinking about her dad and had felt the old sadness plodding toward her on its big, square feet. *Oh no,* she thought, *nope, not here, are you kidding,* and, as fast as she could, she had whirled away from it and chosen anger instead.

Once she had decided to fume, it was easy to start because it was so like Cat, so *exactly* like her to decide to meet Pen again, after so many years, at an enormous party, in front of an audience of strangers and, worse, non-strangers. And it was so like Pen to go along with the idea, to do things Cat's way, instead of suggesting an alternate plan. Even as she thought these thoughts, getting angrier and angrier, Pen realized that they had little basis in fact. Although Cat had always loved parties, she had a firm sense of appropriateness and privacy, especially other people's privacy, and though Pen had been occasionally happy to indulge Cat's flights of fancy, she had never gone along unquestioningly when it came to something really important. In fact, it was the very abruptness and oddness of Cat's request that had caused Pen's uncharacteristic compliance, caused her to send an e-mail saying nothing but I'll be there. Still, however makeshift, the anger felt good, coursing through her like a stiff drink and sending the sadness, shoulders hunched, clomp, clomp, clomping away.

I could be home, Pen growled silently. *I could be in my apartment, right this second, with Augusta.* It had hurt to leave Augusta. It always hurt. Even the usual monthly weekend good-byes set a hard sadness thrumming inside Pen's chest every single time, and this month, there had been more than one good-bye.

Augusta had been okay this time, though, which wasn't necessarily to be expected. She didn't balk often at being left at Patrick's, but when she did, it was invariably high and excruciating drama. Last time it happened had been awful: Augusta wrapping herself around Pen, python-fashion, wailing like a blizzard, Patrick's face crossed with sorrow, Tanya feigning applause in Pen's direction, saying, "Nice. Very nice."

Pen had been especially worried about this go-round because whenever Pen left, Augusta insisted upon knowing precisely where she was going, and, perhaps because she had so little in the way of a past, Augusta had had difficulty comprehending the concept of a reunion. In the end, this had probably worked in everyone's favor, since, inside her imagination, Augusta had tidily substituted the unwieldy reunion idea with one of her own and decided that Pen was going to meet friends at the Union Street bakery in Wilmington where Augusta had loved to go with Pen's mother.

Pen had driven Augusta over to Patrick's in the early morning, with long, pink-stained clouds still floating low in the milky sky and with her child, bread-warm and messy-haired, sleeping in the backseat, and had prayed that the powers that be not mistake her recent uptick in leave-takings for a lack of love. *This is it,* she had vowed. *It, it, it. For a long time, all summer; except for Patrick's weekends, this is the last time I'll spend a night away from her.* On Patrick's doorstep, as carefully as Pen had tried to make the transfer—one palm cupping the weight of Augusta's head, the other arm supporting the curled rest of her—Augusta had awakened and reached for her. Pen had held her breath, but, instead of launching into a tantrum, Augusta had smiled, blinked extravagantly like a cat, and said, "You will bring me some jam-spot cookies like I like, right, Mama?" And Pen had asked Patrick, "How can I, how could *anyone* walk away from that?"

But she had. Because Cat had said that she needed her, Pen had left Augusta, and now here she stood, mute and rigid as a stump, her head full of noise, remembering the curve of her child's perfect skull in her hand, and waiting for someone who was either taking her damn time (Pen hadn't worn a watch in years and her satin wristlet bag was too small for her phone, so she didn't know how long she had been waiting but knew it was unforgivably long) or who was never arriving at all. *God, I must be insane,* she thought, *or stupid.* And then she turned her face—what was it? fifteen degrees? ten? less?—and saw Will.

He wasn't looking at her, was at such an oblique angle to her that his face was little more than a sliver, but she knew him at once. "It was like reading," she would try to explain later, and she wasn't talking about phonics. She didn't break him into syllables—shoulders, hair, shirt collar, hand, nose, cheekbone—and put him back together again; she didn't sound him out. He was a language she knew, and it was whole-word recognition: Will.

He looked at her and smiled, not a wry or wary smile, but an easy, sudden gift of a smile, like someone handing her a pear, a smile that only a crazy person would fail to return. But that's just what Pen did. Not only did she fail to return it, but she stared at Will, frozen, for a long time, a fiery blush shooting up her neck and face, finally lifted one finger in a forlorn and inane gesture meaning *I'll be right back*, then spun around and went careening—erratic, batlike—through the crowd of people and out the back of the tent.

Once outside, she kept walking, blindly, cursing herself, cursing the ridiculously high heels that sent her wobbling, knock-kneed, across the grass like a baby giraffe, then teetering down a brick sidewalk, clicks echoing like gunshots in the night.

"Idiot!" She bit the word out through clenched teeth. "Idiot, idiot."

After a few more steps, she stood still, squeezed her eyes shut, and a thought came to her that was perfectly calm and in the voice of her mother, *You are overwrought and you need to sit down.* She opened her eyes and got her bearings: a long, beautiful serpentine wall made of bricks, a white gate. One of the university gardens. "Let it be unlocked," Pen whispered, and it was.

Inside, plum trees stood in a row, flowers lifted their pale throats to the moon and stars, a magnolia held its tight-closed buds like white candles in its green hands. The place was so orderly, so full of grace that Pen hated to disturb it with her idiocy and her burning face and her raucous pulse, but then she saw a white bench, so she sat down.

She hadn't walked far, but she felt like she had. The party was still there, right around the corner. She could hear it but not see it, and she took a few seconds to imagine it as a big, white, hoop-skirted ghost floating away over the grass or one of those Mississippi riverboats, its paddlewheel turning languorously in the brown water, carrying the music and laughter, the corseted women and wild-eyed gamblers farther and farther downstream. *You are weird, girlfriend,* thought Pen, shaking her head. *As weird as they come. A closet weirdo.* But the ghost and the riverboat called her back to herself enough so that she could sort out just what in the hell had happened back there at the party, to enumerate all the reasons (and she was sure there were legions of them) why she was an idiot.

It had happened fast. What had happened fast? Will had done a small, normal thing: he had looked at her and smiled. But as soon as he did it, the instant Pen really and truly saw him, she was overtaken, sucker punched, not once but twice: first by a terrible, rawboned loneliness, then by desire. For Will. Desire for *Will.* Although *desire* was too breathy a word for what she felt, and too narrow. Because it wasn't just sexual desire (although it was that, too), but a voluminous, all-purpose longing. If Will hadn't, by the grace of God, been too far away to hear her, she might have said it out loud: "I want you in every way a person can want someone."

"Holy shit," Pen whispered, panicked, into the stillness of the garden. "What have I done?" And then she remembered that, apart from running out of the party like a lunatic, she hadn't really done anything. "Calm down, sweetheart," she told herself, doing her best to channel her mom. "Chill the cluck out. Think."

After briefly undertaking what she imagined to be yoga breathing, she did think, taking on the loneliness first, touching it cautiously, examining it, and she discovered that the loneliness was nothing new, but had been there all along. It was just that, before the moment at the party, she hadn't been aware of its magnitude. She hadn't been conscious of all the pieces of it—loneliness upon loneliness—all at the same time: her lost friendships, her misbegotten hopes for Patrick, her father's dying (and, for a bad split second, sitting in the garden, she was that woman again, her father's girl, kneeling next to him, asking him to wake up), her lonely windswept desert of a heart at her father's funeral, the lost, folded-in-on-itself solitariness she felt when she rode her bike, the way she missed her mother, the way she missed Augusta every time she left her.

Stop it, she told herself, disgusted. *Cut the crybaby crap. You have*

Jamie. And Amelie. You have Kiki and plenty of other people. And for God's sake, you have Augusta.

It was true that there was no way to be with Augusta and to feel alone. Just the sight of her girl holding a cup with her two hands, just the sound of her voice in the hallway outside their apartment not only connected Pen to Augusta, but turned Pen's boundaries deliquescent, let some of the world flow in. But the rest of the time? *The rest of the time,* Pen understood, startled, *I am outside of life. I am sad. I spend so much time missing people.* She turned the idea over, parsed it out, tried it on—"Penelope Calloway is a sad and lonely person"—and found that it fit. How in the world had she let this happen?

For a few bleak seconds, she reeled, before snapping back to herself, or to herself-as-her-mother, or, more specifically, to herself-as-her-mother-on-an-especially-impatient-day. *Don't be silly. You will fix it,* she told herself sharply. *Of course, you will. It's not too late.* Pen would do whatever people did to fix themselves, and even though she had no clear idea of what this was or where to start, just thinking the word *fix*—the short, no-nonsense briskness of it—made her feel competent. She sat up straighter on the bench. She clapped her hands together like Mary Poppins: spit-spot, that's done.

As for her wanting Will, just because something felt like a revelation didn't mean it was one. Wanting a man she hadn't set eyes on in six years? *You don't even know him,* she told herself meanly, but she didn't really believe it. In any case, whether she knew him or not, whether the desire was a fleeting or a permanent condition, wanting wasn't nothing, but it wasn't all that much, either. It wasn't love. *You have always loved Will,* a voice in her head reminded her. *That's different,* she shot back with fierce practicality. *And you know it.* Then the garden gate creaked and there he was.

Neither one of them said hi. After a single, superfast, peripheral glance, Pen didn't look at him, not even when he sat down on the bench next to her. She sat gazing vacantly at the flowerbed, unmoored, possibly not breathing, thoughts fluttering like moths through her brain— *Are those daylilies? Are daylilies supposed to bloom at night? Who are you, the daylily police?*—and listening to what might have been a mockingbird braid its long, rippling strands of shine in the magnolia tree (*Were mockingbirds supposed to sing at night?*), but mostly listening to the annoying bass line of her heart in her ears. Will was so still that, for all Pen knew, he might have been doing the same (daylilies, bird, even her own heart because it was that loud).

When the mockingbird finished singing, Will said, "So, are you gonna eat that?"

For the first time, Pen noticed that she still had the small Chinet plate. It sat in her lap. A piece of ham the size of a silver dollar sat on the plate, all that had survived her mad rush from the tent to the garden. *Intrepid ham scrap,* was her desultory thought. *Scrappy scrap.* She envisioned herself, trailing hors d'oeuvres; then as her mind cleared enough for Will's question to register, she smiled.

"It's all yours."

"Awesome."

She laughed and gathered herself and looked at him. To her relief, she wasn't gobsmacked by desire. She didn't burst into tears. There was Will, sitting on the bench, chewing ham, and the sight of him made her happy.

When he finished, he grinned a semi-shy, close-mouthed grin and said, "Hey, Pen."

At the sound of her name, Pen flashed back to the Pen of a few minutes (five? twenty? more?) ago, hightailing it out of the tent in her cocktail sandals, and groaned.

"What?" Will asked.

"I guess I was hoping you wouldn't recognize me."

"You? Oh." And then he smiled his true, guileless, transfiguring smile, the one he had given her back in the tent and so many times (how many?) before that, back when his smile was just an ordinary part of her life, like her books or her coffeemaker or the view from her window. "I would know you anywhere. Sorry about that."

Pen shrugged. "It's okay."

"But, hey, did you see that woman back at the party? Blue dress? Ran out of there like a jackrabbit."

"Whew." Pen rolled her eyes. "Total nutjob."

"Maybe, but fast. Her speed, and not just her speed, her *acceleration* was *very* impressive."

"You think?"

"Oh yeah. In heels? And with a death grip on that little white plate? Not a lot of people could've pulled that off."

Pen considered kissing him, then, not kissing him-kissing him, which would have been madness, but leaning over and kissing the plane of his cheek because, with an impossibly light touch, he had gotten them through it, set them both safely down on the other side. Not kissing him-kissing him, but kissing him because he was kind and funny, because he was a man who deserved to be kissed. *Ha! Forget it,* Pen told herself, derisively. *I don't trust you as far as I can throw you.*

Instead of kissing Will, she placed her hands in her lap, fiddled with the tassel on her satin bag, and said, "Have you seen her?"

"Not yet. Have you?"

"No." Then Pen had a thought. "You mean you haven't seen her here or you haven't seen her since she left?" She'd almost said "left us" but stopped because it sounded both too plaintive and too final. "Left us" made it sound like someone had died. "I mean, since she moved away."

"Both."

Pen let slip a sigh, a drawn-out sigh, an *oceanic* sigh, of relief.

"Hey," said Will, surprised. He looked at her until she looked back. "You didn't really think we were out there somewhere being friends without you, did you?"

"Oh, no. Of course not." But she found that her voice was shaky. "Okay, maybe. Once or twice, in my darkest hours."

Will didn't say anything. Then he said, "I'm sorry."

"It's not your fault."

"No. I'm sorry you had darkest hours."

Pen swallowed. This wasn't the time or place to talk about her darkest hours. There might be a time and a place later; she even hoped there would be, but not here in this serene and otherworldly garden, not now.

She said, "I just got an e-mail from out of the blue. It didn't say much."

"Mine said, 'I know it's been forever, but I need you.' "

Pen's eyes widened. " 'Please come to the reunion. I'll find you there.' "

" 'I'm sorry for everything.' "

"What did she have to be sorry about?" asked Pen, and immediately wished that she hadn't, since who among them should be sorry and for what were untouchable topics, the very last ones she wanted to discuss.

Maybe Will felt the same way because he jumped in quickly with, "Weird how she sent us identical e-mails."

"It is weird. And that e-mail just didn't sound like her."

"I thought the same thing."

"It was flat."

"And colorless."

"And not at all long-winded." Pen and Will exchanged a quick smile because Cat's long-windedness was legendary, but then Pen frowned. "Honestly, the way she said what she said worried me more than what she said."

"I know. I don't like to think about what might have happened to Cat to make her write a flat, colorless, short-winded e-mail."

Pen shivered and said, "You know what? We should . . . ," but before she finished, they were both standing up.

"Yeah," agreed Will. "We should go back to the party, see if she's there."

But as they left, first Pen, then Will, and as Will closed the gate behind them, Pen felt her heart sink a little.

"I like that garden," she said, picking her painful, tottering way across the bricks. "I could live in that garden. Pitch a tent under that big magnolia tree and live there. Just so you know."

Will nodded. "I can see how you would. Although if you're planning to live in a tent, you should probably consider some different shoes."

Pen said, "Ha ha, very funny," and slapped Will's chest with the Chinet plate, and poof, there they were, the Pen and Will of ten years ago, twelve years ago. Then, without breaking stride or making a big deal about it, Will offered her his arm, and because when someone offers you his arm, you take it, that's what Pen did.

IF WILL LEAPING, AFTER SIX YEARS, INTO A FULL-BODIED, RADIANT being out of the chaos of a party was one thing, Will leaning back on his elbows in the grass under an ordinary noon sky turned out, to Pen's profound relief, to be quite another. Longing didn't jump up and seize her by the throat; she was not a voice crying in the wilderness; the "come live with me and be my love" nonsense from the night before did not evince itself for a second, having been washed out, apparently, by a flood of normalness and daylight. Even when she checked in with her body (*like a person poking a rattlesnake with a stick*, she thought), it seemed to be behaving itself.

It wasn't that he didn't look as good in the light of day. Pen knew that his austere angularity wasn't everyone's cup of tea. (Once, in the throes of taking Intro to Architecture, Cat had declared Will's looks as "either totally Bauhaus or totally Frank Lloyd Wright!" "Better figure that out soon," Will had advised. "I *will* be on the midterm.") Strictly speaking, he wasn't even Pen's cup of tea, since her taste in men had always leaned toward the lush-featured and swarthy. But, in a detached way, on the rare occasions when she'd thought about it, she had always found him oddly beautiful. Now, plopped down next to him on the grass, she had to admit that, while pretty much anyone could look good in a moon-soaked garden, Will was holding his own in the sunshine, and still, no fuss, no lust. All she felt was happy.

Cat never had shown up the night before. But, after sidling uneasily up to the party, an interesting thing had happened to Pen and Will: they had had fun. They'd eaten; they'd mingled. Will had run into a hallmate of his from freshman year, a guy they had all called Huey and whose dual claims to fame had been wearing cowboy hats and the ability to quote *Raising Arizona*—not bits and pieces, but the entire script—by heart. Now, Huey went by his given name, Paul, was a nurse-anesthetist with Doctors Without Borders, and was headed, in three weeks, for a two-year stint in Sierra Leone.

"You make me feel like a deadbeat, Paul," Will had said.

"Don't worry about it, man," Paul had replied. "I make everyone feel like a deadbeat." Then he squinted his eyes and drawled, " 'Son, you got a panty on your head.' "

"Thanks," said Will. "That helps."

Pen spoke with three separate women named Jennifer, one of whom now owned a designer resale shop in Richmond called Déjà Ooh!, a woman named Lane Lipton whom everyone had known would become a high-powered Washington attorney and was one, and a very drunk redhead whom Pen remembered not at all, but who tearfully apologized for having told "at least ten people" that a friend of a friend of hers had walked in on Pen, Cat, and Will having a threesome.

"Forget about it," said Pen.

"I can't!" the woman wailed. "Were you? Having them?"

Afterward, in the sleepy, easy quiet of Will's walking Pen to her car, Will said, "I hate to even say this, but what if she doesn't—" and Pen cut him off, saying, "I know. I hadn't even considered that. I mean, until right now."

"She'll come," said Will.

They walked a few more steps and Pen said, "My stupid feet are on fire," and she stopped and slipped off her shoes, and, fleetingly, considered throwing them at something, the streetlamp by the side of the road, a passing car.

"Where the hell was she?" she almost yelled, making her voice angry even though what she really was was disappointed and worried. "We come all the way here and she doesn't *show*?"

For a few seconds, she and Will stood rooted to the sidewalk, not looking at each other. Pen stared at their two shadows stretching down the sidewalk as though they'd been flung from a bucket, then at the streetlamp that was casting them, shining yellow through a haze of bugs.

"That," she said, "is a lot of bugs for this early in the summer." Her eyes were filling with tears, which annoyed her.

"It is a lot of bugs," agreed Will in a tired voice. "She'll come."

"What will we do if she doesn't?" The childishness of this question deepened her annoyance, but she waited for Will's answer anyway.

"We'll think of something," said Will. "And anyway, she'll come."

They started walking again. Pen's shoes dangled from her fingers. A car quaking with bass trundled by, and Pen saw a child-skinny arm dangling out the passenger-side window, the orange pin-dot glint of a cigarette.

Finally, Pen said, "She might not."

"Yeah," said Will. "She might not."

But when Pen got back to her hotel room, she found the gumdrop of a message light on the oldfangled phone blinking, and even though, when she hit the button and braced herself for the sound of Cat's voice, it never came, relief washed over her because it was a message from Cat all the same. The man working the front desk read it to her: "Sorry I couldn't make it tonight, but I will see you at the barbecue tomorrow."

"Is that a note that someone dropped off?" As she asked, Pen was already slipping her shoes back on so she could run down and get it, was already seeing Cat's curvaceous handwriting, capital "S" like a swan, but the man said, "No. Jonah the guy with the shift before mine took it. I'd know his chicken scratch anywhere. Must've been a phone call."

Pen opened her satin evening bag and took out the napkin with Will's cell number on it. When she saw that he'd written "Will W." above it, she smiled. As if she wouldn't know. As if she'd been collecting phone numbers from men named Will all night. And then she smoothed the napkin with her fingers and felt a twinge, below her sternum and on the back of her neck, of what she had felt when she had first seen him in the tent.

"Don't be a sap," she snapped. "It's a *name* on a *napkin*."

Then she called Will, said, "Listen to this," and read him the message.

"I got the same thing," he said, and for a moment, they basked in their shared relief, not saying anything. Then Will said, "Hey, you didn't bring your bike with you, by any chance?"

◆ ◆ ◆

Pen had forgotten how quickly it happened, how you round a corner, pass a Shell station and the Kingdom Hall, go up a hill, and enter another world: sloping wooden porches, dogs chained to stakes in yards, dense trees, steep, thigh-burning hills, and the occasional valley farmstead opening up like an exhale. Once, years ago, Pen had hit a broken patch on the road and fallen and, with her bike on top of her, had been amazed to see children—white blond hair, knobby heron legs—materialize from between the trees to call, shyly, "Hey, lady! Hey, lady! You okay, lady?"

Pen and Will took a lunch break in the yard of the ancient gray church, leaning their bikes against an oak tree, tossing down their helmets and sprawling gratefully on the hard, balding lawn. Will had stopped at a deli on the way to pick up Pen at her hotel, and after he'd caught his breath, he unzipped his backpack and started to hand Pen a sandwich wrapped in white paper, but when she tried to take it from him, he got a look of concern on his face and didn't let the sandwich go.

"What's wrong?"

"I should've asked."

"Asked what?"

"About your current relationship with brine-cured meat."

"You got me a sauerkraut-less Reuben?"

"I did." Will's expression turned unexpectedly shy. "But, you know, it's been six years. I shouldn't assume."

"My love for brine-cured meat has endured the test of time," said Pen, yanking the sandwich out of his hand. "My heart belongs to brine-cured meat now and for all eternity."

The Reuben was slightly leaky but otherwise perfect.

As Will began unwrapping his sandwich, Pen said, "You're a whole other story. No love. No loyalty. Total sandwich promiscuity. You could have anything in there."

Will grinned and bit into ham and Swiss with hot mustard on pumpernickel. "We're talking about sandwiches," he observed, after an interval of chewing. "We haven't seen each other in six years."

"You're right." She watched two dark birds wheel against the powder blue sky. Vultures, she figured, although they didn't look ominous or even hungry, just lazy. An idea hit her and she slapped her palm on the ground. "I thought of a way to do this."

"Do what?"

Pen raised an arm and made impatient, circular, flapping motions with her hand. "*This!* This-this. What other this would I mean?"

"Okay. So what's the way?"

"Four sentences," she said smugly.

Will waited, then popped the stopper of his water bottle with his teeth and drank.

"Brilliant, right?" said Pen.

"Four sentences. That's all you're going to say."

"Oh, come *on*."

"I got nothing." He held out his empty hands.

"You used to be better at connecting the dots."

"It's been a while since I've been around your dots, remember?"

Pen sighed. "Six years in four sentences. No questions, no comments. Four sentences from each of us and we consider ourselves caught up."

"Fine," Will said slowly. "You first."

"Oh, no," said Pen. "I thought of it. I did the legwork."

Will laughed and kept eating. "No questions or comments," he said. "And that would apply to the person who did the legwork, too."

"Right."

Pen was suddenly nervous. As she redid her ponytail, she felt a rising urge to babble her way into and through the silence of Will's thinking, and instead of fighting the urge, she decided to give in.

"My hair's hot." She petted her head. "You know how you have those things that you measure the start of a season by? Not you-you, but people-you. One, I guess. *You* might or you might not. But anyway, like if you wear gloves *and* a scarf, that means it's winter? Like that?

Well, even if, technically, it's not summer, not, you know, summer sol-stice summer, I always feel, personally, that it's summer when I sit in the sun and my hair gets hot."

"I write books for kids, for a living," said Will. "I live in Asheville, North Carolina, sometimes with my now-sober yogi/painter mom, sometimes by myself. When I get mad, I no longer go apeshit. My dad, whom I haven't spoken to in about four years, has a girlfriend who had a baby last year, so I have a little brother I've never met, whose name, apparently, is Randall Junior, a.k.a. R.J."

Pen absorbed this for a moment, her heart in her throat. *It's been so long,* she thought. *It's been no time at all.* In a soft voice, she said, "Am I allowed to say that I love your books?"

Will ducked his head, smiling. "No."

Pen lay back on the grass with her eyes shut, feeling the sun on her face, pressing like warm thumbs against her eyelids, thinking how she could fall asleep there, with the sun and with Will and that old church watching over her, and it would have been so easy to do, even for Pen, who had trouble falling asleep in her own bed, but, instead, after a minute or so, she started talking, without sitting up or opening her eyes or even imagining what Will was thinking as she spoke.

"I have a daughter named Augusta who turns five in July. I am not now, nor have I ever been married. Augusta and I share an apartment in Philadelphia with Jamie. My dad died two years ago." It wasn't hard after all. She released the sentences carefully, evenly, like someone placing leaves, one by one, onto the surface of a stream, letting the water carry them slowly into the trees and out of sight.

Will didn't make a sound. Pen couldn't hear anything except the tide of her own breathing and the sequined clamor of birdsong, but as she sat up, she kept her eyes closed, thinking, *Please don't let him be crying. If he's crying, I might cry, I might roll over on the ground, bury my face in my arms and fall to pieces, and he will feel like he needs to say something or hug me, but he won't know if I want him to, and it will be a disaster.* So great was Pen's need for Will not to be crying that it ceased, for a few seconds, to matter that he almost certainly wouldn't be. Will had never been a crier, not even when he was a kid.

This was something Pen knew, and, sure enough, when she opened her eyes, he wasn't crying. He was almost not moving. The only giveaway that he was sad (a thing Pen had forgotten about Will until this very second) was a pair of parentheses etched into the corners of his mouth.

"Am I allowed to say I loved your dad?" Will said finally.

Pen caught his eye and smiled. "No."

A red pickup truck with a German shepherd in the bed drove by.

"It's been a long time since I've seen a dog riding in the back of a truck," said Pen. "Is that even legal anymore? You'd think not, with all the seat belt laws and car seat laws and so forth. I remember how when we were little, we'd take, I don't know, ten kids to the pool in my mom's Volvo station wagon. We'd lie in the back, head to foot, like sardines. Not that I'm not all for the new laws. They're great. I just wonder if they apply to, you know, dogs."

Pen stopped for breath, and Will said, "No feet."

Pen looked at him quizzically.

"Sardines."

"Oh. Right. Anyway—"

"So hold on," Will broke in. "You *live* with *Jamie*?"

"Hey! No questions! Remember!" But Pen was laughing, and even though she knew that Will didn't really expect her to explain why she lived with Jamie, that it was just his way of breaking the tension and navigating them away from the towering subject of Pen's father's death, she answered it anyway, surprising herself by beginning at the beginning, with Will and Cat leaving and with Patrick's knack ("perverse knack" she said, even though she had found his arrival lifesaving, or close to lifesaving, at least once) for showing up at Pen's most vulnerable moments.

"You didn't meet cute," said Will, resurrecting their old joke right on cue. "Tell me you didn't."

"I wish I could. *I* was sour and mopey, but pretty much everything Patrick does is cute. We met cute and irresponsible and slightly deceptive, which is Patrick in a nutshell." Guiltily, she jumped in with a revision. "Well, except for the deceptive part. Well, I mean, he *is* deceptive sometimes, but he doesn't really plan to be."

"Spontaneous deception is much better," said Will.

"I had just finished up my last requirements for my master's in education," began Pen.

"I remember you were studying to be a reading specialist. Congratulations."

"Well, and I was feeling sorry for myself because I didn't have anyone to celebrate with." She shot him a look.

"Yeah. Sorry about that."

"I guess I could've found someone. Jamie or one of the people in my program or someone, but I really just wanted to wallow. I did a fair amount of wallowing after you and Cat left."

"I'm familiar with wallowing," said Will.

"And I'm drinking coffee as morosely as I can and reading a book, a really sad book about a child murder because if you're feeling glum you might as well go all the way, and this person sits at my table and says, 'Is it okay if I sit here?' Except he was already sitting, so I said, meanly, 'I guess, but there's a seat right over there,' and he said, 'Oh, I know, I was just sitting in it.'"

"You're right. Cute." Will pretended to gag.

"See? And then he said, and this was the deception part, 'I was waiting for a friend who never showed, and I hate to drink coffee alone.' And I said, 'On the other hand, I like drinking coffee alone,' and he said, 'Not to be insolent or anything, but you don't look like you're liking it. In fact, you look miserable.' And it made me laugh that he said 'insolent' so we ended up talking."

"I get how that was nauseatingly cute and spontaneously deceptive, since I gather he didn't really get stood up, but how was it irresponsible?"

"His wife had thrown him out of the house just five weeks earlier. They had a three-year-old daughter. And while he was busy hitting on a random girl in a coffeehouse, he missed a meeting with his attorney regarding their breakup."

"Wow," said Will. "That's hard-core."

"I know. But I was worse because even after I found all that out, I didn't send him away."

"I wouldn't say worse," said Will. "He was the one with a wife and kid."

"I know, but he's just *like* that. Careless. I'm not, but I threw myself into it, even though I knew better. I allowed myself to become criminally smitten."

Will smiled at "criminally smitten."

"I even let it affect my career. One day, Patrick said there was a reading specialist job at his old private school in the suburbs, the one he went to from the age of four until he graduated, and because it was his school, I applied for it. I'd been all set to work in a city school, and I got all goo-goo-eyed and dropped that idea in a flash. I think I'd known him for two weeks."

"Still: wife, kid."

"We were together five months that time, before I made him go back."

"You felt guilty?"

"Yes, but also, he was pining for them, both of them. Anyone could tell that."

"What do you mean 'that time'?" asked Will.

Pen kept going, leaving out nothing, or almost nothing. How Patrick and Tanya had shown up at her school, Patrick's alma mater, one day without warning, Patrick having forgotten to mention to Pen—having possibly forgotten altogether, knowing Patrick—that he and Tanya had always planned to send Lila there. How the admissions director stopped into the reading center as part of the tour and how Pen had kept her cool, pretending not to know them, but how Patrick had turned into a red-faced, stammering idiot so that Tanya knew something was up, and how the next day, the headmaster suggested that Pen take a semester's leave of absence. Pen could still recall the way the icy doom settled in her stomach as she walked down the hallway to his office.

"Did you go back?" asked Will. "After that semester?"

"No. I found out I was pregnant soon thereafter. But I'd decided not to go back even before I knew. I was—disheartened."

"I'm sorry you were disheartened. The whole thing sucks."

Patrick had come back after Augusta was born. He hadn't come to the hospital for her birth, which had earned him Pen's parents' and Jamie's disdain until the end of time, but which was actually a relief to Pen. Patrick slouching among the nurses and Pen's family members, with his uneasiness and his big hands in his pockets and his guilt-stricken eyes, asking her for whatever it was he needed from her—and there would've been something—while Pen tried to give birth would have been a distraction, one thing too many. Plus, there was a tiny, barbed part of her that had been glad he was missing it, glad that their baby's sliding whole and gorgeous into the world would never belong to him.

It was ten days later, less than an hour after Pen's mother had gone home ("What were you doing, spying on us?" Pen had asked. "Yes," Patrick had replied.) that Patrick had shown up on Pen's doorstep, un-shaven and gaunt, his nails bitten to the quick, and Pen, her edges worn down by ten days of sleep deprivation, breastfeeding, and titanic love, had let him in and, when he begged to stay, had let him stay. Pen didn't tell Will how Patrick had set his daughter gently back into her bassinet, then had fallen onto his knees in the bedroom, sobbing, how she could still close her eyes and remember the sight of him in the half-light with his face in his hands, and the raw and honest sound of his weeping.

"I didn't really love him. I didn't even feel the charmed infatuation I had felt when I met him, but we spent our days in Augusta's glow. She made things seem possible. So when he asked me to marry him, even though he wasn't divorced yet, even though I didn't have that much faith that it would work out, I said I would."

She broke off a piece of her Reuben and tossed it to a couple of brown birds that were hopping near by. With affronted squeaks and a melodramatic agitation of feathers, they bounced backward and flew away.

"I shouldn't have done it," said Pen, sighing. "It made him really happy, though, and Patrick when he's happy is just this big, positive force of nature, so I let down my guard and let myself start to be-lieve in our happy little family, and as soon as I did that, the next day maybe, Tanya threatened to take Lila."

"What do you mean 'take' her?" asked Will.

"She said she'd say anything; she'd lie and get other people to lie. She'd do whatever it took to get full custody. The day Patrick found this out, I came home to find him on the couch, looking like he'd been run over by a tractor, and even before he told me, I knew he was gone."

"Man, Tanya sounds like a piece of work."

"The thing is, though," said Pen, "he would've left anyway. I like to think I would have come to my senses and broken it off eventually, but even if I hadn't, I don't think he would've gone through with it."

"Why not?"

"He loves Tanya. It's a fact. He loves Lila, too, of course. Lila alone might have been enough reason for him to leave us, but he is stone-cold, crazy in love with Tanya."

"What about you? And Augusta?"

"Oh, he loves us, too. He told me one time, at a really low point, that he was cursed to be in love with two women. But he loved Tanya first. And best, which in a way is only fair because she loves him back in a way that I never did."

Then, in a thin, strained voice, Pen said, "He did come back one more time, though." She started talking fast to get it over with. "He showed up at my dad's funeral, which wasn't a bad thing because I was a wreck that day, and Augusta was three years old and needed a parent who didn't collapse into tears every five minutes."

Pen swallowed. *You got this far,* she said to herself. *Don't fall apart now.*

"He came back to Philadelphia with us, and somehow he just stayed." She caught herself. "On my couch, I mean. He told me he was thinking he'd made a mistake, that he wanted to try again. I don't know why, except that maybe I was such a mess that he thought I needed him, and he loves to be needed. I didn't say yes or no. I hardly heard him. I was so tired and sick at heart. He took care of us for a week, maybe a little more, cooking and doing everything for Augusta, and then Jamie showed up, and got furious (you wouldn't even have recognized him), and threw Patrick out, and took me and Augusta home with him, and sent some guys later to pack up our stuff. And we ended up staying. Somehow, it worked. It works. For now, anyway."

Will didn't say anything for so long that Pen began to get anxious. There she went again, handing everything over, entrusting, like a five-year-old, and to what end? *Good grief. Did you really think,* she asked herself, *did you honestly think that you and Will could just pick up where you left off?*

"Maybe we should go," she said stiffly, and started to clean up, brushing crumbs off her bike shorts, balling up the white sandwich paper in her fist.

"Wait," said Will. "Can I say something?"

Pen's hands stopped moving at the sound of his voice, which was grave and formal. *Oh, God,* thought Pen. His jaw, his shoulders, even the skin around his eyes looked taut; he had the aspect of a man steeling himself. *Just say it, say that this is all too much,* thought Pen. *Get it over with.* Then he shook his head and laughed, a short, self-mocking sound, more like a bark than a laugh, but it did the trick, dissipated the tension and Pen's worry, sent them evaporating into the bright blue air.

"I'm not used to being nervous when I talk to you," said Will. "I'm not used to talking to you."

"Well, and I threw a lot at you: the rise and fall of my doomed love affair, the birth of my illegitimate child, my near breakdown after my father's death. My life as a Russian novel. Way to give a guy some breathing room, Pen." Pen gave Will a quick glance, then began the careful and important project of unballing the sandwich wrapper in her hand and smoothing it flat against the grass.

"You don't have enough names for a Russian novel. You need to have at least six names," said Will.

"And three nicknames."

"I wasn't talking about that, the breathing room thing. I was going to say: no pressure, but—"

Pen looked up at him.

"You can say no to this," Will started over, riffling his hair with the palm of his hand, "and if you were thinking we'd just hang out here and then go back to business as usual, post-reunion, that's fine. Or not fine, but I'd respect it. I mean, of course, I would. But I was just going to say that I think I should meet Augusta, before she turns into one of those what-do-you-call-'ems, girls with ironed hair and Ugg boots, who text instead of talk."

"Tweens," Pen said. She smiled. "She already has Uggs because Patrick has no freaking idea of how to say no to her. But okay."

" 'Okay'? That's it?"

"If I said more it would be something like, 'Your meeting Augusta is not only okay, but would right a grievous and cosmic wrong,' which might sound overblown."

Will shrugged. "I'm okay with okay."

"Good," said Pen.

THE BARBECUE WAS TURNING TO SAND IN PEN'S MOUTH.

"What if she's sick? What if she has cancer? What if there's some complication with her epilepsy? What if she's crazy? Not Cat-crazy, but seriously mentally ill? We've been here an hour, Will. What if she doesn't come?"

Pen's voice was shrill, about to tip over an edge into frantic and desperate, but she couldn't help it. The tent tonight was smaller, and, at some point earlier in the evening, humid air had rolled in from someplace, the Amazon rain forest maybe, and the party, just an hour old, had already hit the glazed-face, mosquito-y, warm drink, sticky-red-checkered-outdoor-tablecloth phase that every summer party gets to if there are enough people and if it goes on long enough. And still, no Cat, no Cat.

Flushed and tugging at the neck of his white T-shirt, Will said irritably, "What do you want me to say, Pen?"

Pen saw him, then, striding purposefully, eyebrows hawkishly lowered, toward them through the crowd. He was a little thinner than when she'd last seen him, softer bellied, but still big, blond, and boy-faced.

"Oh, for the love of God."

Will didn't turn around to look, but put down his knife and fork and stared at Pen. "Cat?"

"Cat's husband," said Pen drearily.

"Pen. Will. It's been a while." Same voice.

Will stood up to shake his hand. "Hey, Jason. You want to join us?"

"Oh, I do. Most definitely." Jason pulled out a chair and sat down. Pen didn't like the look on his face: smug, challenging, a little mean. She didn't like his pink, short-sleeved button-down or his sunburned ears or his hammy forearms, either. How, oh how, could Cat have married this person?

"Where's Cat?" demanded Pen.

At the question, Jason's demeanor cracked, just briefly, a flinch, a flash of alarm in his eyes, before the bravado was back.

"You tell me," he said. "That's"—he made two guns with his fingers and pointed them at Pen and Will (*God, you're an idiot*, thought Pen)—"why I brought you here."

Chapter Ten

"Y OU." PEN EXHALED THE WORD MORE THAN SPOKE IT.

"Yup," said Jason, with an upward, confirming chin-jut jerk of his head. "Me." He leaned back in his chair and crossed his freckled arms.

Pen wished with all her heart that she could say, "I knew it!" or "I thought so," or at least, "I didn't really believe that e-mail came from Cat," or even, "As much as I wanted to believe Cat had written that e-mail, as much as I expected, every second, to turn around and find her standing next to me, I harbored, nevertheless, a small, slender, vaporous sliver of suspicion that it wasn't really from her at all." But none of those would have been the truth. The truth was that she had fallen for Jason's trick hook, line, and sinker. The truth was weeks of happiness and worry and anticipation and nervousness and waiting and hope like a blazing light.

Pen wanted to hit him. Not just hit him. Pen who had never hit anyone in her life (since childhood anyway, and then it was only Jamie) wanted to slam Jason over backward in his chair, leap on him like a wolverine, and beat the crap out of him with her fists. She was picturing it, filling in the details (the clonk of his head against the ground, his nose fountaining blood), when, suddenly, she became aware of Will across the table, perfectly unmoving, his silence hissing like a live wire, his hands flat on the table at either side of his plate, and hitting didn't seem like such a good idea anymore. *Don't,* she thought in Will's direction. *He's not worth it. You've come so far. Please don't.*

But when she forced herself to look at Jason, the urge to hit and for him to be hit came back. Belligerent and neckless, hair like toothbrush bristles. The way he lolled his head to one side and had his hands shoved under his forearms so that his biceps strained against the sleeves of his shirt made her want to scream. *You are not LL Cool J, you posturing moron!* she imagined herself yelling. *You pink, doughy, unripe strawberry of a man! Yup? Yup?*

"You shit," she said instead. "You complete and total asshole." She didn't scream it. Her voice was low, but she could feel herself gathering steam. "You must be pretty proud of yourself, right? Sending us down here, worried out of our minds about Cat? What was it, some kind of joke to you?"

"Pen," said Will.

"Some kind of sick game to get back at us for—what? *Not liking you* six years ago, you stupid overgrown baby?"

Jason's face went from hostile to stunned to enraged. He turned alarmingly red, clamped his lips together, and began to breathe hard out of his nose. *Bull!* thought Pen.

"Pen," said Will.

"I left my *daughter.* I left my job. I drove all the way the hell down here for some cat-and-mouse bullshit *game?*" When she said "game," Pen slapped her hand down on the table, making the plates jump and her nearly empty plastic water bottle flop over and roll across the table. It stopped in front of Jason, who didn't even look at it.

It wasn't until Will put his hand over her hand to stop its trembling that Pen realized it was trembling, not only her hand, but her entire body. *I am shaking with rage,* she marveled.

"Hey," said Will gently.

She looked up at him and he gave her a little encouraging nod, so she took a deep breath and began to count backward from ten, like the child in Will's book. By five, Will's hand was gone—she wished it weren't, even with all that was happening, she had the momentary presence of mind to wish it weren't—and he was staring at Jason with piercing eyes. Pen remembered, then, how Will could narrow his already long narrow eyes an almost imperceptible bit and turn their gaze to steel. "Like Clint Eastwood looking down a gun barrel," Cat used to say. "The eye equivalent of gritted teeth."

"Cat left you," said Will. Even before what he said sank in, Pen admired the flatness, the absolute, matter-of-fact calm of his voice.

Then what he had said sank in, and Pen thought, *Of course, she left him!* followed by, *Wait. What?*

"No," Jason shot back viciously.

"She left you, and you thought she came to us."

Pen stared at Will, bewildered. Then she heard it again, the part that had gotten lost in her outrage at Jason for tricking them into coming, in her sorrow at Jason's being Jason instead of Cat: her own voice asking, "Where's Cat?" and Jason's answer, "You tell me."

"You don't know where she is," said Pen in a wondering voice.

"You don't know shit," said Jason.

"She left you," said Will again.

"Not *me*," said Jason, pointing at his own chest with both forefingers. "She might have left, but she didn't leave *me*. She thought I was"—he paused, searching for the word—"awesome."

Will shifted his gaze from Jason to the tablecloth, the trail of water.

"We were happy," said Jason. "You might not believe it, but fuck you. We were a happily married couple." And at "happily married couple," even Pen, who still hated him, had to look away because he sounded so querulous, querulous and defensive and about six years old.

Maybe he sounded this way to himself, too, because, with one windshield-wiper swipe of his arm, the water bottle flew off the table, and he was standing up.

"Forget it," he said. "I don't have to defend myself to you shitheads."

But he just stood there, not leaving, breathing hard, rubbing his forehead with one hand, and staring out over the party, looking, with his sunburned ears, exactly like a guy in a lifeboat, scanning the ocean for land or boats or dorsal fins. As Pen watched him, she found herself remembering the e-mail, the words she had thought for so long were Cat's, but were really Jason's:

```
I know it's been forever, but I need you.
```

"Wait," she said to Jason.

"*You* wait," he said. He jerked his arm back as though she'd touched him, even though she hadn't.

Pen sighed. "Just—sit. Okay? Please." The "please" was an afterthought, a giving in, a tiny offering to his childlike blustering and his sad red ears. But she didn't think he would sit, not immediately, anyway. He was the kind of guy who would sit later, on his own terms.

"I need a beer," said Jason. Pen watched him stomp his way toward the beer table in his shorts and loafers, his arms slightly bowed at the elbows, his hands in loose fists. She recalled his vow in his old apology letter to never drink again and wondered what other promises to Cat he might have broken.

"I can see what Cat sees in him," Pen said, nodding. "Absolutely."

"'*You* wait,'" said Will. "Nice comeback."

Pen slumped, cradling the sides of her face in her hands and looking wide-eyed at Will. "Holy, holy, holy shit."

"I know."

"I can't believe it was him all the time."

"Yeah. Not only did I think it was her, I thought she'd be here. Even when she didn't come last night, I would have bet money she'd show up before it was all over."

"You think we should've suspected?" asked Pen.

"I don't know. I think we really wanted it to be her."

"And not only is she not here, she's missing."

"She left," Will said quickly. "That doesn't mean she's missing."

"I hope not. He's worried, though. You can see it in his face. And think about that e-mail. He's scared."

After a somber moment, Will grinned. "He should be scared. I thought you were about to jump up and break your chair over his head."

"Remember that night when you lost your marbles and pounded him into the Crater? I miss that night."

"Me, too. But maybe we should try to be nice, so he'll tell us what happened to Cat." Will shook his head. "What happened *with* Cat, is what I mean."

"He's a hard man to be nice to."

"Just until he tells us about Cat. Then you can clobber him."

"Here he comes."

This time, Jason didn't just sit, he yanked the chair around backward and straddled it, a startling gesture that would have been more impressive had it not placed him too far away from the table to put his beer down. After one attempt, he propped it on his knee instead. *Stumpy arms,* thought Pen. *T-rex.*

"Sorry I lost my temper," she said, attempting a smile of mollifying self-deprecation. "It was a shock, you showing up instead of Cat." At least this was true.

"Yeah, I'll bet," snorted Jason. "You guys always hated me."

Pen almost said, "And this is all about you." Instead, she didn't confirm or deny what he'd said. Neither did Will.

"Please tell us what happened," said Pen.

"Her dad died, like, six weeks ago, give or take," said Jason, darting his eyes from Pen's face to Will's, as though watching for their reaction.

Instantly, Pen's eyes filled with tears, both because her eyes always filled with tears at the mention of dead fathers and because the dead father in question belonged to Cat.

"She was crazy about her dad," said Will.

"How did it happen?" asked Pen, trying not to picture her own father, curled on his side, his cheek slack against the cement.

"Heart attack," said Jason. He squinted at them. "You're telling me you didn't know? Her dad died and she didn't tell you."

"How would I know?" said Will. "I haven't talked to Cat in six years."

"Neither have I," said Pen.

"Yeah, right," said Jason snidely. "I forgot."

"What's that supposed to mean?" asked Pen.

"It means I don't believe that, no matter what Cat said. I'm not an imbecile. Not one phone call? Not one e-mail?" said Jason. "It means I think you're all a bunch of liars."

"Cat, too?" snapped Pen, forgetting to be nice. "Cat who thinks you're awesome and would never leave you? You're calling her a liar, too?"

Jason tensed and opened his mouth, but nothing came out. His right knee started to jitter, causing his beer to slosh out of the glass and down his leg. "Fuck."

Will handed him a napkin, and he slapped at his leg with it.

"Her dad died," prompted Will. "Go ahead."

Jason tossed the napkin onto the table and said, "She lost it. It was weird."

"Weird to lose it when your dad dies?" said Pen. Will shot her a look.

Jason glared at her. "Believe it or not, I was *sensitive* to the fact that she was grieving. I was *there* for her. And, at first, you know, she was dealing with it the way you'd expect."

Pen tried to imagine how Cat would deal with something as big and final and grim as death, Cat of the twinkling eyes and sly sweetness and witty quips. Cat, who so much of the time, had seemed to float.

"I don't know what I'd expect," said Will. "I haven't seen her in a long time, and when I remember her, she's usually laughing."

A cloud passed over Jason's face. "Well, you know, she's an adult now. No one stays like that."

"So tell us," said Pen, "how she reacted."

"When she first heard, she was sad. Understandably, right? She said stuff about how she didn't know him that well, even though he was the only family she had. Which was true, by the way. She thought he was the greatest thing since sliced bread, and I guess he was charming and all, but he wasn't exactly a guy who showed up, if you know what I mean."

Pen thought that she did. She and Will had only met Dr. Ocampo twice (which in itself said a lot), once at their graduation and once in

Philadelphia when he came to lecture at a medical conference at Penn, and both times, Pen had liked him. It was impossible not to. He had been one of those compact people who fill up a room, a person who shimmered with charisma. It was there when he shook your hand, there in conversation, when he talked and even more when he listened, giving you his steady, absorbed attention, his eyes alive with intelligence. She still remembered the conversation they'd had about neuroscience and teaching kids to read. "You have learned, through experience and fine-tuned observation," he had told her, so animated he seemed to crackle, "what science is only just beginning to give us!" Pen had felt understood, cherished, and at the same time, gleeful, like a baby tossed into the air, and all the while, there had been Cat, rapt, flamelike and flickering in her father's presence, her face full of dazzle.

But he was the kind of father who was good in the flesh, but bad at a distance, who almost never returned Cat's phone calls, who sent extravagant birthday gifts two weeks late, who forgot the classes Cat was taking, the names of her friends ("Persephone!" Cat told Pen once, hooting with laughter. "He thinks you're the Queen of the Underworld!"), and, at least twice, the day and time of her arrival home for Christmas break (she called him from baggage claim, he sent a town car). "It's not his fault. He never learned *how*!" Cat had once explained. "Blame my mother, who kept track of everything, everything, everything for him!" Later, alone with Pen, Will had said, "Cat's mom died when she was two. The guy's had seventeen years to learn how," but neither of them said it to Cat.

"She said she thought they'd have a lot more time to get to know each other, but then he died. Plus, she said she was an orphan, which is big, having no family. There's her mom's sister out in Oregon or someplace, but Cat hardly knows her. So she was sad," Jason went on. "For like forty-eight hours, she even let me take care of her, which you guys know isn't easy for a person like Cat."

Pen's and Will's eyes met, and Pen knew that he was thinking what she was thinking and that he was thinking it in the same way, without a trace of resentment, *What was ever easier for Cat than letting someone take care of her?*

"But then we flew to Houston for the funeral, and she was her old self and then some. Totally took charge of the arrangements, organized this big after-party at her dad's house, ordered the food, flowers, talked to all the people, shaking hands like frigging Jackie O. No crying. She was amazing." Even in the midst of her shock at hearing about this unfamiliar, take-charge Cat, Pen had to smile at "after-party."

"That does sound amazing," said Will.

"It does, right? And then I flew home and she stayed for another week or so, getting his estate in order and whatnot. Meeting with his lawyer, sorting through his stuff, getting the house ready to sell—"

Jason broke off, stared into his nearly full cup of beer, bolted it the way you'd bolt an espresso shot, and then stared into the empty cup. Pen waited for him to crumple the cup in his fist, but he didn't.

"I couldn't stay," he said, looking at them defiantly. "Cat was a student, so she could leave for a week, get incompletes or whatever, but I had a *job*."

"Makes sense," said Will.

"I'm an accountant," said Jason. "This was April, for God's sake."

"What was Cat studying?" asked Pen. She was surprised to hear that Cat had gone back to school because, as smart as she was, Cat had loved everything about college *except* school.

"Physical therapy. She thought about nursing, but it would've taken forever. As it was, she had to take a bunch of undergrad science courses before she could even think about PT."

If Jason had said that Cat had gone back to school to be an elephant trainer or a pole dancer, Pen could not have been more flabbergasted. (In point of fact, pole dancing was a stretch only because it did not, as far as Pen knew, involve costumes covered with spangles and feathers; she wasn't even sure if it involved costumes at all.) In Philadelphia, Cat had worked as a salesperson in an upscale men's clothing store, a job she had adored. "It's like a game!" she'd said. "A dance! A play!" And Cat wrinkling her nose at the fit of a pair of pants, recommending charcoal over navy as though the fate of humanity depended on it, saying, "You would be completely out of your mind not to buy that tie," *that* was Cat. But Cat healing the injured? Cat laying her tiny, perfect hands on imperfect bodies? Cat taking *science* courses? Pen's mind boggled. As a physical therapist, she would wear what? Sweats? *Scrubs?*

"Anyway, she came back different," said Jason in a very tired voice.

"Different in what way?" asked Pen.

"Every way. She basically stopped eating. Not even candy. Not even *pastries.*"

Pen smiled, remembering Cat, sighing with bliss over éclairs, napoleons, palmiers, chocolate croissants, and, especially, scones, the ones from her favorite Rittenhouse Square bakery, hockey-puck-heavy, studded with currants, and blanketed in Devonshire cream.

"And she didn't sleep," said Jason. Cat, who could sleep anywhere, on a kitchen chair, on a subway, at a Phillies game, as instantly and peacefully as a cat in a shaft of sun.

"She got really careless about her medication."

"For the Cat we knew," said Will, "that wouldn't have been much of a change."

"Yeah," said Jason. "It's not like she was ever great about it, but she got worse. In fact, she got really bad. I even yelled at her about it once, that's how bad it got, and she just gave me this thousand-mile stare. It was spooky."

Pen felt a pulse of something uncomfortably like affection for Jason, so obviously still riddled with guilt for having yelled.

"But if she wasn't crying, she was like that, a million miles away, even when she was right there. Distracted. And then she'd leave for hours, say she'd been driving or at a friend's. Then a few days before she left, she got better. Still really distant, but she got calm, started taking care of herself. And then whammo: she left me a note saying she had to get away for a while, to please not try to find her."

"But you did." Pen sounded judgmental, although she didn't mean to. She wasn't even sure if she felt judgmental. She knew from experience that just because someone wanted to be alone with grief didn't mean they should be. But maybe Cat didn't want to be alone; maybe— and this was abundantly easy for Pen to believe—she just didn't want to be with Jason.

Jason's face hardened. "Have you seen her? That's all I want to know."

Pen shook her head.

"No, man. Sorry," said Will.

"And she didn't tell you where she was going."

Pen and Will shook their heads.

"I guess I have no choice but to believe you."

"Guess so," said Pen.

"Then it looks like my work here is done," said Jason.

"Will you let us know," said Will, "when you find her?" Pen could tell by Will's face what it cost him to ask this favor of Jason.

"Oh, I'll find her," said Jason, lapsing into a cocky nonchalance that, again, filled Pen with the urge to slug him. "No worries there. I got it covered."

He started to drum on the back of chair and look around the party. He actually yawned.

Why doesn't he leave? thought Pen. *What's he waiting for?*

In the midst of her exasperation, a thought began to take shape.

"Hold on," she said. "Give me a second."

Will and Jason looked at her. She closed her eyes.

"You know what?" she said to Will, opening her eyes.

"What?" he asked.

"It doesn't make sense." She reached across the table and took hold of Will's wrist. "It doesn't."

"Okay," said Will, waiting.

"Think about it," Pen said, getting excited. "If he really suspected we were with Cat or had seen her or knew where she was, how could he have thought his trick would work? 'I know it's been forever, but I need you.' See?"

Will looked puzzled; then his face cleared.

"We wouldn't have believed the e-mails were from her," he said, "because we would've been in touch with her."

"That's right! We wouldn't have come down to see her if we were *with* her or knew where she was!" Pen dropped back in her chair, breathless.

"Everything happened so fast I didn't even think of that," said Will.

Pen's heart started to race. What if Jason was insane? What if he had hurt Cat and was just pretending she'd left him? Then she remembered that the only reason she thought Cat was missing was that Jason had said so. Maybe she wasn't. Maybe she was. Maybe Jason was a psychopath. Psychopaths existed. Maybe Jason was one of them. Pen felt sick to her stomach. But when she turned to face Jason, he didn't look like a psychopath. She reminded herself that this didn't mean he wasn't one. But, red-faced and squirming in his seat, Jason looked embarrassed, near tears even, like a third-grader who has been caught in a lie.

"What the hell?" said Will in a flat voice.

Jason opened and closed his mouth a couple of times without saying anything.

"Did you do something to her?" blurted out Pen.

Jason's eyes went wide. "No! Of course not. God!"

"What, then?" said Will.

"I figured that—" Jason ran a hand down the center of his sweating face. "I figured that if she was with you, she'd make you come, okay? To see who was pretending to be her. Except more than likely, she'd know it was me. Even though I didn't use my own e-mail address, she'd figure sending that e-mail to try and find her would be something I'd do, and she'd send you to the reunion. Or maybe she'd even come with you."

"Why would she do that?" asked Pen, whose head was beginning to hurt with trying to follow Jason's train of thought.

"To laugh at me. Why else? You three could have a big old chuckle together at my expense. But at least I'd get to see her, maybe talk her into coming home."

Pen and Will sat staring at Jason for a long, stunned moment. Then Will said, "You sent e-mails to us pretending to be Cat so that Cat would know it was you pretending to be her and would come down here, even though she'd left and asked you not to look for her? Jason, that's"—Will scratched his head—"pretty complicated."

With wonder, Pen noted that there wasn't a single mocking note in

Will's voice; more than anything, he sounded kind. *Wow,* thought Pen. *Kindness? Now?*

But Jason didn't seem to hear it that way because he jumped up and hissed, "You know what? Go to hell."

At this, Pen flared. "That must be some marriage you've got, Jason."

"Fuck you, you condescending fucks," said Jason, spit flying out of his mouth with each "f." He threw his plastic cup on the table and left.

For at least half a minute, Pen and Will just stared at each other, or in each other's general direction, since they were both lost in their separate, if overlapping, thoughts, with the party whirling to a blur around them. A woman came up and asked if she could take Jason's chair, and Pen didn't even look at her, just nodded.

"I think he likes us," said Will finally.

Pen sighed. "I'm sorry."

"Why are you sorry?"

"That last thing I said about his marriage. It was a low blow."

"It wasn't anything he didn't know," said Will.

"I know, but he's a sad and desperate case, setting this whole thing up the way he did. He's lost."

"We believe him, then?"

"I don't know," said Pen. "I'm confused. I'm dumbfounded."

"Maybe we should get out of here," said Will, "take a walk. Unless you wanted to stay, hang out, have a beer, maybe go for a whirl on the dance floor." He smiled.

"That sounds fun," said Pen, standing up, and together they walked out of the tent.

"Do you mind if we don't talk for a little while? My brain is so full it hurts," said Pen.

"Brain indigestion," said Will.

Even outside of the tent, the air was so humid that Pen felt as though she were wearing the night like a coat of paint. They ended up at the university chapel, a small, stone Gothic Revival structure that Pen had always loved, perched moodily as it was, all its eyebrows arched, amid the gleaming neoclassicism. As if by agreement, she and Will stopped walking when they got there, Pen dropping onto a wooden bench, Will standing around awhile like a person waiting for a bus, then sitting on the brick walkway in front of her, elbows hooked over his knees, arms dangling.

"We're mosquito bait," he said. "You know that, right?"

"Little vampires." Pen sighed heavily. "I'm too discombobulated to care."

"You want to talk about what we're thinking?"

"Maybe," said Pen. *No.*

"What are you thinking?"

"You first."

Will leaned back on his elbows and looked at the sky. Pen waited for Will to start the conversation about Cat and Jason but wished he wouldn't. She wanted to keep it at a distance for a few more minutes.

Will said, "I'm thinking it's way too muggy for June. That moon looks like it's suffocating."

Pen looked at the hazy moon. "It looks like an Alka-Seltzer dissolving."

"You're right. So what else are you thinking?"

She closed her eyes and rested her head against the back of the bench. "I'm thinking how I've always liked this chapel."

"And your little friend who lives in it," said Will. Pen could hear him smiling.

"Edith," said Pen.

For the most part, the chapel's stained-glass windows were lovely but generic, sporting geometric patterns or expressionless religious figures with blue robes, iconic noses, and bony, rectangular feet. But the first week Pen had arrived at college, before she met Will and Cat, when she was homesick and drowning in lonesomeness, she had wandered into the chapel and found herself drawn to one high, almond-shaped window (she'd find out later that it was called a *mandorla*, a beautiful word) that seemed different to her: a girl's face, intimate-eyed and human and looking straight at Pen. Pen figured that she was supposed to be an angel, but to Pen, she looked like a regular person, a girl like herself, shy, brown-haired, smart, out of breath, slightly lost. Something about the girl, about being alone with her in the dim, high-ceilinged hush of the chapel made Pen feel less lost, befriended even.

Though she knew that having an imaginary friend at the age of eighteen meant she'd hit a point so humiliatingly low that she must never, ever tell anyone about it, one night, she told Cat and Will. They made fun of her, of course, but they liked it, and, straightaway, the two of them, especially Cat, wove the girl into the fabric of their friendship. "Edith says hi," Cat would say, or "I couldn't finish my sandwich, so I gave half to Edith." On the bench under the fizzy moon, Pen held Cat's voice in her head, cradled it in the palm of her memory.

"I miss her," Pen said sadly, a sob in her throat. "I was so sure I would see her."

"It'll be okay," said Will quickly, and Pen remembered how worried he'd always gotten when anybody cried.

"I know it will," said Pen, rubbing her eyes and sitting up. "You know I was always a crier."

"You always were," he agreed. "I was sure we'd see her, too."

"You want to know the truth?" Pen said. "The truth is that, all these years, I have missed both of you more than I can describe. I have pined for you. I wanted you back the whole time."

Pen felt lighter after she'd said it. She had not planned to say it. In fact, she had planned *not* to because what in the world would be the point? To make herself as vulnerable as a newborn chick? To make Will uncomfortable? To put him on the spot? And still: this lightness. Something about the night, about having listened to all that Jason had said and to be sitting in this precise spot under this precise sky thinking about Cat with Will made saying what she harbored in her heart feel natural. She didn't expect him to say it back or to even acknowledge it. She just wanted him to know.

"You know what," said Will after a long moment. "I was in town for my friend Gray's wedding a couple of years ago, not at the chapel, at an inn down the road, and I stopped in to see Edith."

"You didn't."

"Yep. I did, and there happened to be a tour going on, so I asked the tour guide about her."

"You asked about Edith?"

"Turns out she's special."

"Of course, she is!"

"Hers is the only Tiffany window in there. The others were made by someone else. And it also turns out that she's a real person."

"Of course, she's a real person."

"I mean, she was. The window's a portrait of a real girl. Who lived." Pen considered this information. "Was her name Edith?"

"No."

"Then don't tell me about her. I don't want to know."

"Well, yeah, I was pretty sure you wouldn't."

Pen thought about Will stopping in to see Edith, asking about her, two years ago, four years after Pen and Will had last seen each other. She thought about how there was more than one way to say, "I missed you, too."

"Thank you," she told Will, "for checking on her."

"No problem."

"Do you believe Jason's story?" Pen asked. Time to dive in.

"I think I did, until you pointed out that his reasons for getting us to come down here made no sense. That made me doubt everything he'd told us."

"And the thing he said afterward. When you described it back to Jason—how he pretended to be Cat so that Cat would know it was him pretending to be her, et cetera—it sounded so convoluted. Convoluted to the point of crazy."

"Can you think of another reason, though? His real motive for setting us up?" asked Will.

"No. I tried. It made my head hurt."

"I had one idea," said Will slowly. "It's pretty far-fetched, though, and grim."

"You think he hurt her?"

"It's probably just too much *Law and Order,* but I had the thought that if he did something to her, looking for her afterward would be a way to make it look like he hadn't done it."

Pen shivered and wrapped her arms around herself. "Do you think he would hurt her?"

"Do you?"

Pen thought about this and said, "No. I don't, and not just because I can't stand to think it. Remember that letter he wrote after he left her in the Crater? As much as I loathe being around him, I think he's decent at the core. What do you think?"

"I think he loves her," said Will. The word *love* coming out of Will's mouth caused a brief fireworks display to go off in Pen's chest. She ignored it. "When he was talking about her, that's the impression I got. It's what I always thought about him: he's a huge pain in the ass, but he loves Cat."

"Still," said Pen, "maybe we should check out his story. Maybe Cat's safe at home, and he made all this up for a mean joke. Because he hates us."

"After all this time?" said Will.

"Maybe," said Pen. "Maybe the thought of us wanting Cat not to marry him rankled and rankled his soul for six years. Probably not, though."

"I hope she's safe at home," said Will. Then, in a hesitant voice, he asked, "Do you know where home is? Do you know where Cat lives?"

Pen's rib cage tightened at the question and her cheeks got hot. She looked down at her hands. "We weren't supposed to look for each other. We weren't even supposed to google. Those were Cat's rules."

"I remember."

"I guess you could say"—Pen paused and took a breath—"I broke them."

"Oh."

"For the first year, I googled you both. Often. Obsessively often, I would go so far as to say. I didn't know you'd moved to Asheville, but I know you ran a 10K there in March of 2004. For example."

"How'd I do?"

Pen smiled. "Not bad, but not great. 42.47."

"I was out of shape," protested Will. "My friend Jack—I moved down there to work with him after I bailed out of Wharton—he *made* me do that race. I'm way faster now."

"Sure, Will. Sure you are," said Pen.

"What about Cat? You find out anything about her?"

"Not really. We knew she and Jason were moving to Tampa when they left Philly. I saw their wedding announcement, I guess, but after that, nothing, and, as I said, after a year, maybe a little more, I stopped. I started following the rules."

"Any particular reason?"

"Augusta was born. I got busy, and also"—Pen gave a nervous laugh—"I was on the verge of becoming a stalker. I wanted my daughter to have a mother with a little more dignity than that."

Pen could remember the day, typing `Catalina Rogers` (Cat had sacrificed her musical name for Jason's, a semi-tragic misstep, in Pen's view) into the narrow box, then looking down at Augusta asleep in her Moses basket next to Pen's desk. Augusta had stirred, her arms flying outward, her hands startling open into two stars, and for some reason, that had been the sign Pen had been waiting for without knowing she'd been waiting. "Enough!" She had said it out loud and had not only deleted the name, but had turned the computer off altogether, then had rested her forehead on the desk in front of her.

"But then you went and became a famous writer," said Pen, grinning, "and all bets were off."

"You started stalking me?" Will asked hopefully.

"No, but I buy all your books, and I looked at your website a few times."

"Yeah?"

"It's nice, all those interactive games and great graphics, but there's no picture of you. That was kind of disappointing."

"Don't want to scare off the kids."

"Ha ha," said Pen. "So, anyway, I don't know if they're still in

Tampa or not." Then, tentatively, she asked, "What about you? You ever break the rules?"

When he answered, Will's voice was odd, tight and fast, as though he wanted to put the question behind him, get rid of it. "No. It seemed easier that way."

"Oh."

She waited for him to say more, but he didn't, and Pen felt rebuffed, even though she couldn't think why he would resent her question, when he had just asked her the same thing. In the brittle lull that followed, Pen watched a couple walk past about thirty yards away, coming from the direction of the reunion, the man talking fast and eagerly, telling some kind of story, his hands in motion, the woman walking with her head tilted back, languidly fanning herself with a newspaper. *Give it up,* Pen thought about telling the man. *No way she's interested.* And because she was distracting herself from the little wall—not wall, she thought hopefully, hedge, low hedge—that had sprung up between herself and Will by imagining the inner lives of these strangers, she didn't realize that the man walking a short distance behind them, his shoulders slightly bunched, his hands in the pockets of shorts, was Jason, until he was cutting across the grass toward them, a stone's throw away.

"Jason," she whispered to Will. "Behind you."

When he got to them, he didn't sit down, but just stood, a few feet away, and there was something about him, not his face, which Pen couldn't really see, but his posture—duck-footed, slump-shouldered, backward leaning, his hands in his pockets, his elbows jutting—that was so old-mannish and forsaken that Pen wanted, almost, to hug him, to put her arm around him and lead him back to the bench.

"I'm glad you're back," said Pen kindly. "We were just talking about you."

"Yeah, I bet," said Jason. "My ears were burning."

Because his attempt at belligerence was so halfhearted and because she remembered that his ears really were burned, hot pink and peeling, Pen's heart softened a little bit more, and she said, "You want to sit down?"

"That's okay," said Jason. "I just want to say something."

"Go ahead," said Pen.

"The thing I told you back there, about why I e-mailed you. It wasn't the real reason."

"We wondered about that," said Pen.

"You know, I thought there was an off-chance all that would happen, that she'd know it was me and come down here with you. An off-off-chance. But really what I wanted—" He pulled a hand out of his pocket and slapped at his arm. "Damn mosquitoes are out for blood tonight," and then he looked at Will and Pen and smiled. "Literally. Since they're mosquitoes, right?"

"The little suckers," said Will.

Jason chuckled. "So anyway. It was the reunion that made me think of it, of getting in touch with you guys. After Cat left, I happened to find the stuff about the reunion that came in the mail, and thought, *Okay, so maybe this is the way to go.*"

"The way to go?" asked Pen.

"Backward, I guess," said Jason. "Into the past. Because the present wasn't really panning out."

"What do you mean?" asked Will.

"I'm really worried about her," said Jason. "Running off that way, all distraught."

"That is worrisome," said Pen. "I agree."

Jason squatted down next to the bench. "So the deal is I was hoping you could help find her."

Pen and Will looked at each other.

"I guess I'm wondering," began Will carefully, "why ask us? We haven't seen her in a long time."

"Trust me," said Jason sardonically. "If I hadn't exhausted all my other possibilities, I wouldn't have. I talked to a cop buddy of mine, but there's no sign of foul play, and he said that a wife's allowed to leave her husband, *not* that that's what this is. Anyway, they might've checked into it, but she got in touch with this friend of hers, who told me she's okay."

"She did?" Pen said, startled. "Well, then why don't you just ask her friend where she is?"

Jason snorted. "It'll shock you to hear that Cat's friends aren't all that fond of me. Samantha won't tell me a thing, apart from that Cat's supposedly safe."

"Jason," said Pen, "maybe she just needs a little time. Maybe you should just wait for her to come home."

Jason squeezed his eyes shut and shook his head. "The best I can explain it to you," he said, "is that I have a sense of foreboding."

"You do?" asked Pen, impressed at his use of the word *foreboding*.

"Look," said Jason, standing up again, "you guys knew her better than anyone. I think she's in trouble. I want your help." He took a deep breath and held out his hands in a gesture that could only be called beseeching. "I'm *asking* for your help. Please."

Ten, maybe twelve seconds went by, a few heartbeats—Pen and Will looking from Jason to each other, getting their bearings—before Jason was taking off across the grass so fast he was almost running.

"You know what?" he yelled over his shoulder. "Forget it. My bad."

"Jason!" called Pen, jumping to her feet. "We'll help!"

Jason slowed to a walk, then stopped, his back still to them, his arms hanging at his sides.

Pen turned to Will, saying, "We'll help, right?" but he was already moving past her. She watched Will run his long, loping run to where Jason stood, watched him put a hand on Jason's shoulder, talking to him, turning him around, bringing him back.

Chapter Eleven

"KIKI CALLED," SAID AMELIE, "WANTING TO KNOW WHETHER the three of you, um, connected."

She lifted one sculpted eyebrow and smiled.

"Ha," said Pen. "Kiki's never used a euphemism in her life. What'd she really say?"

Amelie sorted through the phone messages, which were written on random scraps of paper, napkins mostly, a few receipts, the front page of the *Philadelphia Inquirer*. It was one of Amelie's quirks: to be meticulously organized in some ways and almost pathologically messy in others. Once, Pen had found a used paper coffee cup on her desk with "Call your (yummy!) brother" scrawled across it in lipstick, along with the precise time and date he had called.

"Here it is." Amelie plucked a take-out menu from the pile. "'Need details on the group sex, pronto, Henny Penny. Hope you didn't turn chickenshit on me.'"

"Charming," said Pen. "Subtle."

Amelie tapped her pencil lightly against her pursed lips and looked at Pen.

"What?" said Pen. "No!"

Amelie put the pencil down and sighed. "No?"

"No. I told you the whole story. Cat wasn't even there."

"So you're saying that if she had been there—?"

"No!"

"Fine," said Amelie lightly. "Fine, fine, fine. The subject of you, Cat, and Will is officially closed."

Sure it is, thought Pen. She waited, watching Amelie pretend to sort through the phone messages, then to examine her fingernails, which were perfect. She looked up at Pen, opened her mouth, closed it, then searched for a pencil and tucked it behind her ear.

"Oh, for crying out loud," growled Pen. "Just say it."

Amelie leaned back in her chair and folded her hands on the desktop. "I think you should tell me what happened between you and Will, way back when, why you stopped being friends. I think it's time."

"You do, do you?"

"Not for me," said Amelie, her eyes widening with empathy. "For you."

"Gosh," said Pen, "you're so thoughtful."

The weird thing is that Pen found that she wanted to tell. She had never, in six years, told anyone, not Jamie or her parents, not the therapist she had seen a handful of times in a tired, haphazard, halfhearted (not even half: quarter-hearted, sixteenth-hearted?) manner at her mother's insistence after her father's death, not Amelie all the other times she had asked. But suddenly, she felt like telling.

She didn't know why. Maybe it was because, after the reunion, the story of the end of Pen's friendship with Will was no longer the story of the end of Pen's friendship with Will. Maybe it was because she needed to set the story free from her own head, where it had circled for so long like a fish in a bowl, getting bigger and bigger and more and more neurotic, and send it swimming out into the narrative of her life with everything else. Maybe she needed closure or release or absolution so that she could move forward. Mostly, what she felt was, "Oh, go ahead and tell, for cluck's sake."

Pen knew that, in the grand scheme of things, it wasn't such a terrible story, not especially shocking or sordid. Even so, it was the story of the worst thing Pen had ever done. If she could go backward in her life and change one thing (excluding—oh, God—everything she had done, everything everyone had done on the day her dad died), it would be pushing Will away, even though, she reminded herself, the real problem hadn't involved pushing away, but pulling toward (her hand against the back of the man's neck, her fingers in his hair), when she should have done anything but.

A COLD MARCH, CAT TWO WEEKS GONE, TWO WEEKS OF PEN feeling as empty as Cat's closet, as relinquished and obsolete as Cat's twin bed, which drifted, with its flower-splotched Marimekko comforter, like a parade float in the middle of her empty room. Pen avoided her (their) apartment, went to classes in sweatpants, sat through gloomy meals of take-out food and self-blame with Will. With sadness, she noted that the two of them, unused to being the two of them, were awkward around each other for the first time ever. "Patience. You will adapt," Pen's mother assured her, and Pen believed her. He was still Will, after all; she was still Pen. But it hurt her, how moments of quiet between them felt, for the first time, like silences.

Things got better in the car. Even though Cat's absence rode along with them the way her presence always had, unbelted, leaning forward between them from the backseat, even though the bottle of wine in the paper bag in the trunk was Cat's favorite Pouilly-Fuisse (she'd left it in their refrigerator, further proof, Pen told Will glumly, of her eagerness to get the hell away from them as fast as her little legs could carry her), Pen and Will regained something like their old ease.

Maybe it was the act of putting the city in which they'd been a trio (the word they had long ago agreed upon, less loaded, God knew, than *triangle* or *threesome* [although *threesome* got Cat's exuberant vote], less commanding, but more accurate than *triumvirate*, Pen's personal favorite) behind them. Maybe it was the near impossibility of face-to-face conversation, of reading each other's eyes. In any case, Will's old red Saab, which, even in their college days, had hovered somewhere between being a classic and a piece of crap, was on its best behavior, and as they flew along the road, the still-bare trees and billboards and pearl gray sky streaming by on either side, Pen was glad that Will had suggested going to his family's summerhouse on Boston's North Shore for a few days. "It'll be colder than here and grayer than here," he'd said. "It might suck. But at least it won't be here."

They talked. Their conversation veered and backpedaled and bounced and stalled out and, from time to time, rocked to a rest, featherlike, before taking off, herky-jerky, in some unforeseen direction, which is to say that it was, for them, an ordinary conversation, apart from the fact that it was between two people, instead of three. Pen realized that others had often found the way she, Will, and Cat talked to each other annoying. "It's like goddamn conversation bumper cars," one of Cat's boyfriends had said. "I get motion sick just listening." But for Pen, talking this way with Will, the faint, familiar, pleasant-bad cracked-leather-dusty-attic-with-a-hint-of-street-vendor-peanuts smell of the car around them, the chilly air wailing through the permanently one-inch opened right rear window, was relaxing. More than relaxing. A homecoming. For the hours of the car ride, Pen was a creature in her natural habitat.

And though they didn't exactly skirt the subject of Cat, they didn't do what they'd been doing nearly every day back in Philadelphia: wallow in it, throwing around anger and sadness and what-ifs until the very furniture seemed saturated with regret. They talked about Cat, yes, but also about Roald Dahl, their favorite smells (Pen: the cold cream her mother used and bread baking; Will: coffee and the ocean), dyslexia, whether watching television makes kids overweight, Lance Armstrong, the Salem Witch trials, and why some people love horror films while others don't.

When a solemn, smoke-colored dusk began to fall, Will brought up the subject of his parents' marriage, a drawn-out, ugly thing that had recently begun coming to what would surely be a drawn-out, ugly end.

In mid-January, while Will's father, Randall, was on a three-day business trip to San Francisco, in a burst of initiative and activity that shocked everyone who knew her, Will's mother, Charlotte, had changed the locks on the family home, hired a lawyer, and enrolled in a painting course at the local arts college. She was two weeks sober, which didn't sound like much, Will said, until you considered that it was two weeks longer than she had ever stayed sober before.

"Two weeks!" Pen had blurted out, then, "Do they recommend that, making so many life changes so fast? She didn't waste any time cleaning house, did she?"

"Not unless you count the thirty years she spent married to the guy," snapped Will.

Since then Pen had trodden lightly. Will had visited his mother in Connecticut twice, and both times had come back bearing a hopefulness in his face that was so simultaneously glowing and cautious that it broke Pen's heart a little to see it. But right after he got back from the second visit, Cat had left, and, as they rode in the car together now, as Will said, "So Tully says the lawyers have made it so my dad can't get anywhere near my mom's money. Which is going to kill him," Pen realized, with shame, how long it had been since she had asked about his mother, the extent to which she'd let Cat's leaving usurp every other thing.

"You sound pretty busted up about that," said Pen.

"We all are," said Will. "Philip actually opened a bottle of champagne. I just wish I'd been there to see my dad's face when he got the news."

"No, you don't. Remember: *he* was there when he got the news."

"You're right. I wish someone had taken a picture of his face and sent it to me."

Even as Pen saw Will's smile flash in the growing darkness, she noticed his right thumb thrumming against the steering wheel, always a sign that something was wrong.

"How's your mom?" she asked.

"It's getting cold in here," said Will. "You want to stop and get your jacket out of the trunk?"

"I'm wearing it," Pen said, holding out her arm to show him. "You got it out for me at the last rest stop, remember? You said, 'Pen, time for this.'"

"Your teeth were chattering, and your lips were turning blue. Science tells us that these are signs it's time for a coat."

Pen was beginning to get nervous. From long experience, she knew that the intensity of Will's worry would be directly proportional to the length of time he spent on aimless chatter, rather than on answering her question. *Go ahead, Will*, she thought, *give me an answer*.

"Damn window," said Will, giving the window a baleful glance over his shoulder. "I should get it fixed."

"It's been broken for seven years."

"I've been taking the laissez-faire approach," said Will. "I'm the Ayn Rand of broken windows."

"You hate Ayn Rand." *Please don't let it be that she's drinking again*, thought Pen.

"Okay, then I'm the Alexander Hamilton of broken windows. Nobody hates Alexander Hamilton."

"Except that one guy."

"Except for him, but he was just one guy."

"He was," said Pen, truly scared now. "He definitely was."

Then Will said, "Tully's worried."

Pen shivered inside her coat. "Oh. Does Tully think she's—" Pen found that she couldn't say the word.

"She doesn't know. She hasn't found direct evidence. Those were Tully's exact words, 'direct evidence.'"

Will's sister was in law school, a superfluous, if necessary, step, Will and his brother, Philip, liked to joke, since Tully had been born a lawyer. "When has Tully *not* been in law school," Will had said when he got the news she'd been admitted. "It's like Mephistopheles and hell. Wherever Tully is is law school."

"But if she's drinking," Will went on, "she's different from how she used to be. Tully's word was 'agitated.' Never sitting still, talking in long bursts, not sleeping, starting things and not finishing."

"Like paintings?

"Paintings, meals, gardening. She dug holes in the side yard to plant bushes or something, which had to be hard because it's still so cold, and then she left them there, empty, for days. The mailman stepped in one."

"Oh, no."

"Nothing broken and my mom's lawyer says she's in the clear because he shouldn't have been walking across the yard in the first place. Not that the mailman threatened to sue. Actually, he was apparently really nice about it."

"But she checked with a lawyer anyway? That maybe sounds a little paranoid."

"Tully checked with the lawyer," said Will. "Tully was born a little paranoid."

"So maybe Tully's seeing a problem with your mom when there's really not one?"

She heard Will draw in a long breath, then let it out. "It's not just Tully. I talked to my mom a couple of days ago. She said something odd."

"What?"

"She said she doesn't know how to live."

Pen thought about this and said, "Without your dad? Because that would make some sense. Yes, he was jerk, but they were married for a long time."

"That's what I asked her. I said, 'You mean without Dad?' "

"And what did she say?"

"She said, 'I mean period.' Her voice when she said it—" Will broke off, shaking his head.

Without thinking, Pen unhooked her seat belt and reached out to hold on to Will, her forehead on his shoulder, her arm across his chest. It's what she would have done for anyone she loved, for Jamie or Cat or her mother, and for a few seconds, everything was normal. She smelled the cold wool of his coat, felt its roughness against her face and her hand, and then something happened: Will took one hand off the steering wheel and rested it against the back of her head.

Pen knew that it was nothing Will would not have done for Tully or Cat or anyone, something he probably *had* done for Pen herself, without her blinking an eye. She knew that it was an acknowledgment, a thank-you, Will being nice, but the fact of her knowing these things did not stop the touch from feeling different from any way Will had touched her before. It startled her. She tensed. Within seconds, she was detaching herself from Will, pressing her back against her seat, her hand lifting involuntarily to the spot on the back of her head where his hand had been, even as she scolded herself for being so foolish, ridiculous for imagining weirdness into Will's hand on her hair, especially at a time like this. *He's thinking about his mother,* she thought. *He's worried. He's not hitting on you, you ridiculous person.*

"Thanks," said Will, and for a moment Pen thought he meant for understanding that he hadn't been hitting on her. Then she realized he meant for the hug.

"*De nada,*" she said.

With her peripheral vision, she saw him looking at her. "Hey," he said.

"What?" said Pen too quickly, pulling her hand off the back of her head and slapping it into her lap.

"Buckle up."

Because Pen worried that the quiet that followed might be awkward, even though Will seemed fine, because she was concerned that, distracted by the hug/hand/hair event (non-event), she had dropped the subject of Will's mother prematurely, Pen decided to say something, and because she wanted to say something appropriate and natural, she fell headfirst into cliché.

"She'll be fine eventually." She hated the stilted sound of her own voice. "It will take time. Change is hard."

"Don't worry about it," Will said, his sarcasm making everything the way it should be. "I didn't know what to say, either."

THEY HAD NEVER ARRIVED AT THE HOUSE IN THE DARK BEFORE; they had never come in March. Usually, it was early evening and spring or summer, the sky like a slice of nectarine to the west, low light striping the porch boards, the air smelling like black dirt and flowers. Pen had always loved the moment of arrival, the way the place opened its arms to her. She expected it to be different at night, with nothing in bloom, nothing singing in the trees, and, on the surface, it was different, drained of color and still. But the outline of the roof against the sky, the sigh of the wooden screen door were so familiar, Pen could have cried, and the house's essence, as it settled over her, was the same as ever: clean and old and incandescently peaceful.

Pen dropped her bag in the hallway and leaned against the wall.

"I love this place," she said.

Will was fiddling with the thermostat, and Pen heard the radiators start to hum.

"I called and asked Lacey and Roy to turn the heat on for us," he said, "but I think their idea of warm enough might be different from yours." Lacey and Roy were the caretaker couple who lived in town.

He turned around and looked at Pen. "You always say that as soon as we get here," he said, "that you love it."

"Because I always love it." Pen turned around and planted a kiss on the wall, loving its chalky, bleached-seashell whiteness, the bumps in its thick plaster.

"Cat was less sold," said Will, smiling.

"She loved it *some*. Definitely, she loved being here with us. You know Cat can't love any place entirely that doesn't have central air," said Pen. "Comes from growing up in Houston."

Will walked through the house, turning on lights as he went, the heavy switches thunking. Pen stayed in the hallway with her eyes closed, breathing the place in. The house seemed to breathe, too. *Leave it to this house,* Pen thought, *to not feel shut down or forsaken in the winter, to just be sleeping.*

"Are you hungry?" called Will.

"No," Pen called back. "I'm too tired to be hungry."

"Are you hungry if there's a pie?"

"Are you kidding?"

At the enormous, scarred dining room table, they ate shamefully large slabs of Lacey's apple crumb and drank the milk she had left in the refrigerator. Basking in gladness, Pen took in the room around her as she ate, the tall windows, the defunct brick fireplace, the great bronze, low-hanging octopus of a chandelier. The house wasn't a showplace by most standards, but it was perfect nonetheless. The kind of house in which you'd look up to see sprigs of dried lavender in a glass milk bottle exactly, smack-dab, where sprigs of dried lavender in a glass milk bottle should be. The kind of house whose cramped, hot kitchen was rendered moot by the faded hydrangea-print wallpaper in the guest room and the sleeping porch's view of the backyard.

"This and my parents' house are the only places I drink milk," said Pen.

"Same here," said Will.

THE NEXT DAY WAS SERENE, SUNLIT, AND CONSUMMATELY BEAUTIFUL. Pen woke up to white curtains full of light, and she and Will spent the daytime hours in an easy weaving between being together and being apart. They went for a morning run, parting ways after mile four, then drove to the market in town and bought green beans, new potatoes, and lamb for Pen to butterfly and rub with olive oil, garlic, and rosemary from the backyard and for Will to throw on the grill for dinner.

In the afternoon, Pen sat on the porch in a trapezoid of sun and read an ancient copy of *The Golden Bowl*, turning the frail, sepia-colored pages with care and, stopping, now and then, to unknot a sentence, reveling in the opulent commas and old-book smell. Afterward, while Will worked at his computer, she walked on the rocky beach with a bucket to search for sea glass, an addictive, squatting, neck-kinking enterprise that consisted of Pen vowing to stop, then finding, at the last second, something rare—an aquamarine kidney bean frosted over with nicks, a needle of saffron-yellow—and keeping on until her eyes swam with black spots and shooting stars.

It was only after dinner, when Will and Pen sat down to watch *The Graduate*, one of the DVDs from the crazily random selection (*Mad Max, To Kill a Mockingbird, The Unbearable Lightness of Being . . .*) that had accumulated at the summerhouse over the years, that a little awkwardness set in, at least for Pen. While Will crouched in front of the television cabinet, coaxing into action what could have been the DVD player prototype, Pen got herself a glass of water. When she came back into the living room, Will was sitting on the sofa, and Pen stood, water in hand, socked feet rooted to the rug, immobilized by uncertainty about how to sit in front of a television with Will without Cat.

Don't be stupid, she berated herself, *you've done it before.* Even though she knew that this was true, had to be true many times over, standing there, she couldn't remember a single instance. What she remembered was Cat, with her instinct for cuddliness, plopping her head into Will's lap and throwing her legs across Pen, Cat curling against one shoulder or another, Pen and Will sitting on the sofa with Cat on the floor, her arms hooked over their knees. When it came to sitting in front of a television or a fireplace or on a picnic blanket at an outdoor concert, they hadn't been a triangle; they'd been an "H." Now, every place Pen considered sitting seemed either too close to or too far away from Will. Too close to Will? Before this moment, such a thing had not existed. Pen didn't understand why it should now. From the edge of the living room, she watched Benjamin Braddock ride the moving walkway, the white tile wall gliding by behind him, Ben's shell-shocked profile going nowhere.

"What's up?" asked Will. "You're having second thoughts about the movie?"

"No," sputtered Pen. "What do you mean? Why would you think I was having second thoughts about the movie?"

Will gave her a mild, squinty "Are you crazy?" look, and said, "Because you're not watching it?"

"I'm listening to the sounds of silence," said Pen. "Hold your horses." To show herself who was boss, she strode across the room and sat next to Will on the sofa. There was about two feet of space between them, maybe two and a half, not that Pen was keeping track. *Calm yourself, missy,* she thought.

When Benjamin took Elaine, with her shining hair and lily-white jacket, to the strip club and she looked up in mute misery, the tears in her big, angelic brown eyes rendering them bigger, more angelic, more brown, Will said, "Remember how Cat used to say you were Elaine?"

"Cat and her backhanded compliments," growled Pen. "The passive-aggressive midget."

"I'm glad she's gone," said Will, throwing a pillow into the air and batting it toward the television like a volleyball.

"Oh yeah," said Pen. "Way glad. Cat never did see my inner bad girl."

"Hello, darkness, your old friend."

"Damn right."

"You don't really have an inner bad girl, do you?"

"Nope," said Pen. "But I'm working on it."

"Uh-oh," said Amelie, when Pen got to this part of the story.

"I know," said Pen. "Famous last words."

The next day, after a leisurely breakfast and another trip to the market, Pen and Will filled travel mugs with coffee, a paper bag with a lunch of leftover pie, packed up a blanket and the newspaper, and drove to the sandy beach on the other side of the peninsula. With the lambent bay before them, flat and silver as a platter, they sat back-to-back and ate and read, silently trading sections of the paper. Then they walked along the shore and talked about plovers, whether Will should quit business school, and Cat. In the almost-heat of the afternoon, Will rolled up his sweatpants and waded into the water, and Pen took off the Irish wool sweater she'd found in the guest-room closet and tied it around her waist. After a while, they walked back to the car, where Will stripped down to shorts, put his running shoes on, and took off down the road. Pen drove home, wrapped in tranquility and the smell of warm mothballs.

From the road, even before the blond stones of the driveway were crunching under the Saab's tires, Pen saw the car, a long gray Mercedes with Connecticut plates. Before she had time to consider who it might be, a note of unease began sounding in her head, faint, barely audible, but throwing the harmony of the past thirty-some hours out of whack. She wondered who it was, although anyone would've been less than welcome in Pen's opinion, now, when she and Will were leaving the next morning.

"You couldn't have waited just one more day?" Pen asked the Mercedes, as she pulled up next to it.

If someone apart from herself and Will had to be there, she hoped it was Philip, whom she loved for being a goofier version of Will, or Tully, whom she loved for being part twenty-three-year-old girl, part cranky old man ("Andy Rooney in Juicy Couture" is how Cat summed her up). But the man sleeping in the rocking chair on the porch with his feet, in gigantic, beat-up, paint-splattered black Chuck Taylors, propped on a milk crate wasn't Philip or Tully. He was older, maybe late twenties, with a long narrow face, Frida Kahlo eyebrows, and a head of oil-black Shirley Temple curls. One hand was tucked inside his toffee-colored Carhartt jacket; the other one dangled off the arm of the chair and was large and elegant and stained with something purple.

"Excuse me," said Pen.

Possibly it had something to do with his oversized hands or his extravagant hair, but Pen expected the man to wake up dramatically, maybe kick over the milk crate or shout with surprise. But he didn't move at all.

"Excuse me," she said again more loudly, and, this time, the man lifted a hand very slowly and rubbed the back of it back and forth across his still-shut eyes. It was only after he'd dropped the hand heavily into his lap and had, with great languor, tilted his head from side to side, as though working the kinks out of his neck, that he opened his eyes. They were an unexpected cloudy bluish gray, like the eyes of a newborn baby. The man smiled at Pen, a fast-twitch smile that made the cheek muscles in his thin face pop out like two golf balls.

"You caught me napping," he said. Actually, what he said was, "Yih cawt me nappin'," all the edges of his words smoothed away by a southern accent so lush it was almost comical.

"I see that," said Pen. She couldn't help smiling back at him. He was at best an interloper, at worst a serial killer, but he was cute.

He stood up. Due to his immense height, this was a multistage unfolding activity that reminded Pen of setting up a music stand. The man rubbed his hands down the front of his jacket and offered the right one to Pen. "Damon Callas."

Pen shook his hand. "Pen Calloway."

"What sort of a name is 'Pen,' if you don't mind my asking?"

"A nickname. For Penelope."

"Good Lord, girl, you're Greek!"

"No. Sorry."

"Where'd you get a name like that, then?"

"It's from *The Rise of Silas Lapham,* a book no one in the world but my mother loves. Penelope is Silas's daughter, the plain, brainy one."

"I'm sure only the latter adjective applies to you." Somehow—maybe it was the accent—he could say this without sounding like a complete phony. "Does she get her man?"

"She does, actually."

"I believe it." He winked. Pen was not a fan of winking, and she averted her gaze, but Damon was the kind of person whose eyes never leave your face during conversation. When she looked elsewhere, he leaned so that he could keep looking at her.

"Hmm," sniffed Pen.

"Sounds like she got a better deal than the other Penelope. Mrs. Odysseus."

"Yeah," said Pen, "you really never want to be the one who gets left behind."

"I was thinking more about the loyalty, the fidelity." He sagged his bony shoulders and made a bored face, "The chastity."

"The never-ending sewing project." Pen smiled.

"That, too." He smiled back at her, not a quick smile like before, but a molasses-slow, whole-face event. He crossed his arms across his chest and kept smiling.

"So," said Pen.

"Right," he said, still smiling. "So are you one of Charlotte's neighbors?"

Partly because of the way Damon pronounced "Charlotte," partly because Will never referred to his mother by her first name, and partly because Pen never suspected that this sublime scarecrow of a man could have anything to do with Will's mother, it took Pen several seconds to figure out what Damon was asking.

"Oh," she said finally. "No. I'm a friend of her son Will. We're just up for a few days."

"Will." Damon nodded. "The one in Philadelphia, right?"

"Yep, him."

Damon continued to nod. Pen thought Damon might be the most unhurried person in the world. Standing before her, nodding in the sun, he had the aspect of someone who could stand there nodding in the sun all day long.

"Are you a friend of Will's mother?" she said.

"I am," he said. "We're visiting for a few days, too. She's upstairs having a little lie-down. Long car trip and all. Plus, we were up late last night."

Something about the way he said "we" caused Pen to begin formulating a complicated word problem inside her head: if Will was twenty-six and the oldest child, which he was, and if Charlotte had gone to college, which she had, and if she'd gotten married after graduation, which Pen was pretty sure she had, even if it had been *right* after graduation, which it might have been, and even if she had been slightly pregnant at the time, which Randall Wadsworth liked to insinuate when he was feeling mean, how old would that make Will's mother? Mental math was not Pen's strong suit, but, eventually, her brain managed to eke out a number: forty-nine.

Will's mother was, at the very youngest, forty-nine years old, and, unless Damon were a vampire—which was possible, since he sort of looked like a vampire—he might have been thirty at the very oldest, which would mean he was dating (and this word seemed entirely wrong, although Pen realized it should not), *if* he was dating her, a woman at least nineteen years his senior. And that woman was Charlotte Wadsworth, Will's mother. When Pen, using emotional calculus, factored in the two measly months Will's mother had been separated from Will's father, along with the two measly months plus two measly weeks Will's mother had been sober, assuming she still was sober, plus

Will's sky-high hopes and bone-deep worry for his mother, the only answers she came up with were these: a vision of her friend Will running, fleet and unsuspecting, toward a mountain of fresh worry and her own heart beating out the words, *Oh, Will. Oh, Will. Oh, Will.*

PEN'S FINDING DAMON CALLAS SLEEPING ON THE PORCH OF THE summerhouse marked the point at which things got weird, but things did not progress from weird to surreal until after Pen got drunk.

Pen got drunk. Not falling-down drunk, but not just tipsy, either, which meant that she got drunker than she ever usually got. She didn't plan to get drunk at all, but after she, Will, and Damon got back from their walk to the sea glass beach—a weirdly unweird excursion—while Will and Damon sat in Adirondack chairs in the yard, making conversation in a weirdly normal way, Pen went into the house to get herself an apple and found the bottle of Pouilly-Fuisse on the counter, open and half-empty. It should not have been on the counter, open. It should have been in the refrigerator, unopened, the way Pen knew it had been when the three of them had left the house, with Will's mother still asleep upstairs.

Pen panicked. She could not let Will see the bottle. She could not let Will's mother drink any more of it. With shaking hands, she got a large wineglass, a goblet really, out of the china cabinet in the dining room, poured herself a glass of the wine and gulped it down. Then she poured another big glass, draining the bottle, and hid the bottle in the cabinet under the sink behind dishwashing soap and two boxes of scouring pads. For a moment, she leaned on her hands against the counter, her stomach burning, her head bowed, and whispered an already drunken prayer inspired by the box of scouring pads, "S.O.S., S.O.S., please S.O.S." Then she picked up the glass of wine, drank it, washed the glass, put it away, and walked outside.

◆ ◆ ◆

"WHY DIDN'T YOU JUST POUR IT OUT IN THE SINK?" ASKED AMELIE.

"I should have, but, honestly, for some reason, I didn't think of that."

"That reason possibly being your subconscious desire to have a drink?" said Amelie.

"Or two," said Pen ruefully.

WHAT PEN SAW HAPPEN IN WILL WHEN HE GOT BACK FROM HIS RUN had struck her as both marvelous and chilling: after she'd raced out to meet him on the driveway, giving him a rushed explanation, as much as she had one, for Damon Callas's presence on the porch, and after she'd watched confusion followed by anxiety followed by revulsion followed by anger pass over his face and she'd heard him spit out the words, "Oh, for fuck's sake," he had pulled out what Pen would later describe as "the big WASP guns." He had slid his emotions into some noiselessly opening and shutting WASP filing cabinet, turned his face into a blandly friendly WASP mask, and put on good manners like a suit of clothes.

Instead of pounding Damon's towering, scrawny body into the summerhouse yard, Will had made conversation, which is how Pen found out that Damon taught at the art school where Charlotte was taking a class ("Not my class, of course," he'd told them with a quickness and a reassuring tone that effectively turned "Not my class, of course" into "Will, I am banging your mother."), that he was a painter and collagist, that his hands were purple from dyeing cloth for use in one of his pieces, that he was "six-foot-six in stocking feet" but had not played basketball in high school or anyplace else.

When Damon asked if they'd mind showing him around a bit, Will had taken him to the sea glass beach, the two men walking ahead, talking in mellow tones about the history of the North Shore, and Pen following behind, fighting off the urge to fall to her knees on the stony beach and wail, "Will, let's go home!"

It wasn't until Pen had disappeared the wine and was walking unsteadily out of the house that she saw Will's remote demeanor crack, just for a second. He looked hard at Pen's face and said, "Everything okay?" The question made Pen want to weep.

She scraped together a feeble smile and said, "Should we start making dinner?"

"That reminds me," said Damon, giving his forehead a light smack. "There's a cooler of wine in the car I need to unload. Give me a hand, Will?"

Pen reeled at this, but everything else—Will, the house, the birds in the trees—seemed to stand still. She could see Will's face, which was not full of rage, but of sadness.

"Oh, Will," she said.

He turned toward Damon and said, "I don't think that's a good idea."

"Why not?" asked Damon.

"I guess you don't know that my mom's a recovering alcoholic. She hasn't had a drink in over two months."

Damon drew his heavy brows together, confusion all over his face, then he closed his eyes and sighed. "I'm sorry," he said. "I don't know how to tell you this."

Before he was even finished saying it, Pen had walked over to Will and taken his hand. "Don't," she told Damon.

The screen door sighed its sigh, and Will's mother stepped onto the porch. She was tall and straight and wore a long, loose sweater dress and boots. Pen noticed that she'd cut her hair; it hung at either side of her high-cheekboned face, blunt and expensive-looking.

"Why don't you say I'm a work in progress, Damon?" she said brightly. "Like all of us."

"Mom," said Will. His cheeks were red; he looked the way he looked when he had a fever, but his voice was ice-cold. Pen wanted to put her arms around him and take him away; she wanted to make his mother and Damon and the last couple of hours disappear off the face of the earth. Oh, please, she prayed, let it end, make them leave.

"Hello, darling," said his mother. "I didn't know you were coming. Lovely to see you."

"Lovely to see me?" said Will.

"You and Pen, both," said his mother, smiling. "Hello, Pen."

"Hello, Mrs. Wadsworth."

"Charlotte, please."

"Charlotte," said Will with a raw laugh. "That's great, Mom. Very hip. Like your new boyfriend and your cooler of wine."

"Please don't be rude," said Charlotte.

Will turned to Pen and said, in a low voice, "I need to get out of here before I lose my mind."

"I'll go get our stuff," said Pen.

"No, I mean right this second," said Will. "I need to drive. Or something. I'll come back."

"I'll go with you," said Pen.

"No," said Will, shaking his head and letting go of her hand.

"Why not?"

Will gave her an exhausted look with something scarier hovering behind it, "Because I really can't talk to you right now about why in the hell you're drunk and when you got that way."

Pen took a step back, her eyes stinging. "Will!"

"You have the keys, right?" He held out his hand, and Pen gave them to him.

"Promise you'll be careful. Promise you'll come back," she said, but Will was already turning away from her and running toward the car.

IN ALL OF THE BIG HOUSE, PEN COULD FIND NO PLACE TO BE. SHE'D started out in the guest room, but its door, like most of the doors in the house, was too warped by salt air and age to shut properly, and the music, along with the laughter and voices, poured hotly into the room just as the moonlight poured coolly through the white curtain to pool on the floor and make shadows on the wall. Pen gulped water and tried to read, but the words swam in front of her eyes, and all she could do was lie on the bed, trying not to hear the noise from downstairs, straining to hear the sound of Will's car. Emotions washed over her:

mostly anger—at Charlotte, drinking wine, dancing while her son's heart broke somewhere out in the dark; at Damon for letting her drink, for dancing, for being attractive, for being here at all; at Will for leaving her alone with them—but also sorrow and worry and something else, a cut-loose reckless feeling that might have been desire if it had any suitable object to fix on.

At midnight, Pen could not stand it a minute longer. She pulled on her shoes and the fisherman's sweater, yanked the quilt off the bed, and crept downstairs, wincing at every creak the steps made, wanting to be invisible. From the landing she could see Will's mother in the living room, dancing with surprising grace across the floor to sit in Damon's lap. *How could you?* she thought. *How* could *you?* She had to stop herself from shouting the words. Later, she would remember this righteous indignation with shame.

They didn't see her. Pen let herself out, the sound of the screen door reminding her of how arriving at the house just a couple of days ago had felt like a blessing. She had planned to sit in the porch rocker, but it was too close to what was happening in the house and, when she looked at the chair, she remembered seeing Damon there, asleep, so she went out into the backyard to get one of the Adirondack chairs and clumsily carried and dragged the big, awkward bulk of it to the grass a few yards out from the porch, a spot that gave her a clear view of the driveway. Then she cocooned herself in the quilt, tucked her hands deeply into the cuffs of the sweater, and sat down to wait for Will.

She woke, or half-woke, to the feeling of hands on her shoulders.

"Will," she whispered, with sleepy gratitude. "You're home." She opened her eyes.

Damon knelt on the grass in front of her, his face close. Pen blinked and leaned away from him, confused.

"Hey there," he said, smiling. "You must be cold out here."

"Where's Will?" Her voice was a croak.

"Not back yet," said Damon. He took his hands off her shoulders and put them on the wide, flat arms of the chair and said it again, "You must be cold."

Then he kissed her, and, after a numb few seconds, his warm mouth began waking her up, and the restless free-floating wanting that had been moving through her for what she now realized had been days, weeks even, contracted and concentrated to the point at which their two mouths met. She didn't think about Charlotte or Will or even Damon, because the man kissing her wasn't Damon. Or he was Damon and at the same time wasn't. It didn't matter. When he began to pull away, she put her hand on the back of his neck and pulled him back to her. She kissed him because he was there. She kissed him because he was kissing her.

"TRANSFERENCE," SAID AMELIE.

"What?" said Pen.

"You transferred your desire for Will onto Damon. Clearly."

"Except that I didn't have desire for Will."

"Oh, please."

"Trust me, he was my best friend. I definitely would have noticed if I had desire for him."

"Or maybe," said Amelie smugly, "that's why they call it the subconscious. Because it's subconscious."

SHE MIGHT HAVE PUSHED HIM AWAY. SHE MIGHT HAVE SLID FROM THE chair to the grass, opened the quilt, and pulled him inside with her. Pen would never find out because what broke, ragged, through the night was Will's voice, saying, "How could you do this?" And just as quickly as they'd come together, Pen and Damon broke apart, Damon dropping back to sit on the grass.

"Will, man," said Damon, but Will didn't even glance in his direction. Will stood in the darkness just beyond the circle of porch light so that Pen couldn't see his features, but she knew he was looking at her. In alarm, she jumped to her feet, shucking the quilt off her shoulders and starting toward him.

Will held up his hand. "Stop."

Pen stood still. "I'm sorry," she said.

Will took a step toward her and the light fell on his face. His expression, not closed and angry, as she had expected, but wide open as a child's, stunned and hurt, made her hate herself.

"Him?" said Will.

"I don't know why I did it," Pen said pleadingly. "I'm so sorry."

"You—" Will broke off and just looked at Pen. "That's not something you would do."

"I didn't mean to."

"What does that mean?"

Pen didn't know what to say.

"It means you're down here making out with my mother's whatever-the-hell he is. Boy toy. It means I don't know who you are."

"Yes, you do." Pen was crying. "You know you do."

"Will, brother. It was just a kiss," said Damon, with an attempt at a laugh, and Pen shut her eyes (had he really said "brother"?), waiting for an explosion.

But when Will answered, his voice was simply cold. "My mom is what? Passed out someplace? Seemed like a good time to give old Pen here a go?"

He shook his head in disgust, then ran up the porch steps. Before Pen realized what he was doing, before she could stop him, Damon was trotting up after him. He put one giant, bony hand on Will's shoulder. *Oh, God,* thought Pen, her chest tightening, *whatever you're about to do, don't, don't don't.*

"Listen," said Damon, with a smile that was probably meant to be kind and ingratiating, but under the circumstances, just looked smarmy, "I want you to know that there's no betrayal going on here. Nothing like that. Your mom and I are a no-strings operation, strictly casual."

A frozen second. Then the bottom dropped out of the world, and all of them crashed downward into a roaring nightmare, worse than a nightmare because it was so real, so flesh and blood. Pen's voice screaming "stop" might have been a fly buzzing. Nothing stopped. It went on and on. Until: Will's mother on the porch in a yellow bathrobe, yelling, "William, William"; Will turning his head to look at her; Damon catching him off guard and, like a battering ram, knocking him across the porch and into the corner of a railing.

Will lay still, his head bleeding onto the gray-white boards of the porch.

Pen ran to him—stepping over Damon, who sat slumped against the wall of the house, holding his rib cage and gasping—with a single throbbing thought: *If he is dead, I will die.*

Will's mother got there first. She dropped onto the porch next to him, put her face close to Will's, and pressed her fingers to the side of his neck. "My baby. My darling boy," she cried out. "I am so sorry."

Pen's heart seemed to stop, but she saw Will put his hand on his mother's hand and hold it for a few seconds. When he let go, he sat up, pressed his hand to the side of his head, groaned, then twisted sideways and vomited over the edge of the porch into the bushes.

"Forgive me," said his mother in the most regretful voice Pen had ever heard. "It's all my fault."

"Not all," said Pen. Will took his hand away from his head and stared uncomprehendingly at his wet red palm, and Pen saw that it wasn't the time to sit around talking about blame.

"You're going to the hospital," she said.

Will turned his battered face up to her, and, to her amazement, laughed a short, bitter laugh.

"What?" asked Pen.

"Who will drive me?" said Will. "You're all drunk."

"I'm not," said Pen. "I drank that wine hours and hours ago. I'm as sober as I can be."

She watched the archness fall away from his face and the hurt flash back into his eyes. She knew what he was thinking as surely as if he'd spoken the words aloud: *You kissed my mother's piece-of-shit boy-friend, and you weren't even drunk.* Pen quashed the useless impulse to apologize again and said, "Can you walk to the car?"

Pen heard a long groan from behind her and turned to Damon. "What about you? You need to go, too?"

"I don't think so," he said, working his way slowly up the wall, until he was standing, hunched and still breathing hard. He shot a glance at Will. "You're crazy," he said, with a strange lack of anger. "You're going to get yourself killed one day."

"Maybe," said Will.

"Go inside the house," said Charlotte to Damon. "Go on."

When he was gone, she started to help Will to his feet, but he picked up her hands in both of his and moved them off him, impassively, as though they weren't his mother's hands or hands at all. He reached for the porch railing and pulled himself up, wincing every time he shifted position. Blood was running down his neck and the front of his shirt.

"Wait," said Pen. She ran into the house, catching a fleeting glimpse of Damon on the living room sofa, ran upstairs to the linen closet, and grabbed an armful of thick white towels.

Back on the porch, she handed Will a folded-up towel for his head and took hold of his arm.

"I don't need help," said Will balefully.

"Yes, you do," said Pen.

THEY DIDN'T TALK ON THE WAY TO THE HOSPITAL. PEN DIDN'T TALK because she couldn't think of anything to say that wasn't scolding or apologizing, and she assumed Will didn't talk because he was too busy hating her and bleeding. He had refused to lie down in the backseat and sat with the towel between his head and the front passenger-side window, leaning as far away from Pen as it was possible to lean. The ride lasted twenty minutes, twenty minutes of silence, Pen catching glimpses of Will's unmoving face in the occasional beams of light from outside, and by the end of the ride, Pen found she had reached an odd, wrung-out state that was almost like peace. The tumult of blame, anger, confusion, worry, regret was all gone, everything was gone, except for love, of course, from which there was no relief.

The emergency room was quiet, and the nurse took Will back right away to be triaged. Under other circumstances, Pen would've gone, too, but without asking, she knew Will didn't want her with him.

She sat in the waiting room for what felt like hours, paging through months-old magazines and watching close-captioned CNN, until a nurse came in to say that Will's head was stitched but that he had a concussion and needed to remain there for observation.

"Does he want me?" said Pen.

The nurse gave her a concerned smile, looking, for a second, like Pen's mother. "Not right now," she said gently. "Are you his girl-friend?"

Pen started to cry, mostly from sheer exhaustion. "His friend," she said. "His best friend. But he's mad at me right now."

"I'm sorry," said the nurse. "He said you should go on home, and he'll call when he needs you."

"Can I stay?" said Pen, wiping her eyes. "For a little while more?"

"Sure you can," said the nurse. "He's not the boss of the waiting room, now is he?"

Pen fell asleep, her cheek leaning against her hand. When the nurse shook her awake next, Pen saw on the television that it was 7:05. Morning.

"Hey," said the nurse, "I told Will you were still here. You want to come on back?"

Pen nodded.

The sight of Will sitting in the hospital bed in a blue-sprigged gown, the white sheets over his legs, flooded Pen with relief, even though he looked surpassingly bad, unshaven and weary and the color of oat-meal, apart from a purple, swollen cheekbone and a black eye. Pen saw that a patch of his hair had been shaved on the right side and had a short caterpillar of stitches running across it. But he was breathing. He was safe. She had known he would live, of course, but the ugliness of the night before had shaken her up, twisted her imagination into irrational shapes. Looking at him, she realized she had been afraid, ter-rified even, that she would never see him again. But here he was.

"Hey," said Pen softly, smiling.

"Hey," said Will.

"Nice haircut."

"Yeah. You like it?"

Pen felt fear steal over her because nothing was the way it should have been. The words she and Will said to each other were more or less normal, but everything else was wrong: the distance in his voice and in his eyes, the way he didn't smile back at her. She thought it might have been the first time ever, since they'd met, that he hadn't smiled back at her. He wasn't angry anymore, at least she didn't think so, but he wasn't Will, either. Will would have rushed to meet her halfway. He would have understood that this bright room, everything clean, a world away from the squalor and the bloodstained porch, was meant to be the place in which they would fall back together. They'd had a very bad night, but now it was morning.

She tried again. "You hit your head pretty hard, friend. You didn't, by any chance, suffer memory loss. Maybe lose the last fifteen hours or so?"

Still, no smile. He said, "You didn't have to stay."

"You don't think so?" Pen asked. "Really?"

Will didn't answer. He looked down at his hands, turning them over and back on the sheet in front of him, as though noticing the white bandages on them for the first time.

Pen walked to the side of the bed. She wanted to touch Will but was afraid he would stiffen or move her hands away the way he had his mother's the night before, so instead, she held on to the metal arm of the hospital bed.

"Won't you forgive me?" she asked. "You have to know how sorry I am."

Will turned his tired, faraway eyes on her and said, "Don't ask me that. It's not about forgiving you."

"*What's* not about forgiving me?" asked Pen, gripping the bed rail. "Can there just not be an 'it'? Please? Can we make it go away?"

"I don't want to talk about this right now."

"When, then?" Pen ordered herself not to cry. She wasn't sure why, but she understood that her crying would doom the conversation. She needed to stay calm and optimistic and as normal as possible if there was any chance of ending the moment on a happy note. And Pen thought that if the moment didn't end on a happy note, she would not be able to stand it.

With gratitude, she saw Will's gaze soften a little, and he said, "Soon. All right?"

"All right."

The next second, though, he was all business. "I called Philip. He's on his way."

"So when he gets here, we'll go home," said Pen.

"I can't," said Will. "Phil and I need to stay with my mom, figure out what to do. You drive my car home, okay? I'll take a train later."

At the thought of driving home alone, the panic from the night before came back, the fear that, if she left him, she would never see Will again. On impulse, she placed her hand on top of his bandaged one and carefully curled her fingers around it. "Let me stay. I don't want to leave without you."

He gave her a long, complicated look, his clear hazel eyes taking in her face bit by bit, a look that she would spend hours and months afterward trying to decipher. She would never figure out what he was thinking, but, eventually, what she understood was that, while other good-byes would follow, this look Will gave her was the real end. He leaned over and kissed her forehead.

"It'll be okay. Go home." He smiled at her, then, which should have made her feel better, but it didn't. She didn't want to go home, she didn't think anything would be okay, but she let go of his hand and left.

Amelie said, "Can I stop here to point out the elephant in the room?"

"I know what you're thinking," said Pen. "And why you're thinking it. I've even considered it myself, but nope, it's not there. It's not a real elephant."

"When it comes to your personal life, honey, you wouldn't know a real elephant if it bit you on the ass."

"You didn't know us."

"*You* didn't know you," Amelie said. She sighed. "What happened next? After he got home."

"You know what happened. He left. Eight years of friendship up in smoke."

"Did you try to stop him?"

Pen told Amelie how she had yelled at Will the way she had never yelled at anyone. She had gone on and on and ended with:

"That's it? That's *it*? I watch you totally lose your mind and beat the shit out of another human being, *twice,* which I have to tell you is pretty fucking terrifying, and I don't leave you. I don't not forgive you. I know I shouldn't have kissed that man, that I betrayed you and your mother and probably my mother and God knows who else, and I am sorrier than I have ever been about anything but come *on*! I lose my head for five minutes, after being a goody two-shoes *my entire life,* and you're *leaving*?"

"What did he say?" asked Amelie.

Will hadn't yelled back. He hadn't even been angry. He'd been generous and loving and in pain about how much he was hurting Pen, from the second he arrived back home until the second he got into his car and left Philadelphia for good, but he was immovable as a mountain.

"He said, 'I forgive you. I feel stupid even saying that. Of course, I forgive you. It's not about that.' "

Pen could close her eyes and see him saying this to her and still feel what she'd felt then: the lights going out with a bang, total hope blackout. She knew right then that he wouldn't stay, no matter what she said, but still she asked, "What is it about, then?"

"Pen," he'd said, sighing, "my family is a disaster. I'm a disaster. I hate my dad. I hate business school. Damon"—he paused, and Pen flinched at the sound of Damon's name—"was right when he said I was going to get myself killed one day. I need to get away and start over, figure out my life."

But he didn't meet her eyes, and when she said, "Do you hear how little sense you're making? How none of those are reasons for leaving *me*? Don't lie about this," he didn't contradict her. He leaned back in his chair with his hands on top of his head, staring at the ceiling. *He's trying to think of how to say it,* thought Pen, bitterly, *how to let me down easy.*

After a long time, Will reached across Pen's tiny kitchen table, lightly raked his fingers down her cheek once—a ghost of a touch, there and gone—and slowly and carefully, with such kindness and sadness in his voice that Pen felt that maybe all wasn't lost after all, he said, "The thing is, this won't work, just the two of us."

"We can make it work," said Pen.

"I can't." In frustration, Will pushed his chair back from the table, so that he was suddenly far away, out of reach.

"So—what?" Pen lashed out at him, put words in his mouth that she knew weren't true. "You're saying that Cat's the only reason you and I were friends? If it's just me, it's not worth it?"

"No. No way. Of course not. But Cat kept us—in balance."

Pen was not above begging. If she hadn't been sitting at the table, she might have gotten down on her knees. Instead, she reached out as far as she could and put her hands on the table in front of Will, palms up, as though asking him to take them. He didn't, but she just left them there.

"We're still here, together. Cat's leaving was bad enough. It was a nightmare, but I could stand it if you were still here. You're my best friend," said Pen. "I love you."

She realized they were words that she and Will never said. Cat had said them all the time, and they had said them back to her, but never to each other.

Will didn't say them now. He said, "I don't know how to be with you without her."

"I don't know what you mean," wailed Pen.

"I know," said Will. "And I'm so sorry."

When Pen told Amelie this, Amelie knocked on Pen's head and said, "Hello. Is anyone in there?"

"Stop it," said Pen seriously. "We were friends. It was as big a deal as being in love." She tried to think of a way to make Amelie understand. "It was a revelation, being friends like that. God, it was *holy* to me. But it wasn't being in love."

"Fine," said Amelie. "And what about now?"

"We're talking. We're plotting," said Pen. "Coming up with a plan to try to find Cat. Will's going to talk to a neighborhood friend of hers."

"You already told me that, and you know what I'm asking," said Amelie impatiently. She waved her hands around. "What about *now*? Six years later. You're both adults. Bygones are bygones. No Cat around to distract you at the reunion."

"We wanted Cat around," Pen reminded her. "A lot."

"Still, she wasn't there."

Pen shrugged.

"So how did it feel to be with him again? Different? Come on, it had to feel different."

Pen raised her eyebrows at Amelie. "You want me to say I'm in love with him. After seeing him for two days."

"No, I don't." Amelie grinned.

"You want me to say that I was struck by the thunderbolt realization that he is the love of my life."

"Nope."

"Yes, you do. That's how you are. But here's a thought: it takes two to tango."

"Ha! So you *are* in love with him!"

"Not what I'm saying, and you know it."

"Oh, he wants to tango all right."

"I don't think so," said Pen. "I didn't see a single sign, not that I was looking."

"History tells us you're not so good at seeing signs. But let's put tangoing aside. Were you attracted to him? Simple question."

"I might have been, but not continuously. In flashes."

"Why say 'might'? You were."

"Seeing him again was overwhelming. A shock. I can't be sure of what I felt."

Amelie gave her a skeptical look.

"And even now," said Pen, "I can't quite believe in him."

"You don't trust him?" Amelie ruffled her cropped blond hair in dismay. "Why not?"

Pen shook her head. "I trust him. Or I trust him in all ways except that I'm not completely sure he won't disappear again. But what I meant was I can't quite believe that those two days happened. You know what I did?"

"What?"

"On my way back from the reunion, I pulled off the road to call him because I needed to make sure he was real."

Amelie smiled at her and said, "Was he? What did he say?"

"He said, 'I was about to call you. I just passed a dead possum the size of a Volkswagen. I knew you'd want to know.'"

AFTER HER CONVERSATION WITH AMELIE, PEN WALKED HOME DIS-tracted and brimming with feeling, half of her still in the past, the other half walking homeward through the here and now. Outside her apartment door, Pen stopped to listen to Augusta, who was inside singing a song from her spring concert, when suddenly, above the bubbling clarity of this, she heard one word, like a bird landing on a branch, "Beautiful!" *Oh, my God,* she thought. Pen was fumbling with the key in the lock, when Jamie threw open the door with a smile like Christmas morning.

"Mom?" said Pen, stepping inside.

Pen's mother sat in the leather armchair in a blue T-shirt with Augusta on her lap. The breath seemed to fly out of Pen's body. *Everyone, everyone is coming back to me,* she thought.

"My girl," said her mother, holding open her free arm. "I missed you every day."

"Your heart leaps up, Mama!" said Augusta, clapping her hands. "Right?"

All Pen could do was nod.

"Come here, right this second," said her mother, and Pen went.

CHAPTER TWELVE

$\mathcal{S}$AMANTHA DENHAM-DREW MADE WILL WANT TO SMOKE. NOT in the same way that *Casablanca* made him want to smoke every time he saw it; chiefly because he was sitting on his back steps not seeing Samantha, just talking to her on the phone, but her luxurious, intriguingly placed inhaling pauses and her drawn-out velvet exhales sounded so satisfying that Will could feel them in his own chest. Will had smoked for eight weeks at summer camp when he was fifteen, exclusively on sloped roofs and exclusively at night, which caused him to associate the smell of cigarettes forever after with sliding and the sound of frogs, but, apart from that, he had never been a smoker and had no interest in becoming one. Still, Samantha Denham-Drew was a woman who knew her way around a drag.

Jason had e-mailed Samantha Denham-Drew's number to Will and Pen (not from the Glad2behere address, which was apparently a dummy account Jason had set up to fool Will and Pen into thinking he was Cat, a username choice that Pen called "such a clear case of wishful thinking it makes you want to throw up or cry," but from CoolTaxDude, which Will found equally wishful, if considerably less poignant), and they had flipped a coin to decide which one of them had to call her. Actually, Pen had flipped a coin while the two of them were talking on the phone and had given a short victory cheer that went something like, "I won I won I won," after which she had put Amelie ("friend, business partner, coin-flip witness, hot blonde") on the phone.

"I really am hot," said Amelie. "And she really did win."

"You'd lie for her," said Will. "Admit it."

"All day long." Amelie's voice shifted from snappy to buttery. "But you should be the one to call anyway. You have a great voice. Very commanding. Very persuasive. Any woman on the other end of the line from you would be putty in your hands."

"Oh, yeah," said Will. "Putty. As you and Pen are demonstrating."

"Abundantly," corrected Amelie. "Abundantly demonstrating."

So he had called.

Sam answered the phone by exhaling smoke and saying, "This is Sam."

"Hi, Sam," said Will. "This is Will Wadsworth. You don't actually know me, but—"

Sam cut him off. "If you're calling on Joe's behalf, forget it. Joe's a sonofabitch."

"I'm not calling on Joe's behalf."

"Fool me once, shame on you. Fool me twice, shame on me." Inhale. Will watched a little brown bird with a tail like a tongue depressor take a brief but entire bath in the birdbath Will's mother had put up in his backyard. Exhale. "Tell that to your friend Joe."

"I don't know Joe."

"I don't know you, and you don't know Joe. Is that your story?"

Inhale.

"I guess it is."

Exhale.

"Fine. I'll play along. So if you know neither me nor your sonofabitch friend Joe, how did you get my number?"

"From a guy named Jason Rogers."

"Aha. Jason." Inhale. "There's another sonofabitch." Exhale. Will smiled. It would take more than a colossal lungful of smoke to keep Samantha Denham-Drew from calling Jason a sonofabitch.

"I agree," said Will. "Not that I know the guy all that well."

"If you're agreeing that he's a sonofabitch, I'd say you know all there is to know," said Sam. "So why are you calling me?"

"I'm an old friend of Jason's wife, Cat."

Inhale, quickly followed by a hairball cough. "Hold on. What did you say your name was?"

"Will Wadsworth."

"You are so egregiously full of crap."

Will laughed. "Sometimes. But not right now."

"Will Wadsworth." Sam's voice dropped to a hoarse whisper. "Mother Mary."

"So you've, uh, heard of me?"

"You? Of course! You're a living legend."

"You're not thinking of the poet, are you?"

"What poet? I've never heard of a poet named Will Wadsworth."

"Well, yeah, there's not one, but—"

"You're Will Wadsworth, the friend! College Will! Philly Will! The Pen-and-Will Will!"

Will smiled. "That's the one."

"And you got my number from *Jason*? I thought you and Pen hated Jason."

Will flashed back to Jason standing outside the chapel, his hands open, hollow-eyed under the moon. "Well, I wouldn't say 'hate.'"

"'Despise.' 'Despise' was Cat's word. Although she also said you beat the shit out of him the first time you met him, which sounds a little hotter under the collar than—what's the noun form of 'despise'? Despisery?"

"I don't think so, but nothing else really springs to mind," Will said.

"Huh! I thought you were English majors, you, Pen, and Cat."

Will laughed. "Anyway, it was a long time ago, when I did that."

"You've cooled off, you're saying?"

"Yes, and I shouldn't have done it in the first place."

"Oh, I don't know about that. So how did Jason come to give you my number?"

Will gave her a condensed version of the story, after which she was silent, except for the sounds of smoking.

Finally she said, "Question: Why? Are you and Pen looking for her for you and Pen or for Jason?"

Will puzzled over this. "I don't know. We were worried about Cat because Jason said he was worried about Cat, and he was pretty convincing. But Pen and I haven't really discussed why, even though we talk about finding her all the time."

He thought for a while more, aware of the lengthening phone silence and wishing he had a cigarette to fill it. "So I don't know, but knowing me and Pen, it's for us, not Jason. Or it's for Cat. Cat's dad died. She was distraught. She took off. I guess we didn't discuss why we were looking for her because it just seemed like the only thing to do. If that makes sense."

Will heard sniffles.

"Are you—crying?" he asked nervously. He stood up as though to make a getaway.

More sniffles, one gulp, and then, tearfully: "That just has to be one of the sweetest things I've ever heard. So sweet and *so you*!"

"You don't actually know me," Will reminded Sam.

"I know," she said. A bout of unusually staccato smoking followed. Puff puff puff. When it was over, Sam was calm and snarky again. "Sorry. I'm prone to emotional outbursts, having only recently broken up with my lying, cheating boyfriend." Will sat back down.

"Joe," supplied Will. "The sonofabitch."

"See? You do know him." Sam laughed. "Cat would love it that the two of you are looking for her. She'd be over the moon."

"You think?"

"But she'd be jealous as hell that you guys are back together without her."

"Do you," said Will slowly, "know where she is?"

"I knew where she was going. I know that she got there. Which isn't the same as knowing where she is at this precise moment. And then there's the matter of how she is, which I also don't know. Although not so good would be my guess."

"Where she was going is a start, though. Will you tell me? I would really appreciate it."

More smoking. Unless Sam's cigarettes were a foot long, she'd lit another one without Will's noticing, although Will doubted that a woman who smoked like Sam was capable of soundless cigarette-lighting. He would have imagined a big snapping Zippo or the loud, luscious cinematic *scrape-whoosh* of a match.

"On one condition," said Sam.

"Okay. What?"

"I tell you in person. How could I pass up a chance to meet the famous Will in the flesh?"

"Seriously? I live in Asheville, North Carolina, and you're outside of Cincinnati. That's got to be at least six hours, one way."

"You'd do it, though. You'd make the trip. For Cat," cajoled Sam. "You know you would. You know you would."

Will groaned. "Fine."

"Ha! I knew you'd do it. Cat would love that, too," she said. "But look, I don't have a lot going on right now, to tell you the truth. A long drive could be therapeutic. How about we do a little Mapquest magic, pick a spot, and meet halfway?"

"How about you tell me where Cat is now, and you and I will plan a get-together for another time?"

"Ha! Nope."

"All right, all right. I'll meet you halfway."

"You think there's any chance Pen could come, too?"

For one clear instant, Will pictured Pen in the passenger seat next to him, reaching with one long golden-brown arm to close the air-conditioning vent. "I doubt it. She has a five-year-old daughter."

"What?" shrieked Sam. "Is Pen married? Are *you* married? Oh my God, you're not married to *each other*?"

"Maybe," said Will. "Maybe not."

"You're not telling me? Are you kidding?"

"I'll tell you when I see you," said Will coolly.

"Ah. Payback."

"Not payback. Insurance," said Will. "Three hours each way is a long way to drive just to see me in the flesh. As enticing as I am."

"Modesty! Sarcasm!" Will heard a sound that might have been Sam slapping the table in front of her. "That is just so *you* of you! Can I tell you how excited I am at how you you are?"

"Well, thanks. I'm sure you're very you, too."

"Oh, I am," said Sam. "I totally, totally am."

THE NEXT DAY, AS HE HEADED OFF TO JELLICO, TENNESSEE, TO MEET Sam, Will found himself remembering the conversation he had had with his mother on the day he got home from the reunion. After he'd walked through his front door, but before he had closed it behind him, the phone had started ringing.

"Welcome back, sweetheart," she'd said.

"What do you have?" Will had said. "Spies staking out my house?"

"Intuition," said his mother.

"You're deeply, deeply creepy," said Will. "I just want to go on record with that."

"Done," said his mother. She got down to business: "Now, tell me, did you see her?"

"Yes," Will had said. "I mean, no."

He had told her the whole story. It was the fourth time that day he had told it, since Philip, Gray, and his Asheville friend and former boss Jack, all of whom apparently lacked either his mother's patience or intuition or both, had called him while he was on the road coming home. Unlike the other three, his mother didn't punctuate his telling with "No fucking way," or "Holy shit," or similar expressions of surprise. Unlike the other three, she didn't ask him if Pen was still hot. In fact, his mother had stayed almost perfectly quiet, and when Will had finished, the first thing she said was, "Isn't it interesting how, in the years you've been apart, all three of you have lost a father?"

Will was caught off guard by this and didn't say anything.

"Sad, of course," his mother went on, "but there's also something beautiful there, something synchronous. Maybe you're coming back into each other's lives to help each other heal."

Will had thought about pointing out that his own father wasn't actually dead, unless you counted his heart and soul, or that you had to first have a father in order to lose one, or that his father's exit from his life had left nothing that required healing. But Will suspected that even though his mother respected Will's right to think these things about his dad, it bothered her to hear them. His mother, who had been more despised, more broken by Randall Wadsworth than anyone, had forgiven him.

Once, four years ago, Will had asked her how she had accomplished this. She had reached out to cup the side of his head in her hand, her eyes full of tears, and said, "Oh, my darling, compared to forgiving myself, it was easy."

"How, though?" Will had persisted.

"I did for your dad what I did for me," she'd said. "I didn't decide that his behavior wasn't that bad or erase the memory of it from my mind, but I threw away the idea that he was a monster. I acknowledged his humanness. There's a light inside every human being; I chose to honor his inner light."

"When?" asked Will. "How long did it take?"

His mother had given him a crooked smile and said, "When? Every morning when I get up and every night before I go to bed. Same as I do for myself."

"Like brushing your teeth."

"Yep."

"I'm a long way from that," said Will. "Probably, I won't get there."

"Maybe you won't, and that's okay," said his mother. "But I don't think you're giving yourself enough credit. After all, you forgave me."

She believed that he had forgiven her because she had asked him, once, and he had said yes, which he had been glad about because the answer had made her so happy (nothing he had ever done or said in his entire life had ever made anyone even close to that happy), but, in truth, he didn't know if *forgiveness* was the right word for what had changed between himself and his mother after she'd stopped drinking. He hadn't deliberately forgiven her. He had never thought the word *forgive.* Instead, gradually, without really meaning to, he had turned himself over to her, had begun to love her without wariness or sorrow.

"Oh, come on," Will had said. "Dad is—. You don't need to hear what I think Dad is, but I'll tell you what: he's not you."

"Okay," said his mother, "but for your sake, if not for his, I hope you'll forgive him one of these days."

"I might." Will had shifted uncomfortably, then. "Whether I do or don't, though, I figured something out."

"What's that?"

"I need him gone," Will had told her, looking her straight in the eye. "For good. No seeing him. No more phone calls or e-mails. Nothing." He had braced himself.

"Good," said his mother firmly. "Cut him out."

"Really? I thought you'd be upset."

"Of course not," said his mother. "Whatever you need to do to take care of yourself, do it. And good riddance."

"Hold on," Will had said. "I thought you forgave him."

"I did. I do. I let go of my anger and blame, but I know him." She had given Will a look of such fierce tenderness that he knew he would never forget it. "And you are my child, and, unless that man undergoes a radical change, which could happen because miracles do happen, but which I'm sorry to say seems unlikely, he shouldn't be anywhere near you."

Now, four years later, Will was no closer to forgiveness, unless not caring much anymore counted as forgiveness, and Will's father, if not dead, was as gone as ever, not as gone as Pen's father, as Cat's, but only technically. Will could still see Pen lying on the ground outside the old gray church, could still hear her voice saying, "My dad died two years ago," and he knew that his father was gone in a way that Pen's and Cat's would never be.

But when his mother said that, about how they had all lost fathers, Will hadn't launched into a conversation about degrees of fatherless-ness or grief. Tired from his drive, his head full of Pen and Cat, he had looked out his window and said, "I think my lawn has grown a foot since I left. Is that possible?"

Will's mother said, "Ben Calloway was an uncommonly good man."

"Yeah," said Will. "I wish he hadn't died."

"You wish it for Pen's sake and for her family's sake the most," his mother went on, not noticing, or more likely ignoring, his terseness. "But also for your own. He was more a father to you than your father ever was. I know how you loved him."

Sometimes, he thought, *you are too much.* Time to pull back. Time to set limits. "I haven't seen him in a long time," he said.

"Honestly, William, *time*?" his mother had snapped. "*Distance*? Those things have nothing whatsoever to do with love. Who knows that better than you?"

It happened the way it always happened: Will set limits and his mother rolled over them like a tank mowing down a picket fence.

Will hadn't bothered bringing up his overgrown lawn again. He smiled a resigned smile, shook his head, and said, "Nobody."

IN THE MIDDLE OF THE DRIVE TO JELLICO, PEN CALLED.

"Where are you?"

"Driving."

"Where?"

Will looked around him. Highway. Hills.

"In my car."

"Your *speedy* car," said Pen, who had seen Will's car at the reunion and given him the kind of look you'd give a traitor. "How could you?" she'd said. "This car is shiny and speedy and blue! The only thing it has in common with your old red Saab is that it's German." When Will told her that Saabs weren't actually German, she had refused to believe it, saying, "Why would I have thought all this time that Saabs were German if they're not?" to which Will could find no answer.

"I hope you're not speeding," said Pen.

"If by 'speeding,' you mean exceeding the speed limit, Grandma, then I am."

"I don't blame you," said Pen giddily. "I can't wait until you pick the brain of Samantha Denham-Drew. I bet the anticipation is killing you."

"I wouldn't say 'killing,' " said Will.

A couple of days before, Pen had e-mailed Will a list of fifteen questions for Sam with the instruction that he should add them to his own, checking, of course, for redundancy and preferably arranging them in a subtly rising arc of intimacy and importance. Will had reminded Pen that nobody showed up to a conversation with a list of questions; went on to say that, as far as he could tell, Sam was the kind of person who would talk for hours, in detail, about any subject, especially Cat, *unless* a man were to hand her a list of questions and instruct her to answer them; and had added, "Besides, all we really need to know is where Cat went, right?" To which Pen had hollered, "Are you insane? It's been six years! You have to find out everything! How can that happen if you're *not prepared*?"

Now, as he had known she would, Pen asked, "Did you bring the list of questions?"

"I e-mailed them to her in advance," said Will. "She's putting together a PowerPoint presentation on the last six years of Cat's life that she'll project onto the wall of the barbecue joint."

"Shut up," said Pen, laughing her laugh. "So you'll never guess what happened."

"What?"

"Guess."

"You said I never would."

"Guess."

"Uh, Augusta lost a tooth."

"That's mean, Will," reproached Pen. "If you saw her perfect, little, square white baby teeth, you would know how mean it was."

"Sorry," said Will. "So what really happened?"

"My mother came home."

Something in Pen's tone was familiar to Will, and it occurred to him that maybe the tone was a universal, the way you sounded when your mother came back: like a little kid and so glad that you shine, even over the phone. Maybe he had heard Tully sound that way. Or Philip. Maybe he'd heard himself.

"Wow," said Will, "that's great news! You must be really happy."

"I'm beside myself with happiness," said Pen. "And gratitude. And relief. I just came home from work and saw her sitting there with Augusta, and it took my breath away. It was like someone fixed my television."

For a second, Will considered saying what he figured most people would say to this, something like, "Man, you must really like television," but the fact was that he knew immediately and exactly what Pen meant. "Colors got brighter," said Will. "Edges got sharper."

"Everything gleamed," Pen said. "Like sometimes happens after it rains."

"How is she?"

It took Pen a little while to answer, and when she did, something uncertain had edged into her buoyancy. "You know," she said. "She's fine."

"Good. But if she's fine," said Will, "then why do you sound like that?"

"Like what?"

"You tell me."

Pen sighed. "Worried? A little?"

"About what?"

"Listen, are you driving with one hand while we're talking? Because that's dangerous."

"I have a Bluetooth phone."

"You have to know that I have no idea what that is."

"I just talk. No hands required. So why don't you tell me what you're worried about."

"Okay. I know this sounds crazy," said Pen, "but she's almost too fine. If you had seen her when she left—. I mean, my father had been gone for over a year and a half, but she seemed sadder than she was right after he died. More than just sadder. She was heartsick, despondent." Pen quickly added, "And, Will, you know I would've given any-thing to make things better for her."

Will remembered the last visit he'd made with Pen to her parents' house, how he and Pen's father had just come back from a bike ride and could hear, from the driveway, even before they'd gotten off their bikes, Pen and her mother singing in the kitchen: Michael Jackson's "Ben" at full volume, their voices stretching for the high notes near the end, then collapsing into laughter.

"Sure, you would have," he said. "You don't even have to say it."

"But there's something about her now that's more than what I ex-pected," said Pen. "I expected peace, acceptance. But she seems so *ac-tively* happy. She has this—this luster to her."

"She was in India and Tibet, right? Maybe she had some kind of spiritual awakening. Or maybe she's just glad to be home." Will could see how a spiritual awakening and coming home to Pen could amount to the same thing.

"Jamie, Augusta, and I are driving her home tomorrow morning. She mentioned that she has something she wants to tell us."

"Could be the meaning of life," said Will.

Pen laughed. "I'll keep you posted."

Leave it to Cat, the most dramatic person Will had ever known, to have a friend who walked into a tiny barbecue joint in a tiny Tennessee town at twelve thirty on a June afternoon looking like a head-on collision between Marilyn Monroe and Johnny Rotten: white halter dress, white sandals, red lipstick, orange sea urchin hair. As every person in the restaurant—mothers and toddlers, men nurs-ing beers at the bar, people on their lunch break—turned to look at her, Sam whipped off her enormous black sunglasses and flicked her green gaze over the room. Will started to raise his hand (he was that sure of who she was), but her eyes didn't rest on him for more than a split second before she strode across the room to the bar, grabbed a giant of a man with a ZZ Top beard and a John Deere cap by his copious shoulders, cried, "Will Wadsworth, you are exactly what Cat described!" and kissed him, Euro-style, on both cheeks.

For a second, the man stared at Sam. Then, as the other men at the bar erupted into hoots and laughter, he removed, with great delicacy, Sam's hands from his shoulders, stood up, took off his hat, and said, "Ma'am, I believe you have me confused with somebody else."

Sam's eyes widened, and she gave the man a smile that had the grace to be abashed and that confirmed Will's suspicion, from their phone conversation, that Sam Denham-Drew was a little out there but was overall a good egg. Gesturing toward Will with one red-nailed hand, she said, in a further demonstration of good-eggedness, "Sir, I was playing a little joke on my friend here, pretending I didn't recognize him, and I am mortally sorry if it embarrassed you. I can be thoughtless."

The man, and every other person in the restaurant, looked over at Will, and, feeling suddenly scrawny and overgroomed, Will stood and gave the man a forlorn thumbs-up.

"Me as him, huh?" said the man, chuckling. "That *is* funny."

"See?" said Sam to Will, as though the whole display were part of some conversation they'd been having. "Funny!"

"Hilarious," said Will.

When Will put out his right hand to shake Sam's, she batted it away and grabbed his left.

"Ha! No ring!"

She narrowed her eyes at him. Up close, Sam's face was pretty in a surprisingly ordinary way, bare, apart from the lipstick, snub-nosed, pale and freckled, like eggnog sprinkled with nutmeg.

"Unless," she said, "you're one of the ones who refuses to wear one?"

"I'm one of the ones who refuses to wear one because he's not married."

"God, I hate those guys," seethed Sam. "Expect your wife to sport an 'I'm taken' diamond that can be seen from space but won't wear jackitty shit yourself."

Before he could catch himself, Will laughed.

"What?" said Sam.

"You're just so—mad."

"I know," said Sam, sighing. "Hi, nice to meet you. I'm full of rage."

"Will you hit me if I ask you if you want to sit down?"

Sam appeared to consider this, then wrinkled her nose and said, "Nah, I'll sit."

Will walked around the table and pulled out a chair for her. She stabbed a finger in his direction. "Don't even start with the gentlemanly crap," she said. "I'm in a vulnerable place."

"Sit the hell down," said Will.

"That's better."

A teenaged female server in a T-shirt with a pink pig face on it and the words HOPE YOU'RE BIG ON PIG walked over. Her hair was dyed a sooty, shineless black. Will would've bet money that she hated having to wear that T-shirt. Will waited for Sam to order a drink and was relieved when she asked for a Diet Coke with lemon.

"The lemon's not an affectation," she told Will. "I really like it better that way."

"I believe you," said Will, and ordered a ginger ale. As the server walked away, Will saw that the other end of the pig was on the back of her shirt. "I think I was expecting you to get bourbon," he told Sam. "Possibly a double."

"Because of the rage thing," said Sam, nodding. She mimicked throwing a drink in his face. "A 'Take that, asshole!' kind of drink."

"And because of the smoking," admitted Will, with a grin.

"Oh, I only smoke on the phone," said Sam. "It's one of my rules."

"I see."

"And when I drink, which I do from time to time, I hate to say it, but I lean toward the pink and frilly," she said and quickly added, "But I know you don't drink at all."

"I do, actually," said Will. "Not a lot, but sometimes." He smiled. "Not in the middle of the day when I have to turn around and drive two hundred miles, but if you'd ordered that double bourbon, I would've had no choice."

"Can't stand to be outdone by a girl?" asked Sam. "Or can't let a lady drink alone?"

"Both," said Will.

"Whoo!" said Sam, snapping her fingers. "Cat would *hate* it that I know you drink and she doesn't. Know, I mean. Not drink. Which she does. Not like a fish or anything, but if you were married to Jason, you'd throw back a glass of wine now and then, too."

"I'm sure I would."

"You said you'd tell me about Pen's kid. So tell."

"Her name is Augusta. She's about to turn five."

"Is she yours?" asked Sam, clasping her hands pleadingly under her chin.

"Nope," said Will. "I've never even met her."

"Oh, yeah." Sam snorted and rolled her eyes. "Like that means anything. Like fathers who have never met their kids aren't a dime a stinkin' dozen. Stinkin' deadbeats."

"Rage, again," observed Will.

"Sorry," said Sam.

"Maybe you should just run over Joe with your car," said Will. "Get it out of your system."

"I just might," said Sam. She folded her hands primly on the table. "Pray, continue. About Pen and her kid. She's married, I take it."

"No."

"Oh, no, she's a widow." Sam pressed her fingers to her lips, a reckless move, Will thought, considering her lipstick.

"Not a widow," he said.

Sam's eyes widened in amazement. "Well, I'll be damned. Divorced? Little Miss Perfect is divorced?"

"That's not a name Pen really embraces," said Will, "believe it or not. And no."

The server came back and handed them menus. "We have a couple of specials today."

Impatiently, Sam waved her away with the menu, as though she were a fly. The server gave Will a look with her black-rimmed eyes that said *What the fuck?* as clearly as if she'd said it out loud.

"Sorry," he said. "Would you mind coming back in a few minutes?"

She lifted one painfully thin shoulder, mumbled, "So be it," spun around on her heel, and left.

"Whoa-ho-ho-ho, Nelly! I am stunned. I am *thunderstruck*," said Sam, her jaw dropping open. After several seconds, she closed her mouth and said, breathlessly, "Our Penelope has joined the ranks of the unwed mothers. Holy frijole."

"He wanted to marry her," said Will and immediately felt stupid for defending Pen, who didn't need defending, although he couldn't resist adding, "She wasn't interested," which wasn't the complete truth but which felt pretty good to say, nevertheless.

"Cat would fall. Over. And die," said Sam and did a dance in her chair.

"Speaking of Cat," prompted Will.

"All in good time, my friend," said Sam with a laugh. "We haven't even ordered yet."

They both ordered the pork barbecue, a.k.a. "enough pig to pop your buttons," which caused Sam to merrily point out that she didn't have any buttons, standing up and turning around to reveal their absence along with a generous expanse of freckled back, which caused the server to appear to contemplate stabbing herself in the jugular with her pencil.

"Take your time," said Will to the server, in an attempt to cheer her up. "We're not in a hurry." It was the only thing he could think of to say.

The server didn't even look at Will, but lifted two listless fingers in a "V" that certainly did not stand for victory. "Your meals come with your choice of two vegetables," she said.

Will ordered fried okra and slaw. Sam ordered French fries and macaroni and cheese. "Mac and cheese," she said, clapping her hands. "My favorite vegetable."

"Got it," said the server in a voice of bottomless despair.

When she had slumped away, Will said, "Okay, we ordered."

Sam began to talk about Cat.

◆　◆　◆

AS SOON AS HE HAD PULLED OUT OF THE BARBECUE JOINT PARKING lot, Will called Pen, who answered with lightning speed and by saying, "How is our girl?"

Will smiled. "How" not "where"—even in the middle of their burning quest to find Cat, "how" came first. *That is just so you of you,* Will thought in Pen's direction. He wished he had a better answer for her.

"Still funny, according to Sam," said Will, deciding to start with the positives. "Still 'the cutest little fairy princess person in the whole world.'"

"I assume that's a direct quote?"

"The entire thing was something like, 'How could you and Pen have let the cutest little fairy princess person in the whole world marry that box of rocks?'"

"We tried! We did everything we could, and it only made things worse," protested Pen. "Did you tell her that?"

"I think the question was mostly rhetorical. When I pointed out that Cat hardly ever made up her mind, but when she did, she was about as easy to stop as an elephant stampede, Sam knew what I was talking about."

"So: funny, stubborn, fairy princess," said Pen nervously. "All good, but there's more to it, right? I can tell by your voice."

"Well, yeah," said Will, "I guess there is."

"Tell me that Jason wasn't hurting her."

"No. Nothing like that," said Will.

"Thank God," said Pen vehemently. "I mean, I didn't really think he was, but thank God all the same."

It felt suddenly wrong to be talking to Pen but looking out the windshield at the highway with its ruffle of flimsy trees and occasional cataracts of kudzu on either side, its green signs and billboards (DON'T LET DARWIN MAKE A MONKEY OUT OF YOU said one). For a moment, Will considered heading north, driving without stopping until he got to Philadelphia so that he could sit in the same room with Pen as he told her what Sam had told him about Cat's life since they'd last seen her. Not that it was an unusually tragic story. It wasn't unusually anything, really, and this had struck Will, as he knew it would strike Pen, as the saddest thing about it: their bright star of a friend spending the last six years living a life of ordinary disappointment.

"Tell me," said Pen, sighing, "plain and straight."

"She didn't like living where she lived," said Will.

"Oh, no. Was it awful?"

"Not by most standards. Strip malls, subdivisions, chain restaurants, typical midwestern suburban stuff."

"Hell, by Cat standards, in other words."

" 'Soul-killing' was what Sam said she called it."

"Except, you know what?" said Pen quickly. "It didn't have to be. You know how it is: places are places, but more than anything, they're the people you're there with. So I'm guessing that means she and Jason weren't happy together."

She said this thing about places as though it were self-evident, when it was something Will had never even thought about before. He wasn't sure she was right, not universally right. Certainly, he knew New Yorkers who didn't really believe life happened anywhere else or people in Asheville who couldn't imagine living without hills and co-op groceries and a shiny downtown like something out of a movie. In truth, he suspected that his own mother was one of those people for whom place in and of itself mattered. But, as he considered all of this, Will realized that he agreed with Pen: there were people he could live with anywhere and have that place be home.

"Will?"

"Sorry. Driving."

"Oh, good. Safety first, sonny boy. I need you in one piece."

Will smiled at this. "Getting back to your question about Cat and Jason. I think Jason was pretty happy. Cat wasn't. Sam said she fell out of love a couple of years after they moved to Ohio."

"Nobody falls out of love," scoffed Pen. "They just realize they were never in love in the first place."

"Nobody?"

"Nope. Nobody, nobody. Especially if they're Cat and they're married to Jason."

Will laughed.

"I hate thinking of Cat unhappily married," said Pen. "Cat *hated* being unhappy. Why didn't she just leave him?"

"Well, she did," Will reminded her.

"I mean earlier. What kept her there? They didn't have kids, right?"

"That brings us to the next thing Sam told me."

Sam had cried at this part of the conversation. When Will had gone to the bar and gotten her a fresh napkin to dry her eyes with, she'd only cried harder and ordered him to "Stop being gallant, goddammit."

"It's like what you said," Sam had told him, once she'd settled down. "When she really made up her mind, Cat was unstoppable. Getting pregnant became a project with a capital 'P.' Nothing mattered more. Maybe nothing else mattered, period."

"They had trouble?"

"It just kept not happening. Or happening and then un-happening. Over and over. It wore her to a frazzle, physically, mentally, spiritually. I hated watching it."

"Was it because of the epilepsy?"

"They didn't think so, but they didn't really know. That was the worst of it, not knowing why. She and Jason tried everything, spent thousands of dollars, tens of thousands, on in vitro. And then there were the charts and the Internet support groups and the herbs—chaste tree and cohosh and whatever the hell else—and the acupuncture and the homeopathy. I think she would've tried witchcraft, if there'd been a witch around to show her how, which there wasn't where we live." Sam had taken a long sip of Diet Coke and eyed Will. "You probably have witches where you live."

"Entirely possible," Will had said.

Sam had begun to tear up again, then, waving her white napkin in front of her eyes as if she was either fanning them dry or surrendering.

"I remember the day—and this was just less than a year ago—when she came over to my house to tell me that the doctor had advised them to give up and start looking into adoption. 'Some things just aren't meant to be,' he had told her, like he knew. Like he was God or Fate or whatever. Cat was completely racked with sobs, this little tiny thing in a flowered dress bent over double. Broke my heart. I just gathered her up in my arms like a puppy."

"I'm glad she had you there," said Will.

When he told Pen about this, she said, "I wish we'd been there, Will. My poor, poor, beloved girl. Thank God for Sam." Then she said, "I'm trying to think of how to say something without sounding cold-hearted."

"Like maybe it was nature's way of saying that a guy like Jason has no business trying to transmit his genes in the first place?"

"Ouch!" said Pen. "Not that cold-hearted. Geez, Will. I was thinking more along the lines of: Why would Cat work so hard to have a baby with Jason, when she didn't even like him that much?"

"Oh, that. Yeah, I said the same thing to Sam. And she had apparently, at some point, *not* when Cat was bent double with sobbing—she was clear about that—asked Cat a similar question. Although what she said was something like, 'Do you want a baby so much because you think it will save your marriage?' "

"Bully for Sam. And what did Cat say?"

"Sam said Cat gave her a look like the thought had never occurred to her, and she said, 'This isn't about me and Jason. It's about being a mother. I've been stockpiling love for my baby for years. You can't even imagine how much.' "

"Oh," said Pen. "That's a little disturbing, right?"

"Kind of makes you wonder where Jason fit in."

"I think I need to put that away and think about it later," said Pen. After a silent few seconds, she said, "And then, on top of everything, her dad dies. It must have shattered her."

"It sounds that way," said Will.

Pen growled in frustration, "How could this have happened? When I think about the Cat we knew—. I mean, who ever gave off more light than Cat? Her future should have been shining; it should have been *resplendent*. Or at the very least, fun. I will never, never, in a trillion years understand why she married Jason."

"I'd like to know," Sam had asked Will at one point in their conversation, "what's your take on why Cat married Jason?"

"Who knows?" Will had said. "He was definitely crazy about her. I thought it was a little creepy even, the way he worshipped her, all the presents and the surprise trips and showing up wherever she happened to be. Borderline stalking is what Pen and I thought, but Cat loved it. So maybe that was it. Except that he wasn't the first guy to fall for Cat that way, and he probably wouldn't have been the last."

"She is inherently adorable in every sense of the word," Sam had declared.

"Exactly. But he didn't just adore her. He deferred to her in everything. He asked her advice about any decision he had to make: what to order for dinner, how to vote. It's true that she was smarter than he was, and he was smart enough to know that. Still, it was kind of nauseating to watch. What amazed us was how Cat ate it up."

"Now, don't get mad at me for saying this," said Sam, "but maybe it felt good because maybe no one had ever treated her that way before."

"We listened to Cat," said Will. "We always wanted to hear what she had to say."

"Of course, you did! I do, too. Her take on things is always funny and kind of weirdly brilliant. But I'm talking about asking her advice, looking to her for wisdom and suchlike. That's different, right?"

Will had sat and considered this for a long time. "I don't know. Maybe," he said. "But the thing is that, back then, Cat was, I don't want to say 'careless'—"

"Impulsive?" suggested Sam. "Flighty?"

"Not a lot of looking before she leaped. She got herself into some tough situations that way. So, if we didn't trust her judgment that much, it was probably because she didn't use it very often." Will felt bad saying this, but it was true.

"You want to know what I think?" Sam had raised one very pale eyebrow very, very high.

"Sure."

"Cat married Jason because she wanted a chance to be the grown-up."

Will had set his fork down and stared at Sam, letting this sink in. When it had, his first impulse had been to get defensive, but when he thought past this urge, he had to admit that Sam might be right. When he told Pen about this part of the conversation, she was quiet for a long time, just as he had been, and he could feel her thinking.

When she finally spoke, her voice was subdued, almost ashamed. "Remember how Jason said Cat took care of all the funeral arrangements after her dad died the same way she took care of everything?"

"I do remember that," said Will.

"We babied her, didn't we?"

"We took care of her," said Will. "Everybody did. She was just that kind of person."

"You know what Jamie said once?" said Pen with an embarrassed laugh.

"What?"

"He said that it was like we were the parents and Cat was our child." Pen laughed again. "At the time, I wanted to kill him, but . . ."

Will didn't know how to answer this.

Pen said, "Listen, maybe we took care of her, but if we did—and I'm really trying not to be defensive when I say this—it's because she wanted us to. It was how things were, and it worked."

"But you could see," Will said carefully, "how it could have stopped being what she wanted. And how she couldn't see any other way out of it but to leave."

"Leave?" Pen said. "But we *loved* her."

Pen's voice filled the air inside Will's car, and the pain and sincere bafflement in it sent Will to where he had, for so long, tried to avoid going: back to Pen's tiny kitchen table, to her telling him, with that same painful confusion, that he could not leave—*how* could he leave?—when she loved him. The second he got there, saw her again, with her outstretched hands and her stunned disbelief, he realized that this was who Pen had always been, a person who believed that people who loved each other were different from everyone else, from the world in general, exempt from the usual pressures of time and change, of growing older or of growing up. When it came to love, Will's friend Pen was that rare and dangerous thing: a true believer.

"I want us to find her," said Pen resolutely.

"I figured," said Will.

"Where did she go? Across town? Across the country? Not that any place is too far away to look."

Shit, thought Will, regretting so hard it felt almost like anger that he didn't have an easier answer to give her.

"Across the world," he said. There was nothing to do but say it. "Cebu City, where her dad was born. The Philippines."

CHAPTER THIRTEEN

*P*EN HAD SPENT TWO YEARS WAITING TO BE HAUNTED, AND IT hadn't happened. True, her father was always there, inside Pen's mind, sometimes standing squarely in its center, everything else side-stepping or flowing around him, other times as a reassuring but nearly anonymous presence, like the lit windows of the apartment building across from Jamie's that Pen would look at, parting the curtains of the window next to her bed for a quick glimpse, when she couldn't sleep. Anything—a windbreaker, a bicycle helmet, a man with his hair parted a certain way, the joke the weatherman on Channel 10 made about fog—could send him flaring like a torch into a three-dimensional, walking, talking memory. But if these moments were vivid and if they bruised and embraced Pen at the same time, they were memories all the same, she knew, incorporeal, evanescent. Actually seeing her father or hearing his voice or feeling his hand on her shoulder, even sensing his physical nearness had never happened, no matter how patient she had tried to be, no matter how much she had longed for him to come back to her, even for a second.

The day she and Jamie brought their mother home, entered, for the first time in months, the house they had grown up in, was no differ-ent, though the house even looked sort of haunted, with every shade and curtain drawn and pale sheets over the furniture making a moon-scape of the living room. Pen knew that the Wexlers next door had been coming over now and then to check on things and to adjust the thermostat so that the pipes wouldn't freeze in the winter, and that they had been sending their teenaged son, Alec, to weed Pen's mother's flowerbeds and mow the lawn, but the house had the hollow, echo-filled atmosphere of a long untouched place. Standing in the dim entryway, Pen imagined cobwebs into the corners, even though she knew there wouldn't be any because she knew that, just as Margaret Calloway would never have asked her friend Astrid Wexler to do a little tidying up from time to time, Astrid Wexler would never have not, from time to time, tidied up her friend Margaret Calloway's house.

As she and her mother went room to room, dusting and vacuuming, raising blinds, lifting or cranking open windows so that light cut pathways across the floors and new air drifted in (with Pen dogged, the whole time, by the idea that doing so should have felt a lot more metaphorical than it did), Pen kept a part of her psyche (small, upright, and hyperalert as a meerkat) attuned to the possibility of her father's presence. She had to admit that it made her feel foolish. She had never believed in ghosts, not even as a kid. It was only in bursts that Pen believed in an afterlife at all.

The thing was, though, that if the dead could come back to visit the people they loved, her father was exactly the kind of person who would do it. Alive, he had been a frequent just-to-hear-your-voice telephoner, a daily, one-sentence e-mailer, a base-toucher, a checker-in. Once, he had stopped in the middle of his crack-of-dawn bike ride to call Pen and tell her he'd just seen a flock of birds flying in the whooshing, shoal-of-fish manner that she loved. Pen believed in her heart that anywhere her father was now, even in the most replete and splendid of all possible heavens, he would miss them.

But all that day, he never showed up. Not when Pen opened her parents' closet to hang up her mother's clothes and saw the leather aviator jacket he'd had since college, not when Augusta came clacking out of the garage with her sneakered feet stuffed into a pair of his old bike shoes, not even when Pen opened the door of his office and the great, polished, barren rectangle of his desktop (no computer, no overstuffed folders, no scarred globe, no road atlases, or years-deep stacks of *Science* and *Sports Illustrated*) rose up to break her heart.

Overall, it was a good day. Pen and Margaret cleaned and talked, sometimes shouting, impractically, over the sound of the vacuum cleaner, the way they had always done. ("Will was crazy enough to suggest that we all fly out to the Philippines to find Cat!" Pen hollered. "How crazy is that?" "Not crazy at all!" roared Margaret. "Do it!" "Listen to you!" shrieked Pen. "Globe-trotter! Jet-setter!" "Why are you shouting?" shouted Augusta. "Because they're insane! Total freaking nutjobs, and they're trying to drive us insane, too," yelled Jamie, unplugging the vacuum cleaner, and continuing to bellow into the quiet. "They must be stopped!" "Nutjobs, nutjobs, nutjobs!" sang Augusta at the top of her lungs. "Totally freaking out!")

Jamie got on the phone and had the mail, which had been forwarded to his apartment, unforwarded, restarted the newspaper delivery, telephone service, Internet service, and cable television, upgrading his mother to a premium package on this last one and having the bill sent to him, so horrified was he at her paucity of channels. In the afternoon, he shopped with Augusta, for whom a trip to the grocery store with Uncle Jamie was heaven on earth, and the two of them cooked dinner, noisily, drinking cranberry juice out of wineglasses (Augusta explaining to Pen solemnly and in an uncanny echo of Jamie's voice, "Because you gots to drink-a while you cook-a."). Augusta stood on a kitchen chair, wrapped like a burrito in Pen's father's barbecue apron, and sliced mushrooms with a butter knife, stopping only to literally dance with joy when Jamie did an extended impersonation of a hibachi chef, a performance that occasioned Pen to predict, "You will either chop off your hand at the wrist or drop dead from cultural insensitivity."

Later, after she had sat in the egg chair in her old room with Augusta and read aloud almost a whole chapter of *The Trumpet of the Swan* (after attempting to read a chapter of *Sideways Stories from Wayside School,* which had made Augusta laugh in an unbridled way that Pen feared would spell sleep-doom if it went on for long), and after lying down in the lower bunk with her and singing "Baby Mine" in her best Mrs. Jumbo voice, twice through, and after, in blatant defiance of every "help your kid learn to sleep" book she had ever read, staying with Augusta until she fell asleep, Pen went downstairs and out into the backyard and found her father.

She was headed, a Tupperware container of vegetable peelings in hand, for what had been her enthusiastic father's but was now her reluctant mother's compost tumbler. Like Jamie, Pen's dad was a gadget man, irresistibly drawn to peanut butter stirrers, bagel guillotines, and ergonomic snow shovels as Jamie was drawn to tiny bike handlebar GPS devices and anything with a lowercase "i" at the beginning of its name. A month before he died, Ben Calloway had come home with a contraption that he regarded as being "as pretty as any yard sculpture out there" but which Margaret thought looked like a giant blueberry with legs. The neighborhood association (and Pen, although she never said so) agreed with Margaret, so that the composter sat in the very back of the backyard, near the brick wall of the detached garage, half-hidden much of the year by a Texas beauty queen ball gown of a weeping cherry.

When Pen was about ten feet from the garage, the motion-activated floodlight attached to its roof came stunningly to life, and so as not to be blinded, Pen turned her face away and found herself staring at a creature of such astounding gorgeousness that it took her a few seconds to register what it was. It burned against the green grass, an impossible long, lean pour of orange (*neon paprika*, Pen thought afterward), with a glorious puffed tail as long as its whole body and nearly as big around. A fox.

Pen felt an instinctive jolt of fear, but then the fox turned its head and looked at her, and something happened that she found difficult to describe later, even to herself. It was nothing so simple as looking at the fox and seeing her father. The fox was altogether foxlike and other: precise black nose; extravagantly upright ears; white fur spilling down its front like milk. What regarded Pen through tilted amber eyes was not threatening or alarmed or even particularly wild, but it was surely not Ben Calloway.

However, as Pen and the fox stood with their eyes locked, Pen was suddenly rushed and lifted by the certainty that her father was with her, and this certainty came not only from the fox itself but from the ground under her shoes and the pulse of crickets and the stones of the garage wall behind her. The feeling effervesced delicately as fireflies in the rosebushes and slid with a startling *whomp* off the canted back roof of the house and into the yard, like sheets of snow. The air was alive with it. Not with it, with *him* just as Pen knew him: funniness, geekiness, bravery, a reserve that wasn't so much shyness as a deep sense of privacy, genuine interest, kindness like an ocean. She felt him prickle along her forearms and down the back of her neck. She felt him everywhere.

Joy was a high-pitched vertiginous singing in Pen's ears.

"Daddy," she said and dropped the Tupperware container.

The fox turned and walked into the trees, dragging its tail with the offhand elegance of a duchess dragging her train, and it was over. Pen stood, shaking, in the empty yard. When she could think enough to move, she leaned over, picked up the container, and stepped away from the garage so that the light snapped off and darkness dropped like a sheet over a birdcage. She sat down on the back steps, container on knees, fists on container, forehead on fists, and breathed.

"Are you sick or praying or just weird?"

Pen gave a convulsive start that sent the Tupperware container flying off her knees onto the walkway in front of her and looked up, a little wild-eyed. It was Jamie, back from his evening run.

"Whoa!" said Jamie, pulling the earbuds out of his ears. "Little jumpy tonight?"

"Stop sneaking up on people." Pen picked up the container and threw it at him. It bounced off his knee.

"Ow," said Jamie amiably. He sat down on the grass and pulled his T-shirt by the collar up over his face, wiping off sweat.

"That grass is probably full of mosquitoes," said Pen. "I hope they bite you to bits."

"Nah. They don't like me. You're the one they like."

This was true, and as soon as he said it, Pen felt one bite her upper arm. She slapped at it.

"See?" said Jamie. "What are you doing out here, anyway?"

Experiencing miracles, Pen thought about saying. Instead, she shrugged and said, "Taking the stuff from dinner to the composter."

"Really? Because it looked like you were sitting on the steps in the fetal position."

"Fetuses don't sit," said Pen. "Fetuses recline." She scratched her arm and eyed Jamie. "Can I ask you something?"

"Nope."

"Since Dad died, do you ever feel like he's—?"

"What?"

"I don't know. Around?"

"You mean like a ghost? Tapping on a tabletop, Ouija board kind of thing?"

Pen recognized Jamie's sarcasm for the wariness it was. Being at this house did it maybe, she thought, put Jamie on guard against sudden plunges into grief. She considered giving up and going inside, but who was there to talk to about this, apart from Jamie? Since her mother's return Pen hadn't really brought up her father much. As suspicious as she was of her mother's new, vibrant cheerfulness, she was afraid of its ending.

"Sort of. I mean do you ever feel him with you. With you, with you. Not just like a memory."

To Pen's surprise, Jamie didn't immediately shoot back a mocking response, but leaned back on his hands and appeared to be considering her question. It was something Jamie could do, take you seriously when you least expected it.

"His voice wakes me up sometimes," said Jamie at last. "It doesn't seem like a dream. And I can call it back up for hours, his voice saying whatever he said to me. Sometimes, after it happens, I can hear him all day."

Oh, Jamie. Pen felt, with a rush of urgency, that she needed to have another child and soon. For Augusta. There were some things with which no one should be left alone. Pen wished she could see Jamie's face, but it was too dark.

"What does he say?"

"Nothing profound," said Jamie, with a slight shift away from seriousness that Pen knew was deliberate. "No insights from the great beyond or anything. Mostly stuff he said to me when I was a kid."

"Tell me."

"Well, like once he said, 'Come look at this, Jamie: Fibonacci's sequence in an artichoke.'"

Pen smiled.

"He was here just now," she said tentatively. "It felt like that, anyway. There was a fox in the backyard, and it looked me right in the eye, and then Dad was just—here."

"Dad was a fox?"

"No, and I didn't see him or hear him, but I felt him all around me. That's never happened before."

She waited for him to make fun of her, but, after a moment, he just said, "Nice," and then, "Lucky."

She could see him nodding. With a groan, he got creakily to his feet. *You're a good brother*, thought Pen, *a good man*. She knew better than to tell him this.

"Looking a little stiff there, Grandpa," she said, standing up, too. A mosquito bit her other arm. "Ow," she said and slapped at it.

"Good mosquito," said Jamie.

PEN'S MOTHER HAD FOUND SOMEONE.

Owing to the fact that Pen was engrossed in watching *Foyle's War*, a show she adored, and to her mother's odd use of the word *found* (and also, possibly, to what Amelie would say was Pen's subconscious refusal to believe that her mother had found someone), Pen didn't immediately understand what she meant.

"Was someone lost?" asked Pen sleepily, rubbing her eyes. What had happened in the yard (she hadn't yet figured out what to call it— encounter? experience? visitation?) had sapped her.

"God, Pen," said Jamie.

When she looked over at him, he was glaring at her. Before Pen could make sense of the glare or of Jamie's tone of voice, he jumped up from the sofa where he and Pen sat, strode across the room, and switched off the television. It happened fast. The bright and everlasting calm of Foyle's blue eyes vanished.

"Hey!" said Pen.

Jamie threw open eyes and hands in a gesture that meant, *What the hell is wrong with you?*

Pen looked at Margaret, whose face was bright pink.

"Found someone?" said Pen, slowly. "You mean you—met someone?" Suddenly cold, she wrapped her arms around herself.

Margaret moved a stray curl off her cheek and tucked it behind her ear, a gesture that meant she was nervous.

"Yes," she said. "And no."

"What's that supposed to mean?" said Pen, mounting alarm turning her voice into a kind of bleat.

"Knock it off," said Jamie to Pen. He looked at his mother. "Hey, Mom. You want to sit down or something?"

"I will if you will," said Margaret with a bittersweet smile.

Jamie sat back on the couch, leaving his mother the armchair. She sighed and sat down. Margaret was short compared to Pen and Jamie, whose ranginess came from their father, but she had been a gymnast when she was younger and was still broad-shouldered and full of energy, even when she wasn't moving. But sitting there, on the edge of the chair, her hands clasped, her face full of worry, she looked fragile.

"This won't be easy for you two," she said, but she was looking at Pen. "And the last thing I want to do is hurt you."

"We just want you to be happy," said Jamie.

Under other circumstances, the grave sweetness in his voice would have touched Pen and made her proud of him, but she felt stony and resentful. *Oh, sure, the old good kid/bad kid routine,* she thought acidly. Her stomach was full of knots.

"Thank you," said Margaret quietly. "I didn't think I could ever be happy again. I didn't go looking for it, certainly."

"You didn't?" said Pen. "Why did you leave, then? You must have been looking for something." She would have liked for this to have come out sounding less childish and bitter, but she *felt* childish and bitter.

"What did you think it was?" Her mother sounded genuinely curious.

Pen gave a cranky shrug. "Tibet. India. Rome. What do people usually go looking for in those places? Spiritual enlightenment, I guess. The meaning of life. God."

Pen's mother's laugh was harsh. "God? I was looking for *God*?"

"Why is that funny?"

"Because I was furious with God, when I could bring myself to believe in him at all, which wasn't very often."

"Why did you choose those places, then?" asked Jamie. "You never told us."

His casual tone impressed Pen because the fact was that she hadn't just left out this one detail but had told them almost nothing. She had given them three days' notice that she was leaving (to be fair, this was no more notice than she'd given herself), had a friend drive her to the airport, and had only made phone calls—brief, static-riddled—every few weeks, facts that had hurt and baffled even Jamie.

Their mother's blue eyes were bright with tears. "Right before your dad died, we were talking all the time about traveling."

"And those were places you talked about going?" asked Pen.

Margaret wiped her eyes. "No. We talked about Wales, Brittany, bicycling through Scotland. The Galapagos, Brazil, Paris, Tanzania, Barcelona. So many more places. Your father and his maps."

Something softened in Pen, then, and she met her mother's eyes. *My father and his maps,* she thought. Her mother smiled at her. "What I did was choose places we had *never* talked about going. It wasn't easy."

"But why go at all?" said Pen.

"I was broken," said her mother. Her voice was steady and tender. "I had lost my capacity for anything but sadness. I don't mean to scare you, but I left because I thought I would die, and there was only one tiny part of me that cared, and every day that part got a little bit smaller."

"But it won in the end, right?" said Jamie quickly, still the kid who would read the end of the book before the beginning to make sure it ended happily. "The part that cared."

"It was like in *Horton Hears a Who!*," Margaret said with a sparkle in her eye. "Remember? The tiny part shouted at the top of its lungs for me to do something to save myself, and I almost didn't hear it, but then I did."

"It told you to leave?" asked Pen, narrowing her eyes.

"My girl," said Margaret, "for whom leaving is always the worst thing."

"Leaving *people*," said Pen impatiently.

"It told me to do *something*," said Margaret. "Leaving was the only thing I could think of. I had some money from your father's life insurance. To tell you the truth, I didn't think leaving was a very good idea, either, and I had almost no expectation that it would help, but I couldn't think of one other thing to do. Please try to understand."

The forlorn note in her mother's voice was like a fire blanket, putting out the anger that had begun to smolder inside Pen with one colossal whack. She looked at her mother and saw that since the conversation had started, some of the youthful, sun-streaked radiance she had been carrying in her face since she'd gotten home had faded, and, instantly, desperately, Pen wanted it back. She got off the couch to sit on the floor at Margaret's feet. She grabbed her hand, which was smaller than her own, and kissed it.

"I do understand," she said. "And, look, it did help: you came back happy."

Pen meant it. She did mean it, and she felt glad when she said it. Even so, when Jamie said teasingly, "All right, all right, cut the bonding crap and tell us about this international man of mystery," Pen couldn't help but give a sharp, internal flinch. As if her mother felt it, she rested her hand briefly, protectively on the top of Pen's head.

"I don't know quite where to start," she said, flustered.

"Then start with where," said Jamie.

"Bossy," said Pen. "As usual."

Margaret laughed a free, fluttering laugh. "In an airport in Mumbai. I was going to Vienna. He was going to Rome. Our flights were de-

layed and we got to talking, and I—I . . ." She broke off, blushing
again. Margaret was a blusher, could go from zero to azalea pink in a
matter of seconds. "I changed my flight."

"Mom!" said Pen, laughing. Pen was aware of sadness, out there
and waiting, a big, foggy shape that would surely overtake her later.
Just now, though, she let herself be carried by the current of her mother's happiness.

Jamie whistled. "Must've been some conversation."

"It was," said Margaret, "although it wasn't as though I had anything particular to do in Austria. I was just going to go. But, yes, it
was a good conversation. And we actually did end up going to Vienna
later." The "we" stung, but Pen closed her eyes and breathed past it.

"So you spent a lot of time together," said Pen.

"Yes. He travels for his job. I went with him."

Pen's impulse was to ask her mother how serious this relationship
was, but she weighed the possible consequences of the question—her
mother having a meaningless European fling versus her mother in love
with a stranger—and held back.

"Okay," began Jamie. Pen saw the trace of uneasiness under his
smile. *Oh, just don't,* she thought, but, of course, he did. "How serious
is this?"

"Oh. Well." The way Margaret drew herself up and pressed the
back of her hand against her mouth, she could have been holding tears
or joy or both in check. Pen couldn't tell, but she knew it wasn't the
gesture of a woman who was about to say, "Not serious at all." In a
moment, she moved her hand away and said decisively, "Very."

"You're in love?" asked Pen. She found that she couldn't not ask it.

Margaret nodded, looking so demure with her lashes lowered and
her hands folded in her lap that for a crazy moment, Pen imagined that
the whole scene was ripped from a Jane Austen novel, with Pen and
Jamie as the stern parents and their mother as the rose-fresh, marriage-
able daughter. *Gloves and a fan,* thought Pen, *that's all she needs.*

After a few seconds, Jamie sent these slightly hysterical fancies
flying out the window by saying, "You know what? Dad would be
glad."

Pen remembered the fox in the backyard, her father's kindness reverberating around her, not passive, but powerful, a force, and she had to admit that Jamie was right.

"I have never thought otherwise for one second," said Margaret.

"Not that what Dad would think should've stopped you." This was such a startling statement that, for a second, Pen wondered who could have made it, declared it, really, in that clear, certain voice.

"Holy cluck," said Jamie, staring at Pen. "Did you really just say that?"

"Yes," said Pen, trying to sound sure of herself. "Why? Do you think I'm wrong?"

"Oh, I think you're right," said Jamie. "I'm just not sure if you're you."

"What do you mean?"

"You know," said Jamie. "*You*. The never letting go of stuff. Ever. The insane loyalty."

At the mention of loyalty, Pen felt a little doubt inch in. "You think I'm being disloyal?"

"Of course, you're not being disloyal," said her mother.

"Jamie?" persisted Pen.

Jamie's face tensed, reflecting what was rare for him: an inner struggle. Pen thought he was on the verge of just agreeing with Margaret, but then he said, "I think you're being loyal to *Mom*, which is the way it should be because Dad's dead and Mom's alive. The living win, automatically. Especially if the living is Mom."

It hurt him to say this, Pen could tell, and she understood because she felt the same way: that just acknowledging that Dad was dead, relegating him to that state, lumping him in, however sorrowfully, with other dead people, constituted a kind of betrayal all by itself. Which made her blithe pronouncement that it didn't matter what her father would think about her mother's loving another man even more puzzling.

She considered Jamie's idea, that the living win, automatically. It wasn't exactly what she had been thinking when she'd said what she'd said, but it was such an elegantly simple statement, so translucent and true, while what she had been thinking had been so scattered and unformed (although nonetheless urgent)—more an impulse than a thought—and also so potentially embarrassing to piece together and articulate in the presence of Jamie that Pen just nodded and said, "Right."

WHEN PEN CALLED WILL LATER THAT NIGHT, WHEN SHE GOT TO THIS part of the story, she added, "I said 'right' because Jamie was right, but that's not really what I'd been thinking." It came out in a rush, unplanned. Pen closed her eyes. *Blurter,* she thought with exasperation. *Spiller.*

"Oh," said Will. "So what were you thinking?"

"Will you promise not to make fun of me?"

"Can't do it," said Will.

Pen sighed.

"How about if I promise not to make fun of you *immediately.*"

"Fine," said Pen. It was more than she would've gotten from Jamie. And because she felt suddenly overcome by shyness, she launched into a little conversation with herself inside of her head:

You want to say this thing, she said to herself.

Obviously. The question is why.

You have no idea why, but you want to say it. You need to hear yourself say it out loud.

But why now? And why to Will?

Because you just figured it out, and now is when you want to, and if you want to, why not to Will? He's as good at listening to the things you say as anyone, isn't he?

"Pen?" It was Will. "You still with me?"

"Yes," said Pen decisively.

From where she was sitting on the guest-room bed, she could see a ladybug creeping up the white lampshade on the dresser, and she remembered a story Amelie had told her about ladybugs infesting her aunt's house, how it became like something out of a horror movie, ladybugs everywhere, a scourge of tiny, lacquered bodies, a plague of cuteness. According to Amelie, they bit. Pen thought about telling this story to Will, along with Amelie's interesting assertion that *"anything in huge numbers becomes horrific,"* but she realized it was no time to dither. *Just say what you have to say as clearly as possible,* she instructed herself. *How hard is that?*

"What it comes down to is that I just don't see it as a choice. I mean, not really," she said.

"You don't?"

"Well, of course, technically, it's a choice. Free will and all that crap. Cartesian, right? Free will? Like the plane, I guess. René. It's a name a man can only pull off if he's French. But just because you get to choose doesn't mean there isn't one right choice. Right?"

"Descartes thought the pineal gland was the seat of the soul," said Will.

"That's disgusting."

"It's not what you think."

"Of course, there are situations in which it's the wrong choice," Pen went on, "for the same reason that anything is the wrong choice: you hurt people, you break promises. Although I suppose that not everyone would agree with that."

"Maybe not."

"But if you're not hurting anyone, then I think you have no choice but to, well, honor it."

"Honor? What do you mean honor?"

"Acknowledge it. Follow it. Chase it. Hold on to it. Whatever."

There was a silence on the other end of the line, during which Pen watched the ladybug fly, a black blur, from the lampshade to the curtain of the window next to the bed.

Will said, "All right, I give up."

"What?"

"I'm not getting it. Your pronoun reference."

"What are you talking about?"

"The 'it.' I need a real noun. The right choice, the thing you follow, hold on to, et cetera."

"Love," said Pen impatiently. "What else would I be talking about?"
Another silence.

Finally, Will said, "So you're saying, 'Love wins, automatically.' "

"No. Well, maybe. Except that makes it sound easy when it's not.
Or not most of the time. It's stringent. Exacting," said Pen. "I think
love is an imperative. It obligates you."

"You think that because your mother fell in love with this man, she
should be with him, even if your father would not have approved."

Pen recoiled from this, leaning back against the pillow propped
against the headboard, but she said, "Yes. Even if it's hard. My mother.
This man. Anyone. And I'm not just talking about being in love. I
mean any kind of love. You don't mess around. You don't walk away.
You can't."

"Can't. Can't is hard-core."

"It's what we're here for," explained Pen. "It's what we're *for*."

Pen realized that her face was burning, that the phone was pressed
so hard between her ear and shoulder that she would probably have
bruises, and that she was clenching the quilt that lay spread over
the bed underneath her until her tendons popped out. Deliberately,
she relaxed, released the quilt, cradled the phone in her hand, but as
the silence between her and Will stretched on, she began to get anxious, fidgety.

"I think this is the good kind of ladybug," she said. "It's a true red.
Like a Red Delicious apple. Or lipstick. Porsche-red. I'm pretty sure
the infesting kind are more orange. And anyway, it's summer."

"Pen."

"They only go inside in groups in the cold weather. What's the
word for that?"

"Hibernation?"

"Overwintering."

"You thought I would make fun of you?"

"Jamie would. Amelie would. Maybe even my mom would. They'd
call me a romantic."

Will laughed. " 'Love is an imperative'? Not exactly hearts and
roses stuff. You make it sound like joining the army."

"I guess."

"And, hey, look at that," said Will. "I was right."

"About what?"

"About what your mom had to tell you. Remember when I was on my way to see Sam and I was talking to you?"

"On your Bluetooth phone," said Pen quickly, "with both hands on the wheel."

"Even if that's not what she went looking for, it's what she brought back and gave you."

"What?" Then she said quietly, "Oh, I know. I remember."

"What?"

"The meaning of life." Pen looked up and caught her reflection in the full-length mirror on the back of the guest-room door. She was smiling. Not even the sight of her face, lit up and smiling into an empty room, made her stop smiling. Pen thought back to the conversation she had had with herself a few minutes earlier, when she'd said that if she had something to say, she might as well tell Will. As if she'd picked him at random. As if she could have told anyone else.

Time to tell the rest.

"You'd think that I would've gotten to enjoy it for a while," she said. "Knowing the meaning of life. You know, rest on my laurels."

"What happened?"

"It got put to the test. My meaning of life! Challenged! Tested! Can you believe that? After, what? Thirty seconds? How unfair is that?"

"What happened?" said Will again, and Pen knew that he wasn't fooled by her joking tone, as he should not have been. Even now, nothing about what had happened next in her conversation with Jamie and her mother struck her as funny.

She told him, then, how Jamie had said, "Do we get to meet him?" and how something in her mother's face after he asked it made Pen remember herself asking, "You met someone?" and her mother saying, "Yes. And no."

Before her mother could answer Jamie's question, Pen jumped in with, "What did you mean before: 'Yes. And no'? What did you mean when you said you 'found' someone? Why 'found'?"

Pen's mother smiled at Pen, the lines of her face holding affection and worry and something that looked like pleading. "You know why, don't you?" she said.

Pen was still sitting on the floor and she shifted, now, slightly away from her mother. "Why, but not who," she said bluntly.

Jamie looked from his mother to Pen and back, confused. "Did I miss something?"

"I was seventeen when I met your dad," said their mother. "It was my gift, my blessing to love him and no one else for forty years. If I had my way, that would have gone on forever."

"You don't even have to say those things, Mom," said Jamie, surprised.

"I want you to understand." She was looking at Pen.

"Okay," said Pen. She knew it wasn't enough, that the moment demanded more from her, but she felt so physically tense with waiting, her rib cage tightening and tightening, that it was hard to breathe. The name hovered around them. The air in the room was thick with it. She just needed it said.

"Who is he? Someone from high school? Someone you grew up with?" Pen asked, and she marveled at this for a moment, the possibility that someone you knew forty, fifty years ago could circle back into your life and make you fall in love with him.

Pen's mother slumped a little at this. She shook her head.

"Could you please just tell us?" said Pen.

"Mark Venverloh."

Pen stared at her mother. She opened her mouth, but no sound came out.

"Mr. V?" said Jamie in a choked voice. "You're in love with Mr. V?"

It seemed impossible, but of course, it wasn't. Pen didn't know why it hadn't occurred to her: that the man wasn't someone from her mother's distant past, that he was someone they all—even their father, their father *especially*—had known.

"Mr. Venverloh," said Pen, who had never called him "Mark" and was only vaguely aware that it was his name at all. Saying the name out loud failed to make her mother's loving him any more plausible.

To Will, Pen said, "Mr. *Ven*verloh. Can you believe that?"

"I can't if you say I can't," he said. "But I don't think I know who that is."

Pen considered this and realized it was true. Her dad hadn't started working for Mr. Venverloh until after Will and Cat had left. Unexpectedly, this realization filled Pen with sorrow, and for once in what seemed like forever, she wasn't sad on her own behalf. Cat and Will had had their reasons for leaving, but whatever they were (Pen still didn't understand them, only believed—still, eternally—that whatever they were, they weren't good enough), they had nothing to do with Ben Calloway, who had loved them unreservedly, just as they had loved him. And they had lost each other all the same. Incidental loss. Collateral damage. But permanent. Will and Cat had missed out on the last four years of Ben's life. Ben had spent the last four years of his life missing them. It was enough to break your heart.

"He loved you," said Pen. "He missed you." She hoped there was no reproach in her voice. She didn't feel reproachful, only sad.

Will didn't say, "Mr. Venverloh loved me?" He said, "I know. I wish I could see him again."

"You know my dad was an environmental engineer for the city for years, mainly in the water department, and he liked it a lot. It suited him: part environmentalist, part science geek. Then Mr. Venverloh started riding bikes with my dad's group about five years ago. He's rich, crazy rich actually, owns a big estate nearby."

"One of the baronets?" asked Will.

It was something she, Will, and Cat had always joked about, how little Wilmington, Delaware, birthplace of more than one gigantic corporation, was like something out of the nineteenth century or earlier, with a true landed gentry. "This place is more Middlemarchian than Middlemarch!" Cat had quipped.

"Yes," said Pen, "but he has a real job, too. Some finance thing. Anyway, he and my dad got to be friends, and when Mr. V's land manager retired, he asked my dad if he wanted the job."

"Land manager. That sounds so—"

"Feudal. I know. But my dad loved it: sustainable agriculture, native plants, eliminating invasive species, and he got to be outside. You know he grew up on a farm."

"I did know that."

"So that's my mom's new boyfriend. Mr. Venverloh. Mark. *Mark.* God."

"I can think of a lot of reasons why that might be tough for you," said Will.

"It's tough for Jamie, too. He didn't let on to my mom, of course, but later he told me that he wished it were someone who hadn't been in Mom and Dad's life. Jamie said that even though he knew it didn't really, he *felt* like it cast a shadow backward, memory-wise. He couldn't really explain that, but I think I sort of know what he means."

"Do you feel like that, too?"

"Not now, I don't think. I don't know. I think I like it that it's someone who cared about my father, who knew him. My dad liked him, too. He's nice, Mr. Venverloh. The thing that hurts—well, a lot of it hurts, to tell you the truth—but the thing that hurts right now—and I know this is probably stupid—is that, on paper, he—" It hurt even to say it.

Will bought her some time by saying, "Does he own a jet? That's all I really want to know."

Pen laughed. "My dad was the best man in the world, you know that, right?"

"Yep."

"But Mark Venverloh looks, to the untrained eye, like a—step up. Possibly even a gigantic one."

"Richer," said Will.

"And better dressed, which let's face it, isn't saying that much. And handsomer."

"Your dad was a good-looking man."

"He was, but he was regular-guy-handsome, not movie-star-handsome. I feel sort of sorry for my dad, and feeling sorry for him makes me feel terrible."

"I bet your mom doesn't think he's a step up."

"Of course not!"

"And I bet your dad could've handed him *and* his ten-thousand-dollar bike their asses in a mass start hill climb."

Pen smiled. *This is why I love Will Wadsworth,* she thought.

"On a platter," she said.

LATER THAT NIGHT, CLOSER TO MORNING REALLY, THE DOUBLE whammy of the fox and Mr. V having electrified Pen's usual insomnia so that the inside of her head was beehive-crowded, bristling with light, and a million miles away from sleep, Pen went downstairs to get herself some tea and was surprised to see lamplight coming from the family room. She looked in and saw Margaret tucked into one corner of the big sofa reading a book, and the sight of her made Pen catch her breath. She looked purely alone but content, as complex and self-contained as a Russian doll, inward and inward and inward. As Pen watched, her mother smiled a private smile at something in her book, and Pen thought she had never seen anything so incandescently lovely as her mother alone, until her mother glanced up and saw her and shut her book and became lovelier still, open-faced and alive.

Pen thought, *You are like me. You like your little pockets of solitude, but you're not made for being alone for long.* There were people who could live on their own and be happy, and then there were people like Pen and Margaret who needed the falling together, the daily work of giving and taking and talk and touch.

Even so, love? Commitment? Again? How much easier to just settle into a life of family and friends, of dating even, of traveling and reading and being at peace. She felt happy for her mother, but she felt scared for her, too.

"Come here, baby," said Margaret, and Pen sat down next to her and rested her head against her shoulder.

"I'm happy for you, Mom," said Pen. "I really am."

"I'm glad," said her mother. Then she added, "Mark wants us all to come to dinner at his house. He wants to know you and Jamie and Augusta, and for us to know his boys. He has three sons."

Agree, Pen told herself, *just suck it up and say yes.* But she pictured them, sitting around an enormous table, a chandelier sparkling overhead, casting its coins of light over them all, turning them into a family, and she could only think, *Oh, Daddy.*

She kissed her mother's shoulder. "Is it all right if I say 'Yes, but not quite yet'?"

"Can you say 'Soon'?"

Pen had to smile. Of all the things her mother was, she had never been a pushover.

"Yes," said Pen, closing her eyes. What else was there to do? "Soon."

CHAPTER FOURTEEN

*T*HREE DAYS AFTER HIS LUNCH WITH SAM, WILL STILL HADN'T told Jason what he'd found out about Cat's whereabouts. He knew that he should. He knew that even Pen, who had, during more than one phone conversation, argued vehemently (and cantankerously) against telling him, knew that they should, even if she hated to admit it.

"We told him we would try to help him," Will had reminded her the night before. "We wouldn't have even known to call Sam if it weren't for him."

"We didn't *promise* that we'd tell him what she said," Pen had countered.

"The promise was implied."

"That's not how promises work," scoffed Pen. "They aren't implied. They're overt. There's a universally accepted method to them."

"And what's that?"

"You say, 'I promise.' Especially if the person asks you to promise, which Jason distinctly did not do."

"Maybe he didn't think he had to."

Will had waited, then, for Pen's innate sense of justice to come to the fore or, if not come to the fore, at least to start nagging her like an itch.

"It *might* be different if we actually knew where she was now," she had said finally, grudgingly. "We only know where she used to be: the name of a hotel, where she's probably not even staying anymore. We don't even know if she's still in the same city. When it comes right down to it, we don't even know if she's in the same country!"

"She told Sam fifty-nine days, which leaves her with about twenty-five to go."

"She's *allowed* to stay for fifty-nine. That doesn't mean she will. She's *Cat*, remember? She's whimsical. She might have changed her mind last week and headed to Australia to see a wallaby. She might be sailing around the world this minute on some guy's yacht."

"Don't you get the idea that this trip was serious for Cat, though? Not some wacky adventure?"

"Maybe. Yes." She made an exasperated cat-hiss noise. "Okay, but even so, she might not be where she was when she called Sam. It's a big country, right? I mean, not relative to this country, but relative to Cat, it's big. I googled it, and it has, like, seven thousand islands. She could be on any one of them."

"I googled it, too, and I'm pretty sure that a lot of those islands don't have people on them. They're basically just bumps in the ocean."

"Really? I didn't know that. What else did you find out?"

"Well, some people say that the number of islands changes, depending on the tide, although that could just be a myth."

"Hmm, I bet it's not a myth. What do you think?"

"I think you should hold it right there, Penelope."

"What?"

"You think I don't recognize a diversionary tactic when I hear one?"

"From what would I be trying to divert you?" asked Pen innocently.

"The fact that none of this really matters. The exact number of islands in the archipelago that is the Philippines doesn't matter."

"Maybe not to you, Yankee," interjected Pen, "but the Filipinos might care."

Will ignored this. "How whimsical or not whimsical Cat is doesn't matter, either. Neither does her exact location at this very second. We still have to tell Jason what we found out. It's only fair."

"What about what's fair to Cat?" snapped Pen. "She doesn't want him to find her. She doesn't like him."

Will had smiled. "Come on, she might *like* him."

In the turbulent silence that followed, Will had imagined that he could hear Pen struggling with her conscience the way he was struggling with his.

"Look, I know she doesn't want him to find her," Will had said finally. "Why do you think I didn't e-mail him right away?"

"No, you're right, you're right," said Pen grimly. "We'd be jerks not to tell him."

"We'll be jerks either way, when you think about it."

"Don't think about it," growled Pen. "Just send Jason the damn e-mail."

"At least if we tell him, we can be jerks taking the high road."

"Great," said Pen. "Very comforting."

However, that conversation had taken place the night before, and it was now almost noon, and Will was still treating his e-mail account as though it were radioactive. Not only his e-mail, but his entire computer, which meant that he was trying to write his novel (about a boy whose scientifically-doctored-with doghouse transports him into the mind of a twelve-year-old giant named Lulu) at the kitchen table with pencil on a pad of paper. This never worked for him before, and it didn't work now. He liked to see the words on the screen. He liked to delete words and have them be gone, extinguished, annihilated. When his pencil lead broke, he threw it across the room, aiming for the trash can, which was closed because it was always closed. It had a stainless-steel, spring-loaded lid, the kind that stays closed. Still, when the pencil bounced off the lid, fell on the floor, and rolled under the refrigerator, Will took it personally.

"Jesus. Fine," he hollered at the trash can.

There were seven messages from Jason in his inbox, their subject headings comprising a tidy narrative of Jason's frustration. The oldest one said "Hey man!"; the second newest, "WTF?" The most recent was the longest: "Once a dick . . . ," which struck Will as mildly funny by ordinary standards and mind-blowingly clever when you considered the source. He thought about opening that one to see if Jason had actually finished the sentence, but he deleted the e-mails without reading them and started a new one. At about the middle of the second paragraph, though, it hit him: Jason might never write back. What was there to stop him from grabbing the information and running? Will had to admit that, after waiting so long to fill Jason in, he probably deserved this, but it wouldn't work. He needed to witness Jason's reaction. He needed to know what he would do.

Will scratched his head, hissed "Shit," shot a malevolent look at his cell phone, and typed, I have some info about Cat. Give me a call, followed by his telephone number, which he stabbed in hard with one resentful but fatalistic finger. After he clicked Send, he got up to get himself a cup of coffee (actually, he jumped out of his chair like it was on fire), but the phone rang before he had even opened the cabinet where he kept the mugs. Cursing under his breath the whole way, he walked back to his office where he'd left his phone.

"Hello," he said and braced himself for a loud tirade, but Jason was surprisingly calm, even—disturbingly—friendly.

"Yo, dude," he said. "I thought you'd never call."

Will decided not to point out that Jason was the one who had called. He said, "Sorry, man. It's been a little crazy around here."

"No worries, no worries. Just glad you're not dead."

"Thanks."

"So . . ." Jason stretched the word out like gum and pronounced it "Sue."

Right there? That? Will told Jason inside his head. *That's why nobody likes you.*

Aloud, he said, "I saw Sam at that barbecue joint in Tennessee."

In an act of blatant procrastination, Will considered how he never used the word *joint* to mean "place," except when it came to barbecue. Or maybe gin. No, not gin. Who was he kidding? Burger? He looked out the window at the birdbath, which was empty, causing him to question, in a perfunctory manner, the hygiene of the local bird population. Jason breathed, audibly, into Will's ear. It still wasn't too late to hang up. Change his cell-phone number. Move.

"Hel-lo?" said Jason. "You saw Sam. What'd you think?"

"I liked her. I mean, she's a little, uh, theatrical, but she seems solid underneath all that. And funny. I can see how she and Cat would end up friends."

"Yeah, she hates me," said Jason casually and with a notable lack of malice. "Thinks I'm a pathetic idiot."

"Oh," said Will. "That's . . . too bad."

"Naw. No skin off my back. No problemo, you know what I mean?"

Neyeeeewww problemo. Will shut his eyes, overcome by nostalgia for the days when a phone receiver was substantial enough to effectively bang against your forehead.

"Anyway, we talked about Cat," he said.

"Take it with a grain of salt, that's all I have to say," said Jason. "Whatever Sam says requires a major grain. Not just grain, *grains*. Many a grain."

"Right," said Will and was busy making a mental record of "many a grain" for when he told Pen about the conversation later when it hit him that, in addition to mocking what Jason had just said, he could use it. "And that's exactly how I took everything she told me. She might know what she's talking about, but then again, she might not."

"She might be full of shit."

"Definitely possible." Will sent out a silent apology in what he estimated was Sam's direction.

"So, uh, what'd she say, anyway?"

Jason did not sound like a person who had begged abjectly for help in the moonlight or one who had shot off six e-mails in three days, jam-packed with escalating anger. His voice was nonchalant, bordering on breezy. It said, *Dude, since you happen to have gotten me on the phone and I have a sec, dude, you might as well, you know, tell me what you know:* the voice of an obsessed and desperate man desperately trying not to sound obsessed and desperate, maybe not the most pathetic sound Will had ever heard, but one of them. How could he tell this sad man where Cat was? How could he not? Will picked up a pen and wrote "Shit" three times on the back of an old envelope.

"She's in the Philippines," he said. "Cebu."

"Motherfucker!" The word slammed into Will's ear, more bark than yell, so venomous, so searingly vicious that Will jerked the phone away from his ear. Jason hung up.

For a dazed second, Will stared at the phone in his hand. Then, hurriedly, he began to flip through the possibilities. Was the expletive free-floating, an expression of frustration in general? At how far away Cat was? Will didn't think so. It sounded personal, directed, like that venom that snakes in Africa spit straight into the eyes of their enemies. But who was Jason spitting at? Will? Sam? Probably not, although Jason wasn't above being a "shoot the messenger" kind of guy. Cat's dad? Will remembered the conversation in the reunion tent, how Jason had said that Dr. Ocampo wasn't exactly a person who showed up for Cat. Pretty clearly, Jason hadn't been crazy about the man, had probably not liked him enough to be thrilled about Cat's going on a pilgrimage to his homeland, but he hadn't seemed to hate him, either, and that "motherfucker" had been all about hate.

Could he have meant it for Cat? Not Cat. Jason loved Cat. But who else was there?

"Shit," said Will again, this being a shit kind of morning, and he scrambled to call Jason back, dropping his phone in the process. As he picked it up, it rang.

"Sorry to hang up like that," said Jason with a hollow chuckle. "Guess what you said threw me off a little."

"Yeah, I guess so," said Will evenly.

"I just pictured my little Cat, all by herself in the tropics. And the traveling? The multiple plane changes and what have you? Forget about it. Cat gets lost on the way to the grocery store. I had this vision of her wandering around the Hong Kong airport like a lost kitten."

Will didn't buy it. Jason's "motherfucker" had been instantaneous, like a gun going off, with no time for him to picture much of anything. Anyway, the Cat Will had known had had as good a sense of direction as anyone. Pen was the one who got lost. Then there was Jason's tone of cheerful concern, which would've been creepily inappropriate, even if it hadn't been so obviously fake. Will knew a thing or two about rage, and he felt the rage seething under everything Jason said. Even as Jason fussed like a mother hen about his "little Cat," Will would've bet that he had just thrown something heavy across the room and watched it smash.

"It makes sense that you'd be worried," said Will neutrally.

"Plus, I thought she was over her dad. His death, I mean. Come to find out she's zipped off ten thousand miles to do what? Mourn at his birthplace? Get to know him? Discover her island roots?"

"Yeah, I guess she's not over it."

"Ya think?"

He's going to go after her, Will thought.

"What are you thinking?" he asked. "That you'll go look for her?"

There was a silence and then, with the good-guy tone turned up a notch, Jason said, "Nah. My wife wants some alone time. I can respect that. I'll just hang out, hold down the fort, as they say, until she's back."

It was exactly the right answer, and Will knew a lie when he heard it.

As soon as he hung up with Jason, Will called Pen.

"Hey, Will," she said. Her voice, hushed and quick, told him she was with someone, probably a client. "Call you back in an hour or two?"

"Sure," said Will. "Wait. Actually—" But Pen had already hung up.

Maybe it was better, Will thought, take a couple of hours, settle down, get some perspective. He could admit that, on its face, his reaction to Jason's reaction had been a little extreme, since all Jason had done was get mad, something Will had done plenty of times himself. A guy who had flat out attacked a whole slew of inanimate objects—and several animate ones—with his bare hands, whose temper had landed him (if not, by the grace of God, other people) in the emergency room more than once, should be able to cut Jason and his single outburst some slack. After all, the poor sap had just found out that his wife hadn't just walked out on him but had pretty much walked as far away from him as it was possible to go—and all without leaving so much as a note.

Still, Will couldn't shake the foreboding. It was as if that single, knee-jerk "motherfucker" had punched a hole in Jason's dopey-guy demeanor, and, through it, Will had glimpsed an interior that was uglier than he would've believed. Will's mother was always telling her kids to "listen to your inner voice," and Will's inner voice was practically shouting that Jason's heading off to find Cat with all of that ugliness churning just under his surface was a very bad idea.

Will looked at the clock: 12:45, about seven hours later than Will's preferred time for a run, especially in the summer, but he had a couple of hours to kill and there was no way he was getting any work done before he talked to Pen. He changed, zipped his cell phone into his pocket, gulped down a glass of water, and headed out. It was so muggy that his shirt was sticking to him before he'd gone a mile, but running had been a good idea. His worry unclenched, stretched and flattened like the hot ribbon of street, resolved itself into a flow of thought that was steady and more or less coherent.

Even though he knew it was the middle of the night where she was, he imagined Cat under the same high white sun that burned above him, making her way through a busy city. He had no trouble bringing Cat to life inside his head, he never did, her black hair and thin wrists and sandals, glamour-girl sunglasses covering half her face, a flowered dress. And even though he couldn't picture the city with any accuracy, had never even seen photos of it that he could remember, he sketched it in around her anyway: fruit stands, traffic, palm trees splayed against the sky, a goat tethered to a stake in somebody's yard. Cat was there, a girl on a mission, walking where her father had walked, looking for what?

Will came to the kind of hill that makes it impossible to think or do anything but force your body up it, but on the way down, inside his head but so clearly that he was tempted to look around to see who said it, Will heard a question being asked in a familiar voice: "How did your dad get to be your dad?" It took him only a second to realize the voice was Cat's.

The last day of sophomore year. Finals behind them and everywhere spring hitting its peak and toppling over into summer: humidity, old oak pollen balled like tumbleweed in the gutters, every kid on campus newly tan and as abundantly, showily happy as the trees were dense and green, except for Will who sprawled sullenly on the grass, the cast on his newly broken hand pissing him off with its whiteness, Cat next to him with her sunglasses on top of her head (she thought it was hideously rude to have a conversation with someone while wearing sunglasses) and her pink skirt tucked primly around her crossed legs.

His parents had swung through town the day before on their way to meet a bunch of other rich couples—friends of his father's—for a golf weekend at a southern mountain resort (the fact that his mother hated the resort, the couples, and golf evidently having no bearing on his father's decision to take her along or on her decision to go). Things went about the way they usually went between Will and his dad, except that this time, after the obligatory post-paternal-visit fistfight with something immovable and hard (in this instance, his car windshield), in addition to the usual breakage (spirit, dignity), Will had thrown in a few cracked metacarpals for good measure.

Cat and Will were drinking iced coffee and waiting for Pen, who was meeting with her nineteenth-century British lit professor to discuss a paper she'd written on images of women's hair in Victorian poetry, despite a horrified Cat's having pointed out to her that nobody, nobody, nobody in all of human history had ever made an appointment with a professor to discuss a paper she'd gotten an "A" on, especially on the last day of school before summer break. "He will be flabbergasted. Flummoxed," warned Cat. "He will almost definitely keel over and die right there in front of you." But Pen had gone anyway.

"How did your dad get to be your dad?" asked Cat suddenly. "Have you ever thought about that?"

"You mean how did he meet my mom?"

"No," said Cat impatiently. "I mean how did he get to be *your dad* in all his awful your dadness? How did he become the man he is?"

Will found that the question irritated him. "Does it matter?"

"Don't get testy with me, mister," said Cat, giving him what Pen called her "mad Persian cat face." "I'm not talking about an excuse because nothing gets him off the hook for being the rat bastard he is. I'm talking about an explanation. Where did he *come* from? How does someone *get* so mean?"

Oddly, Will had never really considered this question before, his father's meanness having always been one of the immutable bedrock facts of Will's life. With his family, Randall Wadsworth was either distant and indifferent or the coldest kind of cruel, and although there had always been moments when Will watched his father talk to other men and change into someone else, joking, backslapping, affable, the real man was still right there—Will could sense him—invulnerable and dangerous and enjoying his power.

"I don't think he *became*," said Will. "I think he was just born."

"Come on," said Cat. "He was a kid, right? He went to school. Drank chocolate milk. Wore pajamas."

"I don't think so."

"Even Hitler was, like, seven once, Will. There had to be a moment."

"A moment when he turned into a fucking, soulless monster?"

"No. A last chance that someone missed. A moment when he could've been saved."

The only evidence Will had that his father had ever been a child was a handful of memories of a visit to his father's mother's house. Will must have been about three or four, and he had stayed, alone, at his grandmother's for what had seemed like a long time, but was probably only a couple of days. The memories were more like fragments, tiny sensory scraps: a turquoise-and-white metal porch glider; the sound of the television going all day long in another room; crescent rolls that popped out of a cardboard cylinder and tasted like heaven; the silky edge of a scratchy blue acrylic blanket; and smoking, a lot of smoking: a cigarette perpetually balanced on the edge of a shell-shaped ashtray on the kitchen counter; his grandmother snapping beans on the porch with a cigarette somehow stuck between her fingers, sending the smell of smoke across the front yard to where Will dug in the mulch with a plastic trowel.

"She wasn't mean? Abusive?" asked Cat, when Will told her about this.

"Not to me."

"You liked her."

"I think so. Her house seemed—safe. Pretty soon after I went there, she died. I don't know how I know that, though. I can't remember going to a funeral or anything."

"What did your dad say about her, over the years?"

"Nothing."

"Nothing?"

"My dad isn't the storytelling type," said Will sardonically. "He doesn't spin yarns. When he does talk about growing up, it's like he's reading his résumé. The boarding school he got himself into in ninth grade, his whole thousand-mile-long record of achievement after that. His mother is nowhere, totally erased."

"What about his father?"

"No idea. Maybe he never had one."

"Maybe it was Satan," suggested Cat.

Will grinned. "That would explain things, wouldn't it?"

Cat's eyes grew serious. She touched her fingertips to Will's, the ones that emerged from the plaster of the cast. "Maybe you'll want to dig a little deeper one day," she said. "If you knew more about him, maybe he'd lose his power to hurt you." Even though Will didn't believe this, he heard the kindness in Cat's voice and felt the force of her friendship, her allegiance to him, and he thought, not for the first time, *You are my family, more than the rat bastard has ever been, you and Pen.*

Now, thinking about Cat searching for her father, Will realized that he had never searched for his, had never taken her advice. He'd had his mother back for years and had never asked her anything about who his father used to be, never even asked about the trip to his grandmother's house. Why had Will gone by himself? Where was that house, apart from inside Will's head, turning itself into myth? It was crazy: to visit a place once and spend your whole life missing it.

I might ask, he thought. *One of these days. Maybe after I come back from finding Cat.*

Which is when he knew that he would go. *Yeah, right.* He could almost hear Cat saying this. *Like there was ever any doubt.*

WHEN PEN CALLED, BEFORE WILL COULD SAY ANYTHING BESIDES, "Hey, Pen," she said, "Okay. I have a story and a question. In that order."

"Is it a long story?"

"What kind of question is that?"

"I have something to say, too, believe it or not," said Will, "which is why I called you."

"I called you."

"You're calling me back."

"Of course. You're right. Your story should take precedence, absolutely," said Pen. "But can I go first, anyway?"

"Okay."

"It is kind of a long story if you want to know the truth."

"Forget it, then."

"I just saw Patrick."

"Is that unusual?"

"I mean I sat across from him at a table at a café and had a conversation with him."

"Which is—unusual?"

"Highly. Ours is an Augusta-drop-off-pick-up relationship. That's about it."

"I see," said Will. "Hey, if I met Patrick, would I like him or would I want to slug him?"

"Yes," answered Pen emphatically, adding, "But I thought you were over the slugging thing."

"Over slugging, not over wanting to. I probably wouldn't want to slug Patrick, though, because I'm guessing Augusta wouldn't like it."

"Augusta," began Pen, and for a second, she sounded on the verge of tears.

"You okay?"

"Possibly. I'm not sure. I just left him about five minutes ago, so I haven't had much of a chance to sort things through."

Will was trying to stay neutral and open-minded, but he had to admit that he liked the sound of "left him."

"You want to talk about this later?" he asked.

"God, no. How will I ever sort it out if I don't talk to you about it?"

She'd been on her way to drop Augusta at day camp and run a couple of errands afterward when he called. When she looked at her cell phone and saw that it was Patrick, she let Augusta answer it.

"I am going to camp right now," Augusta announced in her cell-phone voice, painstakingly enunciated and somewhere between a shout and a bellow. "We are having baking today, but I won't be able to bring you any cookies because, generally, we eat them." *Generally* was her new word. "Iloveyoubyebye," she yelled and handed the phone to Pen.

"Let me call you back after I drop her off," said Pen. She cherished these mornings, walking through the city with Augusta, talking, feeling the delicate, stalwart bones of her daughter's hand inside hers, new light washing the sidewalks.

"Do you have any time today?" asked Patrick.

"For what?"

"To talk."

"You mean in person?"

Patrick gave a halfhearted laugh. "Why do you make it sound like such an outlandish idea? We talk in person all the time."

Pen ignored this. "I need to do a few things, stop in at the office, but I should be home around eleven. Okay if I call you then? I have to pick up a writer at five thirty, but I have some time in the middle of the day."

"Well, yeah. Don't want to put you out or anything." Pen could hear the pout in his voice. "Just call when you get home."

But when she got home, before she even got to her apartment building door, there he was, sitting at a sidewalk table at the café across the street, waving her over.

Will lay on his back on his front porch listening to this because Pen had called just as he was rounding the corner onto his street after his run, and he was too sweaty to lie anywhere else. The porch wasn't particularly comfortable, but Will was too engrossed in Pen's story to mind the porch boards grinding into his spine and shoulder blades. When a fly started buzzing around his head, he swatted at it absently, without fully registering what it was or even that it was there. In the old days, he and Pen had never really gotten the hang of phone conversations; they were together too much. Now, though, they had it down to a kind of art. With not a lot of effort, Will could close his eyes while Pen talked and have what she said come alive inside his head. At times, her descriptions were so vivid, it was almost like watching a movie, so that, in short flashes, he could even picture Patrick, whose face he'd never seen.

Patrick was sitting at the café table nursing a beer, a bad sign, Pen knew, since Patrick never drank in the daytime; it made him too sleepy.

After the waiter brought Pen an iced tea, she said, "All right, Patrick, what's up?"

"What's up is that Tanya got a job offer from this big-time health advocacy group, and she wants to move us to Boston."

Move us, thought Pen, as though Patrick and Lila were pieces of furniture, such a maddeningly apt choice of words that Pen didn't know whether to laugh or scream. She did neither, just sat there for a long, silent moment, feeling like a pond that Patrick had just dropped a rock into.

"What about," she said at last, in a flinty voice, "your daughter? Your other daughter, I mean." She felt the same jolt of anger she'd felt so many other times because she knew that the "other daughter" was who Augusta was and would always be, to Tanya but also—and there was no getting around this, no matter how much he loved her—to Patrick.

She waited for Patrick to defend Tanya, but he surprised her by getting angry instead, angry at Tanya. Patrick almost never got angry at anyone. Pen could never decide if it was due to inner peace or laziness or a kind of emotional ADD, but, whatever the reason, it just wasn't in his nature to get mad.

"It was almost comical," Pen told Will. "Like when one of those adorable, shaggy lap-doggy dogs with chocolate-drop eyes thinks he hears a burglar and starts barking? That was Patrick, except blue-eyed. An enraged Lhasa apso. A choleric cocker spaniel."

"Wow," said Will. "Could you do me a favor and never describe me? To anyone?"

"You want to know the sad thing, though? I liked it. I loved it. I found it so deeply satisfying—Patrick getting all husky-voiced and fiery-eyed and righteous on Augusta's behalf—that it was just this side of a turn-on. How pathetic is that? To be on the verge of throwing myself at a man because he shows, after so many years, a little fire, a little *fight* for his own child?"

"I'd say that if anyone in that scenario is pathetic, it isn't you." Right after Will said this, he wished he hadn't. Even though he was just being honest, bad-mouthing Patrick behind his back made Will feel like a sneak. "Still," he added, "good for him, right? What did he say?"

He had said, "Like I would just pick up and go hours and hours away from Augusta. Like, 'Oh sure, honey, I'll just rip up roots and trail after you like some stupid puppy.' Not to mention Lila, who has a life here, too, in case Tanya hasn't noticed."

Pen had been too thrown off by his anger to do more than nod.

"And here's the thing: this place has been asking her if she wants to work for them for years. She's had what amounts to a standing offer, and she's never said yes. But we've been squabbling lately. Not full-blown fighting, but pretty damn close."

Even though Pen knew Patrick was waiting for her to ask what they'd been fighting about, she didn't. She found herself to be peculiarly incurious, even slightly repelled at the idea of seeing into the cracks in Patrick and Tanya's marriage.

But Patrick went on as though she had asked. "Tanya's just so controlling. Case in point, she cut down my *tree,* if you can believe that." Pen wondered if he was speaking metaphorically, a thought that might have made her smile if her mind wasn't becoming increasingly bogged down with sadness at the thought that Augusta might lose her monthly weekends with her daddy.

"Your tree?" she asked.

"My Japanese maple. My buddy Vince was making some landscaping changes and came over one night with this tree he'd dug up from his yard. Prettiest, most petite thing you've ever seen, almost bonsai-sized, with leaves that turn the best color red in the world every fall. I planted it in our side yard and it was thriving, for God's sake, getting kind of shapely and lacy." He squeezed his face between his hands, like the guy in Munch's *Scream*. "It was a living organism! I put a little stone Buddha under it, you know, so that the tree was sheltering him, and one day, the tree was gone. She took a damn contract out on it and had it disappeared. And not gently, either. Turns out she had some ass-hole chop it down and dig up the roots. Obliterated it from the face of the earth. Because it didn't work with her *colors*, her fucking *plan*. It was too Asian. Can you imagine that? I found the Buddha just sitting there, exposed. A Buddha! It wasn't some damn garden gnome, you know? It was a religious icon."

Pen understood why this would upset Patrick, but it annoyed her anyway, the way he described it like it was the worst thing to ever happen, genocide and desecration rolled into one.

"Well, but it *was* decorative, right?" she couldn't resist saying. "I mean, you're not actually a Buddhist."

"Still," said Patrick, "a little respect. A Buddha's a Buddha. And a tree is a tree no matter how small."

Pen had to smile. Patrick, channeling Dr. Seuss. "You are the Lorax," she wanted to tell Patrick. "You speak for the trees."

Instead she hid her smile inside her glass of tea and then said, "I'm not sure I get it, though, how the, uh, squabbling has anything to do with her wanting to move you to Boston. I'm pretty sure people still bicker in Boston."

He looked surprised, as though he'd thought she would get it right away. "She's worried I'll go back to you."

Pen stared at him.

To Will, Pen fumed, " 'Go back to you.' As if that's all it would take, his showing up on my doorstep."

Will couldn't think of anything to say to this that wouldn't qualify as maligning Patrick, so he didn't say anything.

"But then I thought about it," Pen went on. "How my life might look to Tanya or even to Patrick. I've dated here and there, but, honestly, not much, never anything serious. Nobody Augusta's even met, so Patrick probably doesn't even know, which means that unless Tanya's been having me followed—which is not outside the realm of possibility—she doesn't know, either. And, God, the idea of their thinking that I'm just waiting around for Patrick makes me insane."

On an impulse, Will asked, "What have you been waiting for?"

When Pen answered, her voice was solemn and sheepish. "How did you know? Because you're right. I am waiting. It hits me now and then: that I've been saving myself for something. A sign. A person." She gave an embarrassed laugh. "Mostly, though, I'm just busy."

When Patrick told her that Tanya was afraid he would go back to Pen, Pen said, "Well, that's a ridiculous thing to worry about."

All Patrick's bravado disappeared, and hurt filled his eyes. "*We* never bickered, did we?" he said.

Oh for God's sake, thought Pen.

So quickly that it made Pen's head spin, Patrick began to map out a plan: he would divorce Tanya at last, hire a cutthroat lawyer, file for custody of Lila; the four of them would be together, a family.

"It's what I should have done from the beginning," he told Pen.

There were so many things Pen could have said. "She would die before she let you have Lila." "You're mad at Tanya, but you won't stay that way." "You can't come back every time you get restless or angry or bored with your marriage." "It would be too confusing for Augusta, especially when you leave again, which you surely will."

"But I didn't say any of those things," Pen told Will.

"What did you say?"

"I said the thing that rendered all those other points, as true as they are, moot. I said it for the first time ever."

"What was that?" asked Will.

She had wanted to be gentle. Whether Patrick deserved it or not, Pen found herself wanting to be as kind as possible at that critical moment. She leaned across the table and took, not Patrick's hands, but his forearms, his skin warm inside her hands, and turned him directly toward her. She looked for a sign in his eyes that he knew what she was going to say, but they were hope-blue and as unsuspecting as a baby's.

"You can't come back to me, Patrick, because I don't love you," she said. "I care about you and I will thank you in my heart forever for helping me to have Augusta in my life, but I'm not in love with you. More importantly, I don't want you back, not at all, not anymore."

Will said, "Sounds rough."

"It was. Looking him in the eye and getting the words out was, but once it was over, I felt so good, like I'd been rained on by the cleanest rain in the world." She laughed. "A fat lot of good it did, though."

"Meaning what?"

"He didn't buy it."

"Uh-oh."

"He said, 'I know you're protecting yourself and Augusta. I get it. Why wouldn't you? You think I'll come back and then leave again, but I won't. I promise you that. We'll be so happy.'"

She had let go of his arms and told him, "I don't think you really believe that. I know I don't."

"You're hurt," Patrick said. "You're angry."

"No," said Pen. "I'm really not."

To Will, she said, "He said, 'Don't answer right now,' like I hadn't just answered."

"Did he tell you to sleep on it?"

"He did. He used those exact words. And then, *then* he started talking about how Tanya's moving them to Boston would really not have been that bad."

"Really?"

"Yes. He said, 'I'm glad I'm not going, *so* glad, even though Boston really probably wouldn't have been as bad as it sounds. It's not that far, when you think about it, and I could've kept my job, since I do most of it online and over the phone anyway. We have a lot of long-distance clients, in fact, maybe as much as forty percent of our business. I'd have to come here for meetings and such now and then, but that's it. But then there's Augusta, and, sure, when she gets a little older she could ride the train up by herself, under the care of the conductor or whatever, or even fly, and I'd get down whenever I could, not monthly, but fairly often. But it wouldn't be the same. We'd have solid, quality time, I know that, but I'd miss things, concerts and school plays and . . .' He went on like that for quite some time."

"'Under the care of the conductor.' Sounds like he'd considered the idea pretty . . . thoroughly," said Will. Because this made Will feel weasly again, he added, "Which sort of makes sense."

"Oh, yeah," said Pen dryly. "It all makes a lot of sense. How someone who had never had any intention of moving would consider every angle, in detail, except the one in which he stands up to Tanya and tells her that moving is a terrible idea for everyone."

"You think he'll go," said Will.

"Unless Tanya changes her mind or unless she's just been yanking his chain, which she might be doing, since she's an inveterate chain yanker, he'll go. Even if I said I'd take him back, he would go eventually."

"Patrick being in Boston will be hard on Augusta, won't it?"

"It won't crush her, I don't think," said Pen. "But it will certainly hurt, and I could strangle him for that."

Will was quiet for a few seconds before he asked, "Are you sure about not taking him back?"

"Yes," said Pen. Will knew that he didn't have to tell Pen that she didn't sound sure. She groaned. "I'm sure for *me*," she said. "But how will I tell Augusta that her father wanted to come live with us and be a family and I said no?"

Will sat up stiffly, making the porch boards creak. He looked out across the grass, which needed cutting, and ran a hand through his hair.

"I don't know," he said.

"I don't, either."

"Patrick's still waiting for your answer?"

"I'll say what I said before," said Pen in a tired voice. "What else can I do? But I'm not looking forward to it, I'll tell you that. Which brings me to the question."

"What question?"

"I told you I had a story and a question, remember?"

"Now I do."

"Would it be terrible," Pen began carefully, "would it be a huge betrayal of Cat, if I had an ulterior motive—a very secondary ulterior motive, but still—for wanting to go find her?"

"I can't imagine you ever betraying Cat, hugely or unhugely," said Will. "But I don't really get what you mean."

"I wanted to go anyway, before all this. At this point, it's not even so much that I'm worried about her, although I am. We've just got this momentum, you know? I have never stopped missing her all these years, and, since the reunion, I've thought about her all the time. I want to see her more than ever. You know that, right?"

"Sure, I do."

"But when I found out how far away she went, well, the distance made going to find her seem crazy, even impossible. What is it? Ten thousand miles? More?"

"Something like that."

"But now, with my mom waiting for me to call and tell her I'm ready to get together with her new boyfriend and his entire family, which she wants to be my family, too, and with Patrick waiting for me to call and give his happily-ever-after plan the thumbs-up, which I can never do, no matter how happy it would make my child, well—"

"Ten thousand miles is suddenly sounding less crazy?" said Will.

"It's suddenly sounding kind of great."

"You're asking if it would be somehow unethical or insulting to Cat if you had more reason than just wanting to find Cat for going to find Cat?"

"Exactly."

For what wasn't the first time, Will imagined being with Pen in a faraway place, listening to her talk, her one and only voice shining against a backdrop of new sounds.

"I think Cat would think it was okay. I think she would call you a goody-goody for even worrying about it and then would remind you that wanting to get away from your problems for a while is only human."

He honestly believed this. What Cat would think of his own ulterior motive (he shut his eyes and caught a glimpse of Pen, face, hair, shoulders, the brown and gold gloss of her under a tropical sun) was another matter altogether.

"You want to go?" asked Will.

"I'll go if you go."

"I'll go if Augusta goes."

Pen laughed. "I promise to pay you back for the tickets, although it might take a while."

"I know where to find you," said Will.

As soon as they hung up, Will realized he had forgotten to tell her about his conversation with Jason and called her back. After he finished, she made him say "motherfucker" in the precise tone of voice in which Jason had said it. It took Will a few tries, but when he got it right, she let out a single, flat, doomed "Holy cluck" then went silent.

"Pen?"

"Thinking."

"Sorry."

Will watched a full thirty seconds tick by on his running watch before Pen said, "The question is: do we tell him or not tell him?"

"That we're going?"

"Yes."

"He'll go either way," said Will. "No way he's not going."

"Exactly!"

"You think he'll try to beat us there?"

"Do you think we should try to beat him there?" she countered.

Will's first impulse was to say yes, but after he considered the question for a few more seconds, he said, slowly, "We could, but just because we get there first doesn't mean we'll find her first. Or find her at all."

"You're right, it doesn't. And you know what I hate to think about?"

"I can make a pretty fair guess, but go ahead."

"Jason running like a madman around that island or all those seven thousand islands, give or take, by himself, looking for her and maybe finding her."

"If he's there, we want him where we can see him."

"Yes!"

"So—we should invite him to come with us?" asked Will, and even as he asked it, even though Jason fit nowhere in his being-alone-with-Pen-and-Augusta-in-a-distant-land ulterior motive, he understood that this was the only thing to do.

"I hate to say it, I *loathe* to say it," said Pen, "but yes."

Will hung up, called Jason, had a two-minute conversation, and called Pen back.

"He said no."

"No? Oh, no! Did he give a reason?"

"He said, 'Thanks but no thanks, bro. Like I said, I'm just keeping the home fires burning until Cat finds peace in her heart and makes her return.'"

"He couldn't possibly have said that. Nobody talks like that."

"Direct quote."

"Why didn't he jump at the chance to keep an eye on *us*?"

"If I had to guess, I would say that it hasn't occurred to him, yet, that keeping an eye on us makes more sense than trying to beat us to Cebu. He's not the kind of guy things occur to at the same pace that they occur to other people."

"You think he'll figure it out?"

"He might." Will hesitated for a few nervous seconds before he added, "I told him I'd e-mail him our itinerary, just in case he changes his mind. I don't know if that was the right thing to do, but I had to think fast."

Pen didn't answer immediately, and Will tried to gauge from the quality of her silence whether she was just thinking over what he'd said or was wordlessly cursing him for being a clucking moron and ruining all their plans.

"I could still not send it," he said, "and just say I forgot or something."

"No," said Pen decisively. "It's definitely worth a try. Either he'll figure out that it's a good idea to go with us and he'll call to say he's changed his mind or meet us at the hotel in Cebu or something. Or he won't figure it out and will try to get there first, which, as you said, doesn't mean that he'll find her first and really doesn't make anything worse than it would've been if we didn't tell him our plans."

"Okay," said Will, relieved. "I'll call the travel agent right now."

"Will?" said Pen.

"Yeah?"

"Thanks."

"For what?"

"For being—" she began and paused. The tremor in her voice was so slight that it might have been something or nothing, a phone reception glitch. Will couldn't be sure. "Back," she finished and added, "For everything."

"Anytime," Will told her.

IN THE END, IT SEEMED EASIEST TO MEET IN NEW YORK. ACTUALLY, technically speaking, coming from two different cities as they were, it wasn't very easy at all, not nearly as easy as meeting in Philadelphia and either driving to New York together or hopping on the same New York–bound plane at the Philly airport. But when they were discussing the various travel options, as soon as Pen proposed, shyly, meeting at JFK, they had both jumped on the idea. Will wasn't sure why. Maybe because Philadelphia was still the city in which they'd lost each other. Maybe because they didn't want to risk slowing down their momentum, which was sweeping them forward, into the future. They agreed to meet at the gate.

As soon as Will's plane landed at JFK, before they had even turned off the seat-belt sign or taxied to the gate, Will called Pen.

She answered the phone like this: "Where are you?"

"Just landed," said Will. "Where are you?"

"Still at home. We have almost three hours until our flight. Sorry you have to wait."

"No big deal," said Will. "Listen, I have to tell you something."

"You sound so serious. What's wrong?"

"I'm not a natural with kids. I just wanted to warn you. I'm not bad, but I'm definitely not a natural."

"Okay, forget it. The trip's off."

"Seriously, a lot of people expect me to be some kind of Pied Piper because of the books."

"Have you ever actually read that story? Because the Pied Piper might have played nice music, but, underneath the colorful outfit, he was a big fat brainwashing kidnapper."

"I didn't know that. I never wear colorful outfits."

"Of course, you don't," said Pen. "Look, thanks for the heads-up but don't sweat it. Augusta probably won't even notice. As long as you do whatever she says, she'll be happy as a clam."

"Good."

"See you soon."

As it turned out, he saw them before they saw him. In fact, he saw them coming from so far away that he was surprised he could recognize them. The distance obscured Pen's features, reduced her to nothing but shape and motion. She could have been anyone, any tall woman holding the hand of any little girl, but of course, she couldn't have been anyone but Pen, whom Will would've known anywhere: her uprightness, the delineation of her shoulders, the way her head didn't seem to just rest on her neck like most heads on most necks, but to balance, like an egg on the tip of a finger, if such a thing were possible. Mostly, he recognized the way she moved. Will shut his book and—registering every detail as though he might get quizzed on them later—watched Pen and Augusta come into focus.

Pen wore a white T-shirt, flat red shoes, and the kind of black pants that Audrey Hepburn wore in *Funny Face;* she had a gray sweater tied around her waist. She pulled a wheeled carry-on bag. Her hair was tucked behind her ears. Without making a big, self-conscious production out of it, she made walking through the airport look like ballet. Augusta's hair was bobbed and floating and almost black with a tiny, jeweled tiara riding on top. She wore a bright pink flowered party dress and neon yellow flip-flops decked out with floppy cloth flowers. She had a shiny red purse hooked over one forearm and bore a pink backpack on her back that was big enough for her to climb inside.

When they were maybe thirty feet away, Will saw that the two of them were deep in conversation, Pen looking down, and Augusta looking up, so that even though they were close enough to see him, they didn't. It was a good thing, too, because Will found himself suddenly choked up, which stunned him. He never cried, had just stopped one day when he was a kid (Ten years old? Eleven? Right around the time he'd started getting mad and hitting things) and had never started up again, but here he was with his eyes wet and his throat tightening at the sight of Pen with her daughter. He turned his face, ran his palms over his eyes; when he turned back, Pen looked up and saw him and smiled and became, like she always did, his old friend Pen, the clearest thing in the room.

Will walked up, hugged Pen, took her bag, and offered to take Augusta's, but Augusta wrinkled her nose, shrugged, and said, "I'm good."

"Thank you," prompted Pen.

"Thank you," said Augusta. She put one finger on his arm. "I know who you are."

Will crouched down so that he was eye to eye with her. "I'm Will."

"Will *Wads*worth," she corrected. "You knew my mom before I was born, and you write books."

"Yep."

"I can read." She narrowed her blue eyes at him. "*Books*. Signs. Anything." She raised both eyebrows. "Even bad words."

Will looked at Pen, who shrugged helplessly and said, "Graffiti."

Augusta tilted her head to the side and dimpled demurely, batting her long lashes. "It's a problem," she acknowledged and broke into a tinkling laugh.

Will stood up and stared at Pen. "Whoa," he said. "You know who she reminds me of?"

Pen laughed. "Of course, I do. It's freaky, isn't it?"

"How did that happen?"

Pen put up her hands in bafflement. "Cluck if I know. She just came that way."

"What way?" demanded Augusta.

Will looked back down at Augusta and grinned. "The cutest-little-fairy-princess-person-in-the-whole-world way."

After considering this for a moment, Augusta shrugged lightly and said, "I like that way," and after another eloquent glance from her mother, she added, "Thank you."

"OKAY," SAID PEN, SPREADING THEIR PRINTED ITINERARY OUT ON the table in front of them, "New York to Vancouver, don't get off the plane, then Vancouver to Hong Kong, get off the plane for a couple of hours, then Hong Kong to Cebu. Right?"

"Right," said Will.

Pen glanced quickly at Augusta, who was happily eating a pancake at the airport diner near their gate ("Breakfast for dinner is my favorite forever," she'd told Will) and said in a low voice, "That's a hell of a lot of plane time, isn't it?"

"Are you worried about Augusta?" asked Will.

"Oh, no," said Pen. "It's me. I have serious aviophobia."

"But birds are our friends, Pen."

"Ha ha. I never have actual external panic attacks, probably because of my acute fear of embarrassing myself, but I have multiple internal ones, even on short flights."

"What happens?"

"Sweating, sobbing, disorientation, vomiting, loud outbursts of profanity."

"All internal?"

"Yes."

"Ever try to wrestle open the exit door in midflight and jump out?"

"No, but I will now, thanks."

"What if I keep feeding you drinks, one drink every hour for twenty hours?"

"Could help," said Pen, smiling.

"Or you could just—" Will stopped. "Holy shit."

Augusta dropped her fork and covered her ears, laughing.

"Sorry," said Will.

"Nothing she hasn't heard before. She lives with Jamie, remember? And me. What's wrong?"

"I've read that itinerary. I had it stuck to my bulletin board for four days and I never put it together."

"You never put the itinerary together?" asked Pen. "What's that mean?"

"No. What Jason said, remember? How he hated the idea of his little Cat wandering around the Hong Kong airport. At the time, I thought he'd just chosen Hong Kong at random."

"This is Jason we're talking about. In all likelihood, he's lived his entire life without ever knowing Hong Kong existed." Her eyes widened as she absorbed what Will had said. "He knew. About the flight. Because he *checked* on the flight."

"Maybe. I mean, there have to be a lot of other routes. And he'd be flying out of Cincinnati, right? Or Kentucky. Wherever. Those flights might not go through Hong Kong at all. It's weird, though."

"And this was the conversation where you told him where Cat was, so if he already knew about changing planes in Hong Kong, then he already knew where she was."

"Or guessed."

"Why would he guess that? Cat flying to the Philippines on a pilgrimage to get to know her dead father better is a plausible idea to me," said Pen. "But I wouldn't have thought of it all on my own. And Jason, well, do you think he's capable of that kind of prescience?"

"No, but we don't really know him that well, and we can't forget that he's been married to Cat for six years."

"I wish I could. I tried."

"So did Cat, apparently," said Will. He and Pen exchanged wan smiles: it was a thing they preferred not to think about, that Jason knew Cat, had known her for all the years when the only thing Will and Pen could do was remember her, possibly—okay, definitely—knew things about her that they didn't.

"Whether he knew she was going or guessed, if he researched flights, it means we were right: he's planning to look for her," said Will.

"Maybe he already is," said Pen.

Will didn't know why he picked that moment to look over Pen's shoulder. They had chosen a table at the diner's outer edge, on a kind of pseudo-outdoor patio, so that they would be sure to hear the announcement that it was time to board. Walking toward them from the direction of their gate, across the flow of foot traffic, was Jason. He wore a cheesy grin, brown deck shoes, and a T-shirt emblazoned with an American flag and the words MADE IN AMERICA. *Like there could be any doubt,* thought Will. He shook his head. Whatever Jason's limitations, the guy had a flair for the dramatic.

"It's a good thing," murmured Will. "Just remember that. It's what we hoped would happen."

"What?" asked Pen, knitting her brows.

She turned to see what Will saw.

"Oh, for the love of God," she said, and Augusta put down her fork and covered her ears.

CHAPTER FIFTEEN

*W*HENEVER SHE FLEW, WHAT SENT PEN OVER THE EDGE AND flailing into an aviophobic abyss was an image so sharp and three-dimensional that next to it, every fact or figure she had ever learned (percentage of crashes with survivors; chances of dying in a plane crash; percentage by which your chances decrease by sitting in the tail versus the nose, blah blah blah) paled to insignificance. The image slunk around Pen's consciousness, waiting for its moment to dart in and terrify her. On every flight, she spent all of her energy warding it off in any way she could, reading, meditation, overeager conversation with co-travelers, prayer (if fervent and elaborate bargaining counted as prayer), but, every second, feeling, with her whole being, the image's dark presence, muscular and chillingly patient, like a lion waiting for the baby elephant to break from the herd. Then she would be in the middle of some ordinary, full-cruising-altitude task—reading or watching a terrible, nearly inaudible movie or ripping open a package of Twizzlers, her traditional flight comfort food—and there it was to stop her heart: the plane so flimsy and small, an aluminum gnat, surrounded on every side by an immense, freezing, howling, loveless nothingness.

And as she looked around at her fellow travelers, all of whom she believed were also secretly teetering on the brittle edge of being stark, screeching mad, her one (meager, selfish) comfort was that when the combination of hope and hubris holding them up gave out and they fell, at least they would all fall together.

She had thought it would be worse with Augusta there. It was not Augusta's first flight. Last year, she had gone to Paris with Tanya, Patrick, and Lila, a trip she did not (to Tanya's disgust) appreciate and from which she'd returned cranky, exhausted, with a marked lack of interest in French culture or art but crazy for pastries. However, this was the first flight she and Pen had taken together, and Pen braced herself, figuring that her usual fear would be multiplied by maternal love into something so gargantuan that its very weight might be enough to tug the plane into the ocean. Yet, here she sat, miles in the air, Augusta beside her, book closed, Twizzlers package intact, perfectly at peace.

She remembered, suddenly, the last time she had felt this way on an airplane. She was nine and flying to Florida with her family. It was not her first time on a plane, but at some point between her previous flight (to the Grand Canyon, where she'd fallen headlong into beauty without a single fear of falling into the giant hole) and this one, she had crossed from an age of unconsidered trust into one of watchfulness and worry (an age that turned out not to be an age at all, but a permanent condition, although, thankfully, she didn't know this at the time). When the plane hit a spot of turbulence, Pen found herself on the brink of hysteria, a state she recognized from her third-grade science class when her friend Minnie saw a photo of a real human brain and had to breathe into a paper bag.

It was Jamie who saved her. He sat across the aisle from her, his gray eyes starry in his tanned face (the result of not only baseball and swim team, Pen knew, but assiduous, if clandestine, sunbathing in the backyard), his shoulders inside his T-shirt already on their way to broad, chock-full of lanky grace, and way more beautiful than any thirteen-year-old kid had a right to be, a fact that was anything but lost on him. He flirted with the flight attendants. He swanned down the narrow aisle without touching the seats on either side, giving dropped-chin, faux-shy smiles to anyone female who looked at him. He listened to his Walkman in a way that made you want to hand over your entire savings account to be him for five minutes. Even as she loathed him, Pen understood, with resentment and relief, that no one that full of himself, that purely obnoxious could ever die in a plane crash.

Now, Augusta's presence worked a similar kind of magic on Pen. The child sat there and every single thing about her—the pitch of her voice and the points of her elbows, her messy hair, her radiant curiosity and knobby wrists—made crashing impossible. No harm could come to someone so wholly loved, so at home in her own skin—it was a simple fact.

Pen was so relaxed that, despite her considerable physical discomfort (the curse of the long-legged), her concern (unforeseen and exasperating but undeniable) about being slack-faced and open-mouthed in front of Will, and her long history of never, ever sleeping on planes (how would she get into the recommended crash position, let alone locate her inflatable life vest if she were anything but wide awake?), she spent most of the first leg of the trip asleep. As soon as Augusta, after one chattering, enchanted, snack-filled hour, curled up like a cat with her head in Pen's lap and drifted serenely off, as though she did it all the time, as though she were not the child who, at age five, still failed to sleep through the night in her own bed four nights out of seven, Pen turned to Will, said, "I think I'll just close my eyes for a minute or two," and was out for hours. When she woke up, briefly, the plane was fuzzily dark, pleasantly warm, and, for a moment, Pen was flooded with a sense of connection and comradeship: all those sleeping strangers together, shoulder to shoulder, suspended in a hush that was almost holy.

She woke up for good just before they began their descent into Vancouver. She didn't know what time it was, but inside the plane, it was still night. Sleepily, she turned her face and found the only scrap of illumination in the soft dark: Will, awake and writing in a notebook, head bent, face still, hand moving, entirely contained within his own small, private cone of light. The sight made her ache. *How can I not touch you?* she thought hopelessly, and then she was doing it, her fingers on his wrist. He didn't jump or even look at her, just stopped writing. Neither one of them moved, nothing moved, and the whole thing lasted three or four seconds at most, but when Pen took her hand away and started to breathe again, her chest hurt, as though she had been holding her breath for a very long time.

Will didn't give her a puzzled or dismayed or astonished glance. He didn't pull her face to his and kiss her, even though she could almost feel his hand on her cheek. He smiled his usual smile and said, "Hey," in a quieter version of his usual voice, as though nothing had changed. Pen was amazed. How could nothing have changed when everything had changed?

Maybe because you've touched him a thousand times before? she reminded herself derisively.

But this was a major touch, clearly a turning point touch, she shot back.

Not clear to Will. To Will it was a business-as-usual touch, a "Pen and Will being friends like always" touch. Except on an airplane.

On an airplane in the dark. *How could he not know it was different? How could he know it was different?*

If he wanted it to be different, she said to herself in the smallest of voices, *if he were waiting for it, he would know.*

She felt a lot of things at once, not primarily—not by a long shot—but including relief. No matter how you sliced it, Pen and Will being friends like always was a beautiful thing. In validation of this insight, the lights inside the plane came on, and it was morning.

Pen said to Will, "These seats are insane. I feel like a Poppin' Fresh roll, unpopped."

"I feel like a jack-in-the-box," said Will, "in the box."

"Jesus freaking Christ, please tell me this isn't the way you guys always talk." Jason, standing in the aisle next to Will: loud, looming, big as a barn, American flag T-shirt blazing. "Or I *might* have to change my mind about changing my seat, when the black dude in the sleep mask gets off at Vancouver."

As Will and Pen looked over at him, the black dude on the other side of Augusta lifted his sleep mask, took a long look at Jason, and told them, "Lucky you."

◆　◆　◆

A COUPLE OF HOURS INTO THE FLIGHT FROM VANCOUVER TO HONG Kong, an unlikely thing happened to Will, Pen, and Jason, more unlikely than the dissolution of Pen's aviophobia or the brief, half-asleep, flatly unacknowledged move she'd made on Will: they became a team.

When afterward Pen asked Will to give his best estimate as to where they were when this occurred, he guessed someplace over Russia, which wasn't what you'd call pinpoint-precise, not exactly a zeroing-in kind of guess, but even if it had been accurate, it wouldn't really have been accurate because while there was a single moment of clear-cut coalescence—Will's eyes meeting Pen's in agreement—the moment was more a culmination than a revelation. Their joining forces was a process that had begun back at the airport, not the second Jason had made his smirking appearance, but almost.

As Jason approached, Will had shot Pen a look that said, *Be as nice as you can,* so that by the time he stood by the table at a slightly backward-pitched angle, his hands in his shorts' pockets, thumbs sticking out, his head not so much nodding as bobbing like one of those red-and-white fishing things (later, Will would tell Pen they were called "bobbers") in a manner that made Pen want to grab a pancake off Augusta's plate and smack him with it, Will was standing to greet him, and Pen had turned her chair around enough to see him out of the corner of her eye.

"Well, look who's here," he'd said with a smile so sharky that Pen could tell it set even Will's knee-jerk good manners back on their heels because it took him almost a full five seconds to reach out to shake Jason's hand.

"We figured you'd show up," said Pen, with a cool, sidelong glance, and for a second or two, Jason's face collapsed into a look of injured disappointment that was downright toddler-like.

"Did *not*," he said.

Listen to you, thought Pen, *you are straight out of the clucking sandbox.* It took her breath away a little, how Jason could, in the very same second, annoy the hell out of her and inspire a sympathy that was almost tender. Floundering in the face of these battling emotions, Pen took a prim sip of iced tea.

"Hey, man," said Will, "three heads are better than two, right?"

"I have a head," piped Augusta. "One head."

Before Augusta spoke, Jason hadn't noticed that she was there, and for a few seconds, he seemed confused. Then something happened so quickly that it would have seemed like a magic trick, if it hadn't been so obviously real: quite simply, before Pen's eyes, Jason became a different man. His shoulders relaxed, his chest unpuffed, all the defensiveness and wannabe thuggishness and petulance vanished.

"Really? Are you sure?" he said. "There's not maybe a teeny tiny one you've been hiding someplace?"

"No!" Augusta laughed. "And you know what else?"

"What?" asked Jason.

"Fifty stars and thirteen stripes." She said it like "firteen."

Jason looked up, down, all around, frantically searching. "Where?"

Augusta laughed again and pointed at his shirt. "Right there."

"Whoa," said Jason. "You are one wicked-fast counter."

"No, no, no," said Augusta, shaking her black-dandelion-fluff head. "No one counts that fast. Not even Mommy. Not even *Albert. Einstein.*" She pronounced "Albert" with three syllables: Alabert.

"Then how did you know?" asked Jason.

"I *learned*!" shrieked Augusta with joy. "From my teacher!"

"Learned? Come on. How could you have learned that already? You're only in—what? Fourth grade?"

More shrieking.

It had gone on like this, Jason becoming more starstruck, more unguarded, funnier, kinder, less and less of a horse's ass by the minute.

"Who is that guy?" Will had whispered to Pen, as the four of them lined up to board.

"If you didn't know him," Pen whispered to Will, "you might mistake him for someone who doesn't completely suck."

"Seeing him with her makes it kind of hard to hate him, doesn't it?"

"Don't go soft on me, Wadsworth," growled Pen, but it was Pen who was going soft. In her mind's filing cabinet, she maintained a list of things that she would've otherwise disdained but liked because they made Augusta happy, and she could feel Jason taking his place on it, muscling in with his big shoulders, until he was wedged into a spot well below hair glitter but several notches ahead of chicken fingers and stickers.

When Jason moved his seat in Vancouver, both he and Augusta were in hog heaven for hours. They played I-Spy. They watched the same cartoons and Disney movies on their individual seat-back screens, headphones on, commenting to each other on the action in voices booming enough to generate a flutter of smiling, gentle remonstrance from the ballerina-like Asian flight attendants. They colored in the coloring books Pen had purchased for the trip, Jason scrunching his large form into painful-looking positions in order to chase runaway crayons. They played seemingly endless rounds of Old Maid and tic-tac-toe, until Will offered to read to Augusta, and the four of them shifted seats, so that Will sat between Augusta and Pen and Pen sat next to Jason.

She recognized Will's offer as an act of mercy, one she herself would have appreciated, since her own tolerance for mindless and repetitive children's games topped out at around fifteen minutes, but which appeared to deflate Jason. Once Augusta was gone, he was visibly at loose ends, aimlessly channel surfing, flipping through the duty-free catalog, finally digging out a thick, daunting slab of a hardcover book, which Pen recognized with surprise as a recent, prizewinning presidential biography. When Jason said sarcastically, "Don't look so shocked. We graduated from the same college, remember? I do know how to read," Pen had the grace to be ashamed.

Still, ten minutes into the book, after a period of repeated head lolling and jerking awake, Jason was fast asleep. His left arm was inches from hers, his face maybe a foot away. She never got used to it, the forced intimacy of airplanes, and it took a while for her to look at Jason directly.

"Geez," she whispered to Will. "He looks so vulnerable, like an enormous baby chick."

"Don't do it," cautioned Will.

"Do what?"

"Put that little airplane pillow over his face. Augusta would be bummed." They both glanced down at Augusta, who was sleeping again, tucked under her blue blanket, her feet in Will's lap, and then looked back at Jason. "Plus, it might be too small. You might need something bigger."

"Seriously," whispered Pen, "it's weird to be this close to him."

"Better you than me, pal."

"Thanks a lot."

But she had to admit that Jason's face in repose held a kind of sweetness, smooth cheeks, dimpled chin, blond hair like a freshly mown lawn on top of his head. Seeing him like this, especially after seeing him with Augusta, it was slightly more possible to imagine why Cat married him. Maybe he had reservoirs of goodness under all that bluster. Maybe this face was his real face.

Maybe not, she told herself, sharply. He had lied and misled them multiple times; he had driven Cat away; he said "dude" frequently and without irony. Now was no time to get sappy.

Hours passed, who knew how many? Pen's inner clock had gone helter-skelter, befuddled by time zone switches, the plane's interior darkenings and illuminations, and the indeterminate meals, randomly served (she liked the fish congee, but was it dinner? breakfast? Pen had no idea). Time on the plane seemed to alternate between clotting to an immovable mass and thinning and dissipating, like air on a mountaintop. After that early gift of plane sleep, Pen couldn't even manage a catnap. She read; she watched several episodes of a crime show that made you desperate to be a forensic detective, if only for the sleek, glowing, is-it-a-lab-or-is-it-an-art-installation interiors and scuba-suit-tight pantsuits; she walked around and around the airplane like a panther in a cage; she ate every single thing the flight attendants put in front of her. Mostly, she talked to Will, talked and talked, like a thirsty person at a mountain spring, an enterprise that made time disappear altogether.

It was when she was giving up on her fourth nap attempt in an hour that it happened: Jason, still sleeping, shifted his knees and caused a minor earthquake in his seat, dumping an open bag of caramel corn onto the floor and sending the presidential biography tumbling over the armrest and onto Pen's lap. When she picked it up, it flopped open. Two photographs slid out and rested, facedown, on her knee. Even as her mother's voice told her to slip the photos back into the book without looking at them, she was switching on her reading light and turning them over in her hands.

The first was a wedding picture, Cat on Jason's lap, laughing, her whisper-delicate neck and shoulders rising from the bodice of an upside-down lily of a dress, her button nose pressed against Jason's cheek; Jason's face shining with beatific joy. The second was Cat by herself in leggings and a tiny T-shirt, turned sideways, her arms spread in a gesture that said *Ta-da!*

Because she was taking in Cat's lovely, devilish smile, her long hair (Cat had never had anything longer than a long bob in all the years Pen knew her), it took Pen a moment to understand the significance of the gesture, and then she saw it: an almost imperceptible rise above Cat's narrow hips, what would've just looked like ordinary stomach on anyone less waiflike. A baby bump.

As Pen stared and stared at the photo, her eyes burning with tears, she heard a small sound, the sound of a person clearing his throat deliberately: "Ahem." It came from the direction of Jason. Pen froze. People made a lot of noises in their sleep, but, in her experience, this wasn't one of them. Filling with dread, she braced herself and looked up.

Jason's eyes were on the photograph, and the expression on his face wasn't angry; in fact, it might have been the opposite of angry. Gently, he took the photos from Pen's hands.

"Twelve weeks," he said. "It's as far as we ever got. A couple of days after I took this picture, she started bleeding and, poof, our baby was gone." When he said "our baby," his voice was like the expression in his eyes: honest, bleak, rife with longing. Pen remembered what Sam had said, how Cat had told her that wanting a baby had nothing to do with her husband and everything to do with Cat's wanting to be a mother. Looking at Jason, Pen thought Cat had gotten it wrong. She wasn't the only one who had been stockpiling love.

"I'm so sorry," said Pen.

"She was at the grocery store when it happened," Jason went on.

"And then for, like, weeks afterward, she couldn't go back. Started ordering groceries from this online delivery service."

"Poor Cat. Poor both of you."

For the first time, Jason's eyes met hers. "You know, she didn't even tell me? I'd come home from work and the fridge would be full of food, and I didn't think twice about it. You know how I found out?"

"How?"

"I complained about the bananas." He squeezed his eyes shut for a second or two, as though trying to clear his head of something. "Can you believe that? They were too ripe, all those strings sticking to them when you peeled them. I hate that."

"So does Cat," said Pen, suddenly remembering this fact. "She liked them when they were so green you could barely peel them."

"Yeah, well, right about then, she wasn't eating much of anything, which also took me a while to notice." He shook his head in disgust. "My wife can't walk into a goddamn grocery store without having posttraumatic stress, and I'm complaining about bananas."

"Listen," said Pen with great seriousness, "if you didn't know, it was because she didn't want you to know. It wasn't your fault."

Jason looked at her for a few seconds before he said, with equal seriousness, "Thank you."

They sat in a prickly, awkward silence, until Pen couldn't stand it anymore. She turned to Will, who was facing the other direction, sleeping, and tapped lightly on the back of his head. He swatted at her hand for a few seconds and then turned around.

"Hey," he said reproachfully, glaring at her with half-closed eyes and running his hand across the top of his head, "I was asleep."

"I know and I'm sorry," said Pen. "But someone has to save us."

"Me and you?" asked Will. "From what?"

"Me and Jason," said Pen. "From ourselves."

Will peered across Pen at Jason. "You were fighting?"

"We were getting along," said Pen with a shudder.

"Yeah," snorted Jason, "Pen was *nice*. It was freaky."

"That is freaky," said Will.

Pen punched him in the arm.

"Ow!"

Rubbing his shoulder, Will narrowed his eyes into the Clint Eastwood squint and looked from one face to the other. Then he nodded. "Okay, fine," he said, "but if we're going to do this, we need to clear up a few things."

"Wait," said Jason, alarmed. "Do what?"

"Hey, you started it," said Will.

"We failed to treat each other like radioactive waste for a whole half a minute. So what?" said Pen.

"Yeah," said Jason, "don't get all one-giant-step-for-mankind on us, dude." But under the scorn, he sounded the way Pen felt: optimistic, goofy with relief.

"I'm going back to sleep," said Will, starting to turn away.

Pen tugged on his shirtsleeve. "Okay, okay, I'll tell you what's going on."

"What?" said Will and Jason at the same time.

"We being on the same side," she said.

No one made eye contact. Everyone fidgeted, each in her or his own way.

"Whatevs," said Jason finally. "I guess it only makes sense. We're all trying to find Cat, right?"

"Right!" said Pen. "Absolutely."

But Will was shaking his head. "Not so fast," he said.

"Fast?" said Jason. "Don't forget I hated you for, like, a decade."

Pen chuckled at this, and Will jabbed her with his elbow.

"What?" she protested. "It was funny!"

Being careful not to jostle Augusta's socked feet, which still rested in his lap, Will twisted in his seat to face Jason. "You need to explain something," he said.

"Oh, yeah?" said Jason with a brief flare of his old pugnacity. "And what might that be?"

" 'Motherfucker.' " Will didn't load the word with venom, as Jason had done on the phone, just divided it into two parts and impassively placed them in front of him: thunk, thunk.

Jason sat still, his forehead wrinkled, processing this. Pen watched him figure it out, every step written all over his face. Whatever the opposite of a poker face was, that's what Jason had. Finally, his brow cleared: he got it. But instead of answering, he pressed his lips together and rolled his eyes, hostile and bored at the same time. He looked like a teenager whose parents had just confronted him about the joint in his pocket.

"Come on, Jason," Pen said softly. "Just tell us."

He looked at her, then, and he didn't look like a teenager anymore. Pen saw something private and broken in his gaze. Will and Pen watched him take deep breaths, collect himself, get his emotions in check.

He breathed out. "There was a guy."

"Oh," said Pen. It wasn't what she had expected him to say, but as soon as he did, she realized that she wasn't surprised. Of course, of course, there was a guy.

"It wasn't her fault," Jason said quickly.

"Okay," said Will.

"We'd been doing the infertility thing for so long, her hormones were all screwed up. In addition, she was sad. Losing the baby at twelve weeks tore her up. Even when she was over it, she wasn't over it. She'd never talk about it, bite my head off if I even thought about bringing it up. A thing like that leaves its mark."

"I bet it does," said Pen.

"My point is she was vulnerable." He glared at Will and Pen, as if they might contradict him.

"Things can happen when a person's defenses are down," said Will carefully, "that wouldn't happen otherwise."

"You got that right," said Jason. "And then there was the Freudian shit on top of that."

This was unexpected. Pen and Will exchanged a glance.

"Go ahead," said Will to Jason.

"You know how Cat was about her dad, thought he hung the fucking moon. Dude forgets her birthday every single year, and I'm talking about not even a crappy Hallmark card, but she thinks he's Mr. Perfect. What's it called, the thing where the guy killed his father and then ripped his eyes out of their sockets. But for girls."

Pen winced. "I would hardly say she had an Electra complex."

Jason shrugged. "None of us are psychologists, right? Let's say that when it came to her dad, she was a little off."

Pen started to argue, but Will gave her elbow a surreptitious squeeze and she stopped.

"We all know she was crazy about her dad," said Will, "but what does that have to do with this guy?"

"Armando Cruz," spat Jason. "What kind of soap opera name is that?"

A nice name, Pen mused, like music: Armando Cruz and Catalina Ocampo—it sounded like a poem. As Pen considered the name, a light began to dawn. "Wait. He was Filipino? Like Dr. Ocampo? Is that what you meant by Electra?"

Jason turned the back of his hand to them and shot up a stubby index finger. "Filipino." He raised another finger. "From the same town as her dad." One more finger. "And he was a fucking doctor, to fucking boot. Tri-fucking-Electra-fecta."

A man's face appeared above the seat in front of Jason. "Do you mind?" he said. "I got a kid up here."

"My bad, bro," said Jason. The man disappeared. "Bottom line," Jason continued, "he took advantage of her."

"What do you mean," asked Pen, alarmed, "'took advantage of her'?"

"Not like that," said Jason. "I mean she was vulnerable—all those hormones bouncing around. He should have backed off, irregardless of her having a husband."

Regardless, Pen corrected inside her head. She wasn't about to challenge Jason's version of the story, but she wasn't convinced by the picture of Cat as a manipulated innocent.

"What did he look like?" she asked.

Jason shot her a look. "Why does that matter?"

"I just wondered if he looked like her dad."

"Oh." Jason's mouth worked itself into a hard line, and Pen could tell that he was picturing Armando Cruz next to Cat's short, squat, round-faced father, trying to find some common ground. "Not exactly."

I knew it, Pen thought. *He was beautiful.*

Jason blew out a short, painful laugh. "Put it this way: soap opera name, soap opera looks. The guy was cheesy: expensive haircut, ten million teeth, kind of dipshit who runs without a shirt. Honest truth is when I first met him, I thought he was gay."

"You met him?" asked Will.

"Dinner party some stupid neighbor threw. Out by the pool. Mr. Soap Opera was doing his fellowship or what have you at the hospital where her husband worked. Oh and listen to this," he said eagerly. "You guys are the type who will hate this."

"What?" said Pen.

"She invited him and Cat specifically to meet each other." Jason slapped his hand on the armrest.

"You mean that she set them up?" asked Will.

"Naw," said Jason. "I mean, she just assumed they would have shit in common because they were both Filipino."

"I see," said Pen. "How . . . presumptuous." But what she was really thinking was that Cat and Armando did have some pretty significant shit in common, at least eventually.

"Anyway," said Jason, "I saw him a few times after that. We kind of got to know him even." He scratched his head. "Well, some of us got to know him better than others, obviously."

Will said, "How did you know they had an affair?"

"I told you," said Jason angrily. "He took advantage. It wasn't your typical affair."

"All right," said Will. "But how did you know?"

"She told me," said Jason. The pride in his voice was enough to make you cry. "My wife couldn't stand to keep something like that from me, that's how close we are and that's how done with him she is.

After he left, she came clean, told me everything. They had sex, but never in our bed!" He said it as though forgoing sex in their bed was proof that Cat loved him, and who knew? Maybe it was. "It seemed like she expected me to kick her out, but I would never do that."

Pen turned and caught Will's eye, wondering if he was thinking what she was thinking: that there was a fine line between "expected me to" and "hoped I would." In answer, Will lifted one eyebrow, a fleeting, infinitesimal movement, and flicked his eyes back to Jason.

"Armando left?" he asked.

"His fellowship ended, and he went back to the homeland. Made it seem like it was this big noble thing, too. Who cares? Good riddance, asshole."

Pen waited for Will to ask what had to be asked, but she could sense that he was waiting for her to do it. It was an awful question, since it canceled out or at the very least called into deep question Jason's recent declaration that Cat was "close" to Jason and "done" with Armando, but, since they were on a plane to Cebu, there seemed to be no way not to ask it. When the pause in the conversation started to become unbearable, Will nudged Pen encouragingly. She ignored it. He nudged her again. She kicked him.

"So. Uh. Jason," said Will, "do you think she went to Cebu to be with Armando?"

"Oh, Will," Pen exclaimed, flinching. "'*Be* with him'? God. Could you not do better than that?"

"Hey, it's not like you were asking."

"Well, clearly, I should have."

"And you would've phrased it how?" demanded Will. "'Visit him'? 'Spend time with him'? Come on, we all know a euphemism when we hear it."

"All I'm saying is—" began Pen, but Jason raised his hand.

"Hello? I'm sitting right here," he said.

They both stared at him.

"Sorry," said Will. "I was just wondering if that's why you got mad on the phone that day when I told you Cat went to Cebu. Because you thought she'd gone to see Armando."

"Shit, yeah, that's why," said Jason. "Actually, though? Before you told me where she went, I didn't really believe she would follow him. I thought about it. I explored the possibility. I mean, I'm not completely stupid. But, in my heart, I trusted her." He shook his head. "So shit, maybe I am completely stupid."

Pen couldn't help but admire the grim candor with which he said this.

"Jason," she ventured nervously, "if Cat did that, if she did everything it's looking like she did, well—. It would seem to me that in doing those things, Cat did not have your best interests at heart."

"Ya think?" said Jason.

"I do," said Pen. "As much as I love Cat, I have to say that, if everything happened the way you say, then don't you think that maybe—and this is not rhetorical, I'm really asking—that maybe you should consider—" She broke off.

"What?" said Jason.

Pen sighed and said, as gently as she could, "Letting her go. Moving on."

Jason didn't look mad, just injured, like someone had punched him in the stomach. Injured and, suddenly, ten years older.

"I can't," he said raggedly. "Cat's my girl. She's everything to me." He swallowed and sat up straighter. "And, look, she was a wreck when her dad died, like I told you before. Superfragile. It's that Electra thing driving her: she's looking for her dad, really, not Armando. She doesn't need me to let her go. She needs me to help her."

Everyone should be loved like this, Pen thought. *Well, not exactly like this, but this much.*

Will said, "We'll look for him, then. Dr. Armando Cruz. Start looking as soon as we get there. It might take a while, but I bet we can find him."

Her eyes met Will's, and they both nodded, and, just like that, the three of them were a team. Co-conspirators. Partners in crime. God help them.

"I bet we can, too," said Pen staunchly.

"Oh, I bet we can, too," said Jason, a sly smile sliding onto his face, "especially since when Armando was bragging about how he was heading back to Cebu to work, guess what he told me?"

Pen thought for a second. Then her eyes lit up. "The name of the hospital."

"Bingo."

Jason winked at Pen and put out his fist so that she could bump it with her own, and even though she had never liked being winked at and, until very recently, had never liked Jason and still wasn't sure if *like* was the word to describe what she felt about him, she took a breath, winked back, and bumped.

CHAPTER SIXTEEN

*P*EN NOTICED THE SMELL BEFORE SHE NOTICED THE HEAT, AL-though, when she considered the smell later (and it may have been the first smell ever that she had truly reflected upon), she realized that the two—smell and heat—were all of a piece, inextricably entwined, born of, borne by each other. She smelled the smell before she had even stepped foot outside the small, blessedly uncomplicated airport. It wasn't a bad smell. In fact, she liked it. Charcoal fire and wood smoke, exhaust and hot road and baking earth, with undertones (or so Pen imagined) of leaves and fruit and the ocean. Even as she smelled it for the first time, she knew that it would be one of those smells that would haunt her, knew that she would be walking through some future time and place, get blindsided by the smell, and think, instantly: Cebu.

When they left the airport, after a few preliminary minutes when stepping into the heat/smell was like hurling yourself full tilt into the wall of a thickly padded cell, Pen found her body responding to it differently from the way it responded to hot days at home. The heat wasn't something she moved through; it didn't smother or beat down. The Cebu heat was somehow more personal than other heat. It infiltrated, became part of her, or almost. She wore it, like a dress.

As she, Will, Augusta, and Jason stood glazed over, baffled, and reeling on the pavement outside of the airport's glass doors, she turned to Will and said, "The heat, it's like being enfolded in one of those giant, pleated Issey Miyake dresses they have at the Met, isn't it?"

"Exactly what I was thinking," said Will, his voice the only dry thing in a world of humidity. Pen wondered if she looked as wrung out as he did, his face's topography even sharper than usual, his skin glowless in spite of his tan.

"Ixnay on the damn freak talk already," grumbled Jason. "At least until we're in the air-conditioning."

Augusta tugged on Pen's hand, raised her eyebrows, and pointed her finger at Jason. "Bad word," she said solemnly.

"It was a long trip, honeypot," explained Pen, leaning down to plant a kiss on top of her head. "I think we're all a little cranky."

"I'm not," said Augusta. But Pen recognized the signs that her girl was on the edge: smudgy eyes and a stretched-thin whine in her voice.

"Sorry, sis," Jason told Augusta, his eyes two pools of repentance.

"You're welcome," said Augusta absently. She looked very small, wispy, a spent, slumping point in the center of movement and crackling color, one finger twisting her hair. *Poor baby.* Just as Pen was about to pick her up and cuddle her, despite her own fatigue and the clinging heat, her face colored, came to life.

"Look, look, look, Mama, Mama, Mama!"

In an instant, she had yanked her hand out of Pen's and was flying toward the street, which was clogged with all manner of vehicles, most of them stopped and waiting for passengers, a fact that didn't prevent Pen's heart from leaping into her throat in the same instant that she leaped over Augusta's backpack and ran after her.

"Augusta!" she yelled. "Stop right there!"

Augusta stopped at the curb, possibly in response to Pen's command, but possibly not, since she had skidded to a halt inches away from the object of her desire, an arresting contraption consisting of a motorcycle and a tall, roofed, brilliant orange sidecar decked out in rows of lemon-drop-and-ruby-colored headlights and fiercely, eclectically painted: an ad for San Miguel beer, detailed renderings of both a gold-crowned Virgin Mary and Tweety Bird on his birdcage swing, and, in swirling script, what Pen thought was (but what couldn't possibly have been, could it?) a quote from a Journey song. A man in shorts, flip-flops, and a Baltimore Orioles cap stood next to the contraption (later, Pen would learn it was called a "tricycle"), eating pork rinds from a bag.

"Where would you like to go?" he asked Augusta, smiling.

"For a *ride*," she said, saucer-eyed and breathless.

"Ten pesos." He held up ten fingers. "Per person."

Augusta held her hands up, mirroring him, and turned to Pen, her eyes bright.

"Oh, no, thank you," said Pen to the man, smiling and taking Augusta's hand, which immediately began to twist inside hers like a tiny wild animal (*a gerbil* was Pen's weary, drifting thought). "There are four of us, plus luggage. We need something larger."

"No problem," said the man, hooking his thumb toward the tricycle. "Three on the motorcycle, one in the car with the luggage."

Pen looked at the vehicle dubiously. She had nearly fallen over with guilt and worry when they had checked in at the Philadelphia airport and the airline attendant had told her that Augusta couldn't use her booster seat on the plane because it wasn't FAA approved. But they had survived the flight—*flights*—without mishap, without so much as a spell of airsickness or a spilled drink. No way was she pushing her luck now.

"No, thank you," said Pen.

"Yes, thank you!" Augusta shrilled, her whine escalating incrementally in a way that might have been musical had it not been so piercing. "Yes, thank you!"

Uh-oh, thought Pen. She tried to turn Augusta around and lead her away, but Augusta wrenched her hand loose.

"I want to ride the *thing*!" she yelped. "You *said* I could.'

"Hey, you know what?" said Pen calmly. "Let's find a taxi. I bet they're fancy around here, too!"

At this, Augusta dropped to her bottom on the sidewalk with a thunk, her hands balled into fists, threw back her head, and detonated.

She burst into tears. Tears were the least of it. Wails. Shrieks. Chest-racking sobs. Violent back-and-forth headshaking. A small but potent amount of kicking.

Briefly, Pen observed Augusta with the detached horror and awe she felt when she watched a nature documentary: the shark heaving the gruesome gorgeousness of its body from the water, jagged tail lashing, sad, floppy seal snagged in its teeth, the roiling, roiling sea, the fathomless, stone-cold black eyes. She might have stood there until it was over, doing nothing, but there was Will, at her side, saying, "Can I help?" He had to raise his voice to be heard over Augusta's howls. Pen snapped out of her stupor and saw that the people on the sidewalk had pulled themselves into slightly tighter clusters and were looking discreetly away, for which Pen felt a pulse of gratitude.

"It's okay," Pen told Will, crouching down and wrestling Augusta, who had pinned herself to the ground with the special, dead-weight gravity of an aggrieved child, into her arms. "Maybe just find a cab?"

"Stop! You're *hurting* me!" screamed Augusta, her voice louder than ever, bursting through the ambient sound like a wrecking ball. *Let the people not speak English*, Pen prayed, but she saw heads turning, maternal concern on every face, including those of the men, a girl who could not have been more than seven years old, and a miniature, soulful-eyed pug.

"Save me," whispered Pen hopelessly and to no one.

Salvation came in the form of a tiny minivan (a mini-minivan?) of a variety Pen had never seen. It had gray vinyl seats and smelled nauseatingly of air freshener. Jason presented the driver with the booster seat, but when the man examined it as though it were an artifact from another planet, Pen decided to forget about it. She was too defeated to feel guilty, although she knew she might later. Augusta had turned from fighting her to clinging to her like lichen, and the thought of prying her loose and belting her into a car seat was too much. Besides, unless they were somehow hidden, the van didn't appear to have seat belts. Once inside, tucked into one corner of the backseat on Pen's lap, Augusta quieted almost magically, bushwhacked by exhaustion, her sobs turning to hiccups. In a minute or so, before the driver had even finished loading their bags, she was asleep, her lips parted, her face angelically peaceful.

"I'm sorry," Pen told Will and Jason. "She doesn't usually behave that way."

"What, are you kidding? It was a relief. Totally got it out of my system," said Will with a smile that Pen could have put in her pocket and kept forever. Just like that: she felt better.

From the front passenger seat, Jason turned around to look at Pen. "Hell, yeah," he said, raising a solidarity fist. "Vicarious tantrums all the way."

Pen raised her fist back.

"'Vicarious,'" she said with a grin. "Impressive."

Joking. Joking with *Jason. How did I get here?* she asked herself and then took the question back. She knew how. Pen found that she felt happy, exuberant even, full of well-being, loose and free, and, somehow (ten thousand miles from home, with her carseat-less child in her lap and the traffic nudging in on either side, so close she could study the faces of the passengers in the van next to them) safe.

"More where that came from," said Jason. "I mean, not a lot more, but more."

For a few seconds they were all three smiling at one another, a triangle of grins, before Will said, "Okay, that's enough," and it was.

THE WARM FEELING LASTED UNTIL THEY WERE STANDING AT THE desk of the opulent hotel ("Marble," Pen had whispered to Will as they walked in. "Persian rugs. Flat screens." And he had whispered back, "Cat will be Cat will be Cat."), when the first thing Jason did after they checked in was to whip out a photo of Cat—one Pen hadn't seen before, a headshot—and ask the woman at the desk, in a voice straight out of a police procedural, if she were still a guest at the hotel.

The woman's doe eyes had startled in her cameo face, and she had said, with exquisite courtesy, "I'm so sorry I cannot help you, sir."

"Look," said Jason, jutting out his jaw. "She's my wife. I know she was a guest. All I want to know is if she's still here. Simple question."

"Jason," said Will, "come on."

"It is our policy not to give out information regarding our guests," said the woman, her voice as delicate as the rest of her.

A man in a suit and tie materialized at her side. "May I help you?" he asked.

"All's I want to know is," drawled Jason—('*All's*'? thought Pen. *Are you out of your mind?*)—"is my wife still a guest of this establishment. Period."

"I'm very sorry, sir," said the man behind the desk. "We must protect the privacy of our guests. We would do the same for you and your party, for anyone."

As Pen closed her eyes, vehemently wishing herself part of anyone else's party but Jason's, she heard Will say, "And we really appreciate that. We'll just go find our rooms now."

"And *I*," said Jason, "would really appreciate it if you would tell me if and when my wife checked out of this hotel." His tone grew seedy, conspiratorial. "Me and my friend Ulysses would be most appreciative."

My friend Ulysses and I, thought Pen, and then, *Oh, for the love of God, No. No, no, no.* But she opened her eyes and there he was, waving a fifty-dollar bill under the man's nose.

Simultaneously, the man and the woman took a step back, their faces shutting like boxes, their eyes impassive.

"Hey, man," said Will warningly. "Let it go." He was holding Augusta, her head on his shoulder, and as he said this, she stirred. Will rested his hand, lightly, on the side of her face and said, "Shhh."

If Jason heard Will, he didn't show it. He never took his eyes off the man and the woman behind the desk. From where she stood, Pen could see the back of his neck and his right ear turn scarlet. "Fine. You want to play hardball?" said Jason, banging the fist holding Ulysses on the counter. "She's my *wife*, and she's not well. So, fine, I'll double it. I'll *triple* it."

"If you pull out Ben Franklin," Pen said, her teeth gritted, "I swear to God I will deck you."

Jason dragged his gaze off the couple behind the desk and stared at Pen, bewildered. "What?"

"Do you *hear* yourself?" snapped Pen. "*Hardball? You* are the one who's not well."

Jason's bravado evaporated. He drooped and looked betrayed. "Fine," he said sullenly. "Great." He folded the money and stuffed it into his shorts' pocket, turning to glare at Pen and Will. "Way to have my back, guys. I appreciate it." And he stomped away.

Later, after Pen had unpacked, bathed Augusta, put her to bed, and then stood in the shower for a long time, the hot water pouring over her like hot water but also like divine, transfiguring bliss, there was a knock at the door. She opened it, and there was Will.

"Hey, I didn't wake you up, did I?" he asked.

"No," said Pen.

She saw that he was freshly shaven, his hair still wet. He wore a white polo shirt, open at the neck, and under the lights of the hotel hallway, his hazel eyes seemed to be ten different colors at once. As she looked at him, a drop of water ran from his ear to the V of his shirt, and Pen felt instantly shy, hyperaware of their mutual dampness.

Maybe Will felt the same way because when she asked him if he wanted to come in, he shook his head, glancing over her shoulder at Augusta asleep on one of the two twin beds.

"I'll stay out here," he said. "I'd hate to wake her up."

"I don't think a freight train could wake her up at this point. Jet lag, it's like a drug, isn't it?"

"Yeah," agreed Will, "a bad drug," but he stayed in the hallway.

"It felt a little weird putting on pajamas at three o'clock in the afternoon," said Pen, "but if I don't get some sleep, I think I might die."

It wasn't until she said "pajamas" that Pen remembered what she was wearing: baggy drawstring shorts that used to belong to Jamie and a white tank top. She flushed. *Please don't let him notice that I'm braless. Please don't let him think the shorts are Patrick's.* It took all of her self-control not to cross her arms over her chest and back away. Inside her head, she heard her mother's advice regarding embarrassing situations: *If you act like you don't notice, nobody else will notice.* She didn't believe it any more now than she had as a kid, but she fervently hoped it was true.

"I'll let you hit the hay," said Will. "But I wanted to tell you that Jason and I are taking a little trip to the hospital."

"What?" exclaimed Pen, imagining that Jason had done something ridiculous, cut off his ear while shaving, maybe. Then she remembered: Armando. "Oh. But why not wait until tomorrow? Get some rest? You guys must be as tired as I am, and it's not like a few hours will make a difference."

"Waiting makes sense," said Will. "So obviously Jason won't do it, and we can't let him go alone."

"Well, I guess we could," said Pen. A vision of Jason in the hospital came to her: bursting through operating room doors in his American flag shirt, ears blazing, waving money in front of nurses and surgeons and patients on gurneys. She groaned. "Of course, we can't. He'd get himself locked up for attempted bribery and unforgivable rudeness." She smiled at Will with sympathy. "Sorry you have to be alone with the big galoot. Will and Jason, playing detective together."

"Will and Jason and Jason's friend Ulysses," corrected Will.

Pen laughed. Then something occurred to her. "Hey, how do you know Armando will be there? What if he's off today?"

"Oh, Jason took care of that," said Will.

"Uh-oh. How?"

"He made an appointment. From Ohio. Under an assumed name."

Pen stared at him. "You can do that?"

"Only if you have tunnel vision and no discernible moral compass."

"He made up an ailment?" asked Pen.

"An ailment, a name, an entire medical history. He said he had to cancel his appointment with a doctor in Ohio because of an unexpected business trip to Cebu and didn't want to wait until he got home to get checked out."

"What kind of doctor is Armando, anyway?"

"A thoracic surgeon."

"So Jason said there was something wrong with his—what? Thorax? Do humans even have thoraxes? I thought insects were the ones with thoraxes."

"Well, that would explain why Jason has one," said Will.

It should have been a nothing moment, slightly funny but evanescent, a moment in a long stream of moments. Instead, for Pen at least, it separated itself, became self-contained and revelatory. Pen and Will looked at each other and smiled the kind of smiles people exchange when they have known each other for a very long time, and maybe it was the exhaustion or the fact of time's having been turned on its head, but Pen had the sensation that, right then, they were two bodies caught in perfect balance, the forces pulling them together precisely equal to the ones keeping them apart, Pen on one side of the doorway, Will on the other, and what she understood is that all the forces were love and that she was the opposite of lonely. This could be enough, she realized, this kind of being together. Friendship. In spite of all her longing (her fingers on his wrist), this could be enough.

"You'll have to come back," said Pen, taking a step backward into the room, "and tell me all about it."

"You know I will," said Will.

THE NEXT MORNING, WILL FOUND PEN AND AUGUSTA AT THE HOTEL pool. It was six thirty, which, for Pen, under normal circumstances and time zones, would have passed for the crack of dawn, but which felt remarkably late given the fact that she and Augusta had both been up for a grim, trapped, hungry, television-filled (thank God for the Disney channel) two and a half hours.

Augusta was in the baby pool cooing to the dolphin fountain, and Pen was feasting on warm, dense, cloven rolls called Elorde bread after a Cebuano boxing star (Pen had learned from the waiter that boxing was the most popular sport in the Philippines, with basketball and billiards close behind), sticky rice redolent with coconut milk, and mangoes, palm-sized, kidney-shaped, butter-yellow on the outside, with brilliant, silken, spoonable flesh of such acute deliciousness that, upon taking her first bite, Pen could have wept with joy.

"Was he cute?" had been Pen's first question.

"I wouldn't say 'cute,'" said Will.

"Because you never say 'cute' or because he wasn't?" asked Pen.

"Both," said Will.

"So what'd he look like?"

"The anti-Jason. Take Jason and substitute every single thing about him with its opposite, and you'll get Armando."

Pen considered this. "Jason has decent teeth. Are you saying Armando had bad teeth?"

"Every single thing about Jason except his teeth. I didn't pry open his mouth and go in with a flashlight, but I got the impression that his teeth are fine."

"What else about him is fine?"

"Pen."

Pen sighed. "I knew I should have had you take a picture. What was he like? Funny? Smart? Devastatingly handsome? Did he look great in his white coat? Did he even wear a white coat? Did he really seem like the kind of guy who would run without a shirt? Was he stunned to see Jason walk into his office?"

"Yes."

Pen narrowed her eyes at Will threateningly.

"Yes, he really did seem like the kind of guy who would run without a shirt," said Will.

"No!" yelped Pen, recoiling. "Wait, didn't you used to run without a shirt? I think you did. I seem to remember that."

"I never ran without a shirt. Occasionally, when it was unusually hot, I took my shirt off afterward, when I was cooling down. Totally different thing."

"Sure, Will. Sure, it is," said Pen, patting his arm. "Are you saying Armando was arrogant?"

"A little. Although it was kind of an awkward situation, so maybe he's not always like that."

"Tell me what happened."

"We didn't talk long. He walked into the examining room, where we were waiting—"

"Wait a minute. You went into the examining room with Jason? Didn't anyone find that odd?"

"He told the nurse we were brothers and that he had a tendency to panic in hospitals."

"You look like brothers," said Pen.

"So anyway, Armando walked in and we all shook hands, and Jason asked about Cat, and Armando said he preferred not to discuss it at work, and Jason said, 'I don't think you're getting how important this is,' and Armando said that, yes, he did, and then he invited us to his house, and then he said the thing that made Jason go apeshit, and Jason yelled, and before they could throw us out, we left."

"Hold on. You *shook hands*. Just like that? I mean, I know you; you'd shake hands with Attila the Hun right before he chopped off your head, but *Jason*? With Armando the motherclucker? Armando, his sworn enemy?"

"I was impressed, actually," said Will. "He was literally quaking—or at least kind of vibrating—with, I don't know, rage or a lust for vengeance or something, before Armando got there, but the second the guy walked in, he pulled himself together. He had that 'gotcha' look on his face he gave us when he showed up at the reunion, but he was strangely polite, even kind of dignified."

"But what about Armando?" Pen asked. "Wasn't he shocked?"

"No. He didn't miss a beat. It was crazy. Or at least, I thought it was crazy until the end, when he said the thing that made Jason go apeshit."

"Oh, boy."

"Right before we left, Jason said something like, 'BTW, way to play it cool, bro. It's like you were expecting me.'"

"He said 'BTW'? What is *wrong* with him? Nobody says that."

"A lot of things are wrong with him, remember?" said Will. "So then Armando gave him this arrogant smile and said, 'I *was* expecting you,' and Jason turned the color of Hawaiian punch the way he does and said, 'No, you weren't.'"

"He's such an infant," said Pen, sighing.

"And Armando said, 'First of all, you called from Ohio. Second of all, you called yourself "Clark Kent." ' "

Pen's eyes widened. "Jason really did that? Why?"

"Apparently, he's been a huge Superman fan his whole life."

Pen covered her face. "Oh no."

"Right. Then Jason said in this sneering voice, 'Why would that mean anything to you? You don't even *have* Superman here.' "

Her face still covered, Pen opened her fingers and peered out. "He is the ugliest American in the whole history of ugly Americans."

"Armando didn't refute the Superman thing, just gave Jason this sort of pitying look, and then said, 'I knew it was you because Catalina told me about your comic book predilection. She told me how embarrassing it was that you always made restaurant reservations under the name "Clark Kent." ' "

"Ai, yi, yi!" shrieked Pen.

"Ai, yi, yi!" echoed Augusta from the pool.

"That's when Jason turned purple and started yelling that Armando was full of shit and how he knew what 'predilection' meant and how Cat hated being called Catalina and loved it when he made reservations like that and how Cat called him 'her Superman' when they were alone." Will shuddered. "It was sad."

They sat and watched the lemon light pour through the coconut palms and skim across the serene blue pool, paying tribute to the sad, angry, devoted, appalling, lunkheaded hunk of humanity that was Jason with a moment of silence.

"I'm a mermaid, Will!" called Augusta.

"I can see that," said Will, smiling.

"So, hey," said Pen excitedly, "I'll meet him."

Will made a pained face. "You sure you want to be there? It could get ugly."

"Are you kidding? After you stopped by yesterday—or whenever it was—I got so jealous that you were meeting him and I wasn't that it took me thirty whole seconds to fall asleep."

It had taken her longer than that. She had lain for a long time, contemplating the familiar, easeful, uncluttered holiness of friendship and the memory of Will in the doorway with his damp hair and beautiful eyes, looking like all the Wills he had ever been. There was peace in it, in being the same old Pen who wanted, above all other things, for nothing to change, but still, her body had stayed awake, wired, her skin tingling, until sleep hit like a snowstorm, whiting out everything.

Will smiled. "Poor Pen."

"Pen's not poor!" corrected Augusta sternly, from the pool's edge. "Pen's rich!"

"True," said Pen.

"Armando's sending his car for us today at five," said Will.

"Fancy," commented Pen through a bite of mango. "I guess I'm not the only one who's rich." Then she sighed. "Poor Jason. Poor, poor, poor, poor Jason."

Augusta didn't say that Jason wasn't poor. She had left the world of adults. In joyous self-absorption, she leaned back like the bathing beauty she was, her toes pointed, her face to the sun; then she sat up and slid into the water like a seal.

THE INTERIOR OF ARMANDO'S CAR WAS ICE-COLD AND PRISTINELY, almost spookily clean, but it wasn't, to Jason's evident satisfaction, especially fancy, not a limousine certainly, which is what they'd all either dreaded or hoped for, not even a Mercedes, which seemed to be the luxury car of choice in Cebu, their slick, dignified shapes jostling incongruously through the city streets with tricycles, mopeds, and jeepneys (public conveyances of surpassing gorgeousness, flashing with chrome, dazzlingly painted, studded with hood ornaments, religious icons, proper names, and cryptic messages; Augusta declared that jeepneys were "the best things in the whole, wide world of shininess" and Pen had to agree). Instead, Armando's vehicle turned out to be a Japanese SUV, smallish and silver.

As they'd piled into it, Pen had heard Jason mutter to Will (or possibly to himself or to Armando or Cat, neither of whom were there),

"Not exactly a slammin' ride for Dr. Hot Shit," which had caused Pen to shoot a worried glance at the driver, whose imperturbable face reacted, if it reacted at all, by growing several degrees more imperturbable. When Will had introduced himself to the driver, the young man had identified himself as Ruben, emphasis (charmingly, Pen thought, and distinguishing him forever from her favorite sandwich) on the second syllable. Pen had winced when Jason, in what she knew he hoped was a blatant defiance of normal driver/rider protocol (although who could say for sure?), ignored the door Ruben held open and stuffed himself into the front passenger seat (it had been slid almost as far forward as it would go, presumably to accommodate passengers riding in the back where they belonged), but Ruben hadn't so much as fluttered an eyelash.

"So, uh, Ruben," said Jason, with a conspiratorial glance back at Will and Pen that made Pen want to strangle him, "you cart old Armando everywhere, do you? Where I come from grown men generally drive themselves, unless they're, like, extremely elderly or paralyzed or whatnot. It's a point of pride."

Pen had the urge to stick her fingers in her ears and sing "Mary Had a Little Lamb" at full volume. Instead, she stared pointedly out the window. They passed roadside fruit stands with their big, glorious, fanned bunches of bananas overhanging careful pyramids of red, green, and gold orbs. Sometimes, the traffic slowed enough for Pen to make out individual fruits, gorgeous and strange: giant green brains, strawberry-colored sea urchins, golden hedgehogs. She wanted to ask Ruben about them, but Jason was still talking. "No offense," he began, words to make your heart sink.

"No offense, but personally, you couldn't pay me to ride in the back while another dude drove. I'd feel like an I-don't-know-what. A toy poodle."

"Toy poodles ride in the backseat while another dude drives?" asked Augusta skeptically. "By themselves?"

"Of course not," said Pen. "Jason's just making stuff up."

Jason aimed a look of irritation at Pen and seemed about to start talking again, when Ruben said, "Dr. Cruz drives himself. I am the driver for the family."

Jason widened his eyes at this, his blond brows shooting up his forehead. "Dr. Cruz has a *family*?"

"Yes," said Ruben.

"This I did not know," said Jason, nodding, and adding in an inexplicable and heinous French accent (inspired by Hercule Poirot? Jacques Clouseau? Cousteau? Impossible to say), "Zee plot thickens!"

"Look at the kids, Mama," said Augusta, pointing. "All dressed the same."

They were schoolchildren, lovely in their uniforms, walking serenely along the dusty, busy street, some of them so young that Pen marveled at their being out alone, until she saw that they weren't alone. They walked in threes, fours, arms linked or loosely wrapped around each other's waists, each one connected to another, the little ones in between the bigger ones.

"Little kids in school uniforms," said Jason. "Doesn't get much cuter than that."

Pen caught Will's eye and telegraphed, *So clucking weird how he can do that, shrug off asinine-ness like an ugly jacket and get real and wistful.*

"All those kids," Jason went on. "You know something? It hit me last night that maybe that's the reason all this is happening."

Will looked at Pen, who shrugged.

"The kids?" asked Will.

"Yeah," said Jason. "One anyway. Hell, why not two or three? We've talked about it. Or I have. Cat wasn't ready to give up, I guess."

"You mean adoption," said Pen.

"It's a Catholic country. Highly Catholic," said Jason. "Some people are surprised by that, an Asian Catholic country."

"We know it's primarily a Catholic country," said Pen, hoping against all odds that he wasn't about to say something hideously insensitive in front of Ruben.

"So we're talking no birth control. Families with seven, ten kids. Cat and I could adopt some, take them home, give them everything they'd never get here."

Ruben didn't speak or shift his gaze from the road.

"What's birth control?" asked Augusta in a loud whisper, and Pen hushed her with a kiss.

"People say there's a reason for everything," Jason said. "And I'm thinking that maybe the reason for all this pain and upheaval is to give us the babies we've been wanting for so long. Because, as God is my witness, we would totally do right by them."

Jason was still staring out the window at the children. Pen didn't know what to say to him, but, looking at him, she could see that it didn't matter: he had forgotten they were there. The car kept nosing slowly forward, so full of burgeoning sorrow and longing, Pen thought the windows might blow out.

ARMANDO'S NEIGHBORHOOD WAS IN THE HILLS. PEN HAD NOT EVEN been aware of hills, until the car passed the guard stand at the neighborhood's entrance and began to wind up them. The houses weren't mansions but were bigger than any houses Pen had seen so far, a far, far cry from the plywood and aluminum shanties they'd seen on their way from the airport to the hotel. ("Squatters" the driver had explained; Pen hadn't known exactly what he meant by that and hadn't asked, but she hoped it had something to do with temporariness, hoped that those shanties were a stop on the road to someplace better, though she worried that they weren't.) As in the rest of Cebu, there were flowers in profusion, lopping over walls, bordering every doorway, banked against buildings, flaring along the roadsides: fiery pink bougainvillea, bushes thick with yellow bells, the white stars of sampaguita, which Ruben told Pen was the national flower. Here and there, bony dogs sprawled in scraps of shade.

"They look feral to me," said Jason. To Pen, they looked haggard and introspective.

Ruben stopped the SUV in front of an iron gate set in a long white wall and beeped the horn, and, after thirty seconds or so, the gate swung open and they drove through. When Pen turned around, she saw two small boys in flip-flops pushing the gate shut.

The house was the kind of house that instantly made Pen want to live in it, fine-boned, graceful, but solid and comfortable-looking, with pebbled steps leading down through a steep, tiered garden to a deep, shadow-pooled lawn. It glowed white as a shell in the mellowing sun.

Ruben opened the car door and lifted Augusta out and set her feet on the ground in a gentle, but matter-of-fact manner that led Pen to think he must be a father. Through the open door Pen saw a man standing on the salmon-colored tiles of the verandah, and even before he began to walk toward them, she knew he must be Armando. He was maybe five-foot-ten, compact and lean, with wavy black hair and the bearing of a prince. He wore stone-colored cargo shorts, leather fisherman sandals, and a loose, short-sleeved linen shirt in a periwinkle blue that offset his skin so impeccably that Pen suspected a woman (Cat?) had chosen it for him.

"Hi," he said with a smile. "Welcome."

He shook hands with everyone and was composed and convivial, as if he were greeting old friends, instead of the large, volatile, cuckolded husband of his former (or not former) lover and the cuckold's pals. As the five of them stood on the verandah, Pen saw the two boys who had closed the gate peeking their glossy heads around the corner of the house, and then a young woman, possibly a teenager, appeared with the boys in tow. They wore striped T-shirts and lovely, shy grins. The oldest could have been no more than eight; the smaller one a few years younger.

"Ask her," the woman said to the boys, her hands on their shoulders pushing them gently forward. "The way I told you."

Slowly, the boys approached Augusta, ducked their heads in miniature bows, and the older boy said, "My name is Paul, and this is my brother Nando. Would you like to play?"

After gaping at them with an expression of dewy-eyed enchantment, Augusta curtsied and said, "My name is Augusta," and looked up beseechingly at Pen, who nodded.

"Sure, as long as you stay in the yard."

"Yay!" she shrieked, breaking the spell, and the children bounded like terriers across the grass, the young woman following behind.

Pen smiled at Armando. "They're beautiful," she said. "Are they yours?"

"Beautiful maybe, but extremely loud," said Armando with a chuckle. "They're the sons of Lana, our cook."

"You have a cook?" blurted out Jason. Pen glanced quickly at him and her heart softened at the regret she saw on his face: he hadn't meant to sound so impressed.

"In the Philippines, a lot of middle-class households have helpers," explained Armando. "Nannies, cooks, drivers, housekeepers. Maybe it's because so many people are in need of employment. It's that way in many developing countries."

"Oh," said Jason grudgingly. "Makes sense, I guess. Must've been tough back in Ohio, huh? Fending for yourself and all."

At the mention of Ohio, everyone seemed to stiffen, social awkwardness setting in like rheumatism.

"Not so tough," said Armando finally, a slight chill in his voice, and for a second, Pen thought he was talking about Jason.

Will was looking down into the yard. "That's an amazing tree," he said.

They all looked, and Pen knew what tree he meant right away: some sort of palm, but not like any she had seen before, tall and flat and wide and shaped exactly like a showgirl's feathered fan.

"A traveler's palm," said Armando. "Although not a true palm tree, more closely related to a banana tree. Indigenous to Madagascar, so a non-native species."

Pen caught a glimpse of the arrogance Will had noticed at the hospital. Armando was a man who liked to know things and liked to tell people what he knew.

"I like it," said Pen defiantly. "Non-native or not."

Armando laughed. "I like it, too. I think it's cool."

Just like that, he was warm again. Maybe it wasn't real arrogance; maybe he resorted to didacticism in moments of social stress, the way she resorted to babbling and Jason to being a jerk (even though it could be argued—Pen had argued it herself, although she was less convinced of it than she once had been—that being a jerk was Jason's natural state). Armando walked to the front door and opened it, with a welcoming, if slightly officious sweep of his hand. "Why don't we go inside where we can talk?"

They all filed in, Pen and Will immediately, Jason after another leisurely look at the lawn in an act of rebellion for which Pen supposed he could not really be blamed. Still, it was embarrassingly transparent: Armando might have a cook, sculpted cheekbones, an affair with Jason's wife under his belt, and a fancy tree, but he couldn't make Jason go inside before Jason was good and ready. *You're not the boss of me.* Pen could almost hear him say the words, sandbox voice and all.

They walked into a smaller version of Patrick and Tanya's great room: kitchen, dining room, living room. It was nice, full of low, carved wood furniture, tall Chinese (at least, Pen assumed they were Chinese) jars, cushions in shades of gold, but it struck Pen as a little sterile, too tidy, as though most of the real living in the house took place elsewhere. Even the kitchen appeared pristine, unused. As she sat down on the sofa, she caught a glimpse of another room around the corner, kids, maybe teenagers watching television, its blue light washing over them, before one of the kids saw her looking and, with a smile, closed the door.

Armando called something in what Pen assumed was Cebuano, and a young woman—a different one from the one who had taken the children to play—appeared with a standing fan. She plugged it in and set it on rotate. When the stream of air hit Pen, she realized how hot she was. Pen smiled to herself, remembering how Cat used to say that if there were gods of fire and water and earth, there should be a god of air-conditioning because it was that elemental to human existence. She had joked about naming her firstborn child Freon.

"Can I offer you a drink? Coke? A beer?" asked Armando.

Pen would have loved a glass of water, but before she could ask for it, Jason said, "Let's cut to the chase. I know Cat's in Cebu, and it's crucial that I find her. If you know anything about her current location, you should tell me. ASAP. Time is of the essence."

Here we go, thought Pen. She wondered if Jason thought people really believed he was a detective when he talked like that.

For a moment, Armando's face grew contemplative. Finally, he said one word, calmly, like a person making his move in a chess game: "Why?"

Jason's face began to redden. "Why what?" he spluttered, and then said, "No, wait. Forget it. You don't get to ask questions. Just tell me what I need to know."

Coolly and as if he hadn't heard Jason take back the "Why what?" Armando said, "Why is it crucial that you find her? Why should I tell you where she is? Why is time of the essence?"

Jason rocked up out of the chair to his feet, one hand on his hip, the other pointing at Armando, and said, "Because she's my wife."

Pen was impressed by the simplicity of the answer, but she didn't like the wild look in Jason's eyes, which only grew more intense when Armando got up from his chair, too. He didn't move toward Jason, just stood there, but still managed to look quick, wary, and light-footed, like a boxer. Pen looked over at Will. He was still sitting, but Pen saw that he was full of coiled energy, his hands poised on the arms of his chair.

"I think you should sit down, Jason," said Will in a low voice.

"Fuck that," said Jason loudly, never taking his eyes off Armando. "What do you know about Cat?"

"Have you considered," said Armando coldly, "that if she wanted you to find her, she would not have left in secret, without telling you where she was going?"

"Shut up!" shouted Jason. "You don't know what the hell you're talking about."

Pen waited for it to dawn on him that he was wrong about this, that, clearly, Armando did know what he was talking about, and, sure enough, after staring into space for a few seconds, he jabbed his finger at Armando again. "You've talked to her. You wouldn't know that if you hadn't talked to her."

Armando seemed to consider his next move, before he raised his chin an inch or two and said, "Sure, I talked to her. We had dinner together the day after she arrived in Cebu."

At the same instant that Jason lunged across the coffee table toward

Armando, Will stood up as fast as a striking snake and grabbed him, his arm thrown across Jason's wide chest.

"No, Jason!" said Pen, but Jason was struggling to get himself free. He wasn't in shape, but he was a lot bigger than Will, and Pen knew it could be only a matter of seconds before he broke away. Without thinking, she lifted the delicate china bowl off the perilously positioned coffee table and cradled it in her lap.

"You son of a gun!" A great, loud bark of a voice, heavily accented.

All eyes turned in the direction of the voice. Standing in the entrance to the room was an elderly woman, very elderly, frail and tiny inside her loose batik housedress, but bristling with electricity. With her short gray hair puffed around her head like a nimbus, her ferocious black eyes, and her raised fist, she looked unreal, iconic, like a miniature goddess of vengeance.

"Coming into my house, yelling!" raged the woman, walking toward Jason with remarkably steady steps. "Throwing yourself around like an elephant!"

Jason had stopped struggling as soon as he had heard the woman's voice. Now, as the woman advanced upon him, he wilted inside Will's grasp, and Will let go.

"Sorry about that, ma'am," Jason said with hangdog politeness. "I-I didn't know this was your house. I didn't know you were here."

"Where else would I be?" scoffed the woman.

"Lola," said Armando softly, "it's okay."

He walked toward her and, with exquisite tenderness, took her hand in his. "I'm sorry we disturbed you."

"Ehhh!" said the woman. "You should be sorry!" And she reached up and cuffed Armando across his head, but Pen saw that her eyes had grown soft. "No more yelling!"

He smiled, kissed her cheek, and turned her around. "No more yelling, Lola. I promise."

"You, too, elephant!" said the woman, glaring at Jason over her shoulder.

"Me, too, ma'am," said Jason.

When the woman was gone, Armando turned back to them and said, "My grandmother."

"You live with your grandmother?" asked Jason. He didn't sound hostile, just dazed.

"My grandmother, my parents, my brother, Rey, who is in medical school, two of my younger sisters."

"Oh, so, they're the family Ruben meant," said Pen. "He said he was the driver for your family."

"That's right," said Armando.

"No wife?" asked Jason with a hint of snideness.

"Not yet," said Armando, chin up, eyes challenging.

"Jason and I are going out for a walk," said Will. "Get some air."

"I'm not leaving here until he tells me what he knows about Cat," said Jason in a blunt but thankfully unpetulant way.

"You guys go check on Augusta. I'll stay and talk to him," said Pen quickly, "if that's okay with you, Armando."

"No problem," said Armando amiably.

When they left, Armando slumped down onto the sofa, ran his hand through his hair, and gave a low whistle. Pen liked him for this open display of relief and vulnerability. A pattern seemed to be emerging: his aloofness and pomposity would push you away; his humor and humanness would pull you back—and just in the nick of time. Pen thought that she could only take this state of affairs for so long before it exhausted her, but she could imagine Cat's finding it exciting. She had always had a soft spot for thorny men with soft underbellies. Behind their backs, she and Pen used to call them echidnas.

"I think that went well, don't you?" said Pen.

"He's big, isn't he?" said Armando, widening his eyes. "You can forget how big and then he charges you like a bull and you remember."

"I've thought that before, that he's part bull," said Pen, smiling.

Armando sat up, gave her his out-of-the-blue, disarming white crescent of a smile, and said, "Thank you."

"For what? Showing up here with Jason so that he could disrupt your entire household?"

"For saving my mother's bowl."

Pen looked down at the bowl in her lap, which she'd forgotten she was holding, and laughed. "You're welcome."

"I should thank Will, too," said Armando. "Has he always had those ninja reflexes?"

Pen placed the bowl back on the table as she considered this. "I guess he has. He just used to use them for jumping on people instead of for jumping on the people who jump on people. But he reformed a while back."

"Lucky for me. I was surprised to find you and Will traveling with Jason. I didn't think you liked him."

"You know who we are?" asked Pen, startled.

"Of course. Cat and I talked a lot, and after I left, we e-mailed a lot. I've even seen pictures of you two. You're the friends."

"That's right. We're the friends. Jason's the husband. And you're the—?" She waited.

"I'm the guy who lives on the other side of the world," he said.

On impulse, Pen leaned forward with clasped hands and said, "I wish you would tell me about you and Cat."

She expected him to get supercilious and distant, to say it was none of her business, with which she really couldn't argue except to say that she loved Cat and missed her and that collecting what she could of Cat's story was her only means of feeling close to her. But instead, Armando's eyes lit up with eagerness, and for the first time since she'd met him, he looked young. Pen realized, with a start, that he was young.

"From the very first day, it was like we'd always known each other. We talked about our families, our pasts. It was easy. We both noticed that, how easy it was."

He was so boyish and warm and open-hearted. *Oh*, marveled Pen, *he loves her.* She hadn't expected him to love her.

"You were friends?" she asked cautiously.

"Yes, friends. Real friends." His tone took on a note of defiance, as he said, "It's true that we were both lonely. I was a long way from home, working all the time, and she was unhappy in her marriage, in her work, but that's not why we were together. We could have met under any circumstances and been—"

Pen watched him search for the word. His English was fluid, even formal, eloquent. It wasn't his command of the language that was failing him, she saw; it was that when it came to love, sometimes language just failed.

"I understand," said Pen.

"Thanks," said Armando.

"What job was she doing that she didn't like?" asked Pen.

"She was training to be a pharmaceutical rep. She thought it would be glamorous, the dinners, the parties. You must understand that she was much less happy than when you knew her. She found her life very drab." He said it as though he was apologizing for Cat's desire for glamour, as though glamour wasn't imprinted on Cat's DNA as firmly as her black hair, her tapered fingers.

"And it involved travel, of course," he continued. "She was always wanting to be someplace else, away."

"Away from Jason, you mean," said Pen.

"Of course!" Armando knit his straight black brows in disgust. "She didn't love him. How could she? He's ridiculous, unsophisticated, a—bonehead!"

Even as Pen suppressed a smile at the word *bonehead* coming out of Armando's mouth, and despite having known, for nearly a decade, the way she'd known that the sky was blue, that Jason was indeed a bonehead, she felt the unexpected urge to defend him, but she couldn't figure out how.

"He loves her," said Pen at last. It needed to be said.

"No, he doesn't. He wouldn't know how to love someone like Cat."

Pen would not be deterred. "I'm sure you're right that he doesn't love her the way she wants to be loved, but he loves her," she said. "Yes, he's a bonehead. Yes, I spend most of my time with him wanting to strangle him. But he loves Cat. She's the reason for everything he does."

"That's why you're here with him? You want him to find her because he loves her?"

Pen faltered. "I don't—know. I mean, no. We came because—" She made a frustrated sound. "It's a long story, but now Will and I are here for ourselves. We miss Cat. We've never stopped missing her all these years."

Armando's face softened. "And she never stopped missing you."

"But." Pen hesitated. Why not just leave it alone? Since when was she Jason's champion? Since never. Still. Pen sighed. "On this trip with Jason, I've come to realize that it matters that he loves her. I've tried to deny it, but I can't." Gently, she added, "And Cat did marry him, after all."

Armando shut his eyes. When he opened them, he looked young again, young, conflicted, and even regretful.

"We shouldn't have done it," he said quietly. "It was a mistake."

"Why?" asked Pen.

"Because, for one thing, I was never going to stay."

"Couldn't you have stayed? Did you try?"

"My city needs me," he said, with a touch of the old pomposity. "The Philippines needs me. There is a brain drain in my country; those with talent and skills leave as soon as they get the chance. The United States has plenty of good surgeons. Not so many here. I swore from the beginning that I would come back."

"I see," said Pen, feeling awkward. "Well, that was good of you."

"Also," said Armando with a grin, "I promised my mother that I would."

"Ah! If she's anything like Lola, I can see why you'd be afraid to break that promise."

"You got that right."

"What's the other reason?" said Pen. "You said 'for one thing.' Why else?"

Armando's head dropped for a second. "Because they were married, as you said. I believe in marriage, in taking vows. We made a mistake."

Pen felt suddenly annoyed at his ostentatious regret. "A mistake? You make it sound like an accident, like the two of you just tripped and—oops!—fell into bed. You must have discussed it. Even if you didn't, it was deliberate. I'm not saying it was wrong or that I haven't done things like that myself, because I have, sort of, but own up to it, for heaven's sake."

Armando stared at her. "What did you say?"

"Look, I didn't mean to sound judgmental. Or maybe I did mean to. But I shouldn't have. I'm sorry."

"Why do you think we fell into bed?"

"Because you just said so, for starters."

"We fell in love. That was our mistake. That's what I meant."

Pen felt flustered. "Wait. But you had an affair."

"No, not technically. Not the physical part."

"You mean, you didn't have—sex?" Sometimes, a thing needed to be spelled out.

Armando looked embarrassed. "No. I wouldn't." He corrected himself: "I mean, *we* decided not to."

We, thought Pen, *ha!* She knew her Cat better than that.

"You should not assume," said Armando, scolding.

"I didn't," snapped Pen, and then it hit her: Cat had lied to Jason. Women all over the world trying to hide affairs from their husbands, and Cat had gone and made one up and handed it to her husband, a mean lie dressed up as an act of humility and contrition, an act of trust.

"What do you mean?" asked Armando slowly.

"I mean that—" She tried to sort out exactly whom she would be betraying by telling Armando what Cat had done. Cat? Jason?

Armando watched her struggle with what to say and asked with bewilderment, "She told him that?"

Pen gave a resigned shrug. "That's what he said."

Armando looked like a kid trying to figure out a Rubik's cube, turning his thoughts this way, that way.

"If Cat isn't here with you, where is she?" ventured Pen, hoping to take advantage of his bemused state. "Can you tell me, please?"

"Will you tell Jason?"

Pen wanted to say no. "Yes. I have to. We're sort of in this together, now."

"In that case, why should I tell you? Why should I help him find her?"

"You would have every right not to," said Pen. "But Will and I love her and want to see her so much."

Armando folded his arms and looked at her. Her heart was pounding. They were so close; to lose Cat now, when they were so close, she would not be able to stand it.

"Also, you know that what she did wasn't really right," said Pen.

She may have said it in order to manipulate him into telling her, but as soon as she spoke the words, she realized that they were true. The more she spoke, the more she understood that she was speaking her own heart. "I hate to say that because I do love her, but it's true. I don't mean leaving him. That would've been all right. But leaving him the way she did. She tried to make him so angry that he would leave her or throw her out. When that didn't work, she sneaked away, just disappeared."

"Why would she do that?"

He asked it, but she could tell he knew the answer. She and Armando sat across from each other in his perfect house and in the same difficult spot, caught between loving Cat and admitting that she wasn't as good as they wanted her to be, that she had done a thing she should never have done.

"Because she chickened out," said Pen sadly. "She knew how he felt about her and she couldn't stand to see him fall apart when she told him she was leaving, so she ran away. She should have faced it, don't you think?"

"Yes." Armando turned his face in the direction of the fan, let the cool air flow across it. It seemed to help him decide his next move because, afterward, he looked Pen in the eye and said, "That's why she left the way she did," he said. "But she could have run anywhere. She came here for a reason."

"To see you, right?"

He shook his head. "I saw her. She had dinner here, at the house, with everyone. But I'm not why she came to Cebu."

"Then why?" asked Pen.

"Yes, why?" demanded a voice. It was Lola, stepping from the shadows into the room.

Armando shook his head and smiled. "She came to find her family."

CHAPTER SEVENTEEN

*M*AYBE IT WAS THE FOOD OR THE MUTED LIGHT OR THE CEIL-ing fan's slow, hypnotic paddling of the air or maybe it was simply that every journey—and Pen had come to see herself as a person distinctly on a journey (in rare, solitary, un-ironic moments, "seeker" did not seem too strong a word, although what she was seeking, apart from Cat [and she was sure there was something else] she couldn't say)—has its land of the lotus eaters, its drowsy slowdown in momentum. There would be time to winnow out the reasons later, but as she sat in the living room of the house in which Cat's father had grown up, surrounded by someone else's family—Cat's family, the one she had flown across the world to find—with a plate of food on a tray in front of her, all Pen knew was that she wanted, with her heart, to become part of the place, to unpack her bags, hunker down, and stay.

Jason had wanted to call Dr. Ocampo's sisters right away, the same night they'd left Armando's house, right after Pen had recounted her conversation with Armando, giving Jason and Will a nutshell version (with a covert look at Will that meant she would tell him the rest later) that left out just about everything but Cat's real reason for coming to Cebu. As soon as she had told Jason that she had the sisters' phone number, he had stuck out his bear-sized paw, palm up, demanding it, and had gotten mad when she'd refused. Cat's aunts were elderly, she told him, it would be much more considerate to wait until morning,

but the truth was she wasn't sure that Jason's making the call at all
was a good idea, since having him talk to anyone about anything, especially Cat, was almost never a good idea, and she wanted time to
discuss the matter with Will in private.

"Who died and made you queen of the world?" Jason had protested,
loudly, in the hotel lobby. "You're not the boss. You don't get to say
what we do!"

He had been so whiny and Pen so groggy and irritable, emotional
exhaustion and jet lag's undertow pulling her down and down, that it
was on the tip of her tongue to call him names, to say something low-
down and cutting (*Your wife didn't jump in the sack with Armando
after all, moron; she just wanted you to think she did!*—an incongruous
put-down if Pen ever heard one), but before she could, a little, niggling,
adult voice inside her head reminded her that, blowhard or not, the guy
had already been hurt pretty wretchedly in ways he knew about and in
ways he didn't and it would take an exceedingly mean-hearted person
to hurt him more, at least right at that moment. Pen sat there trying to
gauge whether she was mean-hearted enough and came down on the
side of "No" but just barely. So all she said was, "Of course I'm not the
boss, but I need to put Augusta to bed. Let's have breakfast by the pool
tomorrow and make a plan. Okay?"

When Jason had begun to sputter at this, Will had said, "Take it
easy, man, you're scaring Augusta," which of course were the magic
words.

With a guilty glance at Augusta, who was sitting in a chair playing
with her new favorite toy, a bunch of miniature bananas, each one no
more than three inches long, a gift from Armando's Lola ("*You* are the
tiniest!" "No, *you* are the tiniest!" "*You* are the tiniest and have three
brown spots!"), and looking not the least bit scared, Jason mumbled,
"My bad. See you in the morning."

In the end, it was Pen who called. She spoke to an aunt named Lita,
a short conversation but one full of radical highs and lows—yes, Cat
had been there; no, she was not there now; yes, she might be back; yes,
they knew where she was; yes, they might be willing to tell Pen—and
ending with an invitation.

"Come to the house tomorrow," said Lita, simultaneously bossy and kind. "As Catalina's friends and husband, you are welcome. Let us meet you and plan from there."

She hadn't said, "Let us meet you and judge your worthiness and sanity so that we can decide whether or not to entrust you with information regarding the whereabouts of our beloved Cat," but Pen had understood that this was what she meant.

Now, as she sat across from the three women, Lola Lita, Lola Fe, and Lola Graciela ("Lola" having turned out to be not a proper name, as Pen had assumed when she had met Armando's lola, but a word meaning something like "grandmother" or maybe "respected elderly female relative," since the three women could not [could they?] all be grandmothers to all of the people in the house—and there were lots of them—who called them "Lola"), their bright, dark eyes upon her, she knew she should have felt anxious, judged, but what she felt instead was intense contentment, a warmth that started someplace in the center of her body and radiated outward. As she bit into her second empanada, a golden half-moon stuffed with beef, raisins, potatoes, and heaven, she acknowledged that it was just possible that this central place was in the vicinity of her stomach.

The Lolas had thrown them a party. At least, Pen was fairly sure that this splendid profusion of food and people was a party, even though when she thanked Lola Lita for it, Lita waved her hand in the air, irritably, as though swatting away thanks along with the ridiculous notion that anyone had gone to any trouble, and scoffed, "It's nothing. Relatives and a little food. Lunch. Nothing special!"

But there was nothing "nothing special" about it: great piled tangles of noodles rife with bits of vegetables, meat, and shrimp; a concoction of eggplant, okra, green beans, squash, and bitter melon called *pinakbet;* banana blossom salad; whole fish, crispy and gleaming with sauce; thin eggrolls called *lumpia* that Pen could have eaten like popcorn; and, glory of glories, down the center of its own special table, a roasted suckling pig, burnt orange, glistening, dizzyingly fragrant. Pen had a momentary qualm at seeing it whole—snout, ears, tail, the small, poignant hooves ("even-toed ungulate" is the phrase that appeared, unbidden, in Pen's mind)—but once dismantled, the sublime combination of hard, crackly skin and nearly white, meltingly tender meat caused such rapture in her mouth that she gave hearty thanks to God that she was not a vegetarian.

Still, as astonishing as the food was, Pen knew that the source of her contentment was not solely, or even chiefly, gustatory, but had to do with her fellow partygoers. She would learn that nearly all of them lived there, if not in the main house, then in one of the two other houses that sat on the edges of the dusty backyard. Each tiny house was flanked by a riot of high-gloss green and flowers like little shouts of joy and faced a central space that bore a banana tree, a lanzone tree with cascading clusters of brown-yellow golf-ball-looking fruit, and, queening over everything, a green mango under which slept two black dogs. It was a compound, Pen supposed, although as un-Waco-like as it was un-Kennedy-like, surrounded by a high wall the top of which was spangled with broken bottles embedded in the cement. Despite this hint at a dangerous outside world, Pen felt that she had never been anyplace safer. Even the sharp shards of glass were pretty, glowing with mellow color under the sun.

Although she, Will, and Jason were introduced to each person individually, from the littlest, wobbly-legged toddler, to the skinny, pop-star-haired teenagers slouching in corners, to smiling adults, some chatty, some with shy lowered chins, Pen found that she could not keep straight how each was related to the others, how they all fit in. The titles (tito, tita, cousin, grandson, sister) blurred inside her head. But it seemed to her that specific relationships—who was married to whom, whose children were whose—mattered less here, in this household, than they would have at home.

What was clear was that they were a family, each person belonging to the other, held together by an intergenerational web of talking, teasing, scolding, feeding, pulling onto laps, shooing away, holding close. At the center of the web were the three Lolas. If Pen was initially impressed with their sameness—short gray hair; broad, brown, remarkably unlined faces; delicate hands; voluminous generosity; intelligent black eyes—she quickly began to see differences between them. Lola

Fe was jolly, effusive, the one the kids came to when they wanted someone to say yes. Lola Graciela was quiet but watchful; she seemed a little younger than the others. Lola Lita was the boss.

After dessert (Pen, Will, and Jason had slices of leche flan, wondrously eggy and bathed in caramelized sugar; Augusta dove headfirst into a bowl of deep violet-colored ube ice cream, which Pen later learned was made from a variety of yam, a fact that she did not share with Augusta), the party scattered, people going back to their usual Sunday afternoons. Except for the roaming pack of small children into which Augusta had been immediately and thoroughly absorbed, they were alone with the Lolas.

Lola Lita began. "We have been discussing the three of you, and we have a question."

"If you don't mind," added Lola Fe, giving her sister (if she was her sister; Pen wasn't sure) a look of good-humored remonstrance.

"Of course," conceded Lola Lita with a nod. "If you don't mind."

"We don't mind," said Pen.

"Sure," said Will.

"Fire away!" said Jason. His voice was jocular and too loud. Pen stole a glimpse and saw that he wasn't just stained red from collarbone to hairline; he was sweating and as antsy as a two-year-old. With reluctant but now familiar compassion washing over her, she thought that she had never seen him so nervous.

"Here is the question," Lola Lita said, her voice perfectly calm but her eyes burning like coals. "Do you think that Cat would want you to find her?"

The Lolas leaned back in their chairs and folded their hands. Pen and Will and Jason all looked at one another.

"Please," said Lola Fe quickly, sensing their uneasiness, "do not feel that one of you must answer for all. Maybe it would be best if you each spoke only for yourself."

Silence. The ceiling fan went slowly round and round. Pen saw a lizard, pale brown and no more than three inches long, dart up the wall. Then Will's voice, clear and easy: "I think she would. I don't know if Cat told you about us, about me and Pen—"

"She did," said Lola Lita with a droll look at the other Lolas. "She told us her life story. In some detail. You were included."

"Well, then maybe you know that when the three of us last saw each other, we were basically kids," said Will. "We meant well, but we were a little stupid."

"Hmm," sniffed Pen.

Will shot her a half-grin and continued, "Some of us were more stupid than others, but the thing is that each of us, in our own way, thought that if we couldn't keep being friends in *exactly* the way we'd always been friends, then everything would fall apart."

Did I think that? thought Pen. *I don't know if I thought that.*

You have always hated change, have resisted it with everything you're worth, she reminded herself, and she had to admit that this was true.

"I think we were wrong about that," said Will.

"You do?" said Pen, startled.

"Yeah," said Will, reddening. "I think we should've taken more risks, had more—faith, I guess. And now, I think we could use another chance."

"You think Catalina would agree?" asked Lola Lita.

Will nodded. "I do." He paused, smiling. "Plus, nobody loves surprises more than Cat."

Lola Fe laughed, a sweet, husky sound that filled the air inside the house.

"Thank you, Will," said Lola Lita.

Pen expected Jason to jump in then, but he just sat, staring at nothing, jiggling his knee, looking like he might cry or run out of the room, so Pen took a breath and stared into the faces of the Lolas. A trinity of Lolas. *The three Graces,* she thought, *the three Fates.*

"Cat would be as glad to see me as I would to see her," said Pen finally, and was mortified to hear the trembling in her voice. "She would. We were like sisters. We loved each other." She shook her head impatiently. "Not loved. Love."

"Love?" asked Lola Graciela, speaking for the first time. "Even after so many years?"

"Yes," said Pen staunchly. It was true. She felt the truth of it shine on her like a light. "Of course."

In unison, the Lolas rustled like a flock of doves, nodding and humming murmurs of assent and approval, at Pen, at one another, before settling down again, their eyes sparkling. Pen felt a rush of elation, as though she had passed a test.

Everyone turned to Jason. Pen braced herself, waiting for belligerence or bravado, an oversized, embarrassing burst of something, but Jason didn't say anything right away. He seemed to be willing himself not to fidget, with his knees pressed together, his hands gripping the sides of his chair seat. He opened his mouth and shut it again. Pen wasn't sure he was breathing.

Suddenly, Lola Graciela, who had been so quiet, came alive. She slapped her knee with one hand, and said, with an edge of anger in her voice, "The question is ridiculous for him! She is his wife, no matter what. Naturally, he must find her!"

The other two Lolas did not seem surprised at this outburst. They exchanged a knowing glance between them, and Lita reached out and put her hand over Graciela's.

"We know that you feel this way, Graci," said Lita kindly, and, at her touch, the tension seemed to leave Graciela. She lowered her lids and nodded.

Jason cleared his throat.

"Jason would like a chance to speak, I think," said Lola Lita.

Lola Fe gave him an encouraging thumbs-up with her tiny thumb.

"So, uh, contrary to popular belief," said Jason, "I'm not an idiot."

The Lolas shifted their gazes ever so slightly in the direction of Pen and Will who shrugged and nodded their apologies; then everyone turned back to Jason.

"I know how it looks, Cat leaving without telling me. And, hey, you probably even know about the Armando thing, too."

The Lolas nodded, as Pen squirmed inwardly, wondering which story Cat had told them, wondering what was worse, having a wife who cheated or one who lied in order to hurt you so much you'd throw her out, and wondering, too, not for the first time, whether she was obligated to tell Jason the truth. So much was getting fuzzy lately—Pen's loyalties, her obligations. She felt a jolt of anger at Cat for having lied, at Armando for having told the truth, at both of them—and she knew this wasn't really fair—for making her the keeper of a secret she did not want.

"I'm not gonna lie to you," Jason continued. "We've had our share of problems. The infertility stuff royally sucked, pardon my language, and, yeah, I know Cat wasn't happy with where we lived and whatnot. It's probably also the case that she wasn't always happy with me."

"No marriage is happy all the time," said Lola Graciela softly.

"She's too good for me." A bittersweet, affectionate smile appeared on Jason's face, flickered, and was gone. "I've always known that."

Pen thought, *Too smart, too funny, too sparkling and bewitching and quick, but maybe not too good,* and felt instantly ashamed, until she understood that she didn't mean that Cat wasn't good, but that, in some highly unexpected, mostly imperceptible, but fundamental way, Jason was.

"So I'd have to say it's possible she doesn't realize she wants me to find her. She might even, uh, actively think she does *not* want me to find her."

Pen had to admire his honesty. Maybe it was the Lolas, before whose clear and rock-steady gaze it was difficult to do anything but speak the truth. Maybe it was that Jason had nothing left to lose. Maybe, probably, it was that he was braver than Pen had given him credit for.

"But here's the deal." Jason's voice tensed. "When I find her, as soon as she sees me, she'll be glad I'm there. No lie."

"How do you know this?" asked Lola Lita sternly.

Jason's blue eyes brightened. "Because that's how it always happens. I mean, let's face it; Cat's thought about leaving me before. She even did it a few times, and there might even be times I don't know about. Probably there are. Anyway, she'd pack a bag and go to a friend's house or check into a hotel, or even just drive around aimlessly, with the bag sitting in the front seat." He lifted his weighty chin. "But she always came back, every time, and she'd see me in our house—I'd have, like, gotten her note or whatever and be just sitting there—and her heart would melt."

Oh, God, thought Pen.

"That's what she'd say. She'd say, 'I can't help it, little boy. No matter how mad I am, I see you and my heart melts.' She calls me 'little boy' which is hilarious when you consider how big I am compared to her."

If anyone found this hilarious, they didn't let on. Unexpectedly, Pen found herself thinking of Augusta. Augusta and her addled sleep habits, how on any one of thousands of nights her sobbing and shouts of "Mama!" would drag Pen out of sleep, two, three, even four times, how by the last wake-up, usually near dawn, Pen would be shaking with exhaustion and a resentment so acute it was almost rage. Her head throbbing and full of static, she would throw off sheets and comforter and stomp down the hallway to Augusta's room, muttering expletives, even threats (threats that, no matter how empty, would make her reel with shame in the light of day), but within seconds of arriving at her child's bedside, as soon as she saw the pale, wet face, the skinny shoulders, her anger would dissipate, lose itself in the warm, Augusta-scented air of the room. Her heart would melt. Pen would lie down next to Augusta and pull the small, baby animal bulk of the girl into the curve of her body, and give herself over to the business—her life's work—of loving this person who needed her.

Maybe Cat feels something like that; maybe that's why it was so hard to leave him, thought Pen, which should have been a nonsensical thought, since Jason was a full-grown (even, it could be argued, an overgrown) man, but Pen found that it made an absurd, sad, slightly unsavory kind of sense to her.

"Thank you," said Lola Lita, nodding elegantly, like an empress. "Thanks to all of you. Thanks and apologies; we do not usually interrogate our guests."

"That's okay," said Will and Pen.

"No prob," said Jason. "Totally understandable."

Pen wondered if the Lolas would retire someplace, perhaps to an inner fate-deciding sanctum, to discuss whether to tell them where Cat had gone, but they didn't budge, just set about wordlessly conversing through nods, raised eyebrows, almost imperceptible shrugs, and some of the mild dovecote sounds like the ones they'd made when Pen said that she and Cat still loved each other. Pen didn't feel impatient. She believed that she could sit and watch the three of them do that forever.

When the cooing and humming had concluded, Pen expected Lola Lita to speak first, but instead it was Lola Fe.

"Fine, but if we are telling them where Catalina is, I think we must also call her to let her know they are coming," she said.

"No!" said Jason, so loudly that Pen jumped.

The Lolas did not jump, just turned their heads in unison to gaze at him. He reached up and wiped the sweat from his brow. Seeing this, Lola Graciela leaned over to turn the electric fan in his direction.

"I mean, please," he said. "Could you—do you think you could just not tell her?"

The Lolas exchanged a complicated, lightning-quick set of looks.

"Why do you ask this?" said Lola Fe.

"Uh, like Will said," said Jason, forcing a grin, "Cat loves to be surprised."

Lola Fe did not react, except to keep her eyes trained on him, waiting for more.

"And, you know, like I said, she might think she doesn't want to see me. She might even leave if she knows I'm coming. Probably not, but it's possible. When I show up, though, she'll be very happy, rejoicing even. I swear to God."

Pen saw Lola Fe's eyebrows go up. She wondered if it was a good or bad idea to swear to God, here in this house that had an Augusta-sized Virgin Mary statue standing, wistful and blue-robed, in the yard and a crucifix—at least one—on nearly every wall.

"We should honor his wishes," exclaimed Lola Graciela with fervor. "He is her husband!"

Lola Fe stirred in her chair and seemed about to speak, maybe even speak loudly, but after a second, her face relaxed into cameo-blank inscrutability. Her eyes met Lola Lita's gaze and held it. Lola Lita closed her eyes and nodded, before turning to Will, Jason, and Pen with a smile.

"You must wait until tomorrow to go find Catalina, in any case," she said. None of them asked why this was so. The fact of her saying it was enough to make it indisputable. "We hope you will consider spending the night here, since you are Catalina's friends and family. I'm afraid our home isn't luxurious, but we would be most honored if you would stay."

"Oh, thank you! We'd love to," cried Pen, without so much as a questioning glance at Will or Jason and so hot on the heels of the invitation that Lola Lita laughed, a deep, buttery chuckle. Pen turned sheepishly to Will and Jason. "I mean, if it's okay with you guys."

Will smiled a smile that managed to be private, in spite of the other people in the room, and said, "You like it here. It's a Pen kind of place."

"I do," admitted Pen.

"We'd be honored to stay," said Jason.

"Good," said Lola Lita. "Now, why don't you go to pick up your things at the hotel? My nephew Everett will be glad to drive you."

"Great," said Will. "Thank you."

"Sounds good," agreed Jason.

Pen tried to imagine herself getting up and walking out of that house, even just for a short trip, and failed utterly. "Please," she said to the Lolas, "may Augusta and I stay here, while the boys go to the hotel? If I promise to stay out of your way?"

"Of course!" said Lola Lita. "If Will and Jason are willing."

"Would you mind?" she asked Will. "Our stuff is pretty much together. If you could just throw it all into my suitcase and Augusta's backpack?"

"Sure," said Will, shrugging. "But if I come back and you've polished off that pig? You're dead meat."

"Ha!" said Jason. "Pig. Dead meat. Get it?"

"Got it," said Pen, and all the Lolas nodded.

TUCKED AS SHE WAS INTO A SHADY CORNER OF THE BACKYARD, despite the children playing tag and screeching, despite the cold glass of calamansi juice in her hand, despite the tart perfection of the juice itself, Pen might have fallen asleep. Time changed in that yard. Minutes flowed by with rich, honeylike slowness. Pen's body felt more and more deliciously heavy. But before she could drift off, she opened her eyes to find Lola Lita sitting next to her, fanning herself with a large, woven palm-leaf fan, and regarding Pen with an amused affection that reminded Pen of her mother. Pen shook the sleepiness from her head and sat up.

"Sorry," she said, laughing. "I don't usually go falling asleep in people's yards, at least not people I've just met."

"Perhaps it means you feel at home here. I'm very glad."

"It's a marvelous place."

"Thank you," said Lola Lita, looking about her. "It isn't fancy. It's even a bit shabby, but it's home. My family moved here after the war, when we were all quite young. Manuel was no more than a baby."

"Manuel?" asked Pen. "Oh. Cat's father."

"Yes," said Lola Lita sadly. "My baby brother."

"I'm so sorry for your loss," said Pen and felt ashamed and surprised at herself for not having offered her condolences earlier, when they had first arrived. It wasn't that she had forgotten about Dr. Ocampo. It was just that this place seemed to Pen to be a world away from grief.

"Thank you," said Lola Lita again. She reached over and touched Pen's hand. "We have made a decision regarding your wish to find Catalina."

"You have?" Pen held her breath.

"We will tell you where she went," said Lola Lita.

Tears prickled Pen's eyes. She blinked. "Thank you. Thank you so much."

"She is visiting a resort island, quite enchanting as I have heard. We have secured tickets for you on the ferry for tomorrow morning, and we have made hotel reservations, as well. Our niece's friend from college is a travel agent, which made it possible for us to make the arrangements on a Sunday."

"Oh, that's wonderful! I can just imagine it, seeing her across the hotel lobby—" Pen broke off, overcome with gladness.

Uneasiness swept over Lola Lita's face and she gave Pen's hands a squeeze. "I am afraid that it won't be quite so simple."

"It won't?" asked Pen, worried. "Why?"

Lola Lita sighed. "We can be so stubborn. Fe, Graci, and I, we are usually in agreement, but when we're not, well, it can be—difficult."

"I can imagine," said Pen.

"The problem is that we have decided, after much discussion, to abide by Jason's wish that we not tell Catalina you are coming."

"I see," said Pen. "Well, it might be for the best. She might leave if she knows that Jason's coming."

Lola Lita's eyes glinted. "The best for Jason, maybe, and for you and Will. Possibly not the best for Cat."

"I guess you might be right," admitted Pen uncomfortably.

"But it also presents a problem for you because we know where she is but not precisely where."

"Oh."

"Bohol Province is composed of a large island and many smaller ones. We know that Catalina was planning to stay on Panglao Island. We also know which region of the island, but we don't know which resort. We're not even sure that she is still there, although I think she probably is."

Pen sipped her juice, then pressed her glass against her forehead.

"We have reserved rooms for the four of you at a resort on Panglao Island," Lola Lita continued, "but if we don't call Cat to say you are coming, we can't find out exactly where she is."

"Can't you call her to ask where she is, without mentioning us? Or call her travel agent and try to get the information from her?" Even as Pen said it, she realized how sneaky it sounded.

Lola Lita shook her head. "No. I'm sorry, but no. We can only tell you what we know about where she went, and even that feels—"

"Disloyal?"

Lola Lita smiled tenderly at Pen, "You must understand that this trip was very important to Cat. She wanted to be—undisturbed."

Pen's heart sank. "But we might not find her."

Lola Lita made soft hums of comfort and brushed a lock of hair away from Pen's cheek. "It is not a large beach, not even a kilometer long," she said. "And you can go to some of the Bohol tourist attractions that Cat will surely visit. I have heard that you do not want to miss snorkeling along the black coral reef."

Pen had her doubts about the snorkeling, fearing sharks and figuring that one sure way to decrease your chances of finding someone was to immerse yourself in the Pacific Ocean. She envisioned Cat swimming toward her, through shoals of brilliant fish, waving wildly, her hair floating like seaweed around her face. She smiled.

As if Lola Lita had read Pen's thoughts, she said, kind reproval in her voice, "I know you want to find Catalina, but who knows when you and your daughter will come back to the Philippines? So many people never get to go anywhere. Allow yourself to really be here. See what there is to see."

Pen nodded thoughtfully. Ever since she had arrived in the Philippines, Pen had been dazzled by a sense of improbability. *We were there*, she had thought, *and now we are here. How could it be true?* But it was true. The world was big and Pen was in it. The least she could do was pay attention.

"Okay," she agreed. "But can you tell me something?"

Lola Lita nodded her empress nod.

"Do *you* think we'll find her?" Pen held her breath, waiting.

Pensively, Lola Lita narrowed her eyes, sending sunbursts of wrinkles shooting from their corners. *No one can see the future*, thought Pen, breathlessly. *But if someone could, this is exactly how she would look.*

"Yes," said Lola Lita, "I do."

PEN DIDN'T KNOW WHAT WOKE HER, BUT SUDDENLY SHE WAS SITTING up, her senses prickling, her chest full of rising, undefined emotion. In near perfect darkness, in the bed next to hers, Augusta shifted, sighed, and drew herself into a tight ball, like an armadillo. Pen waited for her daughter's breathing to ease back into its cradle-rock rhythm and then noiselessly swung her legs over the side of the bed. They were in a tiny inner room, windowless and square. What light there was slid in over the tops of the room's walls, which did not quite reach the ceiling. Pen knew that Will was sleeping in the matching room next door. All around her, in every room, enfolded in the same heat, the same velvet silence, people slept.

Pen found the closed door, sliding her feet across the smooth tiles, and walked out into the narrow hallway that she knew would take her to the front of the house. Light from the front windows turned the darkness gray. Uncertainly, Pen rocked on the balls of her feet in the center of the living room, weighed down by what she now recognized as sadness. She knew that she needed to sit down, to be someplace solid and solitary when it overtook her completely, so she let herself out the front door onto the narrow, L-shaped porch. Her body felt separate from her, like a brittle, wounded thing; with care, she set it down on a wooden bench. Then she stepped off an edge and into the sadness and was lost.

After several minutes or thirty or an hour—it was impossible to say—Pen was called back to herself by the sound of the front door opening. Someone sat down next to her, someone put an arm around her shoulders, someone said, "Poor child." Pen wasn't sure who it was and for a moment, didn't think to ask or check. The person was pure kindness, consolation embodied, and Pen buried her face in the person's shoulder until she was calm. The shoulder was the most comforting spot Pen had ever been. It smelled like baby powder.

"I'm so sorry you are sad," said the person. Lola Fe.

Pen sat up and wiped her face but didn't pull away. "I'm sorry I woke you up."

"Don't be silly," admonished Lola Fe. "It is just what happens when you're my age. Your body forgets how to sleep."

"Does it also forget how to be tired?"

"No," said Lola Fe with a chuckle. "That it remembers very well."

They sat in companionable quiet, until a voice from the front yard, somewhere near the Virgin Mary statue, proclaimed, loudly, "Tuk-o!"

Pen looked at Lola Fe.

"Listen," said Lola Fe, pressing her finger to her lips.

"Tuk-o, tuk-o, tuk-o!" The voice began to slow, stretching the space between the syllables, like a toy running down; then it squawked and started over again, "Tuk-o!"

"Was the Virgin Mary doing that?" asked Pen. She hoped it wasn't a terrible joke to make.

Lola Fe laughed. "Not her. Her pet, our friend the tuko lizard."

"I like him," said Pen. "Or her." The sound of the lizard was like so many other things in this place, completely strange and, at the same time, completely natural, even inevitable. She hadn't felt the absence of the lizard before it began to sing, but as soon as it had sung, she understood that nothing would have been complete without it.

"My father died two years ago," said Pen, breathing the words out in a long stream into the quiet that was somehow different from the pre-lizard quiet, more resonant.

"I am very sorry," said Lola Fe. "You must miss him."

"I do," said Pen. "And this place, your home, makes me miss him more than I usually do. Even though he's never been here. Isn't that odd?"

"I don't know," said Lola Fe. "Maybe it's a place he would like."

"It is," said Pen. "He would love it, maybe for the same reason I do."

"The empanadas?" teased Lola Fe.

"Yes," Pen said, smiling, but her thoughts were solemn. It seemed important for her to articulate to Lola Fe what this place meant to her. "I just feel that the way things are here is the way things should be."

Lola Fe did not dispute this. She nodded and asked, "What do you mean?"

"A lot of things, but mostly I'm talking about the way everyone is together. Nobody leaving, nobody gone. Do you know what I mean?"

"I think so," said Lola Fe. She smiled at Pen. "You're wrong, of course. So many have left. Manuel and my sister Maria who died when she was just a girl and my parents and my cousin Gigi, who lives in New York, and my nephews and nieces who have gone to the States or to Canada or Dubai or Australia to live and work."

Lola Fe turned her smooth face to the dark yard, her eyes alert and tender as though she could see all of the missing standing out there among the shrubs and flowers. Then she looked back at Pen and said, "But you are right that nobody's gone."

Pen nodded, wanting her to go on.

"What is that saying? Gone but not—?" asked Lola Fe.

"Gone but not forgotten," said Pen.

"Yes, but it's more than that. Gone but not gone." Lola Fe laughed. "Gone but here. It must be why the house feels so small. We keep them all."

Gone but here, thought Pen. "How?" she asked.

"I don't know," said Lola Fe with a touch of crustiness. "How not? It's how things are. Just because someone happens not to be here doesn't mean he is lost." She said it as though the very idea of people being lost was ridiculous.

"Oh."

"You just make room for more. Always room for one more!" She laughed her wonderful, sandpapery laugh again.

"So you keep everyone?" asked Pen.

"Sure," said Lola Fe with an impatient shrug. "What else?"

Chapter Eighteen

*I*T WAS EVEN BEFORE SHE WAS ACTUALLY IN THE OCEAN, BEFORE she was surrounded on every side by streaming, swirling, darting, infinitely varicolored glory, while she was still riding in the snow-white water strider of a boat (delicate outriggers arching over the blue water) that took them from Alona Beach to Balicasag Island that Pen realized it: sometimes there is nothing to do but surrender yourself to wonder. You must stop searching for one small, dark-haired woman in a world of small, dark-haired women. You must stop missing your father. You must stop measuring—over and over—the line between loving and being in love. You must offer yourself, whole, to the cobalt starfish (and the orange one and the pale pink one and the biscuit-colored one with the raised, chocolate-brown art deco design) and to the clear, clear water and to the sweep of shining sky and to the silver scattershot of leaping fish (an entire school skipping across the ocean like a stone).

It's what they were all doing, Pen could tell. Will with his legs stretched out and his face to the wind. Augusta, who had, that morning, sobbed inconsolably upon learning that the naked children—hair bronze-streaked, skin mahogany from a lifetime of living outdoors ("*Badjao*," a woman next to Pen had whispered. "Sea gypsies!")—standing in small *banca* boats, hands outstretched, begging (there was no other word for it) the people boarding the ferry to Bohol for money or food were naked because they owned no clothes, was now consoled a thousand times over, her face singularly radiant, as she tilted it over the edge of the boat to look into the translucent ocean, searching for stars. Even Jason, who had grown brooding and taciturn since they'd left the Lolas' house, in spite of their being so close to finding Cat, or maybe because of it, was happy under the brim of his baseball cap, waving at passing boats with a broad, magisterial, welcoming smile, as though he owned it all: boat, sky, country, the sea and everything in it.

By the time they got to the coral reef off the edge of Balicasag ("coast" seemed too large a word to apply to Balicasag, which was tiny and, as their captain, Pedro, told them, "round like a *peso*" and boasting a single restaurant, owned by Pedro's cousin Nonoy), Pen had plunged so deeply into the beauty of the day that when it came time to plunge into the ocean (or at least to float on its turquoise surface), she found she had no room in her heart for fear. Even if she had been afraid, it wouldn't have mattered in the face of Augusta's cute but unconquerable desire to "snorgle with Mama."

There was no snorkel small enough for Augusta, so she held her breath and wore a pair of ordinary swim goggles, the kind she wore for the swim lessons she had been attending regularly, if sometimes wildly reluctantly, since before she turned three. Pen was grateful that Augusta was water-safe because it was clear that there was no keeping her out of that ocean. As soon as they landed at Balicasag, Pedro's friend Jing Jing appeared with a little paddle-powered *banca*, a pink peapod of a boat, to take them to the reef (it was a fish sanctuary; no motors allowed), and before the boat was even fully stopped, Augusta was lurching over its side, and Pen had to hold her back.

They snorkeled holding hands. The water was so salty that they almost didn't need to swim, just bobbed on its surface like corks, kicking slightly to propel themselves from one spot to another. The first time Pen put her face in the water and opened her eyes, her senses were so thoroughly and instantly overloaded that she emitted an involuntary yelp, which was a mistake, considering her snorkeled and undersea state. She lifted her head and coughed so long and hard that

Jing Jing leaned over the boat to give her a considerate, if ineffective, underwater clap on the back.

The second time, more prepared, she stayed long enough to understand that the coral reef off Balicasag Island packed more gorgeousness per square centimeter than any other place she had ever been. At the same time that it was exactly like something she had seen on a nature show, it was like nothing she had seen on a nature show because everything—from the imperious butterfly fish trailing their scarves to the brown undulating ribbons that Pen assumed were eels (but might not have been; it frustrated her not to know) to the neon blue coruscations, so penny-small and quick that they might have been tricks of light— each thing, every individual scrap of embodied beauty, was palpably, unmistakably *alive*.

So were Pen and Augusta, alive and in the thick of it. Pen had expected to look down and see fish, and she did, but when she looked to the side, there they were, too, suspended next to her face or flowing by in iridescent streams, and, when Will swam over to take Augusta to see an anemone clownfish and Pen dove downward, the fish were above her as well. She knew that she was an intruder, but she didn't feel like one. She felt like just another living creature, glowing and streamlined among the corals, corals like ferns and hair and platters and Queen Anne's lace. She stayed as still as she could and watched a parrotfish glide by, stippled, striped, and marbled with so many luminous pastels that it looked like a fish-shaped painting by Monet. *Showoff*, thought Pen and wanted to laugh with joy.

Later, Jing Jing paddled them into the deeper, darker waters beyond the steep drop-off in the coral reef wall, and, without warning, stopped. They all looked at him, and without actually understanding why, Pen was immediately, spine-tinglingly aware of vast movement under the water.

"Jackfish!" said Jing Jing excitedly. "Very good to eat!"

He pointed and they all looked down and saw them, under and around the boat, a great, circling body of bodies, lithe and flashing platinum, and, suddenly, the thought that had been skirting the edges of her consciousness since they'd boarded Pedro's boat at Alona

Beach—and probably before that, maybe as soon as they had arrived in the Philippines—hit Pen with the force of an epiphany, knocking the breath out of her. She turned to Will, who sat behind her. One glance at her face and he was pushing his sunglasses to the top of his head.

"What?" he said, resting his hand on her shoulder. "Are you okay?"

Pen nodded, struggling to put words to the thought.

"Hey," said Will, worried.

She shook her head and smiled to let him know she was all right.

"It's nothing," she said, but it wasn't nothing, although she realized it might sound that way. "It's just that—*all this time*. When we were home, driving our cars, drinking coffee."

Will leaned closer, trying to understand.

"This." Pen gestured toward the ocean around them. She meant the jackfish. She meant all of it. "All this time, every second: *this*."

Will stared down at the fish, then back at Pen. "It's not just when we're here. Is that what you mean? It's going on the whole time, at the same time as our lives."

"At the same time, in the same world," said Pen. "And I never knew."

She had never known, and, even now, she could just barely believe it. In a few weeks, Pen would describe what had happened to Amelie, and Amelie would nod and say, "That is *so* Soto Zen. 'All is one and all is different.' Or some people might call what you experienced the 'oceanic feeling.' Although not Freud, of course."

But there in the boat, Pen didn't call it anything. She licked the salt off her lips and wrapped her arms around herself, rocked by awe and the ocean, as the jackfish swirled beneath her like a typhoon or a galaxy or like a swirling school of silver fish.

THAT EVENING, AUGUSTA WANTED PIZZA. SHE DIDN'T JUST WANT IT; she was hell-bent on pizza, running in place on the porch of her and Pen's tiny "villa" and piling on the "pleases" to the rhythm of her feet in a way that Pen had seen before and knew spelled trouble. Under other circumstances, Pen might have given in. Augusta had been a remarkably good sport about eating unfamiliar foods on the trip, had even developed such a taste for the noodle dish *pancit,* shrimp and all, that Pen had vowed to learn how to cook it at home, even though it appeared to involve an awful lot of chopping. Plus, Augusta had been a trooper on the snorkeling outing. But this was Bohol; Bohol did not have pizza.

"We're going to walk down the beach," she told Augusta, "to one of those restaurants *right smack on the beach,* and we're going to buy some delicious fish, and eat it. *Outside!*"

Augusta stopped running in place. "Fish, like the ones we saw today at the reef?"

Uh-oh, thought Pen. "Well, not those exact fish. Those fish live in a sanctuary, where they stay safe and no one catches them. The fish we would eat would be different fish."

Augusta grew stony-faced. "They are still fish. They might have got lost and swum out of the sanctuary. Or they might be *relatives* of those fish." Pen could tell that, even in the throes of her pre-tantrum, Augusta was proud of the word *relatives.*

"*Relatives* is an awesome word," said Jason, who was standing nearby. He walked up to Augusta, crouched down, and lifted his hand. "High five on the vocab, baby girl."

Augusta gave his hand an obligatory pat, but then turned her face away. "I just want pizza, Mama. Pizza is the only thing I want in the whole world."

"I would give it to you, if I could," said Pen, cupping her daughter's pointy chin in her hand, "but there is no pizza in Bohol."

Will had slipped away as soon as the "pleases" had begun and slipped back maybe fifteen seconds later. Now, he stood behind Augusta and mouthed to Pen, "There is pizza in Bohol."

"Really?" said Pen. "Where?"

"According to the Americans sitting at the bar," said Will, gesturing in the direction of the resort's outdoor bar, "on the beach, about fifty yards from the beach entrance to the resort."

"Right smack on the beach," said Augusta with relish. "Right smack!"

It was good. Not chewy, as Augusta observed, but crisp and dotted with salty shavings of ham. After their long day on—and in—the water, they ate with gusto, washing down slice after slice with San Miguel beer, in the case of Jason and Will, or with mango shake, in the case of Augusta, or with bottled water, in the case of Pen, who thought she had never been so thirsty. It was a happy meal, although Pen could tell that, for Jason, the carefree feeling that had carried all of them through the long day was seeping away. As the meal waned, Pen observed him becoming increasingly fidgety and impatient. While Pen, Will, and Augusta watched the sunset, Jason watched, while pretending not to watch, the passersby on the darkening beach.

When they were getting ready to leave, Jason said, "So, hey, I was thinking I'd go take a look around for Cat, maybe inquire at some of the other resorts whether they've seen her."

He saw Will and Pen exchange concerned glances and lifted his hands, three fingers raised. "I'll be on my best behavior. Scout's honor."

"What about Ulysses and Ben?" asked Will.

"They stay in the old walleto," said Jason, patting the buttoned pocket on his cargo shorts.

"You were a Scout?" asked Pen.

Jason shrugged. "Briefly. Until the fake bear scat trail/pile of rocks incident." He waved his hand sheepishly. "That story's a little convoluted."

"I bet," said Pen.

"But high five on the vocab," said Will.

THEIR RESORT WAS ONE OF THE SMALLER ONES ON ALONA BEACH: an open-air restaurant, a pool, and a wide crescent of one-bedroom/one-bath cottages, or villas, with nipa roofs and miniature covered porches. Pen and Augusta's villa was a twin, with Will on the other side of the wall, and after Pen put Augusta to bed, she came out onto the shared porch, where Will sat, drinking his second San Miguel.

"That was quick," said Will.

"Yeah," said Pen dryly. "It turns out that all Augusta needs to fall asleep at night is a coral reef. Maybe I should get one."

"She's slept like a pro the whole trip. Maybe you should get a Philippines, put it in your backyard," said Will. "Tonight, she conked out before I could even go to the bar and get you a drink."

"Here I am," observed Pen. She pointed across the pool. "And there's the bar."

The night seemed as hot as the nights in Cebu, but now and then, a breeze pleated the lit pool and stirred the bushes next to the porch. Voices and laughter drifted toward them from the restaurant. Someone seemed to be singing "Waltzing Matilda." ("This place is crawling with Aussies," Jason had observed earlier. "Apparently, they come for the diving," and Will had said, "Because they don't have any coral reefs back home.") Pen sipped her drink, icy calamansi juice spiked with Tanduay rum, and swore that it was the best drink she had ever had.

She told Will about her conversation with Lola Fe, including an only slightly edited version of her own crying jag.

"Do you think it works that way?" asked Pen. "Keeping everyone? Gone but not gone?"

"Hey, you won't catch me arguing with Lola Fe," said Will. "I might get hit by a thunderbolt."

Pen smiled. "The earth might open up and swallow you."

"Anyway, I kept *you* all those years, you and Cat. Even when I tried to shake you, you stuck."

"Like burrs," said Pen.

"Leeches," said Will.

"Oysters," said Pen. "Did you know that scientists are studying the way oysters adhere to each other in hopes of making better glues?"

"Oh yeah," said Will. "Who doesn't know that?"

Pen laughed, and maybe it was the drink or the heat or the thought of the Lolas or the jackfish epiphany or the sight of Will's face, which always looked most like his face when he was smiling at Pen the way he was doing right then, and which, paintbrushed with shadows and washed in the lunar light of the pool, made her heart leap, but, suddenly, Pen felt brave.

The bravery filled her and she said, "Can I tell you about what happened to my dad?"

She had never told anyone. Actually, she had told a lot of people, back when it first happened, but only because she had to, and even then, it wasn't her story that she had told. It was only facts, which belonged to no one. She had used as few words as she possibly could, and the words had been no one's, too.

"Sure," said Will quietly. "Of course. Whatever you want."

"We were visiting my parents in Wilmington, Augusta and I. We did that a lot back then. It was before we lived with Jamie, of course, and I think we were lonely." Pen smiled and corrected herself. "I was lonely. Augusta has never been lonely for a second of her life. She makes friends like that." Pen snapped her fingers. "With other kids, dogs, waiters, mean old ladies, police officers, Jason, the occasional schizophrenic in the park."

"Bananas," Will reminded her, and if Pen had had even the slightest doubt about telling him the story, it disappeared with this single word. Will knew what tone a situation called for; it was one of the things about him that she loved.

"Bananas," agreed Pen. "Very small ones. So we were at my parents' house and we'd just had dinner, and my mom had made a strawberry pie, and she realized she was out of ice cream."

"Breyers," said Will. "Vanilla bean."

"You remember," said Pen with gratitude.

"The no-apostrophe in the name drove you crazy, your whole family. But you loved it anyway."

"So my dad and I drove over to the Acme. You remember that Acme?"

"You called it the Soviet Acme because it was always running out of things."

"Like bread! And toilet paper. But that night, they had the Breyers, so we bought it, and on the way home, my dad says, 'I need to make a quick stop at the ATM, sweetheart.'" Pen's throat had gone dry, and she took a long sip of her drink. "I knew what he meant."

She looked up and met Will's eyes. "We were so broke. I was doing the author escort work with Amelie, but it had been slow, and rent and babysitting seemed to eat up everything that Patrick gave us. I probably should have asked him for more, but I was the one with custody of Augusta. I hated asking him."

"I can see how you would."

"My dad gave us money every time we visited or they visited us. He'd never say anything, just slip it into my bag or the kitchen drawer where I kept my car keys, and I would just hug him or something the next time I saw him. He knew what it meant."

Pen prepared herself for the next part of the story, and Will waited. Two buff-colored lizards, no longer than a finger, skittered around the edge of the villa and froze in the light.

"They eat insects. Mosquitoes," said Will, and Pen nodded and went on with her story.

"We went to the bank at the intersection across from that bar that's always changing its name. The one near the drugstore."

"I remember it," said Will.

"My dad parallel parked in front of the bar, like always, but he had to go a little way down the road because of all the cars. So I couldn't see him. I couldn't see the ATM from there. And he was taking a long time, but I wasn't really worried because sometimes there's a line at that ATM because of the bar, you know. It took longer and longer, though, so I called him on his cell phone, thinking maybe he'd run into someone he knew and started talking. He didn't answer, but even that didn't worry me all that much."

"He was the kind of guy who probably wouldn't answer his phone during a conversation," said Will.

"Yes," said Pen, smiling. "If he even remembered to bring it with him at all." She took a breath. "Finally, I got out of the car and went to find him."

Pen was crying now, quietly, and she wiped the tears off her face with both hands. "He was on the sidewalk in front of the bank behind one of those big potted plants that public buildings sometimes have. A hibiscus with white flowers, big as saucers. But he wasn't really hidden and the light from the streetlamp was shining right on him. I remember that, his face in the yellow light. He was lying on his side with his legs bent, like he was sleeping."

Pen closed her eyes and let herself see him. It was the first time that she had let herself see him without trying to chase the memory away.

"His face was his face," she said. "It looked peaceful, just the way it looked when he was sleeping, so it took me a few seconds to understand. Even when I did understand I didn't really because I thought he must have had a heart attack. But then I saw the blood on his shirt and pooling under his head, and I started talking to him and kissing his hands, begging him to be okay and to wake up. Telling him that I loved him. I was beside myself. I talked to him until the ambulance came."

She opened her eyes and stared out at the pool and at the moonlight resting on the peaked roofs of the villas. "He wasn't dead. He died almost as soon as the ambulance got him to the hospital, but when I was talking to him, he was alive. He didn't respond to me, his face never moved, but I don't know that that means he couldn't hear me. I think he could. I hope he could, even though it would have upset him to hear how distraught I was and to not be able to comfort me, but I hope that the last voice he heard was mine and not—"

"Pen," said Will.

When Pen looked at him, she saw that his face was full of sorrow and love and that he was crying. Even through her own sadness, she felt wonder at the sight of Will crying. He brushed his eyes, roughly, with the back of his wrist and then reached out and cradled her cheek with his hand.

"I'm sorry," he said. "I'm so sorry."

"Don't cry," said Pen. She turned her face to kiss his palm.

They sat like that for a little while, before Pen pulled carefully away and wiped her eyes.

"They caught him," said Pen. "The kid who did it. It wasn't hard. Between the video camera outside the bar and the one at the bank, they got the whole thing."

"A kid," said Will.

"Nineteen," said Pen. "A nineteen-year-old out of his mind on meth."

"He's in prison?"

"Yes. There wasn't a trial. They made a deal. He'll stay in for a long time, but not forever." Pen sighed. "I tried so hard to hate him. I wanted to hate him every day, every second of every day, for the rest of my life because of what he did."

"You couldn't?"

"His sister called me. After it was all over, months after."

"And she talked you out of hating him?"

"Sort of, but I was already giving it up, even though I tried so hard not to. I found out later that my dad told the kid, Joseph Cort, that he'd give him his wallet if he'd give my dad a minute to talk him out of it, out of ruining his life, which, as far as I can tell, was already a complete shambles. My dad was actually holding the wallet out, ready to hand it over, when the kid freaked and hit him. Joseph Cort killed my father with one of those little wooden bats they give away at baseball games. Every time I felt the hate slipping away, I would think about that bat. But even before I met with his sister, I knew I couldn't keep it up."

"You should not have had to meet her." Will sounded angry. "It wasn't fair of her to ask you."

"I know, but she needed it so much, for me to know who he used to be. Her little brother. Maybe I needed that, too." She gave a grim laugh. "I guess I'm not so good at hate."

"That's okay," said Will. "You're good at everything else."

"I've never told anyone that story, not since I told the police. I'm glad I told you, though. I feel better, clearer. Talking to you has always made me feel clearer."

Will nodded.

"You know, I wanted you, at my dad's funeral." Pen hadn't intended to say this, but once she started, she kept going. "I was so sad and sick and empty, and I wanted you and Cat so much, but mostly you." As soon as Pen said "mostly you," she realized that it was true. "I even thought you were there."

Will glanced quickly over at her. "What?"

"I mean, you weren't, but I thought that you were. I even looked for you."

Will looked stricken. "I wish I had known that you needed me."

"No, Will," said Pen soothingly. "How could you have known? Please don't look like that. I didn't mean that you let me down."

"I would have gone to find you if I'd known. I swear."

"You don't have to swear. I always knew that," said Pen. "But thank you."

"Don't thank me."

"I'll thank you if I want to thank you."

She nudged him with her elbow and smiled at him, and kept nudging and smiling until he smiled back.

She told him, "I e-mailed my mom this morning from the Lolas' computer."

"The Lolas have a computer?"

"They do. I e-mailed my mom from it and told her that when I got home, we should all have dinner: me, my mother, Augusta, Jamie, Mr. Venverloh and his sons, the whole gang. I told her to put it on the calendar."

Will gave her his sudden, lovely, open smile, all the regret from a moment before gone.

"So I guess you decided to keep everyone," he said.

Right at that second, as they sat there, somewhere in the dark ocean, and in Cebu, and in Wilmington, Delaware, all over the world, countless living bodies were living their countless, precious, mysterious lives.

"I guess I did," said Pen.

CHAPTER NINETEEN

HE FAMOUS CHOCOLATE HILLS OF BOHOL DID NOT LOOK PAR-
ticularly edible to Pen, as they bubbled up, brown and smooth,
out of their flat, green, ruffled surroundings, turning the landscape
into something out of Dr. Seuss, but her first thought upon seeing
them was that of all the people she could think of who would love
them (Jamie, Patrick, her mother), Cat Ocampo would love them the
most. She would complain every step of the way up the long, steep
flight of stairs to the overlook (Pen stopped counting at step 110), but
once she arrived at the top and beheld that crazily whimsical view,
she would squeal, jump for joy, and, almost definitely, grab the person
closest to her and kiss him (or her, but probably him).

After the snorkeling trip, they had spent two days searching for
Cat, splitting up, going to the other side of the island and into the city,
scouring beaches, restaurants, shopping malls. Nothing. Now, they
were doing as Lola Lita had suggested, hitting all the tourist stops,
beginning, at Augusta's request, with the Chocolate Hills.

Augusta had been exploring the overlook with Will, but now she
appeared, pink-cheeked, wild-haired, dressed in a rainbow of color.

"Can we do it, can we do it, can we do it?" she squealed. She was
jumping straight up and down with her arms pressed to her sides, a
specifically Augusta variety of overwrought jumping that Jamie called
"popcorning."

Pen smiled. "Maybe. Do what?"

"Check this out," said Will, and he took Pen by the wrist, leading her down some stairs toward a crowd of people, a camera on a tripod, and a large screen that turned out to be a giant, slightly washed-out photograph of the Chocolate Hills. Pen looked from the wan photograph of the view to the view itself, sunlit, rich with color under the blue sky, and unmistakably real.

"But . . . ?" she said.

"Wait," said Will.

As they watched, a college-aged couple stood in front of the backdrop and, at the photographer's cue, jumped into the air, arms raised in victory.

"Oh. My. Goodness," said Pen blankly.

"It makes a *picture* that looks like they're jumping over the hills!" cried Augusta with joy. "They print it out *right here,* and you can take it *home* with you!"

"Is that right?" muttered Pen.

"You can also use brooms," said Will, pointing to a couple of skinny, brown, witchy looking items leaning against the guardrail, "to make it look like you're flying."

"Fabulous," said Pen.

"Just exactly the kind of thing you like," said Will, deadpan except for his wicked eyes.

Taking this exchange as a yes, Augusta squealed, clapped her hands, skipped to the back of the line, and resumed popcorning.

Pen stared at the background, then said, slowly, "Not me, but I can think of someone who would love it."

Will nodded. "It's true. She never met a piece of kitsch she didn't love."

An idea lit up his face, and he pointed to an easel-propped bulletin board on the other side of the backdrop from where they stood. It was covered with photo samples.

"You don't think . . . ?" said Pen.

"Probably not," answered Will, but they were already on their way, squeezing behind the backdrop, mumbling "Excuse me" to the sight-seers in their path. When they got to the easel, Pen turned to look at Augusta, who waved and blew kisses, movie-star-fashion.

"Stay right there," mouthed Pen, pointing.

Augusta gave her a thumbs-up. Pen knew that Augusta wasn't going anywhere, wouldn't get out of that line for all the miniature bananas in the Philippines.

It was a big bulletin board. Some of the photos were faded and dog-eared, but some looked new.

"You start from the top," said Pen. "And I'll start from the bottom."

"Don't bother," said a dreary voice. Jason. "She's not there."

Jason looked even worse than he sounded, moist and slump-shouldered in his light blue golf shirt. In the merciless sunlight, Pen could see his scalp, shell-pink and vulnerable, through his pale hair, and when he took off his sunglasses, Pen saw that his eyes were blood-shot, watery, underslung with dark circles. They were the saddest things she had seen in a long time.

"I think I'm going crazy," he said hoarsely, squeezing his head between his hands, hard.

Uncertain of what to do, Pen turned around to look at Will, who said, "You know what? I should probably go stand in line with Augusta."

"That's great, thanks," said Pen out loud. She narrowed her eyes and whispered, "Weasel!"

Ignoring her, Will clapped Jason on the arm, said, "Hang in there, man," and vanished behind the backdrop.

When Jason walked to the rail of the overlook and leaned against it, heavily, with both hands, the people around him discreetly moved away. Maybe they could sense his desperation or his need for breathing room. Maybe they noted his size and feared for the stability of the guardrail. In any case, the sight of him standing there, alone, was too much for Pen. She moved to his side and, after just a moment's hesitation, her arm hovering in the air behind him, she placed the arm around his shoulders, which were shaking.

"Hey, Jason," she said softly. "It'll be okay."

He shook his head. "I've been scanning faces for so long that it's literally making me sick. I feel like I might puke."

"Well, why don't you give it a rest for a while?" said Pen quickly, resisting the urge to take a step away. "Because you know what? If you're anywhere near her, she'll see you first anyway." She gave his shoulders a squeeze. "You don't exactly blend in, you know."

Jason mustered a feeble smile. "I'm like the Stay Puft Marshmallow Man walking around this place. You know, from *Ghostbusters*."

"Except he was mean, wasn't he? And you're nice."

Jason gave her a skeptical look. "You think I'm nice? Honestly?"

"Honestly?" Pen shrugged. "I think you're a lot of things, nice being one of them."

"Fair enough," said Jason. "So here's another question for you: do you really want me to find her?"

"Yes."

"Come on. Yes? Just like that?"

Pen took her arm away so that she could face him squarely.

"Yes, I want you to find her. I think you need—. I think you *deserve* a conversation, at the very least. You need a chance to be at peace, one way or another."

"Because I'm her husband, you mean."

"Because, as far as I can tell, you have loved her with a true and open heart for as long as you two have been together. And because no one should ever, ever leave without saying why."

To Pen's horror, Jason started to cry, to weep, his face crumpling, his body quaking, the tears pouring out from under his sunglasses, which he took off and handed to Pen, before pulling the collar of his shirt up and over his face, so that he was inside it, his fists clutching the blue fabric against his forehead. Jagged gasps and awful, puppylike whimpers came from inside the shirt. Pen looked around helplessly for Will and Augusta, but she couldn't see the photo line from where she stood. She thought about putting her arm around Jason again, but he was so pulled into himself that touching seemed like the wrong thing, so she stood there, gazing out at the rows and clusters of funny brown peaks because sometimes, she decided, all you could do for someone was stay.

After a little while, he slowed and sputtered to a stop, and Pen handed him his glasses, and he put them back on.

"Thanks," he said. "Sorry."

"Don't apologize."

"It's just that you were right. I have loved her to the best of my ability, and, fuck, do I hate that."

"Why?" said Pen, surprised.

"Because if I'd been an asshole, cheated or slacked off, well, there would be something for me to fix, right? There'd be hope." Quickly, he added, "Not that there's no hope. I totally believe that she loves me and that I can get her to come home. Okay?"

"Okay," said Pen. *Sure you do,* she thought.

"I'm just saying that if she *does* want to end us, well, then I got nothing. Zip. No leverage." He whacked his forehead with his fist, once, twice, three times, leaving a vaguely butterfly-shaped red mark on his forehead. "If she doesn't want me, then loving her to the best of my ability all those years was about the most stupid-ass thing I could have done."

"Stop it," snapped Pen, giving his shoulder a shove. "Right now."

Jason stared at her. "I just had a freaking nervous breakdown. You're not allowed to boss me around. Or *push* me."

"Too bad. Listen to me: you're wrong."

"Wrong, huh? Like you know."

"Everyone knows."

"Knows what?"

"That no matter what happens, loving someone to the best of your ability is exactly the right thing to do. It's the only thing to do."

Jason seemed about to dispute this, but then he shut his mouth and stayed quiet for a long time, staring at his hands on the railing instead of at the view. Finally, he said, "You really believe that bullshit?"

"Yep."

He let go of the rail and turned his hands over, empty, palms to the sky. "What will I do if she leaves me?"

The answer was so clear, so obvious that Pen had to fight to keep the impatience out of her voice.

"You'll love someone else."

AT THE BOTTOM OF THE HILL, WHILE THEY WERE WAITING FOR LUIS the tour driver to bring the SUV around, Augusta ate ice cream, and Pen, Will, and Jason came up with a plan.

"How about if we narrow our tour down to the places that Cat's most likely to go?" said Will, getting out the itinerary that the bartender/concierge back at the resort had made for them. "Then we can spend the rest of the time looking for her back at the beach."

"Good idea," said Pen.

"This is futile. We know that, right?" said Jason blandly. In the aftermath of his conversation with Pen, he seemed calmer, but whether this was because he felt better or because he was simply exhausted Pen couldn't tell. "The chances of running into her at one of these tourist attractions is, like, practically null and void. Even the beach is a shot in the dark. I checked at all the resorts I could find. No sign of Cat and not one damn person, no matter how much I sucked up to them, would tell me anything."

Will's eyes met Pen's, and she knew what he was thinking: that the whole trip to Bohol was a shot in the dark. It was a lot easier to believe in the hand of fate when you were sitting in the Lolas' house with the Lolas' sage, tranquil faces in front of you than when you were actually out in the world, searching.

"What should we do?" said Will to Jason. "If you want to go back to Cebu, we'll do it. Your call."

After staring up at the sky and frantically fiddling with the change in his shorts' pocket, Jason released a hard, drawn-out, sagging sigh and took the itinerary from Will.

"'Church of San Pedro,'" he read. "'Early seventeenth century. Spanish.' Blah blah blah. Boring. Forget it. 'Hanging Bridge.' Nope, she doesn't like heights. 'Loboc River Cruise and Floating Restaurant.' Cruise, restaurant? She'd be all over it. 'Tarsier sanctuary.'" He looked up. "What's a tarsier?"

"A monkey!" sang Augusta. "A weensy, teensy, a-dor-a-ble monkey!"

"We found it online, back at home when we were looking up the Philippines," explained Pen. "It's not a monkey, really, but it is a primate, almost the smallest in the world."

"How small?" asked Jason, squinting his eyes in concentration, as though the specific degree of smallness could make all the difference.

Pen held out her cupped hand. "Baby kitten-ish, give or take."

"Cute?" asked Jason.

"*Yes!*" shouted Augusta.

"Huge, round golden eyes; button nose; round head; long, grippy fingers; soft brown fur. And a smile," said Pen.

"Hell, that sounds like Cat," said Jason dryly.

"A smile?" said Will.

"In the pictures we saw, it was smiling. No lie," said Pen.

"Like this!" said Augusta, pressing her lips together and curling up just the corners so that her mouth was a prim, sideways "C."

"Beautiful," said Will.

"A tiny, big-eyed, smiling monkey," said Jason. "Are you kidding me? Wild horses couldn't keep her away."

THE RIDE TO THE TARSIER SANCTUARY WAS SO LONG THAT BOTH Augusta and Jason fell asleep, Augusta nestled into an ancient, threadbare booster seat (Pen had nearly kissed Luis when she saw it) in the SUV's third row and Jason in the front seat, snoring over the saccharine stream that poured, ceaselessly, out of Luis's radio. Bafflingly, the Philippines had turned out to be a bastion of old R&B and soft rock love songs ("Air Supply is all out of love everywhere but here," Will had noted, with grim awe, on the second day). Pen and Will sat in the second row, looking out of the thankfully untinted windows at the Bohol countryside: hardwood forests, houses on stilts, nipa huts, thickset palm groves, gas stations, stunningly green rice fields.

"Isn't it as though that rice field satisfies some little piece of your soul that's been waiting for that specific shade of green all your life, without your knowing it?" Pen said, solemnly and without stopping for breath, to Will, who laughed and said, "I was going to say that it's like the whole field is one of those glow sticks we used get at the beach when we were kids."

Children played in the yards of long, one-story school buildings, some of which had big, glassless windows, so that you could see straight through to the green on the other side. Slow, curved-horned water buffalo swung their bony hips along roadsides or through fields. Women hung laundry or cooked in the open air. Despite her efforts to not romanticize the place (none of the lives she glimpsed looked at all easy), Pen couldn't help feeling that a kind of peacefulness, a hazy, emerald quietude permeated everything she saw.

"It's beautiful here, isn't it?" she said.

"Yeah. It really is," said Will.

"Too bad Jason is missing it."

Will looked at the back of Jason's head and said in a low voice, "It's good, though. Poor guy needed a break."

"Wouldn't it be terrible," whispered Pen, "to love someone so much who didn't love you back?"

In the silence that followed her saying this, they drove past an entire rice field, one backed by hills and patchworked with bright quadrangles of water, more water winking like sequins between the dazzling shoots of rice.

"Will?" Pen said finally. "Are you there?"

"Sorry," said Will. "I was just thinking about what you said."

"Oh. So tell me."

"You're right: it would be terrible. But there are worse things."

"What do you mean?"

Will stopped looking out the window and looked at Pen instead. Against the lushness of Bohol, the clean-lined precision of his face was startling. It's what happened when beauty became familiar: you saw it and saw it and saw it without seeing it and then, suddenly, there it was to make your heart stand still inside your chest

"At least he did it," said Will. "Went all out. Gave her everything. He'll always know that about himself."

Flushing, Pen said, "I just told Jason almost that exact same thing, back at the Chocolate Hills, and I believe it. I always have. The really great thing is to love someone, no matter what." She smiled ruefully. "But I guess it's a lot easier to have philosophies than to put them into action because I look at him, and all I feel is sad, and all I want is for her to love him back. God, can't she just *do* that?" She stopped, feeling disloyal to Cat. "I mean, I want her to be happy, but I want the thing that makes her happy to be being with him."

Will nodded. Then he said, "And what about you? What's the thing that makes you happy?"

Look at him, Pen told herself.

She looked at him and thought: *Oh, just* look *at you*. The words flooded through her, but she didn't say them. How could she? That wasn't the language she and Will spoke to each other.

She said, "This trip. Augusta. Knowing you again."

"Well," he said after a few seconds, "that's good."

He smiled an unreadable half-smile at her, and the SUV kept moving and the two of them kept riding in it, and, through the windows, the green world kept offering them its extravagant loveliness, mile after mile after mile.

HAD THE MAN AT THE VISITORS CENTER NOT HAD PUPPIES, THINGS might have turned out differently, but there they were in a fenced-in square of yard just outside the tiny museum's open side door: black-and-white bundles, with fur so fuzzy it looked electrified. They were nothing like most of the dogs they had seen in Cebu, not bony and listless, but round-bellied and tumbling with a mild, watchful, well-fed mother nearby, whom Pen would've bet had more than a little border collie dog-paddling around in her gene pool. The second that Augusta spotted the puppies, everything else flew out of her head, displaced by rampant joy and utter besottedness. With one smiling nod from the visitors center man, whose name was Mr. P, she was in among them, sitting flat on her bottom on the grass, and she would not come out, not for love or money or even tarsiers.

"Mama, you said we can't touch tarsiers because they're dindangered," she explained. "But you can touch puppies! Touch and touch and touch!" Since her arms were full of them, it was hard to argue with this.

"How about just a quick look?" said Pen. "Mama wants to see the tarsiers."

Mr. P was as bright eyed and rotund as the pups and exuded grandfatherly kindness, but there was no way Pen was leaving Augusta with a man she had just met or even with Luis, who was leaning against the SUV, texting with fast, expert thumbs.

"I'll stay with her," said Jason.

As soon as they had pulled up to the sanctuary, it had been clear that they wouldn't find Cat there. Luis's SUV was one of three cars in the dirt lot, and the visitors center was tiny, one well-lit room full of tidy displays, photographs, informative signs, and an eerie and delicate little skeleton with enormous eye sockets. Unless you counted Mr. P and a young man sweeping the porch, they were the only visitors in sight. After noting this, Jason didn't get upset or seem eager to leave. He just shrugged and sat down on an outdoor bench near the puppy pen, looking like a man who had either achieved patience or had completely thrown in the towel.

"That's okay," Pen told him. "You should go see the tarsiers."

"Nah," said Jason, waving his hand dismissively. "You guys go on."

Mr. P nodded to the young man, who had stopped sweeping, and the man took off his straw hat, tucked it under his arm, and reached to shake Will's hand.

"I am Monching."

"Nice to meet you, Monching," said Will. "I'm Will, and this is my friend Pen."

They didn't have far to walk. Monching explained that the tarsiers lived wild throughout most of the sanctuary but that there were a few who had been rescued from captivity and were living in a small portion of the forest surrounded by a high fence. These were the tarsiers that they would see.

"It is not like a zoo," said Monching, perhaps anticipating disappointment. "The space is large, and they live as they do in the wild. But they are a little less shy than the ones out in the rest of the sanctuary."

"This is fine," said Pen.

Monching nodded and entered the dense forest. Will followed him for a few yards, then turned and held out his hand to Pen, and she didn't stop to wonder why or to consider the implications of taking it. She just took it, and this was how they walked down the narrow path, until Monching stopped, pointing.

"There," he whispered.

And there it was, just a few yards away, clinging to a low branch, its face turned away from them.

"And there." This one was closer and seemed to be sleeping.

"There will be more, if you are quiet," he said. "Please do not touch, but you can go close to them, take pictures."

Pen realized they had left the camera in the SUV, but it didn't matter. She was following the advice of Lola Lita: really being there, seeing what there was to see.

"I will wait," said Monching, pointing, "just there, beyond the edge," and noiselessly, he disappeared into the leaves.

Pen and Will looked at each other. Under the canopy of trees, it was shadowy and so hushed that it felt as though they stood in the very heart of the woods.

Will nodded toward the closest tarsier and whispered, "Go ahead. You first," which was exactly what Pen wanted.

Advancing slowly, placing her feet as silently as she could, Pen walked until her face was no more than a foot and a half away from the tarsier, close enough to look it in the eyes, if its eyes had not been closed. The creature was perfectly motionless and so exquisitely constructed, from the delicately wrinkled forehead to the flaring, rose-petal-shaped ears to the strong, knobby, shockingly human-looking hands. Pen stared and stared, happiness pouring through her, her heart beating so hard she could feel it in her wrists, and then the tarsier opened its tremendous eyes, and looked at her, giving her the gift of its wild gold regard, and she could have sworn that it wasn't just she, but the whole forest that caught its breath.

It wasn't cute. It had nothing to do with cute. It was strange and dignified, and Pen believed that she had never in her life felt so honored to be in anyone's company. She had come across the wide, tilted, spinning world and landed here to become one of two animals, looking at each other in a deep green wood. She was overcome. She longed for the moment to never end, but the ending was right there, waiting. *Stay,* she wanted to tell the tarsier, but it couldn't stay. *It's endangered,* she thought, and the thought broke her heart.

You are endangered, she thought with grief.

So are you, said a voice impatiently. *So is everything. But we're here now, aren't we?*

Then the tarsier turned its head, hopped from tree to tree to tree, and was gone.

Afterward, she would admit, readily, that no conversation had ever taken place. Tarsiers didn't talk, not even silently. She didn't need Amelie to tell her that the voice answering her own inside her head was also her own. It was a thing she did all the time: talking to herself. But she also knew that, at the time, in the brief, wide, fathomless moment that it happened, that wasn't how it felt at all.

She turned around and saw Will.

It would have been so easy for the two of them to simply fall together, to give in to gravity, but Pen wanted it to be clear, to be the very clearest thing they had ever done.

"I love you," she told him.

"I love you, too," he said, moving toward her.

She held up her hand. "I'm not talking about in a Will-and-Pen-business-as-usual kind of way."

He smiled. "Then how?"

But he was already reaching for her, and when she kissed him, the rest of the world didn't fade or fall away around them. It stayed, with Pen and Will firmly planted in its center, holding on to each other, all the Pens and Wills they had ever been but especially the ones they were now.

Before they left the forest for good, Pen said, "Listen, because of Augusta and Jason—God, especially Jason—we should probably, for now anyway—" She couldn't think of how to say it.

"Play it cool?" said Will, kissing her fingertips, her inner wrist, the palm of her hand.

"Yes," said Pen. "But I want you to know that if I ruled the world, I would never stop touching you."

"You don't rule the world?" said Will.

"Tell me that you love me," commanded Pen.

"I love you," said Will.

CHAPTER TWENTY

*T*HEY WERE SITTING POOLSIDE AT THE RESORT EATING A DESSERT called halo-halo and listening to Celine Dion sing the theme song from *Titanic*. It was not, by a long shot, the first time they had heard the song since arriving in the Philippines, but it was certainly the loudest they had heard it, Celine's voice raining down upon them from the tree-mounted speakers, escalating from breathy to tremulous to so thoroughly full-throated and throbbing that Pen thought the ground might start to shake.

"Holy freaking hell," moaned Jason. "What's this song called, anyway?"

" 'My Heart Will Go On,' " said Will absently, eyeballing the contents of his raised spoon. "This has beans in it."

He looked up from the spoon to find Pen and Jason staring at him.

"What?" he said. "I like it. It's good. I'm just saying: it has beans in it. A dessert with beans in it. That's not something you see every day."

"How do you know that?" asked Pen.

"They're right here," said Will, holding up his spoon. "Beans."

"No. How do you know what this song is called?" asked Pen. "Nobody knows what this song is called."

Will looked from Pen to Jason.

"Sorry, dude," said Jason, "I have to go with Pen on this one. Everyone just calls it that *Titanic* song, if they even call it anything. Except, you know, *you*."

"So tell us," said Pen, raising an eyebrow. "How do you know?"

"I just know," said Will. "Come on, it's not like I *like* it."

"Man, you keep right on telling yourself that," said Jason, giving Will's shoulder a comforting pat.

Pen was happy to see that Jason was perking up a bit. Over the last twenty-four hours, the air of resignation he had adopted at the tarsier sanctuary had gradually deepened into a true, blue, dismal funk. Just a few hours earlier, on the floating restaurant cruise down the Loboc River, he had hit what appeared to be rock bottom, failing to go for even a second helping at the all-you-can-eat buffet and hardly noticing when, right in front of them, three little boys jumped what had to be thirty feet from the top of a coconut tree that leaned out over the river into the river itself and came up next to the boat, laughing.

Now, he seemed as close to lighthearted as he had since they'd arrived. Maybe it was the halo-halo, which was delicious. Maybe it was because they were leaving the next morning, going back to Cebu on the ferry, and Jason had resolved to return to the Lolas and ask them, one last time, to reunite him with Cat. ("I'm trying to think of the right approach," he'd told them, and Will had suggested, "Ritual supplication. Burnt offering. Maybe a small animal sacrifice.") In any case, with a playful gleam in his eye, Jason leaned over and tapped the shoulder of a man sitting with a group of people at the beer-bottle-covered table next to theirs. Pen recognized the man as one of the Australian divers.

"Sorry to interrupt," said Jason to the man. "We were just wondering if you knew the name of this song."

"Oh, wait, don't tell me," the man said, squeezing his eyes shut in concentration before guessing, " 'Total Bloody Shit'?"

"I think it's from the album *Songs That Make You Want to Rip Off Someone's Face*," sang out another man at the table.

After the Aussies had recovered from the hilarity into which these remarks had caused them to dissolve, the first man pointed to a woman across the table from him. "Addie here just presented us with the question of what we would listen to right now if we could listen to any song in the world," he said. "And now I am presenting it to you: What song would you listen to right now if you could listen to any song in the world? Please discuss." And he turned back to his friends.

Pen said, " 'Wild Honey' by U2."

Jason said, " 'The Climb' by Miley Cyrus," followed by, "What? It's inspiring!"

Will said, " 'Consecutive Seconds' by Thelonious Monk."

He said this partly because he loved the song, but mostly, Pen knew, so that she would make fun of him, which she did.

"Horrifyingly pretentious," she said. "Choose again."

"Oh, okay, sorry," said Will, abashed. After a moment's thought, he said, "Bach's Goldberg Variation Number 25 by Glenn Gould," which cracked Pen up, as he had known it would, and caused Jason to ask, "Do you want me to kick your ass? I mean, are you *asking* me to kick your ass?"

It amazed Pen, how they could sit there talking like they had always talked, as though the world had not been utterly transfigured, as though she and Will had not spent every waking hour of the last twenty-four driving themselves crazy trying to keep their hands off each other. Even as they sat, talking in the late afternoon sun, laughing, giving each other crap the way they always had, Pen was adding to the list inside her head of parts of him she wanted to taste: his sternum, the back of his neck, the skin beneath his left ear.

She loved him. She ached with loving him. He was her best and oldest friend and, also, he was a miracle to her. She looked at him and thought, *I would give you anything you wanted.* She wanted to tell him this, and then wondered if maybe, at some point, she already had because she realized that it had always been true. There was never a time, since the day she met him, when Pen hadn't loved Will. He was her clear-eyed conscience, her kind, wry, sharp, beautiful man. No one had ever come closer to reading her mind than Will. When she tried to examine, with a clinical eye, what had changed, she realized it boiled down to two things: she wanted to touch him as often as possible and in ways she had never wanted to touch him before; and she wanted to be with him every day, to live with him, in the same house, for the rest of her life.

◆ ◆ ◆

THAT EVENING, THEY WENT TO THE PLACE ON THE BEACH WHERE YOU could choose your own fish, the afternoon's catch displayed like necklaces (sapphires, rubies, diamonds) on a bed of crushed ice. Augusta took one look and chirped, " 'One fish, two fish, red fish, blue fish.' Pizza, please," and, under Pen's disapproving eye, Will had taken off down the beach to get her some and bring it back.

It was a good meal. The outdoor café was full of people and festive, with Christmas lights strung all over the bar and winding up the trunks of the palm trees like twinkling snakes. People strolled by on the beach, music played at a reasonable volume, and their waitress was so devastatingly pretty—the Filipina Lana Turner of waitresses—that Jason even made a couple of goofy but not totally unsuccessful attempts at flirting with her. They ate at a table not twenty yards from the water's edge with their feet in the sand and the ocean spread before them, the sun melting into it like a fat scoop of mango ice cream.

They didn't talk about Cat. They talked about Pen's newly formed and still mostly hazy plans to go back to teaching. They talked about Florida, where Jason had grown up, and about how when you read the news, every bad, crazy, unlikely thing to ever happen seemed to happen in Florida but how when you were there, it was wonderful. They talked about Will's books, and this part of the conversation gave way to a moment in which Jason said, "Dude, that sounds like a pretty awesome gig. Getting paid to sit around in your underwear, drinking coffee and making stuff up."

Will grinned and said, "Yeah. Plus, it's portable. In case anyone ever wants to, you know, transport me someplace."

Except to abruptly stop breathing, Pen didn't move a muscle, and Will didn't even glance in her direction. It was Jason who looked at her, at her, at Will, and back at her.

With his eyes on Pen's, he said, "I bet before long somebody will."

Jason, giving them his blessing. Pen didn't answer, just held his gaze, grateful, but after about three seconds of this, everything began to feel too serious, and Pen cast around for something to say, but nothing came to her, which left her with no choice but first to hum and then to sing the opening lines of the song Jason had said he would listen to if he could pick any song in the world.

"God, do I love this song," said Will, covering his ears.

"Aw, jeez," said Jason, laughing and leaning back in his chair, "I'm telling you, it's a great song!"

After a second, he joined in, then Augusta, and for a corny, beautiful minute, all three of them were singing the song (which Pen had to admit really was pretty inspiring), a song about how not the arrival but the journey is the point, until they were actually stopping traffic, people turning to give them amused and pitying glances, Will sinking lower and lower into his chair. Pen tapered off after a while, unsure of the words, but Jason and Augusta sang it through to the end. Jason's voice was unexpectedly good, deep and resonant, and when they were finished, the people at the neighboring tables applauded, with the Lana Turner waitress clapping hardest of all.

They walked on the beach, Augusta on Jason's shoulders waving, like the Queen of England, to passersby; Pen and Will walking several yards ahead of them, studiously not touching and thus whipping up around them such an atmosphere of buzzing, whirling sexual tension that Pen told him it was like walking inside a swarm of bees, a simile that made Will smile and shake his head and say, "Only you."

"See? How did you live without me for six years?" teased Pen.

"Poorly," said Will in a way that said he wasn't entirely kidding.

They came to a resort that was more glamorous than any of the others, subtly lit so that it seemed to glow from within, with a wide white stretch of palm-tree-dotted beach leading up to elegant, Japanese-style villas and one of those pools that was designed to appear endless when you were in it, as though it wasn't a swimming pool at all but an extension of the ocean itself.

"Look at that," said Pen in a low voice. "Now, who do we know who would stay in a place like that?"

Will looked and his eyes widened. "Should we say something? Go up and see if she's there?"

Pen shook her head. "He probably already checked there anyway."

"Yeah, but what if someone checked who wasn't acting like a seedy private eye and flashing cash?"

Pen took a quick glance back at Jason, who was talking up a storm and walking with a light step, in spite of the forty-pound child on his shoulders.

"You think we should leave it alone?" asked Will.

"He just looks so happy." She sighed. "Maybe on the way back."

The fancy resort marked the end of the strip, and, as they walked away from it, the beach grew darker. The moon had risen by now, though, and was nearly full—a big, silver, low-hanging plum—so there was still enough light to see by. Even so, Pen should not have been able to tell that it was Cat. Even with the moonlight above and its reflection on the water and the residual light from the strip behind them, it was too dim to make out much more than an outline—two small people, their arms linked—and still, without knowing how she knew (was it her walk? a fragment of barely heard conversation carried through the night air?), Pen knew.

"Will," she said, and she grabbed his arm and started walking faster.

"What are you doing?" asked Will.

"Hey, guys!" called Jason from behind them. "Yo! Slow up!"

"Cat," gasped Pen, pointing.

Will squinted into the dimness.

"Holy shit," he breathed, and together they broke into an almost-run.

Their approach was quiet, their hearts pounding more loudly, or so it seemed to them, than their footfalls, which were muffled by the sugary sand. Still, Cat must have heard them coming because before they got to her, before they could call her name, she stopped, let go of the arm of the person she had been walking with, and turned around, and even though Pen had pictured herself finding Cat and running straight into her arms, had pictured it over and over again, as soon as she saw her face, she slowed down, tugging Will to a stop, so that the first time Cat said her name it was across a distance. The space between them might have been six feet, a body length, but it felt wider than that, and Pen felt suddenly shaky, filled with doubt. From where Pen stood, Cat's face appeared completely impassive, chilly, registering nothing, not even bewilderment or curiosity. What if Pen had been wrong when she had told the Lolas that Cat would be happy to see her? Pen was still holding on to Will's arm, and, as she looked at Cat across that distance, she held on harder.

Then, in a very small voice, Cat said, "Pen. Will. Oh, how can this be?" and she covered her mouth with her hands and sank to her knees in the sand.

"We came to see you," explained Pen, but she found she couldn't move, so it was Will who walked over to Cat, held her gently by the shoulders, lifted her to her feet, grinned, and said, "Hey, sweetheart."

Cat came alive then, shouting, "Oh, my God," and throwing her arms around Will's neck, before dashing over to Pen, catching hold of both of her hands, and saying, "My sweet, sweet friend, my sweet, sweet, sweet, sweet friend," before pulling her into a hard hug.

It's okay, thought Pen, overcome with relief. *She loves me.*

Pen felt a tug on her skirt, and Augusta piped, "Mama, what's happening?"

Cat froze in Pen's embrace, and Pen extricated herself from the hug so that she could scoop Augusta into her arms.

"'Mama'?" whispered Cat. She stared at Augusta, and her face blossomed into awe.

"My little girl," said Pen, filled with awe herself, as sometimes happened at the sight of this glorious, full-fledged person who belonged to her but belonged mostly, and more and more, to herself, "Augusta."

Slowly, Cat lifted one of her pretty hands (the sight of that familiar, flower-delicate hand brought tears to Pen's eyes) and brushed the hair back from Augusta's face.

"She is breathtaking," said Cat, her eyes filling, too. "Imagine: Pen's little girl."

"Thank you very much," said Augusta, and she leaned forward and kissed Cat on the lips.

Cat touched her fingers to her own mouth, and then told Pen in her old irresistible, teasing way, "She receives compliments so gracefully. Guess she got that from her dad."

It was an old joke between the three of them, Pen's embarrassed ineptitude at handling praise. Once, back in college, when she was dressed to go out and Will told her she looked pretty, she had erupted into such a red-faced, stammering series of self-reproaches, disavowals, and disclaimers that Will said, "How about you just hit me in the head with a hammer and we'll call it even."

"Hold on one red-hot minute!" cried Cat, snapping her fingers, whirling around, and pointing at Will. "Augusta. She's not . . . ?"

"No," said Will. He shrugged. "I'd take her, though."

"You can *borrow* me," corrected Augusta.

Everyone laughed, and, afterward, a breathless, trembling silence swooped down upon Pen, Cat, and Will, as if each of them understood, in the same instant, that the three of them—Pen, Cat, and Will, *Pen, Cat, and Will*—were standing, in the year 2010, on a beach, in the Philippines, together. As they stood there, for the first time since she had seen her walking on the sand, arm in arm, with Cat, Pen became aware of the stranger. She stood a few feet away, a short, fine-boned woman, with long black hair and a bemused smile. Cat followed Pen's gaze, gave a little jump, said, "I'm so sorry!" and held out her hand to the woman, who took it.

"Does anyone have a drum?" asked Cat mischievously. "Because not to undercut the solemnity of the moment? But this would be a really good time for a drumroll."

"Nope," said Will, holding his arms out to demonstrate his drumless state.

"Sorry," said Pen.

"Um, Cat?" said Augusta. "We don't really *have* drums on vacation?"

Cat gave a theatrical sigh. "Oh, fine," she said. She let go of the stranger's hand, took a step to the side, and made a sweeping arc with her arm.

"This is Marisol Ocampo," she said, her face soft and starry-eyed, "my sister."

Marisol was nodding her head, princess-fashion, a slow, wide smile emerging on her face, when a voice boomed, "Your *sister*?"

There was Jason. Pen realized that he must have been there all along. Of course he had, hovering behind them in the shadows, watching, probably gathering his courage, keeping quiet, even though his heart must have either leaped up or cracked in two at the sight of his wife. Caught up in Cat, Pen and Will had forgotten all about him.

Jason took a few steps forward and stopped, his shoulders back, his feet spread apart like a gunfighter or a football coach. Pen couldn't bear to look at his face, but the sight of his hands alone was enough to make her heart hurt. They were clasped together in front of him, his fingers interlocked so tightly that, from where she stood, Pen could see the veins bulging in his arms. When she finally got up the nerve to look at his eyes, she saw that they were full of hope.

"I get it, now. You found out about her in your dad's will, didn't you? And you left home and came here to find her." His voice was husky with tenderness.

Cat stood as still as if she had been turned to stone.

Jason unclasped his hands and reclasped them on the top of his head. "Aw, babe, you could have told me that. I would have understood."

Cat did not tell him that her heart was melting at the mere sight of him, as he had predicted she would. With firm, deliberate steps, she walked until she was standing in front of him, and in a voice so cold that it didn't sound like Cat's at all, she said, "Jason, you don't understand a single thing. You never have. And you should not have, you should *never* have come here."

Pen wanted to tell Jason, "For God's sake, just let her go!" She wanted to tell Cat, "Be gentle with him!" She wanted to step between the two of them, but she couldn't be sure which person she wanted to shield from the other. In the end, she did none of these things because it was painfully clear to her that she shouldn't even be there; none of them—Pen, Will, Augusta, Marisol—should be there. If the world worked as it should, Cat and Jason would be alone, with their shared, messy, intensely private story, the years upon years of plans and disappointments, love and anger, the trying and the giving up. This was a scene that wanted no witnesses. Still, there they all were.

Pen thought, *She didn't call him "little boy,"* and when she looked at Jason's face, white under the white moon, she saw that he didn't look like a little boy at all, but like a man who had lost everything.

"ONE: I MARRIED THE WRONG MAN, BUT YOU KNEW THAT ALREADY. He's a good, decent man, just abundantly, inalterably wrong for me. Honestly, not to place blame, but what were the two of you thinking, letting me marry him? Two: When my father died, I felt like that guy in the David Bowie song, floating in space, cut off from everything, as lost as lost could ever be. Loster. Three: To make matters worse, I found out about Marisol and that my dad had had this other life, another life, another wife, before I was born and that he had *left* his *child*. God, here I had spent the last five years trying desperately to have a baby—and I know what you're thinking: why have a baby with a man I don't love? But I thought, well, I would do it and have it and then I would leave, and we would raise her (I always felt in my heart that it would be a girl) together but apart, the way so many other people do because even though Jason was all wrong as a husband, I knew he would be an excellent, no, a *stupendous* father—and all the while, my own father, whom I spent my life worshipping, had walked away from his daughter, left her thousands of miles away and kept her a secret, and I was so angry at him. I was sick with fury and disillusionment. Four: But one day, it suddenly came to me that I needed to come find her, that everything happens for a reason and here was the reason: I was meant to find my sister. And I found her, but not just her, although she would have been enough all by herself; I found my home, my true home and my true family, the one I had yearned for all my life."

It was the morning after they had found her. As they had planned before they had left her and Jason alone on the beach, they were having breakfast at Cat's resort. Marisol was sitting in the sun, reading, on the other side of the endless pool, in which Augusta swam, loping like a dolphin through the water, blissfully untouched by the adult drama that had unfolded around her. Before they had left to meet Cat, Pen had peered through the window of Jason's villa and had been relieved to see him there, sleeping.

After she told her story, Cat tilted her head thoughtfully and said, "I think that's it. The bare bones, I mean," and she scooped a forkful of sticky rice from her plate and popped it into her mouth.

Helplessly, dizzily, internally reeling with myriad, conflicting emotions, Pen looked at Will, who was smiling. She kicked him under the table.

"Ow!" said Will.

"What is the matter with you?" demanded Pen. "That was heart-wrenching!"

In truth, heart-wrenching was only one of the things Pen thought it was. Disturbingly cold-hearted (*husband as sperm donor?*) was another. Even as she thought this, though, she knew that it didn't change anything. Cat was flawed. So what? They were all flawed. Cat was a person Pen loved.

"I know!" said Will. "My heart's wrenched. It's just funny." The smile came back.

Cat was smiling, too, a smile, like Will's, full of barely contained laughter.

"What's funny about it?" asked Pen.

"Six years in four sentences. She really thinks that was four sentences."

Cat made a face at him, nose wrinkled, tongue out.

Pen gave them both a disapproving glare.

"Come on, Pen," said Will, "don't be mad." He started to reach for her, but stopped and set his hand down on the table.

"Oh, go ahead!" scoffed Cat. "Like I couldn't tell from the very first moment I saw you."

"You could?" asked Pen, too stunned to be embarrassed.

"Heck, yeah. I noticed, however, that you both left it out of your four-sentence biographies. It was all the more conspicuous for its absence, too. The unspoken fifth sentence: we are in love." She fluttered her lashes and sighed.

"All right, all right," grumbled Will.

"Cat. Be serious," said Pen. "Is it okay? With you, I mean?"

"That matters to you?" said Cat. "After all this time?"

Pen considered this. "Yes," she said, then added apologetically, "not that there's anything we can do about it, if you don't like it."

Cat smiled. "I do like it. There was a time, of course, when I would have hated it, when it would have seemed like the end of the world."

" 'Total friendship apocalypse,' " supplied Will.

"Exactly. But I knew that it would happen, once I left."

"Six years after," Will pointed out, "give or take."

"Slowpokes," said Cat, smiling. "Even so, I knew it would happen."

"No, you didn't!" said Pen, dismayed. "How could you have thought that?"

Cat turned her face to Pen, a face full of affection and entirely, exclusively Cat's.

"You never saw how things were," said Cat sweetly. "That's part of what made you so wonderful. You thought we all loved each other in the same way."

"We did," insisted Pen, suddenly near tears. "You make it sound like our friendship wasn't what it seemed to be."

"Our friendship was the best thing under the sun," avowed Cat. "I was wrong when I said that I had only just now found my family because you and Will were my family. You were the lights of my life."

"Oh," said Pen, wiping her eyes.

"But even in families, people have roles, spots that they fill. You and Will were the wonder twins. You were so in tune with each other, so connected." Cat linked her forefingers together, the forefingers that Pen had loved, as she had loved everything about Cat.

"We were *all* connected!" protested Pen. "I adored you."

"Of course, you did, both of you," said Cat. "I'm adorable! I was your darling, your angel, yours and Will's, which is precisely what I wanted to be. But you were the ones who belonged together. I was meant to leave, eventually, to go away and grow up. You two were the ones who were meant to go the distance. Will, back me up here."

Will said, "You don't need backup; you're doing fine."

"You think she's right?" asked Pen reproachfully.

"Why are you sad about this?" said Will. Under the table, he grabbed her hand. "I mean, I know why you're sad about this, but you don't have to be. It doesn't take anything away."

"Maybe not," said Pen doubtfully. "I need more time to think about it."

"I wish we had more time," said Cat sadly.

Pen blinked. "But we do. We can. We can change our ticket back to Cebu. Or you can come back with us."

Cat was shaking her head. "I need to be with Marisol, now. It wasn't easy for her to leave her job and her family to come here with me. We're heading off to a different island for a few more days. It might be the only time we have to get to know each other, alone, for a while."

"She has a family?" asked Will, then said, "Oh, the Lolas. Is that where she lives?"

Cat smiled. "'The Lolas.' Aren't they magnificent? Jason told me that you were there."

"They're goddesses," said Pen.

"Exactly what I thought when I met them," said Cat. "Yes, Marisol and her husband and her little boy, my *nephew,* if you can believe it, live in the small house in back, the one painted yellow."

"You know, we might have met them," said Will. "We met a lot of people."

"You did meet her mother. Jason said so," said Cat. "Lola Graciela."

"So, wait a minute," said Pen, confused. "Your father was married to Lola Graciela? They lived at his family's house?"

"Briefly," said Cat. "That is, they were married briefly. But she's lived at his family's house for close to forty years."

"Wow, so even after he left, she stayed, she and Marisol," said Will. "That's pretty amazing."

"They don't find it amazing, I don't think," said Cat. "Marisol and her mom were part of the family by then. It's just how they do things here."

"You're lucky," said Pen a little wistfully, "to be part of that."

"I am straight-up blessed," said Cat with fervor.

She stood up and waved to Marisol, who began to gather her belongings, and Will stood, too. Pen knew he couldn't help it, that it was his dyed-in-the-wool courtliness kicking in, but she felt betrayed. There they both stood, as if standing up were fine, as if anyone could possibly be leaving.

"Wait!" said Pen, flustered. "Sit down! We need to make a plan. When will we see you? When are you coming back?"

"Oh," said Cat blankly, "I thought I told you. I'm not."

"You mean never?" said Will.

"Well, I don't know," said Cat slowly. "I'm extending my visit for as long as I can, and then, well, I'm thinking of applying for permanent residency."

She didn't meet their eyes but began rummaging through her tote bag. She took out a small, bright red leather case, out of which she pulled a card.

Reluctantly, Pen got to her feet. *She is not actually going to hand me a business card*, thought Pen, but that's just what Cat did. Pen stared down at it without really seeing it.

"It's my e-mail address," said Cat.

She walked around the table and hugged Pen.

"I loved seeing you," she said. "Be happy together—that's an order!"

Pen pulled back to look at Cat. "You're saying good-bye?"

That's when Pen saw it, a glimmer of impatience passing over Cat's vivid, black-eyed, smiling face. *She has moved on*, Pen understood with bewildered shock. *We are only part of who she used to be, not of who she is now.*

"I might have to come back to deal with the divorce or pack my things or something," said Cat. "In which case, I will definitely and absolutely call you."

Pen knew when she was being thrown a bone, but, still, she said, "But we only just found you!"

"I know," said Cat regretfully.

She put her arms around Will and kissed his cheek. Then she put her sunglasses on and gave them both a winsome, affectionate smile.

"And I will stay found. I promise," she told them. "But I also have to stay here."

CHAPTER TWENTY-ONE

$\mathcal{B}$ECAUSE PEN AND AUGUSTA HAD A SIX-HOUR LAYOVER IN NEW York and, more significantly, because Pen and Will could not stand the thought of saying good-bye to each other, when their plane landed at JFK, they rented a car and drove to Philadelphia. It was just the three of them, Jason having decided to remain in the Philippines for "a few more days."

"I'm not staying because I think I can talk Cat into changing her mind," he had told them. "I know when I'm beat. I guess I just can't stand the thought of going home to our empty house, yet."

Will and Pen hadn't really believed him, but if they had learned anything about Jason, and they had learned a lot, it was that, once he had made up his mind to do something, there was no talking him out of it.

"He's steadfast," said Pen admiringly, "persevering."

"Delusional," added Will, "quixotic." But Pen could tell that Will admired him, too.

Jason had gone with them to the airport in Cebu, and before she had left him, after Augusta had cried and covered his face with kisses and Will had shaken his hand and told him to keep in touch, Pen had grabbed him by his enormous shoulders and said, "Listen to me: you keep the faith, all right? You will find someone who loves you the way you deserve to be loved. I know it," and he had given her a crooked smile and said, "Isn't it weird how you kind of like me, now?" and Pen had agreed that it was.

At a rest stop, Will called a hotel near Jamie's apartment and reserved a room.

"You could stay with us," Pen told him.

He had leaned in almost close enough to kiss her and, with a wicked gleam in his green, gold, orange eyes, said, "Or—you could stay with me."

When they were about half an hour away, Pen called Jamie on his cell phone to tell him they were coming.

"Did you find her?" he asked.

"We did," Pen told him, settling in. "It's kind of a long story, but basically, she went there to (a) leave her husband and (b) find her—"

"Yeah, yeah. Details later," said Jamie cutting her off. "Cut to the chase: Is Cat still smokin' hot or what?"

"You're a degenerate," said Pen.

"Just hurry up and bring my Gusty girl home, okay? I'll leave work early."

Pen smiled. "You miss the crushed goldfish crackers all over the floor, don't you?"

"And I'm getting way too much sleep," said Jamie. "It's completely out of hand."

As soon as Pen opened the door of the apartment, Augusta was a blur of hair and skinny legs and wild screeches, rushing Jamie like a miniature linebacker.

"Oof!" he said, staggering backward. "What were they feeding you in the Philippines?"

"Pizza!" shrieked Augusta. "And *pancit*! And the weensiest bananas you never saw!"

"You're right," said Jamie pulling her onto his lap and smiling at Pen through Augusta's tangled hair. "I never did."

For a moment, Pen just stood, watching them, until she noticed the flowers on the table, calla lilies, tall, white, posing like fashion models in a curvaceous vase.

"Jamie! You bought us flowers!"

Jamie gave the flowers a sidelong glance. "Uh, yeah, well, welcome home, right? Hey, where are the rest of your bags?"

"Oh," said Pen, with a wink at Augusta, "they'll be here shortly."

"Shhh," Augusta told Jamie. "It's a surprise."

When Jamie saw Will, he set Augusta on the ground and stood up. "Will Wadsworth, as I live and breathe. So good to see you, man."

"Good to see you, too, Jamie," said Will, grinning. "You got me flowers and everything."

"Come here, you little ray of sunshine," said Jamie, and he walked across the room and clenched Will in a hug that caused him to grimace and say, "I guess you started working out since I last saw you."

"Being famous must agree with you," said Jamie. "You look good, brother."

"Not 'brother,'" Pen said quickly. "Anything else but 'brother.'"

Jamie stared at Pen, and then a smile started in his eyes and spread across his face. "Well, maybe 'brother-in-law' would be a better choice?" he said, raising an eyebrow.

"Don't get ahead of yourself, big guy," said Pen.

"Smartest thing you've ever done. One of the only smart things you've ever done," said Jamie to Pen. "What happened over there? Did you get hit on the head with a coconut?"

"Anyway, I was thinking I'd move in here, too," said Will, sizing up the apartment. "You don't mind, do you?"

Pen knew he was joking, but for a few seconds, she was transported back to the Lolas' house, grandmothers, babies, nephews, sisters, everyone together, and she felt a pang of longing.

"Hey," said Jamie, opening his hands in welcome, "always room for one more."

LATER, PEN WOULD WONDER IF WILL HAD PLANNED TO TELL HER right away, as soon as she arrived at his hotel room, because when he opened the door, he wasn't smiling. His face was unusually serious, taut and focused and full of intention, but overcome by her own intentions, Pen didn't let him say anything, just stepped inside and pulled him into her, sliding her hands under his shirt, so that before the door was even closed, he was pressing her against it, lifting a fistful of hair to kiss her neck, her collarbone, and a minute went by filled with nothing but the ragged noise of their breathing, before he pulled away and said, "Wait."

"It's okay. I don't want to wait," Pen said, gasping, thinking he was worried about rushing her, his innate sense of chivalry compelling him to slow down, which turned out to be true, but not in the way she thought.

"Before we do this, there's something I have to tell you," he said, and despite his solemn tone, she wouldn't have been afraid, except that when she looked into his eyes, that's what she saw there: fear. He sat down on the edge of the bed.

"Can you sit for a second?" he asked. "And let me talk to you?"

"No," she said, her voice pleading, like a child's voice. "Please. Let's not talk right now."

"We have to. I'm sorry. I should have told you this before."

She shivered, took a breath, and instead of sitting on the bed next to him, she walked over to an ottoman a few feet away, sat on its very edge, and folded her hands in her lap. *Let him not be sick. Oh God, let him not be dying.*

"I was at your father's funeral," said Will.

This was so unexpected that it took Pen a few seconds to understand what he had said. She shook head. "No."

"I didn't follow Cat's rule, about not looking each other up. I read it online, first the newspaper report, then the obituary, and I came."

"So I was right. You were there." For a moment, all she could do was marvel at the fact that she had sensed him—and she had felt his presence in the church more acutely than she had felt anything all that long, numb day—and, lo and behold, she had been right. But as the awful implications of his having been there began to dawn on her, the wonder and satisfaction dissipated, and she demanded, "Why? What was the point of coming if you didn't even let me see you?"

"I came into the church before it got crowded, and I saw you right away, just the back of your head, but that was enough to know it was you. I saw your mom next to you, and I saw Augusta, sitting on your lap."

"Augusta." At the mention of Augusta, she slid back on the ottoman, farther away from him. "Did you know she was my daughter? Did you even know I had a daughter?"

"Not until I read the obituary."

"But if you knew about her before you came, why would that stop you from coming up to me?"

Will looked down at his lap and started to speak, but, like a slap, it struck her and she said, "Patrick."

"He was next to you. He had his arm around you."

Pen tried to remember. "I guess he did. I don't remember."

She looked at Will reproachfully. "But so what? Who cares if he was there? Why should that have mattered?"

"It mattered because I was in love with you." He shook his head in disbelief. "Didn't you know that? Maybe I always had been, but I only really knew it after Cat left."

Pen absorbed this information and realized that she wasn't shocked by it. For years, she had denied how Will felt about her to everyone, especially to herself, but all along, deep down, she had known.

"If you loved me, that was all the more reason for you to come be with me because whatever Patrick did, it didn't work. We were way past the point where he could even reach me. He helped with Augusta, but he didn't help *me*."

A wave of anger surged through Pen. "*You* could have, though. You are the one person who could have, on almost the worst day of my life, but you didn't. Why? Because you were *jealous*?" The word *jealous* came out as a contemptuous hiss. "I needed you!"

She had meant to hurt him, to make him feel guilty, and she could read in his eyes that it had worked.

"I didn't know that!" he said, a note of desperation in his voice. "You looked like a family. I didn't see any place for me there. Yeah, I was jealous. I can be a jerk like anyone else. But if I had known that you wanted me, if I thought I could have helped you in any way, I would have stayed."

Pen sat there, trembling with fury and staring at his face, the face that she loved, and she felt that his beauty was an affront, an indignity. He could have helped her. He could have *saved* her, and he had let her down. Then she thought of something that deepened her anger, turned it from hot to cold.

"Maybe I could have lived with all of this," she said icily. "But do you know what I can't live with?"

"Don't say that," he said. "I know what you're talking about, it's that I didn't tell you before, and I know I should have, but don't say you can't live with it."

Pen leaped to her feet.

"When I told you about Augusta, at the reunion, after our bike ride, you acted like you didn't already know. When I told you that my *father died,* you acted like you didn't know, and don't use the excuse that we were playing the four-sentence game and that you weren't supposed to comment on anything I said because that is such a cop-out." By the end of this, she was shouting.

Will watched her pace.

"And what about the night on the porch in Bohol? I had never told anyone that story who I didn't have to tell, but I told you. I trusted you! How could you not have told me that you already knew?"

He stood up and touched her, ran his hands along her arms, tried to look into her face, but she yanked herself away.

"Pen, I wanted to. I know how lame this sounds; I know it might sound like I'm making it up, but, listen, you were talking and I was with you. I wasn't thinking about the newspaper article. I was listening to you tell the story, and you were so sad, and I wasn't thinking about anything but how terrible it was that you had to go through what you went through. It wasn't until you said the thing about thinking I was at the funeral that it even occurred to me that I should tell you."

"But you didn't tell me, and not telling me is the same thing as lying."

"I'm telling you now."

"Why?"

Will looked startled. "What?"

"Why tell me at all? Why not just let it go?"

He gave her a confused look, as though her question didn't make any sense. "Because I want to be with you, and I don't mean a relationship. I mean a life. How fair would it be to start that with something already between us that I know about and you don't?"

Fair. What a Will thing to say. Pen felt herself soften at this, just a little, but somehow, that wasn't what she wanted. She wanted to stay mad. For reasons she could not explain, staying mad felt good, even hurting him felt good. Her bag was next to the door where she had dropped it. Deliberately, she walked over to it and picked it up.

"What are you doing?" asked Will.

"I can't do this. I have to go."

"Go?" Will sounded stunned. "Come on, you can't really believe that leaving is the right thing."

Pen turned on him, eyes blazing. "What the hell did you think would happen?"

"Do you think I didn't know it was a risk?" asked Will, exasperated, throwing out his hands. "But I thought you would forgive me. I still think so."

"God, do you know how arrogant that sounds?"

"We're supposed to be together. Believing that is not arrogance; neither is having faith in you."

"Faith in me? Like I'm supposed to fix this? You're the one who screwed it up!"

Will flared at this. "I did! I made a lot of mistakes. But what about you?"

"Me. *Me?* I didn't do anything."

"Exactly. You talk about how much you needed me, but I was only at the funeral in the first place because I decided to come. If you wanted me, you could have called me. You know I would have been there in a second."

"You can't be serious. My father was *dead.*" She threw the words at him.

"And I'm not just talking about the funeral. You say a lot about how much you missed me all those years we were apart, but you never called and told me that."

"You are the one who left!"

Will nodded, accepting this. "I know, and I shouldn't have. I wanted our friendship to turn into something else, and I thought maybe you wanted that, too, or that you would at least be open to it, but you had twisted the three of us into an *idea,* this pure, untouchable thing."

"We were." Pen began to cry. "We were special."

"We *were* special. It's not an exaggeration to say that you and Cat saved my life, more than once. But we were three people. We weren't a religion."

"Who knew you could be so mean?" she said. She felt stung, right on the edge of hating him.

Will didn't apologize or even react, just said in a quieter voice, "But I should have stayed, anyway. I should have been more like Jason."

Pen snapped her head up and said, mockingly, " 'Delusional'? 'Quixotic'?"

"Yeah, he carried it too far, but he *tried.* When he finally gives up, he'll know that he did everything he could. I should have fought for you, been less proud, more patient, made deals with the devil, whatever. I should never have left."

"Well, you did. I stayed and you left."

Will made a disgusted sound. "Don't you get sick of that? Feeling abandoned."

"I was abandoned!"

"And you didn't do one thing about it. All you had to do was call. I don't know what Cat would have done, but I would have been there so fast. Why don't you ask yourself why you never did?"

"Stop it," she said bitterly. "Shut up. Why are you doing this?"

Will sighed. "I love you. I've never hurt you on purpose in my life, but we need to say these things to each other."

She glared at him and said, "You shouldn't have told me you were at the funeral." She knew it didn't make sense, to go from being angry that he hadn't told her to angry that he had, but that's how she felt. "You ruined everything."

He said, "I knew you would be mad. I mean, I didn't think you'd be *this* mad." A glimmer of a smile. "The thing is," he said gently, "if you end things between us because of this, you would have ended them eventually anyway."

Pen didn't know how to answer this. She couldn't even process what it meant. She felt knotted and furious and wretched.

"But I don't think you will," said Will.

With two fingers, he touched her temple. He picked up a piece of her hair and kissed it. " 'Love is an imperative,' remember you said that? And this time, I'm not going anywhere."

Pen felt herself giving way, so she searched for a last reservoir of anger and found it, right in the middle of the memory of herself curled like a wounded animal on her childhood bed, a year after her dad had died.

"Fine," she said, "I'll save you the trouble."

She turned and tugged open the door.

"Hey, come on, this is Will. Could you please look at me?"

No way was she turning around. She braced herself for his touch, but it didn't come.

"Stay and get through this with me," he said.

"I feel like you trampled on my father's death, on our friendship, everything that is sacred to me. I'm going home," she said. "You should, too."

BY THE TIME SHE GOT TO THE APARTMENT, THROUGH SHEER FORCE of will, she had stopped crying. It was only seven o'clock. Despite the jet lag, Augusta might have been awake, and Pen couldn't let her see her like that. When she walked in, Jamie was watching television. He switched it off when he saw her face.

"Oh, crap, what happened?"

Pen shook her head. "I don't want to talk about it."

She went into her bedroom, grabbed an ancient duffel bag, and, indiscriminately began stuffing clothes into it. Jamie followed her and leaned against the door frame.

"You really think you're gonna need those long underwear?"

Pen sighed. "All my summer clothes are still in the suitcase."

"So—what? You guys had a fight?"

"Something like that. Can you stay with Augusta tonight?"

"Sure, where are you going? Back to Will's hotel?"

"That's over," said Pen, stomping into the bathroom for her toothbrush. "I want to see Mom."

"Hey! Crazy person!" In the bathroom mirror, she could see Jamie behind her, waving his hands in the air to get her attention. "You need to stay and work this out. People are allowed to have fights without the world ending, even you and Will."

Ignoring this, she brushed past Jamie and headed for the front door.

"Mom can't fix this for you," said Jamie, catching hold of her arm. "What are you thinking?"

Pen spun around to face him. "Could you mind your own business? Is that possible?"

Jamie's gray eyes grew flinty. "How many chances did you give Patrick?"

Pen turned her face away.

"So is that your policy?" asked Jamie. "Special deals for assholes and deadbeats. But for good guys, ones who might actually stick around and not suck, it's one strike and you're out."

"You don't know what you're talking about."

"Because that's brilliant, Pen. Really. That's genius. Way to go."

The phone rang, and even though the last thing she wanted to do was to have a phone conversation, she didn't want to talk to Jamie, either. She answered it.

"Hello."

"Hello." A woman's voice, unfamiliar, friendly. "Hey, this is Pen, isn't it?"

"It is." Pen rooted around in her handbag for her keys.

"Hi, Pen, welcome home. This is Susan, Susan Davis. Is Jamie there?"

"Oh, yeah, he's definitely here."

She turned around, and Jamie was standing there. He picked up her keys off the telephone table and tossed them to her, and by some miracle, she caught them in her free hand.

"Happy trails," he said.

"Don't tell him where I'm going," she said, and she thrust the phone at him and left.

THE ANGER CARRIED PEN ALL THE WAY OUT OF THE CITY, WHOOSHED her effortlessly past the billboard emblazoned with the ballerina's sculpted back, past the X-rated video store, through the narrow South Twenty-Sixth Street tunnel that she had always hated, past the DON'T FLY TO THE AIRPORT sign that she, Will, and Cat had always liked, past the oil refinery with its flames and towers and plumes of steam, and over the bridge, before dumping her onto I-95 and deserting her completely.

For several miles, she didn't think at all. She felt dazed, tingly, bruised, vaguely convalescent. What seeped in first was a baffled amazement: *How* had she gotten so angry? She wasn't an angry person in general, but she had given herself to it so willingly, even with a kind of relish, like a person swan-diving into a burning lake. What had Will said? That he had never hurt her on purpose in his life, but that's just what she had done to him. Hurt him and felt better for having done it. The thought filled her with so much shame that she almost scurried away from it, but at the last second, she gritted her teeth. *You have to understand this,* she insisted, and with deliberation, she began.

She had told Will that the part she couldn't live with was the lie: the way he kept the secret, even through her telling the story of her father's murder. He should have told her, that much was abundantly clear. He had chickened out, failed to step up, turned himself, in one fell swoop, from the most honest man she had ever known into a liar. No matter how you sliced it, he was wrong, ignoble, and she was justifiably aggrieved.

But when she considered the lie now, from within the small, safe space of the car (*hermit thrush*), with her hands on the wheel and the clear black sky overhead, she realized that it was something she could understand. She imagined his struggling with how to say it, how to edge it in, between her heartbroken story and his own grief (tears—*tears*—on his face, his hand against her cheek). If she were in Will's place, she might have wondered how telling would make anything better, how that particular truth could possibly set anyone free; she might have worried that telling would drive away the person she had loved for years. She might have let the moment for truth-telling slip right by.

No, the thing that had pushed her over the edge and into rage had not been the lie of omission, but the thing omitted: he had not been with her at her father's funeral.

Even this, she could understand. She remembered his stricken eyes, his voice telling her that if he had only known she needed him, he would have stayed. She had believed him then, and she believed him now. Still, that didn't change—nothing changed—the fact that Will hadn't helped her, he hadn't saved her from not only that hard, sorrowful day, but from the two hard, sorrowful years that followed it.

And there it was, the reason for her fury: she had made her suffering Will's fault.

It was *his fault!* a voice inside her cried, high and thready, like a child's voice.

But what could he have done? He could have put his arms around her. He could have told her he was sorry for her loss, and the words would have been different from other people's words and would have been in his voice, and they would have soothed her. He could have come back into her life and been her friend and e-mailed her and called her on the phone. He could have flown out for the first anniversary bike ride and the second and ridden beside her and made her feel less lost.

See all the things he could have done? wailed the angry child.

Yes, she answered, *and your father would still be dead.*

Pen had raged against Will with a child's rage because he hadn't fixed it, hadn't made it better, but Pen knew that losing someone you loved was like a virus, and people could make you soup and hold your hand and press cool washcloths against your face, and you might feel better for a moment, but the virus would still be there, on the other side of the moment, waiting, and all you could do was get through it—cough, fever, chills, body aches, crying jags, devouring loneliness, bursts of rage—step by painful step. Pen was getting through it. She was learning how to keep her father, as Lola Fe had said. But she wasn't there, yet, and that was no one's fault, not Will's, not even her own.

Oh, Will, my friend, forgive me.

MAYBE BECAUSE WHEN PEN WAS ALMOST TO HER MOTHER'S HOUSE, she remembered Jamie saying, "Mom can't fix this," or maybe because she suspected that her mother wouldn't validate her breaking up with Will, or because she suspected that she would, or because Pen just wanted to be alone for a little while more (and she knew that as soon as she pulled into the driveway, her mom would be running out the door to greet her), when Pen drove into her neighborhood, with her house still a half mile away, she pulled over, parked in front of someone else's house, got out of the car, slung the duffel bag over her shoulder, and began to walk.

The air rang with the high, heartbeat singing of cicadas. The trees stood tall next to the street. Pen passed house after familiar house. Her mind was loaded with things to figure out, but she was tired after all that concentrated thinking in the car, and for the duration of the walk, at least, she decided to let it wander. She thought about the tarsiers, and the snorkeling, about Jason's face when Cat told him he shouldn't have come. She thought about the Lolas and about the pride in Cat's voice when she said "My sister." She heard the voice in her head that was not the tarsier's saying, *"But we're here now, aren't we?"* She heard Will telling her to ask herself why she had missed him all those years but never called. She heard Will saying that he had wanted their friendship to change, saying, "We weren't a religion." She heard Jamie saying that she only gave second chances to the deadbeats, the ones who wouldn't stay.

The thoughts began to coalesce, to press forward more and more steadily, moving Pen toward a point she couldn't see, but before she got there, she was standing in front of her mother's house. With a touch of peevishness, she noted that she needn't have worried about pulling into the driveway because there was already a car in it, or not a car, but a truck, a dark, slightly battered, mud-spattered pickup that looked as though, unlike most of the pickups around there—and there weren't many—it might actually be used to pick things up. As Pen looked at the truck, a bell began to ring, faintly, someplace in the back of her mind.

Except for the porch light with its veil of bugs, the front of the house was dark, so Pen walked around to the back and saw that the kitchen lights were on, turning the windows to bright saffron squares. From where she stood, Pen didn't have a clear view of the kitchen, but she could sense movement, shadows on the yellow walls, and, without making a conscious decision to spy, she bent her knees, hunched her back, and padded, catlike, to the lowest window, staying close to the ground and close to the brick walls of the house so as to evade the sensors on the garage floodlights.

I love you, house, she thought, with her heart in her throat. *I love you, Daddy.* She stood on tiptoe and looked.

They were washing dishes. If they had been kissing or dancing or even cooking, Pen's reaction might have been different, but they stood there doing the dishes, Mark Venverloh at the sink, his back to Pen, her mother next to him, drying a pan (the old cast-iron skillet she used to make cornbread) with a dishtowel (one of the fish-print ones from the store in South Bethany that sold kitchenware, sandwiches, and the best seafood salad in the world), before holding it up and eyeing it to make sure it was clean. They weren't talking, just working, performing this comfortable, commonplace task in the kitchen in which Ben Calloway had made coffee for his wife every morning—for what had to have been thousands of mornings—since before Pen was born until the day he died. Pen wasn't resentful or jealous or hurt. She understood that she was looking at the bravest thing she had ever seen: her mother, after all she had lost, after she had broken apart and believed she would die, starting all over again, giving herself, plunging in, risking everything.

Pen crept away from the window. She walked back down the driveway, the sight of her mother and Mark still aglow inside her head, and sat down on the brick retaining wall at the edge of the yard. She looked out at the house across the street, at the particular darkness of neighborhoods, easeful, full of families that you couldn't see but knew were there, and, gingerly, took up the question of why she had, for six years, never called Will, who most surely would have come.

You know why, she told herself. *Because of that.*

Because of what?

Because you knew he would come.

Yes, he would have come. Of course, he would have.

He would have come and he would have been there, with you, the way he was with you at the summerhouse after Cat left, the way he was with you in the hotel room in Philadelphia, and you would have had to run away or make him leave.

Or I could have stayed.

And your life would have changed.

I would have had to love him.

You would have had to give him everything.

Jason, Cat, Will, her mother, the Lolas, everyone around her giving themselves away to the people they loved. Suddenly, she heard the unfamiliar voice from earlier that night: "This is Susan, Susan Davis. Is Jamie there?"

Jamie.

Even Jamie. Everyone and Jamie, too.

Pen reached into her bag and pulled out her phone.

CHAPTER TWENTY-TWO

*A*S SOON AS HIS PHONE RANG, WILL KNEW WHO IT WAS. HE turned the music down.

"Pen."

"I'm sorry I kissed Damon Callas," said Pen.

Will smiled. "You mean just now?"

"I'm sorry I never called you, all those years, even though I missed you."

"You're calling me now, right?"

"Will, there are a lot of ways to run away from someone."

"Yes, I guess there are."

"Is that the Talking Heads?" she asked.

"Yes."

"Where are you?"

"In the car."

"You're driving?"

"Yes. I don't have a driver," said Will. "I'm not Armando, you know."

"So you're using the Bluetooth thing?"

"No. This isn't my car, remember?"

"You mean to tell me that you're driving and holding your phone and talking to me?"

Will laughed. *Pen.* "I love you."

"I know, but, come on, Will, hang up and find a rest stop."

"Uh, I don't think there's a rest stop anytime soon."

"Where are you?"

"Where are you?" he asked.

"Sitting on the wall outside my mom's house."

"In that case, I'm about two minutes away."

"From here?"

"One minute and fifty-six seconds. Fifty-five. Fifty-four."

"You mean you're not on your way home?" asked Pen. Will could hear the joy in her voice.

"Not unless you mean you," he told her. "I'm on my way to you."

CHAPTER TWENTY-THREE

*A*NOTHER MINUTE AND WILL WAS GETTING OUT OF THE CAR and walking toward her, the sight of him more astonishing than a blue starfish, than an entire coral reef. *I could watch you do that forever,* she thought, but already she was impatient, fairly leaping off the wall and into his arms.

"How did you ever find me?" she asked.

"Lola Lita arrived on a silver cloud from Mt. Olympus and told me where you were."

"Jamie," said Pen, "the little traitor."

"It wasn't his fault. I tortured him until he spilled."

"I'll bet."

Pen kissed Will's mouth, the skin beneath his left ear.

"Can we start over?" asked Pen.

"If you really want to, but I was thinking we should hang on to all of it, everything that brought us here."

Pen nodded. "You're right. That's what we'll do. Will, I want to say something."

"Uh-oh." He smiled. "Say anything you want."

"Lola Fe was right."

"Of course, she was. About what?"

"About keeping everyone."

"Gone but not gone," said Will.

"Gone but here. Like my dad, Cat, Lola Fe herself, all the Lolas, and you before you came back into my life," said Pen. "And 'gone but here' is a wonderful thing, a gift."

Will kissed Pen's forehead. Soon, the two of them would leave this spot and walk into the house together and see Pen's mother and the man she had found to love, walk into the house and into a whole changed world, but for now they would stay where they were.

"But if you can possibly swing it," Pen went on, "just plain here is better. Here is the best place anyone could ever be."

Will held her face between his hands and smiled in amazement. "And look," he said.

"I know," said Pen, looking with all of herself, with everything she had. "Here we are."

ACKNOWLEDGMENTS

THANK YOU, THANK YOU, THANK YOU TO THE FOLLOWING people:

Jennifer Carlson, agent and precious friend, who does every single thing she does with uncanny insight and clear-eyed grace;

My lovely and gifted gift of an editor, Laurie Chittenden, and all the good people at William Morrow, including Liate Stehlik, Sharyn Rosenblum, Tavia Kowalchuk, Lynn Grady, Mike Brennan, Seale Ballenger, Shawn Nicholls, and Trish Daly.

My treasured early readers Kristina de los Santos, Dan Fertel, Susan Davis, Annie Pilson, Amanda Eyre Ward, and Sarah Davis Brandon (you are all so smart and kind);

Katie Martin for letting me steal *Middlemarchian*, Arturo de los Santos for answering my Cebu questions, John Willis for solving the mystery of the chapel window, and Annabel and Charles Teague for revealing that, in early childhood, both of them believed that the greatest jazz singer to ever live was named Elephants Gerald.

Anna Carapellotti, ballerina babysitter extraordinaire and all-around sweetheart;

My parents for loving me unreservedly and for cheering loudest of all;

Charles and Annabel Teague, brave, exuberant, and funny children among whom I am blessed to spend my days;

And David Teague, best writer, best reader, best friend, best every-thing.

This book is dedicated to my first family, but there have been so many families since, in Charlottesville and Houston and Philadelphia and Cebu and Wilmington and places in between. Some are gone but here. Some are just plain here.

I'm keeping all of you.